Nashville, TN
www.emboldenpress.com
sales@emboldenpress.com
info@emboldenpress.com
www.tealhaviland.com

This is a work of fiction. Names, characters, places, and incidents either are the product of the author's imagination or are used fictitiously. Any resemblance to actual persons, living or dead, events, or locales is entirely coincidental.

Copyright © 2013 by Teal Haviland

All rights reserved. In accordance with the U.S. Copyright Act of 1976, the scanning, uploading, and electronic sharing of any part of this book without the permission of the publisher is unlawful piracy and theft of the author's intellectual property. If you would like to use material from this book (other than for review purposes), prior written permission must be obtained by contacting the publisher at permissions@emboldenpress.com. No part of this book may be used or reproduced in any manner whatsoever without the written permission of the Publisher. Thank you for your support of the author's rights. Printed in the United States of America by Embolden Press, 2013. For information address Embolden Press at info@emboldenpress.com.

1st trade edition: May 2013
10 9 8 7 6 5 4 3 2 1

The publisher is not responsible for websites (or their content) that are not owned by the publisher.

Library of Congress has catalogued the hardcover edition of this book as follows:
Haviland, Teal.
Inception/by Teal Haviland — 1st ed.
p. cm. — (The Reaping Chronicles ; 1)

Summary: One of the most powerful angels ever created. A war spanning thousands of years approaching its end. A past love who has fallen, a new one who is forbidden. And an ancient book that could cause creation's ruin.
A story of love—past and present—fantastical beings, hidden realms, magic, fate, loss, and the fight of good versus evil.

ISBN: 978-0-9881716-0-2 (Hardback)
ISBN: 978-0-9881716-1-9 (Paperback)
LCCN: 2013937499

THE REAPING CHRONICLES

BOOK ONE
INCEPTION

TEAL HAVILAND

Read it and Reap!
Teal Haviland

To my amazing mother, Dixie, for always believing in me and encouraging me no matter what I was trying at the moment. You are truly a blessing from God. He not only gave me a wonderful person to look up to and aspire to be like, He gave me a best friend.

To my beautiful, awesomesauce daughter, Piper, if you only listen to one thing I tell you in your entire life, let it be this—do with your life what your heart begs you to do. It knows the way . . . trust it.

And for dreamers everywhere . . . never, never give up.

"Time. It can shadow what needs to be concealed—forgotten—or cast light on what needs to be revealed. And only as it passes, will we know what we've reaped from those things we've sown."

~ Teal Haviland

Prologue

THE MATTER OF THE BOOK

Elijah stood in front of the fallen angel he only knew as Lek. He hadn't seen him for two days, not since the demon had given him the Book.

That day, Elijah's heart had skipped when he realized what was wrapped in the crimson cloth in Lek's hands—the Book of Barabbadon. Adrenaline had surged through him, knowing that, at any moment, Lek could realize he was being deceived, disappear with the Book forever, and put an end to Elijah's revenge.

Today was already a day past when Elijah had told Lek he would keep his part of the deal and help him return to Heaven. Elijah had considered the torture Lek would inflict when he understood the betrayal, though the physical pain would be nothing compared to the mental anguish Elijah had been trying to keep at bay for months—ever since Ramai had slaughtered his wife and children in front of him. He still woke several times a night from nightmares full of the blood and screams of those he loved, reliving the mental and emotional torture as the light of life faded slowly from their eyes...

Until there was nothing left except blank stares.

That was three months ago. Now, with the Book safely hidden and trusted family told of its location, Elijah looked forward to the moment his life would be brought to an end by this demon's hands.

"I have had a difficult time finding you, Elijah. Why is that?"

Elijah could tell by the demon's accusatory tone and tightly clenched fists that he already knew the answer.

A sense of calm came over Elijah, and he pushed aside regret. He knew if he had just said no to Ramai, this would have ended then, and he wouldn't have to feel guilt for recreating the Book. He and his family would have died either way, but at least the Book would have never existed again. He wouldn't have felt the loss of his loved ones for more than the few moments before his own life faded. Nevertheless, he foolishly thought Ramai would keep his word that he would spare his and his family's lives. Now, Elijah couldn't destroy what he created—he had no way of saving the human world from its power—but he had been able to hide it from Ramai in a place he thought would be safe for a long time.

Hopefully, those I told can keep the secret.

Lek moved slowly toward Elijah who focused on the bulk of the demon, particularly on his arms and his now unclenched hands that seemed to be abnormally muscled—abnormally strong. He wondered how Lek was going to kill him. Would it be with those hands?

Will he rip my limbs from me? First my legs and then my arms so I cannot run—with no defense—as he does whatever else he wants before I die? Is there some other, even more painful or mentally agonizing, way he can kill me?

Elijah was surprised that he remained calm. Even while he imagined such horrible ways he would enter into death, his pulse was steady and smooth, breath slow and deep. As Lek took the last two steps to bring them face to face, Elijah had to look almost straight up to meet his gaze.

Lek's eyes stared into his. Although now that he was so close, they seemed less soulless, more consumed by hatred and darkness. The breath of the demon was as foul as Elijah remembered, even overtaking the stench of his body.

"You knew I would kill you if you did not hold up your end of the bargain, *human*. Yet, you did it anyway. Not smart."

The smell and heat that accompanied Lek's words made Elijah blink rapidly at first, but then he stared back just as hard. He was ready to see his wife and children again, ready to have the sorrow that had been all he had known for far too long leave him, ready for whatever this fallen angel was about to do.

Elijah smiled at Lek. "Sooner or later … we all reap what we sow."

Chapter One

GABRIELLE ✝ THE REAPER

Phalen fumbled with her clothing, stumbling in her flip-flops as she did. Gabrielle laughed from seeing someone who is normally so graceful and sure of herself being so awkward and clumsy.

'*Phalen, please stop acting so uncomfortable. You're going to bring more attention on us than we need,*' Gabrielle thought to her friend as they made their way down the busy boardwalk separating the beach from a strip of shops and restaurants.

'*I am uncomfortable,*' Phalen retorted. '*Why,* exactly, *do I have to wear these things on my feet? There's hardly anything to hold them on.*'

Gabrielle laughed again but continued to silently converse with Phalen. '*Because this is what females wear on hot, sunny days at the beach. Now, seriously, stop fidgeting. We have to see how long I can go unnoticed.*'

'*I still don't know how I let you talk me into this,*' Phalen continued. '*Why would you want to stay in one of these bodies, anyway? They are strange … all these extra emotions and thoughts. It's no wonder they make* so many mistakes—all the contradictory thinking battling back and forth in their heads. I can't tell right now if I need to be concerned about how I look, or if someone doesn't like my appearance, tell them to mind their own business. And that's just the start of the things I have going on in my mind in the few minutes I've been in human form.'

'That's precisely why I need to live in one for a while. I want to know how their senses and thoughts drive them to do the things they do. Why is that so difficult for everyone to understand? And you came with me because the only way I was allowed to try this was under the condition that I have a skilled fighter with me. You are one of the most skilled I know.'

'More like the most compliant angel you know. Why do they think you need me for assistance if there's a confrontation? Everyone knows you can take care of yourself just fine. Compared to you, I'm an amateur.'

'Don't sell yourself short, Phalen. I've seen you in battle, and they have, too. As far as why it's so important to have a comrade with me, you'll have to ask them. I think it's all Amaziah's doing. He's over-protective of me. I probably don't make things easy for him, though.'

Phalen snickered.

'Oh … Gabrielle … there isn't an angel around who would say there's anything easy about you. And, for the record, there's no way I'm questioning them,' Phalen raised a finger toward the sky, 'about me being here.'

'See,' Gabrielle answered through snickers of her own. 'A skilled fighter and honest. What more could a girl ask for?'

'Ahh, but, you're no girl. You're one of the most—'

'Shh! Don't say it. We should stop communicating this way. Speak aloud from now on unless the situation calls for other means. The Fallen will find us far easier if we don't.' Gabrielle glanced at Phalen to see if she understood, but she looked puzzled. "If they are paying close enough attention, which they hopefully aren't, communicating the way we were will be a beacon to them, and they will be curious. It makes our energy vibrate on a much higher level than a human's. Amaziah didn't allow for me to veil myself, and I don't need them finding me faster simply because I am not being careful. He is already sure they will notice me quickly."

Phalen shrugged and a playful expression flashed across her face.

"Okay. But I am not responsible for what might be thrust out by this human tongue." Phalen smiled. "Hey, I sound pretty good … for a human."

Phalen's perpetually good mood was refreshing and a nice counter to the struggle that Gabrielle had with her own constantly fluctuating emotions—trying to keep herself happy and not downright bitchy was proving more of an issue every day.

"You most certainly are responsible. You'll have just as much control as you do in your Divine form."

"If you say so."

"I say so." Gabrielle smiled, hooking her arm around Phalen's as they made their way onto the beach. Both stopped and took off their flip-flops, quickly finding they didn't like the way the sand felt as it slid between human skin and shoe, scratching at their feet with every uncomfortable step. Phalen shot Gabrielle a look that said she was happy to get them off her feet without needing to say a word.

When they resumed their walk, Gabrielle watched as, each time she put her foot down and let her weight rest on it more, the warm, thick sand fell around her foot, covering it slightly. The closer they got to the water's edge, the more compact and damp the sand became, causing the fine grains to become cooler and squish through her toes instead of blanketing her feet like they were before. Once they reached where the waves grabbed at the shoreline with soaking hands, Gabrielle turned and glanced over her shoulder to see the footprints they had left.

"That's something we don't usually see."

Phalen looked behind them as well, smiling in response, and then both faced forward again.

"So," Phalen began, "what exactly are you supposed to be doing now?"

"Nothing. Except seeing how long it takes for me to be noticed by the Fallen. It's Amaziah's way of proving his point."

"Well, he *does* have a point. You're nothing more than a huge target to them, whether you want to face it or not."

"It's not that I'm not facing it. I know the danger I'm in anytime I'm away from Heaven, but I also know the state of things here. We're losing the war with Darkness. Besides ... I can handle myself pretty well."

Phalen let out a chuckle. "That's an understatement of monumental proportions."

A half smile was Gabrielle's only response. At some point, her powers always seemed to be a part of every conversation she had with one of her brethren, which was the main reason she avoided interacting with the majority of them. She didn't like to be thought of as such an efficient and skilled killer—to have so much more power than the others—even if it was true. And she hated the reverence and fear her abilities evoked from most angels. She had no control over the gifts Yahuwah chose to empower her with. Those bestowed on her made her different from her brethren—too different—and it left her feeling she was alone even with the legions of comrades she had in Heaven and on Earth.

Especially now that Javan is gone.

In her periphery, Gabrielle noticed Phalen's gaze fall on her and heard a subtle huff escape her mouth.

"Javan wasn't who you thought he was ... who *any* of us thought he was, Gabrielle. I wish you would stop thinking of him so much."

"Easy. He was my Reyah," Gabrielle said with a slight scowl. "I wish I had thought of him when I was blocking my thoughts so you didn't know he was on my mind at all. And ... trust me ... I want him off my mind more than anyone."

Silence stretched between them as they continued their path along the shoreline leading away from the busiest part of the beach. Phalen didn't have to respond to Gabrielle's statement—all angels knew the pain was constant and endless from the loss of a Reyah. It left a sense of loneliness that was indescribable, and one that Gabrielle often thought a human could never endure. It was too profound to bear even with their limited time to feel it, and an angel felt it for thousands of years. The best that could be hoped for was to learn how to distract yourself from the conscious thoughts of the one who was lost to you.

Gabrielle closed her eyes as they walked, taking in the way it felt on her skin as the brisk, salty breeze carried the spray from crashing waves, lightly coating her face and body—a breeze foretelling the arrival of the storm approaching from the sea's depths. The darkened clouds were becoming more prominent on the horizon, and she was already aware of the soft rumblings of thunder that were too far away for the humans on the beach to hear.

It only took a moment more before she saw what was now a familiar vision behind her closed eyes—the image of a young man. She didn't know who he was, not yet. However, it was always the same blue eyes looking back at her—the same crooked smile. A human so present in her visions would be someone she would help in some way, and this one—who she'd seen so many times she'd lost count—would be easy to recognize when the time came. He seemed somehow ... *different*, more important, for reasons Gabrielle couldn't figure out. What she did know was that she found herself trying to hold onto the visions longer lately. She enjoyed his face. It filled her with happiness. But what she enjoyed most was the peace it brought that was normally elusive for her. He would appear and all the tension and worry that plagued her would drift away like the sand being pulled back to sea by the tide, causing her to will the vision of him to linger. When she finally opened her eyes, she saw something moving toward them on the distant shoreline, and the feeling of happiness and peace disappeared.

She released a heavy sigh.

"Well, that didn't take long," Gabrielle said under her breath.

Phalen looked up from where her own eyes had been searching the sand in front of her and looked at Gabrielle, then in the direction of her gaze.

"How many?"

"Looks like seven, but there could be more. Once they know I'm around, there could be many in route I don't see, yet." Gabrielle didn't keep her frustration from being known in her tone. This would prove Amaziah right and allow him to gain even firmer footing in his argument against her doing what she had been asking for.

"What do you want to do?" Phalen asked.

"I want to release some of the bad mood my work has left me with. Are you game?"

A large, mischievous smile pushed Phalen's human cheeks aside.

"Always. You don't think I came just out of duty, do you? I was hoping for a little action. It's fine to spar with our brethren, but it's much more challenging when I am fighting with the end in mind—whether it's my end or my opponent's."

"Good. We need to move this somewhere I can easily use a veil."

"Okay. Just remember not to take them all out yourself. I'd like to use this to sharpen my skills—if you don't mind."

Gabrielle smiled at Phalen. She was young, especially compared to her, and still eager for combat against the Fallen.

"No, I don't mind. I'll let you handle most of them."

"Where do you want to take this little battle?" Phalen asked with unrestrained enthusiasm.

Gabrielle scanned their surroundings until she saw a small barrier island about a quarter mile out to sea. It was far enough from the beach that there were no swimmers or jet skiers near it, and most boaters were already heeding the threatening horizon's warning.

"There." Gabrielle pointed in the direction of the island. "That will serve us well."

"How do we get there? We can't exactly walk on water or fly to it without causing a commotion."

"I'll handle it."

Gabrielle raised her hand, bringing the progression of human time to a halt. Every living thing stood still—as if they had been created by an artist's brush. The only beings still moving, other than Gabrielle and Phalen, were the demons in pursuit of revenge that they desired for being cast from Heaven—for being denied whatever it was they felt they deserved.

"Wow ... that's something I didn't think I'd ever see. I've heard about it, but so few are bestowed with the ability to interrupt mortal time."

Gabrielle felt her unease rise once more from the attention her powers brought. She had to stop her inner voice from yelling that she was tired of being different. She didn't have time to dwell on those feelings, so she pushed them away. Their attackers, though a safe distance away, were drawing close. "We need to get over there so I can start time again. I'm not a fan of using this ability unless I have to. I worry some bored demon will use the pause to wreak havoc if it's left in place long enough."

Phalen was staring at Gabrielle with an expression of marvel mingling with admiration, furthering Gabrielle's unwanted sense of uniqueness.

"Anyway," Gabrielle said to try to interrupt Phalen's gaze and its accompanying thoughts, "let's go."

The two made their way to the island as Gabrielle took care of what was needed to keep their human bodies from being bothered on the beach. Once they reached the location, Gabrielle placed a veil around it, then resumed time. A glance at the shore they had just been walking on showed their human figures still making their way slowly along the edge of the breaking waves. The dark-haired, olive-skinned body she'd chosen was a stark contrast to the white-blond, ivory-skinned one that Phalen decided on.

That was all she had time to note before the demons were upon them. They were now facing seven of Yahuwah's Fallen, and as much as it pained Gabrielle to know what was about to befall these demons who were once her brethren, she knew their dark eyes matched their intentions.

"Well," said one of the demons, "I take it you intend on letting us have a little fun. Would you like to ... *dance*, angel?"

They'd dropped their Glamours since there were no human eyes to see their true appearance. She wished they hadn't. The empty gazes that once showed so much Light and life weren't that bad, really. It was their unusually large mouths that held ragged, darkened teeth in their confines and over-muscular faces and bodies that were things seen in human nightmares. Their beauty was lost in the fall, mirroring the loss of beauty in their hearts, minds, and souls.

And their odor ...

Evil is vile on more than a mental, soulless level; it consumes the physical as well. If the Fallen didn't mask their stench, it made her insides lurch as they were right now. It was the smell of the hate and decay of the Underworld they inhabited, a cross between sulfur and rotting flesh. It seeped into everything. It showed in every tooth, under every nail. Even their skin showed the greenish-grey undertones of the Darkness of the Underworld.

"I don't think it's going to be as much fun as you might think, demon," Gabrielle said, aware of the others making a wide circle around her and Phalen.

"I know who you are," the demon continued, "and what you are *supposedly* capable of. But we are seven against you and one other. And there are more on their way. Your time is over."

"You seem so sure of yourself. I'm surprised ... *if* you really do know who I am."

"You're Gabrielle. *The Reaper*, as we like to call you," the demon said with more than a little venom pricking into his tone.

That name made her skin crawl, and the Fallen knew it. The Reaper. She didn't cause death, but those who crossed her sometimes wished for it by the time she was done with them.

"The Angel of Karma," the demon continued. "I believe that's what you like to call yourself. I'm much older than you. I fell long before you were created, so I don't hold the same respect for your abilities as those who lived with you in Heaven." The demon glared at Gabrielle, and there seemed to be more than loathing behind his scrutiny—there was curiosity. "Let me guess, *angel*, you're here to try and find a certain book before we do."

Gabrielle's puzzled expression was the only answer she offered. She didn't have time to inquire about what book he was speaking of. "I see. If you had known me in Heaven, you might have made a wiser choice." Gabrielle continued to consider the positions of the others and moved herself to be able to see Phalen. It was true that Phalen was a skilled ally in combat, but Gabrielle would never forgive herself if she was hurt. It would be better to keep her in view as much as possible.

The demon who had spoken and two of the others fixed their attention only on Gabrielle while the remaining demons seemed to be more interested in Phalen. Gabrielle realized the plan must be to take her friend out first so they could then focus all their efforts on her. They were obviously underestimating Phalen. Gabrielle couldn't help but let a smile hint at the corners of her mouth.

Phalen is definitely going to have fun.

"Remember, Gabrielle," Phalen whispered, "you said you'd let me have some of them."

Gabrielle smiled knowingly at her friend. That was all there was time for before the demons began their attack. As Gabrielle suspected, four of the seven focused on Phalen.

They swiftly encircled her as the other three cautiously made their move toward Gabrielle. She was glad they were being wary of her; it gave her the opportunity to see how Phalen would do before her own combat began.

The demons surrounding Phalen presented their weapons; all wielded Dither Swords that gave off a slight silver shimmer. That shimmer would turn blindingly white when it struck another weapon, confusing the opponent by making it difficult to see. The demons smiled, revealing their razor sharp teeth, so sure of their choice and perceived advantage.

Phalen smiled back, and Gabrielle could see her relax with the knowledge of her own abilities. Gabrielle focused her attention back to her own aggressors, keeping her friend partially in view. Phalen closed her eyes and raised her palms to the sky. The demons rushed her friend as a Dither Sword appeared in each of Phalen's open hands. The day lit brighter as Gabrielle heard the crash of the swords meeting. It was as if they were in the presence of Yahuwah himself. Sparks from clashing swords peppered the air around them, creating an amber glow that invaded the white light.

The demon who'd spoken so surely moments before now looked upon the scene with a deep scowl. Gabrielle didn't have to look to know Phalen was proving to be a more than worthy opponent, and smiled as the demons in front of her realized their miscalculation. The space around them dimmed as the racket of opposing swords behind her ceased.

Gabrielle felt the approaching energy of her comrade.

"Was it as enjoyable as you had hoped, Phalen?" Gabrielle asked without looking at her. The sound of Phalen's voice told Gabrielle there was a smile on her face.

"Yes, better than I'd hoped. I'm not sure why Yahuwah allows them to still call Divine weapons, but it sure makes things more fun."

The demon who had acted as the leader released a deep, throaty growl. "Don't get too happy yet, little angel. We aren't done here. Not by a long shot."

Gabrielle's smile faded as she suddenly felt the urge to be done with this, compelling her to make quicker work of her opponents than she had intended. Partially because she didn't want Phalen to be in even more awe of her, to have her then add to the tales of *Gabrielle's might*—there was enough story telling going on already—but, more than that, she wanted to get the *I told you so* from Amaziah out of the way.

"Demon," Gabrielle said with an edge seeping into her tone, "I am most certainly done here. Playtime is over."

Gabrielle did no more than raise her hands. A golden bow appeared in one hand, and three arrows tipped with crackling, white Holy Fire manifested in the other. With a swift motion, she pulled the arrows back as if they were one and let them loose. The targets fell to their knees before they took two steps. Matching expressions that held both pain and surprise gazed back at her. The Fallen slowly began to burn from within, consumed by the fires of Hell they would now never leave.

The only demon who'd spoken maintained his targeted glare at Gabrielle. "*Bitch!*"

Then his form succumbed to the death that came for him, turning him into nothing more than ember and ash.

"For you," Gabrielle said in no more than a whisper to the space where he once stood, "I *was* The Reaper."

Phalen stepped forward and looked at Gabrielle. "So … how many arrows *can* you use on different targets at once, anyway?"

Gabrielle looked at Phalen. She'd tried not to inspire what was behind the look in Phalen's eyes as her friend waited for an answer to her question. Gabrielle just smiled and quickly looked away, focusing back on the area around her.

Satisfied that the lingering stench and ash was the only remaining evidence of her fallen brethren and their conflict, knowing the storm would unleash rain upon the landscape—joining the ash with sand—Gabrielle turned and responded to Phalen's question.

"It doesn't matter. Let's go"

"Sure. Why does Yahuwah allow the Fallen to still use His weapons?"

"Amaziah told me it's some deal He made with Ramai. To keep things as equal as possible with the war." Gabrielle considered the deal Yahuwah had made before continuing. "This war is more about humans than us. He wants humanity to win it for themselves by making the right choices on their own, not through his own power or ours. It would be very easy for us to wipe out the entire population of demons if they had no defense."

"Hmm …" Phalen said. "Hey … do you know what he was talking about when he said he thought you were trying to find a book?"

"No, but I need to. Maybe Amaziah knows."

"*So*," Phalen began, her playful tone lightening the mood slightly, "that demon was pretty sure of himself, asking you to *dance*. What would you do if the Devil asked you?"

Gabrielle smirked. "If the Devil asked me to dance, I'd tell him he couldn't handle me."

As they returned to their human forms, Gabrielle glanced back to make sure everything looked as it had before the fight began. Satisfied, she descended into her temporary body. Together, they continued walking away from the crowd until they found sufficient cover to ascend.

What Gabrielle couldn't have noticed on the island was a flock of crows hidden behind a veil of their own. They had observed the battle as it unfolded and ended—and listened closely to the angels' conversation after it was over. As Gabrielle and Phalen resumed their stroll, the flock took flight—disappearing into the heavy black clouds closing in on the coastline. A flash of lightning lit the dismal horizon as the last crow was enveloped in the storm's roiling shadows—as if it was embracing a lost love.

Chapter Two

GABRIELLE ✝ BATTLE WON

'Then tell me how you expect me to learn how to get through to humans, Amaziah.' Gabrielle found herself trying, for what must be the hundredth time, to convince her closest ally she needed to live as a human. And, once again, her mood wasn't helping her keep her cool. She could feel the negativity from giving out so much bad karma trying to push toward freedom—ready to lash out at whoever was nearest. Right now, that was Amaziah, and she certainly didn't want to use him to ease her edginess. 'Because I have tried everything else I can think of to get them to want to be closer to Light, and all I see is more of them drifting toward Ramai and the shadows of Darkness. As we lose their souls, we are also losing our Asarers.'

Amaziah sighed. Gabrielle knew he understood her need to be on Earth, but it didn't mean he would plead her case to Yahuwah. It was more than a little dangerous for her to be incarnated for any substantial length of time, both physically and spiritually. Being on Earth in any form made her a physical target to the Fallen, but being in a human body would make her a spiritual target in ways she would not be able to control. If her request was granted, she would be there for months, maybe longer.

'Gabrielle, I know the struggles you have had in getting the results you want when you assign karma. And I am well aware of the angels we have lost. Especially our Asarers and the human souls they have bound themselves to. But that doesn't mean putting yourself in jeopardy with only a hope of understanding humanity's motivations is the answer. Why is it that you can't do the same from here?'

'That's what I've always done. It's not working anymore. I've tried to make adjustments for the changes I've seen, but I'm not making any headway. If I can live in a human body, feel and think like a human in different situations, maybe I can get a better grasp on what drives their decisions. Then I can give out karma in ways that will cause them to want to move closer to Light.' She realized her illuminated hands were clenched tightly at her sides. She immediately opened them, but her tension still showed clearly as her energy quivered and took on a light red hue, instead of her normal shimmer of mingling white and silver.

She was weary of this debate, but she needed to calm herself. Amaziah was Yahuwah's closest advisor and one of the only angels who could see Him whenever he needed to. He was her only real hope in being granted the task she sought.

'Gabrielle, you would be in constant danger. The incident that just took place when you went to Earth with Phalen and the quickness in which the Fallen noticed you should have made that clear.'

'I don't need to be reminded of the danger. I am quite aware of it,' she snapped, then took a deep breath. Amaziah's pulsing energy turned a deep crimson—a visual caution for her to be careful. There was no other angel she was as close to as Amaziah now that Javan was gone, no other she trusted and loved more, and she knew he felt the same. They were more than just brethren; they were much like a human father and daughter though angels don't have biological ties like humans. Regardless of their closeness, his patience with her and her moods had limits, and judging by the silent warning, she was pushing it. Gabrielle took a few more moments to get a grip on herself, then continued. 'That doesn't change anything. Would you please just ask

Yahuwah again if He'll let me do this? Tell Him I am willing to take the risk.'

'But He may not be willing to let you take the risk, Gabrielle. You are important to Him. You hold a lofty position, one difficult to fill. One that's too important to risk a new angel with no experience stepping into your role if something were to happen to you. The abilities and powers that go along with it can be ill-used if put in the wrong angel's control. You have gained a great amount of trust with our Lord, and every demon on Earth knows it. They will try to hurt you—kill you—if they have the chance, just to get a taste of revenge on Him for casting them out of Heaven.'

'I could have dealt with what happened earlier even without Phalen.'

'It might not always go so well for you, Gabrielle. Or for those with you. You are not invincible. For an angel who seems to be so wary of attention concerning her powers and abilities, you certainly seem to have every confidence of what you are capable of doing. There are those who have fallen who are powerful., and when gathered in force, they can be even more so. What will you do when faced with an opponent who is, at the least, as skilled as you?'

'They were more powerful. I realize I don't know just how much it would have affected them, but those who were created, at least as powerful as me, would have lost a significant amount of that power in their fall. And I don't know what I will do when faced with an opponent who is a good match or better than me, Amaziah. I suppose I will do what I always have, use the gifts Yahuwah has bestowed on me. But we both know there are few demons I have to be concerned with. I'll see them coming. I can evade them and any threat they pose.'

'But that won't help you against the spiritual attacks. You, alone. Against Darkness. Even you won't see it coming. And it will happen often, quietly, sneaking into the places in your mind that a human body will leave unprotected.'

Gabrielle had no argument. She would not be able to protect herself as well from the dangers to her spiritually while incarnated. Amaziah waited for her to respond, but she took the opportunity to change the subject instead.

'Speaking of the encounter with the Fallen, one of them assumed we were there to try and find a book—a book the demons are apparently seeking. Do

you know what they were talking about?'

His face clouded with a puzzled expression that she was sure was identical to the one she had when the demon spoke the words to her, only Amaziah seemed a bit more taken aback.

'Amaziah, do you know what he was speaking of?'

Amaziah snapped back to their conversation.

'*There are many powerful books, but I don't know of any still in existence that would benefit the Fallen enough to demand our attention.*'

Even as he said the words, Gabrielle could sense that wherever his thoughts had been, he was being pulled back there to search for an answer.

Quiet lingered between them, and she remained still, both in form and communication. The best thing to do was wait. She wasn't sure what to say now, anyway. For the first time, though she didn't know why, she felt the argument was turning in her favor. Amaziah had never before relinquished on this subject, but she sensed his desire to fight what she wanted was waning.

I wonder why?

Something else was brought on by his silence. A feeling of dread washed over her. She shivered. Was the chill just an after effect of being so close to evil or some early foreboding? Something concerning the book? As the silence stretched, Gabrielle searched for a way to shake the dark feeling. It seemed to be taking root, though, making her want to go to Earth even more to find out what the demon was speaking of.

She tried to remember anything she had heard about a book over the thousands of years of her life that may be of some concern. Something that Amaziah had not heard of. That wasn't likely. There didn't seem to be much he didn't know. Regardless, she didn't like the feeling that hung over her. Something was coming—something the Fallen knew and she didn't. And *that* was definitely troubling.

There wasn't much she could do with so little information, but she could make a trip to the realm of the Shifters—to Corstorphine. She could find out if Grayson or any of his fellows had any information, and if they didn't, she could ask for their help in finding out more about it. She felt her heart warm as she thought of taking time out to see her old friend. It had been too long since their last meeting—far, far too long.

Amaziah's voice pulled Gabrielle back from her thoughts. When she focused her attention on him again, she noted his color was back to normal. From the glow cast around her, she knew hers was, too.

'Gabrielle, while you were on Earth, Yahuwah made the decision to allow you to live as a human if you still wanted to when you returned. It seems dealing with the danger you are bringing on yourself, first hand, has not changed your mind as I had hoped it would.'

Amaziah paused, and again, Gabrielle remained silent, shocked to hear Amaziah's words. She never prepared herself if what she was asking for was granted. Now, she not only didn't know what to say, she wasn't sure how to act or feel. Part of her was thrilled but another part of her was concerned. Even if Amaziah didn't think she took the threat seriously, she did.

'However, this is only being granted to you for six months. You will have to return to us and the safety of Heaven after that time has transpired, whether you have accomplished your goal or not. Do you understand?'

Gabrielle took another long moment before she could answer him as thoughts of all she would learn and all the dangers she would face played in her mind.

'Yes, Amaziah. I understand.' She found her thoughts immediately going to the young man in her visions and wondered if she would have enough time to find him. She hoped so. As much as she tried not to, she couldn't help but feel the desire to search him out.

'Good. I'm surprised you don't seem happier about the news.'

She pulled her mind away from the human, worried that she wasn't being careful enough to block her thoughts. *'Believe it or not, I am not happy about the need to do this at all. I have to, though, if I want to help regain the upper hand in this war. I admit I am looking forward to experiencing things I never would otherwise, but this decision is driven by concern and fear of what will happen if I don't go.'*

'Yes, I imagine it is. You have always carried a tremendous burden along

with the position you hold. No other comes to mind who would have done as fine a job as you.'

'Really?' Gabrielle couldn't help but laugh humorlessly at the accolade. '*I wonder. If I had done a better job to this point, there would be no need for me to live as a human.*'

'My dear Gabrielle, if you must doubt something about yourself, doubt your negative thoughts. Don't waste your energy on what doesn't deserve it. You have always been more critical of yourself than needed.'

'Maybe … maybe not. I'd like to believe you are right, though,' Gabrielle responded, but so quietly she wondered if Amaziah heard her at all. In a normal tone, she continued. 'When do I begin?'

'Right away. The location has already been chosen. I can take you now.'

'You're coming with me?'

'Only to make sure you are safe, and I will be there if it is ever needed. You will have to have my Aegis Veil around you, as well as in your mind, at all times while in your human body. It will help protect you from detection but still allow for the most realistic sensations and emotions possible. It's the most powerful protection I can offer without being by your side myself. But it will dull your Divine discernment. You won't be able to easily spot the Fallen. So be even more cautious than usual.'

Gabrielle was still having a difficult time believing this was finally happening. She was moments away from beginning her life in a human body—even if it was going to be brief.

'*Are you ready, Gabrielle?*' Amaziah asked to get her attention. But what captured it more was the undertone of concern she was sure she heard with the words.

'*What? Oh … yes. I'm ready.*' She realized he wasn't just asking her if she was ready to leave, he was asking if she was sure she was ready for all this task would ask of her.

'Then let's get this over with, shall we?'

Chapter Three

GABRIELLE ✟ INCARNATION

As soon as Amaziah felt she was settled, he reluctantly left, and Gabrielle headed to the beach. She then spent the entire day with the sun, sand, sea, and humans, and now her time to be by herself for a while was coming to an end. Being alone was a rarity for her. She was normally surrounded by her brethren.

A bright flash of lightning and immediate crack of thunder sent the few remaining humans scrambling to gather their belongings from the beach as they tried to beat the downpour. Some people had been so eager to get out of the path of the storm—one that seemed particularly angry—that they abandoned some of their things.

Gabrielle scanned the discarded items—bottles of lotion, trash, scattered towels, a beach ball, and an umbrella tumbling away as if trying to outrun the wind. Gabrielle mused that the gusts were trying to push the people, even her, out of the way to safety. The storm was of no concern to her. Nothing that belonged in the human world could harm her. It was the beings who didn't belong among humans who could make her wary, but there were few of those who caused her worry.

Gabrielle turned her attention away from the umbrella's dance into the distance and gave it back to the water in front of her. The intensity of the surging waves had grown steadily. She stood with her feet just within reach of the fingers of water that seemed to stretch to tickle her toes, enticing her with each break of waves against the sand to come in and play for a while. The sun that had given its warmth throughout the day was setting just ahead of the storm, reflecting against the liquid horizon of the Gulf of Mexico. The fiery sky boasted shades of red, orange, and yellow that reflected and mingled on the surface of the stirring waters as gusts of wind roused the fabric of her long black dress, whipping her legs as if urging her to hurry—to move on and take shelter before the storm unleashed its rage.

As terrible as this storm threatened to be, this wasn't the one that she was concerned with. It wasn't a storm of rain and wind and lightning that she was here to outwit—it wasn't the one that threatened her life. Gabrielle closed her eyes and tried to push the thoughts out of her mind, but the new thoughts that rushed in to replace them were no better.

The mental calm the tropical landscape helped her achieve earlier had waned, replaced by a familiar ache as her mind wandered to memories of Javan. She'd been on this beach many years ago. Only that day, she hadn't been alone. She had been with him.

It was a time before humans settled the now overpopulated Florida coastline. Before she lost the only love in Heaven she could ever have. Before she had the empty space inside her she did now that was constant and as loud to her as it was silent to others. Many times she'd heard a human say, 'It's better to have loved and lost, than to have never loved at all.' She'd argue that if it was the kind of love one angel had for another of their kind, it's better to have simply never loved. An angel who lost their Reyah will forever grieve them as if it just happened, without any chance of another in their life to ease the sorrow. It didn't matter if that loss was due to death or if they had been cast out of Heaven, the result was the same.

Gabrielle closed her eyes, sensing the last warmth the sun's rays would offer her face and bare arms on this day.

Now is not the time for regrets.

She pushed the sadness away, focusing instead on the Earthly sounds of seagulls calling to each other in the distance and palm fronds rubbing against their neighbors as they tossed in the wind. When she opened her eyes, the sun was on the cusp of slipping away for another day. She wished it would take the memories of Javan and her love for him with it, knowing it was a lost wish even as she made it. The light the sun lent to create the vibrant colors she'd seen moments before now conceded to the dark blues and purples of dusk—chasing the light into gloom and void. There was still just enough light to make her eyes glint like emeralds and her long waves of dark hair to shine against the ensuing shadows.

A bolt of lightning drew her attention in the direction of not only it but also a human who had been slow in leaving the openness of the beach. The length of his stride told her that he was aware of his vulnerability to the strands of electricity that were almost constantly ripping the sky apart. Gabrielle's body tensed as the man, in his mid-twenties, began jogging toward her and smiled—looking at her a little longer than she was comfortable with.

Am I doing a good job of looking normal?

She felt a pang of worry grip her stomach as she wondered whether or not she was going to fit in here or stand out like she did in her eternal home. The reality of being so different from her brethren was completely inescapable in Heaven. She caught herself hoping, on many occasions, that things would be easier for her on Earth.

Please just let me fit in … at least here.

Another flash and crack of thunder made the man jump, and he pulled his hands quickly to his ears. He glanced over his shoulder at the storm, then back at Gabrielle.

"That storm's going to be a real nasty one," the man said as if he truly was concerned about her safety. A slight scowl reinforced the worry in his tone.

She just smiled and nodded. His concern, though kind, was wholly misplaced. But he would have no idea of that—at least, she hoped he wouldn't suspect.

She looked around to see if she drew any other attention but there wasn't anyone left. They'd heeded nature's threats. Even if they did notice the seventeen-year-old standing at the water's edge, they probably wouldn't take enough time to realize she was, somehow, different.

They don't notice the fantastical side of their world at all.

The thought both relieved and disturbed her.

Gabrielle turned her attention back to the sunset as she, once again, tried to distract herself from her thoughts and recalled her day.

She'd spent the day under a much different sky, one full of sunlight and cotton clouds, experiencing the added sensations her human senses allowed—senses she had no need of in her true form. She was enjoying being incarnated this time more than any before. It was the first time she'd been on Earth for more than a few minutes without drawing the unwanted and dangerous attention of every demon within a hundred miles. All thanks to the Aegis Veil.

While spending part of the day walking slowly in and out of the shops along the road running parallel to the beach, enjoying the protection the veil offered, she discovered the blissful taste of mint chocolate chip ice cream. She loved the way the cold slipped down her throat but didn't understand why it caused her to shiver and get little raised bumps on her tan skin. To her relief, they went away as quickly as they appeared. It had been a nice change from the heat of day, and she looked forward to another scoop before she made her way to her temporary home.

The task ahead was going to be difficult, and she hoped she was doing the right thing. It made little difference if she was one of the most powerful angels Yahuwah ever created if she couldn't figure out how to make humans have faith again. So many from her home, as well as here on Earth, were relying on her success. She and her brethren were losing the battle that had been waged between Light and Darkness for thousands of years. It was beginning to slip through their fingers so fast that Gabrielle was concerned the decision to live here had been made too late.

This was all she could do, though.

This, and handling karma—making sure people receive the appropriate rewards or punishments for their choices. Free will is a wonderful gift, but so many used theirs without a conscience now, and humanity's lack of conscience was the biggest obstacle to winning the war.

Gabrielle breathed the warm, moist sea air into her lungs, stretched them as far as she could and exhaled slowly. She needed to clear her mind of her concerns.

Just concentrate on your goal.

It was difficult to ease her tension. Her job had been affecting her mood more harshly every day. As much as she loved her position as The Angel of Karma, she hated the hostility she found herself experiencing most days—a nasty repercussion of dealing with so much bad karma. Handing out a little more good karma would go a long way in making her less edgy.

Closing her eyes, she tried to listen only to the waves. They were coming in at a more rapid pace as the angry clouds grew closer.

Soon, there won't be more than a heartbeat of time between each break of waves.

Her focus on the sound wasn't what soothed her troubled thoughts. It was the image of the young man. She loved seeing this stranger's face pass into her mind's eye. She loved it, and at the same time, was frightened that she loved it. She didn't know who he was— the young man with the blue eyes she wanted to retreat into. She *did* know the feelings she seemed to be having for this human were forbidden, something she couldn't act upon.

I can't have the love of a human any more than I can have it from any angel other than Javan, unless I join the Fallen ... and that will never happen.

The human, at least his image and the way it made her feel, was Gabrielle's, and no one knew it but her. Not even Amaziah—especially not Amaziah. He would be furious with her if he knew. She would keep the vision of him to herself as long as she could, and one day, he would appear in front of her. She would wait for that day. And, at least for now, he was hers and only hers.

My little secret.

All too soon, the vision ended, and so did the peace it loaned her for that moment. Peace she so desperately needed. Gabrielle took another deep breath, this one involuntary. She huffed out a sharp sigh.

Lightning weaved its white coils across the twilit sky once again, followed instantly by a crack of thunder so earsplitting it made the ground tremble.

"Is that all you've got?" Gabrielle asked the storm defiantly, feeling the desire for a fight. She wished it really was a foe coming upon her instead of rain and wind.

As she turned and moved away from the horizon that had just swallowed the sun and its light completely and began walking toward her new life—a life that would be surrounded by the oppressive shadows of Darkness—she felt a foreboding stirring deep in her core. It accompanied a Knowing she prayed would not come to be.

There was a storm … one that could bring her end, and it loomed on a horizon invisible to the humans it so greatly affected. But Gabrielle could see it. It was coming fast and true. The rain it spilled would be the blood and tears of angels, the lightning from Divine weapons striking, the thunder from the screams of pain born from Yahuwah's angels and the Fallen.

Gabrielle shivered. As her body trembled, she wanted to believe the chill was from the absence of the warm rays her human flesh now missed, but she knew it was from the heaviness that accompanied the Fallen and those who lived in Shadow—from Darkness caused by far more than an absent sun.

Chapter Four

GABRIELLE ✝ FIRST IMPRESSIONS

Time moved so slowly on Earth, at least compared to what Gabrielle was accustomed to. She still hadn't adjusted to the difference. It made her uncomfortable in a way, feeling like she was missing something important back in Heaven. Or that whatever—whoever—was causing the feeling of dread that had settled on her since arriving on Earth two months ago had way too much time to put their dark plans in motion. Regardless, she thought it was possible, even if she spent years constantly living as a human, she'd never feel comfortable with the difference in how time flowed.

She'd been feeling like something or someone was coming. Looking at her reflection in her car's visor mirror, she saw her mouth and brows move in unison as she frowned. Whichever it was, it wasn't good.

"Not good at all," she said to herself.

Even the dreams she now had because of her human form were unpleasant, though she only woke with fuzzy memories of them. At times, she would wake to her screams echoing off the walls of her bedroom, her eyes frantically searching her surroundings, panting and sweating like she'd been running a race.

It was fitting, though. She was in a race against the clock to find out what she needed to in the short amount of time she'd been given. No matter how slow she felt time in her human body was going, she knew it would be coming to end faster than she wanted.

"Let it go, Gabrielle. There's nothing you can do about your damn feelings that *something's* coming," she scolded her image in the mirror. She glared back at herself, as if the stare was going to drive the statement home and make her actually heed the words. In a frustrated swipe of her hand, she flipped the visor up, sending it hard against the roof of the car. She momentarily let the frustration consume her.

She was going to have to calm down before getting out of the car. Earning the reputation as an angry, unapproachable teen on the first day of what was supposed to be her senior year was not what she wanted. Her job wasn't helping to keep that intense side of her from coming to the forefront of her personality, though.

She glanced at the time on her cell phone for what was probably the tenth time in as many minutes. She'd hurried herself this morning, wanting to arrive early to begin observing her classmates.

Now, she wished she'd taken her time.

Her nerves were starting to show but not from being scared. At least that's what she told herself.

Why would The Angel of Karma be scared of a bunch of teenagers?

It was anxiety that stemmed from hoping she had done a good job in her attempt to look like a normal teen. She watched the students milling around campus, scrutinizing their clothes, hair, makeup, and shoes—their mannerisms and how they interacted with each other.

Now ... she was waiting.

Even in the early morning sun, her car was beginning to warm while sitting in Hillsboro High's parking lot. She felt her skin begin to stick to her shirt that was pressed between her and the leather of the car's seat as it dampened from sweat. She turned the car on, switched the air conditioner on high, and put her face in front of one of the vents. The summer was almost over, but unusually high temperatures that had been the norm over the last couple of months in Tennessee continued.

Hillsboro High was one of the older schools in Nashville. It was chosen because of its diversity. There were many races and economic classes represented as well as an eclectic group of cliques. There were the usual ones found at any campus: jocks, cheerleaders, nerds, and brains. But there were many others including goths, punks, rockers, hipsters, thespians, and artsy kids. It was a wonderful group to study, and a great place to get many different backgrounds to supply the varied perspectives, opinions, and conflicts of humans.

Many of Gabrielle's peers thought it better to be in a larger city like Paris, New York, Venice, or London. But she was told Yahuwah felt it was useful to be in a mid-sized city, Nashville, so she could get a better feel for what people were dealing with in a more balanced environment. Nashville was just right. Not too big or too small, too fast or too slow, too exciting or too boring—a happy medium.

So, here she was, waiting for this endeavor to really start. She'd been living among humans for two months now, getting accustomed to her new body and its emotions, but the real test and fun was about to begin—high school.

The decision to live as a teenager was her own. It seemed to be the most logical choice to learn which direction humanity was moving. Though she'd been sure of this plan in the beginning, she'd had doubts over the last two months. There had been several occasions she felt the war was already lost, that her time here was going to be a waste. Later, she would decide that the feeling was caused by her new human emotions and thoughts.

There's no way I will ever give up ... not until my life is over, and the choice to fight is no longer mine.

Light flutters began in her stomach that seemed to grow more intense with every second that ticked off the clock. She wondered what was causing them.

Could one of the Fallen be near?

The nausea she associated with them wasn't present though, so she decided it must be nerves.

This was one of the things she hadn't been able to fully grasp when committing to live here—feeling, understanding, and dealing with human emotions and sensations. She knew she'd deal with them; that was the point of being here. But she didn't appreciate how *deeply* she'd feel them, how much it would confuse and cloud her normally clear thinking. Things like what other humans or her brethren thought of her, whether or not she was going to succeed in this task, worrying about mistakes, wanting the people she met to like and accept her—so many things were exceptionally important to her while in human form.

"Yeah, the acceptance thing won't go away," Gabrielle said to her empty car. It was frustrating. She had hoped it wouldn't be as hard to feel accepted here. Now, she thought it was going to be harder.

The impact and intensity of her thoughts and emotions were felt so markedly in this body. It was jarring to her mind, at times, just how thoroughly things affected her. Even early on in this experience, she was beginning to understand how volatile these emotions and thoughts were and how it could become difficult to make the right decisions with so many differing stimulations. It was increasingly clear how profoundly they could mess with a human's mind, especially when dealing with the desire to have one person in particular in their life.

Gabrielle closed her eyes and brought forth her mental picture of the young, blue-eyed man. She smiled immediately. She could see him whenever she desired. She had practiced over the last two months. Her mind's eye would call for his face, and it would appear. She did it often, especially when she needed to calm herself.

The intensity of the wantings it dredged up in her was confusing ... and worrisome. There was a desire to be near him, protect him, know him—hold and kiss him. The last sent a chill through her, and she let her eyes open slowly as the thoughts of living in the real world came into her mind—the world she lived in where angels weren't allowed to have that kind of relationship with a human. And yet, she thought she was finding herself wanting one with him—a relationship that was absolutely forbidden.

"Okay ... don't get carried away. You haven't even met him."

She didn't know what to make of it. Was developing this urge simply because of her human body's emotions and thoughts?

Yeah ... that must be it.

One thing was obvious to her after two months. There was going to be a lot to get used to. Humans have more to deal with than she'd ever given them credit for. She took a deep breath as she watched the other students arrive, and after many of them made their way into the school, she decided it was time to immerse herself in teenage life.

Cutting the engine and gathering her things, she took one last look at her reflection in the mirror. Intense green eyes stared back at her. It was funny how much she found herself interested in her appearance now. Just one of the many things angels didn't concern themselves with. Satisfied her makeup was still where she'd put it and her long dark hair was still placed in a loose, messy up-do, she gathered her things and opened her car door.

"Whoa! Watch it!" a male called out, agitation edging into his voice.

Startled, Gabrielle looked up and saw the person the voice belonged to. A tall, dark-haired teenager. His eyes—the blue ones from her visions—fixed upon her, and she saw the crease between his brows begin to relax. The straight line of his mouth was replaced with a slightly crooked grin. Her breath hitched, and Gabrielle couldn't stop a smile from stretching her face while they stared at each other as if entranced. The flutters that filled her stomach seemed to be waging an all-out war as they pinged around out of control.

It's him.

It was the human she'd been catching glimpses of in visions and dreams. The one whose face alone brought her unexplained happiness, whose smile made her own fixed. It was hard to believe, after all this time and countless occasions of seeing him in her mind, that he was standing in front of her. She felt the stirring deep inside of her that had become a part of every thought she had of him. It was like her soul was trying to escape to be with his. After several more moments of staring, Gabrielle snapped out of the spell.

"Umm ... I'm *so* sorry!" Gabrielle said, trying to calm her fleeting pulse. "I wasn't paying attention ... *obviously*. Did I hit you?" The rambunctious flutters increased their chaos in her stomach. Gabrielle had never been so unsure of herself even though he wasn't any kind of threat. He wasn't stronger, faster, more skilled, or more powerful ... he was human. Just a human who could do no harm to her at all, yet she was uncomfortable with what to say, or do, next.

What an odd thing ...

"No, not at all," he said as his smile grew. She could tell just by the shade of his skin that he had enjoyed a lot of time outside over the summer. He looked more like the guys in Florida who spent every waking moment possible on the beach or in the water. She found herself instantly curious about him.

What do you do around here to get a tan like that? Whoa! *Enough, Gabrielle.*

A flood of questions threatened to spill out of her mouth like a possessed inquisitor. Instead, she let herself get lost in them quietly. She wanted to know who he was, where he lived, what he liked to do, and if he had a girlfriend. The last jolted her back to reality. It was dangerous for her to have these thoughts, to feel what she was feeling—dangerous and exhilarating.

Seriously, put a lid on the crazy. A fantasy is just that ... a fantasy.

But he was making that difficult. He was still staring intensely—as if he was able to look deep inside her and was learning more with each beat of her heart. Warmth rose in her cheeks. It left Gabrielle feeling vulnerable though open to his curiosity at the same time. She thought she would tell him anything he wanted to know. All he had to do was ask, and she would give him all the secrets of his world—the one he believed to be reality and the fantastical one that was around him. She saw his expression change to pure curiosity as he returned from wherever his mind had taken him.

"I haven't seen you here before."

"I moved to town in June. Are you sure I didn't hit you?" Gabrielle put her foot on the ground to begin to get out, and he offered his hand to help her. Smiling more broadly as she did, Gabrielle reached for his hand. Not that she actually needed it, but she was enjoying the moment. More than that, she didn't want to do anything that might signal that the exchange between them was over. As she closed her hand around his and began to stand, feeling the heat from his skin joined with hers, a tingle swept through her. It was soothing, but staggering. Her body swayed, and she heard her pulse swooshing rhythmically through her ears.

He moved to steady her, but they stumbled against Gabrielle's car, his body pressing against hers. The backpack that had been in her hand—the hand now on his chest and could feel his heart racing beneath it—had fallen carelessly to the ground. His face was so close to hers that anyone watching would have thought they were about to kiss. Gabrielle's cheeks warmed as the blood that had been thrumming past her ears rushed to her face. The abundance of sensations was unfamiliar and left her even more confused about how to act.

On his face, inches away, a smile replaced the look of concern that had appeared as he tried to keep them from ending up on the ground, saving them from a humiliating beginning to their first day of school. "I guess this would be a good time to introduce ourselves … since I normally don't find myself pressed up against a girl without at least knowing her name." Gabrielle felt his breath warming her cheeks, unless it was her face becoming an even more brilliant shade of red. "I'm Lucas. Lucas Watkins. And you are?"

"Oh … umm, I'm Gabrielle Trayner."

After a few more seconds, Lucas released his grip and moved his body off hers. Gabrielle found herself relieved and disappointed. She liked the way his muscles felt under her hands and against her body. She liked the slow burn that swept through her when they touched.

These things also alarmed her.

"Nice to meet you, Gabrielle. We better be getting inside. They might let you off the hook for being late since this is a new school for you, but I've spent three years here. I can't use the same excuse." Lucas made no move to leave. "Would you like for me to walk you to the office so you can check in, or do you already have a class schedule?"

"Thanks, I already have it. I registered a couple of weeks ago. But I would really appreciate it if you could point me in the right direction." Gabrielle didn't need help; she was simply trying to linger with him. Wanting to remain near him warred with the need to get away so she could regain her composure.

Wow ... he's really thrown me.

She reached to pick her backpack up and grabbed her class schedule out of the front pocket. She handed the piece of paper to Lucas who smiled again and took it, brushing her hand—a simple touch that caused more warmth and flutters to pinball inside her body again.

After looking at it for only a moment, he handed it back. "Your first class is in the main building here." Lucas motioned toward the two-story, brick building in front of them. "Just go through the main doors and take the flight of stairs on your left. Take a right at the top, and the room you're looking for will be on that hall. I'd walk you, but my class is over there." Lucas turned to his left and pointed to a long domed building with a flock of crows settled on its roof—all turned toward Gabrielle and Lucas. Gabrielle's brow furrowed, but Lucas's voice drew her attention away from them. "Gym first thing in the morning kinda sucks, but at least I can wait to take a shower here and sleep in a little." He stopped talking and looked at Gabrielle as if he was waiting for something.

What am I supposed to do?

She just smiled. The sensation of being under a spell returned as she looked into his eyes, and all she could think about was how stunningly blue they were against his dark hair and sun-tinted skin.

The visions did not *do you justice.*

The sound of the first bell breaking the silence made Gabrielle jump back into reality. They both began to laugh.

"Well ... thanks, Lucas. It was nice to meet you. I really am sorry for almost hitting you. Not a good first impression." Gabrielle reluctantly started to back away, turning toward the school and away from Lucas.

"No worries, Gabby. Do you mind if I call you Gabby?"

Gabrielle turned back to him. "No, I don't mind."

She'd never liked her name being shortened. Not for thousands of years. But she didn't think she'd mind so much if it was Lucas. Gabrielle turned back toward the sidewalk that led to the main doors. She was about to turn to say thanks to Lucas again when she heard him calling to her.

"Hey, Gabby!" Lucas said as she turned. "I'll see you in fifth period. We have the same class." With that, Lucas waved and jogged toward the gym.

"*That* was interesting," she said aloud to no one but herself. She hadn't smiled that much in a long time. As a human or an angel. It felt good. She looked toward the sky, closed her eyes, and let the sun warm her skin.

"Thank you," she said to the heavens.

A soft breeze moved across her skin; a breeze nothing else would have felt. It was meant only for her. She smiled again, feeling the familiar sense of Heaven that the wind carried with it.

Remembering the crows, she looked back in the direction of the gym. The crows, and Lucas, were gone.

The flutters in her stomach disappeared with them.

Chapter Five

GABRIELLE ✜ FAST FRIENDS

Gabrielle made it through her first four classes without much of a problem although she noticed, as soon as she walked through the doors of the school, that the other students seemed to stare at her.

A lot.

Every class she entered, she had the feeling all eyes were on her. She found herself wanting to disappear—just *poof* and be gone. She wondered if their attention was just because people recognized her as a new face in school or if she wasn't doing a good job looking and acting like one of them.

If she could have stepped outside of herself to see what the others saw, she would have understood it was her face that drew all the attention and the way she carried herself so gracefully. There were pretty girls in the school, but none with Gabrielle's striking, exotic looks. She had let her hair down and the dark, loose waves fell almost the entire length of her back. It was cut in long layers, the shortest just above her jaw line. Her large eyes, mostly green, were edged in a slight bluish hue. And her olive skin was so smooth she almost didn't look real.

Not knowing this, Gabrielle found herself looking forward to the lunch break, which would begin in moments. She also wanted fifth period to hurry up so she could see Lucas again and wondered if he was wishing for the same thing.

I shouldn't be thinking about him at all!

Staring at the clock hanging on the wall just above the door, she watched the seconds hand spin around the face, urging it to move faster. Finally, she heard the bell, then the immediate sounds of books closing, backpacks being filled, and voices freed to speak once more.

Springing into motion so fast she looked as though she moved before the bell even started, Gabrielle made her way to the door. Just as she was about to pull the door open so she could flee to momentary freedom, she heard a female voice with a fairly strong southern accent call for her.

"Gabrielle! Hey, wait up!"

Gabrielle turned and saw a tall blonde flashing a broad, friendly smile.

"Hi! I'm Nonie Daniels. Did I get your name right? I heard Mr. Friedman say it when he was checking attendance."

"Hi, and yes, you got my name right," Gabrielle said to the bubbly girl.

"Are you going to the cafeteria for lunch?" Nonie asked as they fell in step and entered the crowded hall. Students were going so many directions Gabrielle wondered how they made any progress.

"Is there another option?"

"Absolutely! Juniors and seniors can leave campus and eat anywhere. As long as we're back on time, of course! I was going to meet my brother and a friend at the mall across the street to get pizza. If you want to come along, you can."

Gabrielle studied Nonie for a moment. She was someone the other students would certainly consider pretty, though in a natural way. She wore little makeup. Her hair was long and thick with a slight wave, and her skin had the healthy glow of summer. The effect was stunning against the amber shade of her eyes.

"Unless you already have plans," Nonie continued.

As much as Gabrielle wanted to take a break from all the human interaction and attention from the morning, she had a hard time saying no. Nonie's chipper demeanor immediately put Gabrielle at ease.

"No, I don't have plans. I'd like to go. It's nice of you to ask."

"Great!" Nonie said while adding a hop to her step. "I think you'd be much happier than if you stayed here. If I were you, I'd be getting pretty tired of all the eyes boring through me." Nonie scanned the students. "Has everyone been staring at you like this all day? I noticed it in class, but now that we're out here, I can see their boredom in World History wasn't the reason."

Gabrielle sighed and looked around at the sea of teenagers, their faces gawking back at her, then looked at Nonie and smiled.

"Yeah, I guess they're just curious about the new girl."

Nonie laughed as they began to descend the wide staircase. "That, and possibly that you have to be the most beautiful person to have ever walked through the doors of this school. Maybe any school for that matter. Seriously ... I can hardly stop looking at you myself, and I'm an *only attracted to boys* kinda girl. You're going to be beating guys off with a stick all year long. I'd be jealous, but I don't think that would be fun for more than a couple of weeks." Nonie stopped at the bottom of the stairs, forcing the stream of students behind her to part and move around her like a rock in a river. Several students protested, but most just went around.

Like they are happy to make her life easier by letting her do as she wants.

Nonie just kept talking, kept smiling—seemingly unaware of her effect on others. People were still perplexing. She didn't understand why some were perceived as more worthy or what made one a leader and another a follower.

"You want to ride with me? My car's parked in the side lot, or you can just meet me there."

Gabrielle found she liked Nonie. She had always liked people who didn't beat around the bush. The direct approach was a characteristic she appreciated.

It makes my job easier.

"Yeah, I'll ride with you. Thanks. Not just for the ride ... thanks for being so nice."

Nonie's smile grew. Gabrielle guessed she was someone who wouldn't often be caught without one.

"Well, come on then! If we don't get out of here soon, we won't have time to eat. And, by the way, you don't need to thank me. I have to admit ... *I'm* curious, too!" With that, she pushed open the doors and began to jog slowly toward a bright green VW Bug convertible, top down, gleaming in the sunlight.

Gabrielle caught up to Nonie, her laughter reaching her new friend before she did.

"If I had to pick any car in this parking lot that would be yours, this would definitely be it! It absolutely screams *Nonie's car*, and I've only known you for about five minutes." Gabrielle slid into the passenger seat, and Nonie started the engine. The sound of Bob Marley's *One Love* was in mid-chorus as she put the car in reverse and then pulled out of the school lot.

They were stepping into the mall when Gabrielle saw Lucas. He was far ahead of them, and she could only see his back, but she knew it was him. Even blindfolded, she would have known. She could *feel* him. His energy seemed to stretch out to meet hers like it was seeking her out to pull them together.

She must have had a strange expression on her face because Nonie looked at her with curiosity.

"Gabrielle ... are you okay? You look kinda' funny."

"I'm sorry, I'm fine. Just thinking about something." Gabrielle tried to stay focused on Nonie. It was hard to not turn her attention back to Lucas—where she felt pulled to look. When she did, he was gone.

As they walked through the mall toward the food court, Gabrielle noticed Nonie didn't get caught up in all the clothes and shoes they were passing in the windows. She never even brought up anything that had to do with fashion. That was surprising since it seemed to be one of the main topics of conversation for girls, second only to hot boys, that she had overheard since arriving here. Gabrielle was glad, though. She knew she wouldn't be good at that kind of talk.

I can barely do my hair.

Instead, Nonie told her about the book she was reading—*Stardust* by Neil Gaiman—who she went on to explain was the most amazing author and insisted that she needed to read another book by him, *American Gods*. She asked if Gabrielle read much before launching into the hiking and camping trips she'd been on over the summer. Then, she talked a lot about music and art, mentioning her and her brother's weekly touch football games that started in late September.

Gabrielle laughed to herself as Nonie covered more topics than she thought was humanly possible in such a short time, but somehow, she managed to do so and still breathe.

"Would you like to play on our team? It should be a lot of fun, and you could get to know some really cool people," Nonie said as they turned the corner to the food court.

The merging smells of food—Italian, Chinese, burgers and fries, fresh baked bread from the sub shop—made Gabrielle's mouth water.

"I should be able to." Gabrielle was genuinely interested but had to focus harder to stay involved with what Nonie was saying as her attention was pulled away by food.

"The more the merrier!" Nonie chirped. "I know the guys are going to *love* that I invited you. The girls ... *maybe* not so much, but only because they're going to be intimidated by you."

"By *me*! Good grief, why on Earth would they be intimidated by me?" Gabrielle tried to laugh convincingly. "I've never played football. They'll all be way better than I am."

I wonder if I'll be any good at human sports? Acting like I'm human, *that is.*

Playing ball and running around for fun weren't exactly things her kind did in their spare time. Really, they didn't ever have spare time. There was always something to be done. Even here on Earth, Gabrielle still had her job. Luckily, time worked a little differently for her.

Nonie laughed, and her smile was absolutely contagious. Though if she were straight-faced, Gabrielle thought she'd smile back at her just from sheer enjoyment of how strong her accent became when she got animated.

"Gabrielle, you don't have any idea how gorgeous you are, do you?"

Before Gabrielle could answer, a tall, blond male ran up behind them, grabbed Nonie in a big bear hug, and kissed her on the cheek before he sat her down.

"*Ugh! Nate!* Did you have to slobber all over me? Gabrielle, could you grab me a stack of napkins? Like, *ten*!" Gabrielle could tell she was kidding. She was already chasing the guy. When they made it back around, they were laughing and breathing hard.

Nonie playfully slapped him on the back of the head. And, though he may have wanted to retaliate, he looked up at Gabrielle and immediately stopped.

"*Wow!*" He paused a moment. A smile played on one side of his lips as he stared at Gabrielle. "Who's your friend, Nee?"

"*Oh jeez!*" Nonie rolled her eyes. "*Heeere* we go." She got a light thump on the head in return from the guy. "Nate, Gabrielle. Gabrielle, Nate, my annoying, but loveable, brother. Twin brother, actually." Nonie smiled and pushed her brother toward the line for pizza. "Let's get our food before my brother starts drooling over you and I lose my appetite."

Nate and Nonie did look similar. His hair was darker, more like honey than Nonie's wheat color. Their eyes were the same shade of amber, though, and his smile seemed to come just as easily.

Gabrielle fell in step with Nonie and Nate, feeling Nate's eyes on her, then stopped abruptly.

It's him ...

She looked up and saw Lucas walking toward them. The flutters in her stomach woke again, and a smile spread across both of their faces as their eyes met.

Chapter Six

GABRIELLE ✝ A HUMAN DATE

Lucas took forever to reach them.

At least, it seemed that way to Gabrielle. She liked his confident gait and the way he carried himself, tall and proud—his athletic body all muscles and broad shoulders. She wanted to know what it would feel like to have his arms wrap around her and hold her tightly.

If he did, I don't know if I'd ever want him to let me go.

Gabrielle scoffed to herself. Even if her daydream ever became a reality somehow, he'd have to let her go, one day.

Forever.

She let the dismal intrusion be pushed aside by more pleasant thoughts because, finally, he was there. Standing in front of her—so close.

So very close.

He smelled wonderful, earthy and sweet; she had an almost irresistible urge to move toward his neck and inhale deeply.

Stop! It!

"Hey, Lucas," Nonie greeted him cheerfully. "Lucas, this is Gabrielle. Gabrielle, this is—"

"We've met," Lucas interrupted.

Gabrielle may have thought it was rude if she hadn't been distracted by the silkiness of his voice. It reminded her a little of her own kind.

Nonie seemed a bit taken aback. Gabrielle could see her in her periphery as she shifted her weight. After several seconds, she finally spoke.

"When did ya'll meet?" Nonie asked.

"Just this morning. I tried to maim him with my car door in the parking lot," Gabrielle laughed slightly. "Then he tried to molest me, and—"

"*I* tried to molest *you!*" Lucas's smile grew and his eyes widened "That's not the way *I* recall things! You got the attempt on my life correct, but the other was more like me being your champion, as I believe I rescued you from a very ungraceful face-plant."

"Always the 'he said she said,'" Gabrielle kidded, finally dropping her gaze from his as she felt warmth burning her cheeks.

I hope I get used to this soon. Really. I can't believe I can't keep my cool with humans. Well, at least this *human.*

"Okay, you two," Nonie said, "you can decide who wins the battle of the sexes later. Can we get our food, please? Time's-a-wastin' and my stomach's-a-rumblin!'"

Lunch went by without any more uncomfortable moments. Nonie and Nate bantered back and forth, at times including a jab at Lucas. Gabrielle mostly listened to the other three, enjoying the closeness they shared, wishing she knew what it must feel like to have such ease with others. When she asked how long they'd known each other, they told her they'd grown up together. They'd lived across the street from each other since they were a few months old.

The doors holding back their memories seemed to open as they proceeded to go into 'remember whens', breaking into spontaneous laughter over their adventures. All too soon, lunch ended, and they were walking from their cars, heading back toward school.

Nonie and Nate cheerfully waved and took off in opposite directions.

Gabrielle and Lucas didn't notice, but Nate turned to look back in their direction as he opened the door to the building, then paused. A scowl formed between his brows, his focus directly on Gabrielle as if he wanted to go back to her and say, or do, something. If she had been close enough, she would have noticed how the air chilled around him and maybe the faint odor, present only for a moment. After a few more seconds, he disappeared into the mass of other students.

Now, it was just Gabrielle and Lucas. They made their way to class also but much more slowly than everyone else.

"So," Lucas said, "do you think you'll be able to make the football game? I know it's a month away, and it might be too early for you to know for sure, but I'd really like it if you did."

Nonie told Lucas and Nate that she had invited her but not that Gabrielle had said yes.

"If you need me to, I can pick you up," Lucas continued. "That way you don't have to worry about finding it. Maybe we can get something to eat before we meet up with the others … *if* you want to?" Lucas trailed off at the end.

Her stomach did a little flip. She was pretty sure he'd just asked her on a date.

A human date.

She figured it would help her research.

"I'd like that very much," Gabrielle answered, a little too enthusiastically. Lucas smiled, and Gabrielle worried she was too obvious.

She needed to be careful. Again, she reminded herself that nothing good could come of it if she got too close or if she let him get too close to her. But this was a chance to experience a side of human emotions she had only glimpsed from a distance, to understand how this kind of attraction influenced people. She was sure she could handle it, and that these emotions that seemed to pull her to Lucas were only because of her human body.

This is actually perfect. It's what I'm here for, after all.

The rest of the walk to class was quiet, a few glances and smiles shared between them. Along the way, Lucas got quite a few 'hey mans' with approving, as well as envious, looks from other guys. Some of the girls would see him and act as though they were going to say hi, glance at Gabrielle, take a long look, and pass by. The final bell rang as they entered the room.

"By the hair on our chinny-chin-chins," Lucas said with a smirk and then stopped to glance around the room. "There aren't two seats together. Guess you're on your own."

"I think I'll be okay," Gabrielle said with a flirty side-ways glance and wink. She was a little shocked at herself; flirting was coming very easily. She made her way to an empty seat in the front of the class so she wouldn't have to see the other students frequently glancing back at her.

She was very aware that she could still feel Lucas.

I can't sense anyone else and know for certain it's them like I can with Lucas. Why?

It was very unusual. She was used to being able to pick up on her brethren, even those who had fallen. And, once she met them, she could always recognize them when they were near.

Gabrielle was no closer to an explanation when class ended. Lucas waited at her desk while she organized her things, and they left the room together. Gabrielle found herself sneaking glances at him when he wasn't looking as they made their way into the hall.

She didn't want to admit that something seemed off to her about him. She felt sure she was supposed to help him, and at the very least, she knew she was supposed to meet him.

So, what does this mean?

"I guess I'll see you tomorrow, Gabby," Lucas said as they were about to go separate ways for their next class. "Unless you plan a second attempt on my life in the parking lot after school." A hint of his crooked smile returned.

"Very funny," she responded with a smile on her face and in her tone.

He was about to say something else, but a slender and *very* attractive girl, her hair almost as long and dark as Gabrielle's, cut between them to greet Lucas with a big hug. The girl hung on a little too long, and Gabrielle suddenly felt something that made her more uncomfortable than anything she'd felt in this body, so far.

Gabrielle wanted the girl to get off Lucas and was more than willing to take care of that physically if needed. She wasn't sure, but she thought this feeling was probably jealousy. And she now understood why it made people less than reasonable. She wanted to smack the smile off this girl's face and turn her flirty cooing into sobs of pain. The urge was hard to resist. It would do nothing but make her look like some crazed, jealous teenager. But that was pretty much what she was in this body. Only she was The Angel of Karma, and that made her a crazed, jealous teenager capable of causing this girl a ton of problems.

Wow ... jealousy. This is certainly a first.

Lucas looked at Gabrielle with surprise and embarrassment. Gabrielle tried to smile to make him feel a little better—maybe herself, too—but she bet it looked more like a grimace.

"Lucas!" the girl gushed. "I've been looking for you all day! If I didn't know better, I'd think you were avoiding me!"

Lucas's jaw tensed, and a scowl furrowed a deep channel between his brows. Gabrielle was sure she could see anger, or possibly contempt, raging in his eyes.

"If I was trying to avoid you, Mara," Lucas began, "it would require me to think about you. Which I haven't."

His demeanor suddenly became frigid. The warmth and ease he'd had earlier abandoned him. It was noticeable in the girl's reaction that it wasn't what she hoped to elicit from him.

"Ooh ... feeling a little testy, are we? Are you having a bad day, Lucas? I can make it a *lot* better for you if you want me to." Mara was still very close to Lucas. As she spoke to him, she played with the collar of his shirt then traced her finger slowly up toward his ear.

Gabrielle began clenching and unclenching her fists. If she was in her true form, her color would be turning a deeper crimson the longer that girl continued to hang all over him.

Yes, this is definitely *jealousy.*

Gabrielle did her best not to remove Mara from Lucas. Thankfully, Lucas quickly grabbed Mara's hand, moving his head away at the same time.

He glared at Mara.

"My day was fantastic until about sixty seconds ago. Now, keep your hands off of me. You lost the right to get this close."

He was harsh in both expression and tone. Gabrielle wondered what Mara could have done to make him this angry.

"Fine," Mara said coolly. She turned and looked at Gabrielle. More like shot daggers out of her yellowish-green eyes—the eyes of a camouflaged demon. Gabrielle's breath stopped as Mara looked her up and down with a venomous smile. Gabrielle's irritation at being caught off-guard by one of the Fallen burned through her body. She finally began to feel her stomach's reaction from being so close to a demon—a reaction that should have come much sooner.

This is unacceptable.

She needed to be able to see a demon coming before they were so close. Between the Aegis Veil and a demon's, she was having difficulty knowing when they were around, especially when distracted by human sensations and thoughts. Now, she *really* wanted Mara to get away from Lucas.

The demon is lucky that we are in a school full of witnesses.

"Who's your new ... *friend*, Lucas? She's as pretty as an *angel*." Mara's eyes locked with Gabrielle's. Gabrielle could do nothing to the demon unless she put a human or her own life in danger, and Mara knew it. "Are you going to be rude, or are you going to introduce us?"

Gabrielle fought the profound desire to turn this demon into ash.

Lucas looked at Mara and then at Gabrielle. He reached for Gabrielle's hand and pulled her away.

"Mara ... I'm feeling a bit on the rude side right now." He began moving away from Mara. "I don't think I'll give you the chance to be a bitch to anyone else. At least, not around me." He hastened Gabrielle down the hall.

Gabrielle looked over her shoulder toward Mara just as they were about to turn the corner. Mara's eyes had turned solid, shiny black. Gabrielle's glare made sure Mara would be aware that things would have turned out differently if she wasn't bound by Yahuwah's laws. This wasn't the first time she'd wished she had the free will humans enjoyed, and she was beginning to think that it wouldn't even be close to the last.

Is this why I've been having visions of him? Because he's involved with a demon?

But there were a lot of humans who were unknowingly mixed up with demons. She couldn't understand why that would make him so important.

"What was that about?" Gabrielle asked.

Lucas mumbled something.

"*Lucas* ... seriously. What is it with you and that girl?"

Lucas didn't answer.

Gabrielle jerked her hand away and planted her feet. Lucas stopped, turned, and as if he realized at once that he'd been inconsiderate, his expression relaxed, and he stepped toward her.

"I'm really sorry, Gabby. I hate that you were there for that, but I promise she isn't anyone to worry about. She's—"

"I'm not *worried* about her, Lucas," Gabrielle interrupted. "I'm just really surprised by the way you reacted to her. What happened between the two of you?"

Before he could answer, the final bell for class rang.

"There isn't time to explain right now. Just trust me on this one. Stay away from Mara. She's bad news. We'll talk more later. I have to get out of here pretty quick right after school, so I probably won't see you till tomorrow. So ... can we talk more then?" Lucas looked a little unsure of himself, and Gabrielle found she wanted to reassure him—surprised by how the foul mood Mara caused rapidly disappeared and calm took over.

"Absolutely."

Lucas smiled. For the second time that day, he jogged away.

Gabrielle slowly made her way to her next to last class thinking about the day's events—meeting Lucas and the twins, the confusing and difficult emotions, and the oddity of being able to feel Lucas's presence. But one thing in particular kept coming back up over and over—Mara. Gabrielle needed to know more about her.

Chapter Seven

GABRIELLE ✟ THAT OTHER SIDE

When her last class was over, Gabrielle made her way to her car as fast as she could without looking like a lunatic. All she wanted to do was get out of that place and away from examining eyes. When she finally slid into the leather seat of her car, behind the dark tint of the windows, and drove out of the school's lot, she began to feel better. But real relief came when she pulled into the driveway of her brick townhouse.

It wasn't the safe-haven Heaven was, but she didn't have to hide who she was when she was there. It was really only for appearances and to have a place for her human body to rest. It was cozy, and Gabrielle felt her tension leaving as she looked at the red front door. She placed her forehead on the steering wheel, filled her lungs with air, and pushed out a heavy sigh.

"What a day."

She hadn't been so tired since she began this pursuit two months ago and was looking forward to not being a teenager for the rest of the day—to just being herself. In the years prior to this decision being made, she would have never suspected being human was this taxing. She had sorely underestimated the difficulties she would face daily, and today had been the most exhausting so far.

Gabrielle needed to talk to Amaziah about the way she was feeling toward Lucas, but she was more than a little worried about his reaction. She knew she wouldn't want to do what he would surely suggest even if leaving Lucas alone was the right thing to do. Gabrielle had known Lucas for less than a day though all the visions she'd had made it feel like much longer. It was the only explanation for why she already found herself wanting to be around him more. And that desire was going to present a *huge* dilemma.

"I don't need this distraction. *He's* not why I'm here."

Something tugged at her thoughts after she said those words, though. Something that made her wonder, even if it was only for a brief moment, if he *was* the reason she had been allowed to come here, after all. That maybe, he was the reason Amaziah and Yahuwah had allowed her to come and take on this task.

Gabrielle didn't fight her brows pulling together as the tension came back. The longer she considered it, the more the thought turned into an insistence that Lucas played a larger role in the decision than she knew.

Going over it again and again in her mind didn't seem to help. All that came of her contemplation as she sat silently in her car, heating rapidly in the afternoon sun, was frustration and another sweaty back. Gabrielle decided to let the possibilities simmer.

After gathering her things and getting out of her car, she made her way up the front steps, entered her temporary residence, and gladly shut the door behind her—locking out the rest of the world for just a few moments. Standing there, leaning against the door, she let the cool air in her home bring her body temperature down, letting her mind drift. She'd have to check in with Amaziah, Sheridan, and her troops soon.

I need to try to clear my mind so I can focus on my job.

Reluctantly moving her body off the door, she put her things down on the round table that sat in the middle of her large foyer and made her way into her human home.

The townhouse was decorated erratically. Some would phrase the description more diplomatically and call it eclectic, but Gabrielle was well aware it was nothing more than a hodge-podge of all the things she had found herself fancying while seeing the world for thousands of years. She'd spent a lot of her time, while learning to be human, picking these things up all over the world.

The walls were painted in a soft yellow so she would always feel like she was outside in the warmth of the sun and to remind her of the warm, soft glow that continuously came off everything in her eternal home. The color also set off the wide array of craziness that was her furniture, pictures, rugs, and especially, art. Gabrielle was accumulating too much, particularly since she discovered black and white photography. She'd even picked up a DSLR camera and several lenses so she could take some pictures herself. She had no idea what she was going to do with all of it when she had to leave in four months.

"Just four more months," she said through a sigh.

She felt a pull at her chest with the thought. She wasn't going to like leaving even though she loved her eternal home. She loved it here, too. A different kind of love, for different reasons, but she loved it just the same. Maybe it was harder to think about leaving this place because, unlike leaving Heaven, the departure would be forever. She'd still have to come to Earth from time to time but not like this— not *living* like this. When she left Heaven, she always knew she'd be going back, sooner rather than later.

She stared at her things, thumbing through images of people, flowers, and random things she had found beautiful or compelling in some way and taken pictures of. She loved knowing that, even though these were subjects many people looked at every day, she saw them in a way someone else may not have. She smiled as she looked at her walls since she intended to add a frame to some of her images to hang them.

"I don't know where I'll find a place for all of you. The wall's real estate is pretty sparse."

Gabrielle put the photos back down on the ottoman and headed upstairs to take a quick shower in hopes of re-energizing herself. After shedding her clothes and climbing into the steaming stall, she let the liquid heat flow over her tense muscles. Her body reacted right away, and every second she spent there, she relaxed more. After washing her hair, she stood under the water again and let it take as much stress down the drain with it that she could, picturing Lucas's face to make the peace really set in. It worked, for a moment. Then, another face flashed through her mind, and she sighed. Amaziah had arrived, early as usual.

'Just once, I wish he could be a little late.'

Of course, even if he was, Sheridan would show up early. As soon as she thought this, Sheridan's face made an appearance behind her closed eyes, as well.

She grudgingly turned the shower off, quickly dried, and grabbed sweat pants and a t-shirt from her closet—happy that with her brethren she didn't have to worry about her human appearance.

When Gabrielle made it downstairs, she found Amaziah and Sheridan in their human forms, sitting at the kitchen counter's bar. They were debating something, as was normal for them.

"Ahh, Gabrielle. So nice of you to join us," Amaziah greeted her, doing so without glancing away from Sheridan.

Sheridan simply looked up at her, then the debate resumed. They were always trying to convince the other one that they were right if they found their opinions at odds—which was often. Gabrielle chose to stay out of it most of the time.

It was interesting to see them in human form. She especially liked the body Amaziah created for himself. He was fairly tall with short, dark hair, blue eyes, and quite handsome. Sheridan had a petite frame with green eyes and long, strawberry-blond hair. They were supposed to pass for her parents if the situation ever called for it, but both barely looked old enough to have a child of seventeen.

She plopped herself on a stool on the other side of the counter and rested her chin in her hands. Patiently waiting for the eventual result of the debate—an impasse. It's how it always ended, and Gabrielle learned a *long* time ago to not interrupt them. This was one area of angel lore humans had all wrong—they weren't always peaceful creatures.

Gabrielle certainly wasn't. Today had been a perfect example in that regard. When she was waiting to start her day, sitting in the school's parking lot, she felt so frustrated from the feeling that they were losing the war and there was something ... *coming*, that she thought she might come unglued. Though it didn't turn out as bad as she'd started out thinking it would be.

Come to think of it, as soon as I met Lucas, I felt better.

And that feeling seemed to carry on throughout the day. With one exception—Mara. But the anger she had felt from being caught off-guard and the demon having her hands on Lucas left quickly, too.

I've never had a mood like that just lift *off of me before.*

But if she couldn't give out more good karma than bad today, she may not be so lucky tomorrow. Her mood could be rather unpleasant.

Gabrielle loved her job. Though it was sometimes difficult, it'd been the most important part of her life since Yahuwah appointed her to the position thousands of years ago even if it sometimes had a nasty effect on her personality. Unfortunately, being in an edgy mood had been increasingly common for her over the last one hundred and fifty years.

She was the one that gave herself the title The Angel of Karma. The belief in karma's cause and effect of past and present actions, and Yahuwah's rewards and punishments, were pretty much the same. It was a lot easier than The Angel of You Reap What You Sow.

Gabrielle made her way to the refrigerator to get some sweet tea—some *very sweet* tea. She looked over her shoulder at her brethren as she did. "Hate to interrupt, but anyone want something to drink?"

All she got in response were two shaking heads, then they were back at it, causing her to smile. They were always going to argue, but she knew they respected each other. After filling her glass with iced southern sweetness, she let one cold sip slip down her throat and sat back down to continue to wait.

Thoughts about her job consumed her own mind, and the thing she wondered about most was how she could have done it better all these years. If she had been more efficient, *maybe* the war being fought would be leaning more toward their side instead of Darkness gaining more of a stronghold on humanity.

Maybe I wouldn't have seen so many human souls lost and so very many Asarers die with them.

She didn't know most of the Asarers personally, but it didn't make the cut any less deep or painful. Asarers were a huge step above a typical guardian angel—a sometimes deadly step. They could be from any of the Choirs. They were those of her brethren who chose, on top of their regular duties, to bind themselves to one human in particular. They didn't have to be humans who were important or influential, just someone the angel was drawn to for any reason. It could be that they'd watched them grow from a child and had become attached, had seen them suffer a great loss, or any other reason. They put their own lives on the line, literally, as they try to keep that person they bound themselves to from becoming one of the Fallen's, and thus Ramai's, victims. If they failed to keep their human from Darkness, they would lose their own souls—their Divine lives—to Ramai, as well. Now, more than ever, performing her duties appropriately was vital to the outcome of the battle.

To keep as few Divine lives from being lost as possible.

Her daily task was to take the orders from Yahuwah concerning who He wanted to either reward or punish, along with the level of action He wanted taken. Then she decided in what form it would be dispensed. Once her decision was made, she gave the orders to Sheridan, her second in command, to give to the troops. At times, if it was someone she was particularly interested in seeing karma come back to, whether good or bad, she would take care of it herself.

She wondered, again, what this day's lot would have in store for her, how she'd feel tomorrow, and hoped to be able to cover up her crabbiness on her worst days when she was around the other teenagers.

Especially Lucas.

After several moments of thinking about Lucas, the debate between Amaziah and Sheridan abruptly stopped, and Gabrielle felt eyes on her. When she glanced at her brethren, Amaziah was looking at her. She hadn't realized it, but she had slipped deep into thought about Lucas again. Maybe too deep.

"Who is this *Lucas*, Gabrielle?" Amaziah inquired. "Is there reason for me to be concerned for you?" He waited for her answer.

Amaziah was the closest thing Gabrielle had to a father. He'd been the one to recommend her to Yahuwah for the task of handling His rewards and punishments. Ever since, he made it a personal mission to make sure that Gabrielle not only did her job well but was also happy—knowing the latter could be difficult for The Angel of Karma.

"No, Amaziah. Of course you don't need to be concerned about me," Gabrielle answered, trying to figure out how to explain. "I don't know why I was thinking of him so much, really. He is someone I've had visions of, and I met him today. I suspect I'll have to help in some way in the future, and that's why he's on my mind." Gabrielle hoped the explanation would appease her superior. She was surprised, and uncomfortable, at her attempt at deception. That was new for her, at least verbally, since she had been keeping Lucas to herself for quite some time.

That's deception in its own way, I suppose.

"I see," Amaziah said simply. To her relief, he seemed to let it go. He immediately turned his attention back to Sheridan.

Gabrielle was happy he didn't push the subject further. Sheridan, on the other hand, seemed to be leery of Gabrielle's response. Her gaze lingered on Gabrielle for several moments, and her eyes held questions. Sheridan knew her place, however, and Gabrielle was sure she'd get no inquisition from her. At least not in front of anyone.

Sheridan had been assigned to Gabrielle from the beginning. They'd been through thousands of years of working together, and even though Gabrielle had no proof, she'd always felt that Sheridan didn't approve of her. It was just an instinct, really. But angels rarely, if ever, doubt their intuition. More often than not, it was accurate—and life-saving.

Still, Gabrielle had no cause to doubt Sheridan's loyalty to her directly, and especially no cause to doubt her loyalty to Yahuwah. If she ever went against the orders Gabrielle gave, it would be a transgression against Him. To oppose Yahuwah or his instructions in any way, most often, would mean punishment. Depending on the betrayal, it could even mean being cast out of their home forever.

Javan had rebelled against Yahuwah. Of course, his actions, the most unforgivable from what she had been told, resulted in him becoming one of the Fallen. Gabrielle's chest caught as her heart was gripped by the emptiness the loss left. A rush of emotions forced themselves through her human body. For the first time, tears began to pool in her human eyes, and she shut their lids forcefully to try to keep her sorrow contained.

"I know, Gabrielle," Amaziah said softly. He was suddenly beside her, placing his hand on hers. "We all miss our fallen friend. You, because he was your eternal companion, most of all."

Amaziah had heard her thoughts again. Gabrielle raised her head and looked upon her friend's face, releasing tears from the corners of her eyes when she did.

She was sure she saw some in his, as well.

Gabrielle had excused herself from Amaziah and Sheridan and asked to be left alone on Earth for a while, saying she would meet with them in Heaven when she was ready. She needed some time to let the somber moment pass and clear her mind. When she returned to them a couple of hours later, they were debating a different topic. Both stopped and looked at her with concern. She imagined they both wanted to know the same thing.

'I'm fine.' That was all Gabrielle trusted herself to tell them. She had never let her sorrow show outwardly and didn't know if more emotions would burst forth, even now while she was in her true form. She was eager to get her job taken care of so she could return to Earth and have more time to be alone.

Time ...

She should feel she had a lot, considering she was created to live forever. But she didn't. She'd learned a long time ago that time wasn't a guarantee. Everything can be taken away, everything changes, and even angels die. Her human time would be brief. That was something she had no control over. But, at that moment, she was in 'angel time', so it didn't really matter.

When she was living as she was meant to, as an angel, time passed in a much different way than when she lived as a human. What she did in her job as The Angel of Karma would seem like minutes to mortals, but to her as an angel, it ticked quite a bit of time off the clock.

Now, she could take care of her work without losing valuable time as a human. Then, she could step back to her Earthly life. She wouldn't lose a second that she needed to use for figuring out what compels humans, finding out what Lucas had to do with her being here and how she was supposed to help him, and figuring out what the book was that the demon spoke of.

The realization that she had not put near as much effort as she needed into discovering what the story was with that book hit her, and she decided it would have more importance from that point on. Amaziah didn't seem to take it too seriously when they spoke of it initially, but something told her it was important.

Very important.

Once her lots' karma was decided upon, and the appropriate orders were assigned to her troops or other 'helpers', she could relax. At least as much as she could while concerned about the battle between the Light and Darkness.

All of the tactics she'd used in the past didn't seem to have much effect anymore, and people were progressively lacking in morality. Humanity was losing its humanity. Gabrielle wasn't going to allow Darkness to dominate Light, though. Not while she could still turn the tides and guide people's hearts back toward Yahuwah.

There were many who tried to get in her way—legions. But Yahuwah had bestowed her with many powers to fight them. In addition to the abilities all angels share—telepathy, moving between realms at will, interaction with humans either in angelic or human form, and of course flight—Gabrielle enjoyed a host of others. For obvious reasons, her most utilized ability while incarnated was pausing mortal time. But she also enjoyed having dominion over creatures humans consider to be fantastical—Shifters, the Gentry, and the Qalal. Gabrielle reserved using the last two for the most reprehensible humans; those who truly deserved the kind of suffering they could inflict.

The thing she liked the least about her job was seeing people doubt Yahuwah because His justice seemed to be ill-timed or unfair. People tell each other so frequently that He does things in His own time and not theirs, or that He has a plan for all He does whether they understand it when it happens or not. The truth was, they were right. The problem was, so few truly have faith in the words they speak or hear. Gabrielle wanted desperately to remove their skepticism, to help people see there's a reason to believe, to have hope.

Amaziah and Sheridan were now discussing the final battle of the war. It was coming. No one was sure when. How well their side would do depended largely on Gabrielle. Sometimes she believed she could feel the heaviness of that burden so intensely that she thought it would push her down into the Underworld where Darkness would hold her forever.

Gabrielle captured Sheridan's attention and handed her the last of her instructions. Sheridan could now leave and give them to the appropriate troops. The task was out of Gabrielle's hands and in the care of the thousands of angels assigned to assist her in her duties.

"Gabrielle." Amaziah broke through her thoughts after they left Sheridan and returned to Gabrielle's Earthly home. "Are you okay? Is there something you want to talk with me about?"

Gabrielle didn't know where she could even start. She couldn't tell him about her worries or the human feelings she felt about Lucas. He worried over her so much already, and she didn't want to add to his concerns.

"No, Amaziah. Thank you for asking, but I'm really fine. Just a little worn out from my first day of *school*." Gabrielle gave the most convincing smile she felt she had in her and reached for his hand. It was very warm, warmer than any human's would be. His seemed to be warmer than any incarnated angel she'd touched—considerably so. And his light, when in his true form, was brighter than any angels' she'd ever seen. It was almost blinding. He looked at her for a moment, then smiled and gave her hand a firm, loving squeeze.

"You know, Gabrielle, Yahuwah doesn't expect this of you, and I'm sure He would be happy to have you solely in Heaven once again. If you ever decide this isn't still in the best interest of His Divine purpose, it would not be looked upon by Him, or any of your brethren, as a failure. No other before you has ever taken on such a heavy responsibility without being commanded to do so. You have earned a great deal of respect with your actions."

Gabrielle said a quick prayer of thanks to Yahuwah for giving her such a supportive and loving ally. "This isn't about earning the respect of my peers. You know that." He nodded in acknowledgement. "It's the need to understand why the tactics I've always used are no longer making an impact. If I don't figure out new ways of creating the desire in the hearts of people to do, *and be*, good … Darkness *will* take over their minds—this world. I can't allow that to happen. I *can't* continue to just watch the battle for human souls being lost while our Asarers fall along with them."

Gabrielle felt the need for rest begin to take over her human form. Her mind hurt, eyes burned, and the little perk her afternoon shower seemed to give her had waned. She needed to sleep. As an angel, she had no need for rest, but she had been trying to remain in her human body as much as she could to get in touch with what people deal with on a daily basis.

Amaziah, as usual, knew exactly what she needed.

"Gabrielle," He stood up and lovingly cupped her face with his hands, "I didn't mean for you to feel you had to convince me all over again. I just wanted you to know that there is still another choice, and that you aren't stuck with this decision. It doesn't need to be discussed further. I can see you need sleep. Give your human body a little extra time to rest this evening. I would like to know how your day went and what you may have learned, but it can wait."

With that, he smiled and disappeared like fog being shooed away by a stiff breeze.

Gabrielle went upstairs to her bedroom and climbed into bed. The last image she saw in her mind before she fell into a deep, but restless sleep was Lucas.

Chapter Eight

Javan ✟ An Angel

Javan had just finished pouring a shot of whiskey when Mara walked into his loft. Liquor was the only thing he had to numb the emotions the human body inundated him with. Human emotions were a nuisance he hadn't bargained for. He downed the shot and grabbed a second glass as Mara made her way to him, filling them almost to overflowing.

"Mara. I wasn't expecting you. Why are you bothering me?"

A smile barely showed as she grabbed her glass, downing its contents.

"I can leave," she said and turned to make her way back to the door. "I just thought you'd want to know there's a pretty little angel posing as a student at school. But I can see now it wouldn't concern you, so I'll see you later."

"Wait."

Mara continued to the door. He hated when she tried to be flippant. It irritated him. He was in front of her so fast that it startled her, and the indifferent expression rearranged back to the one of servitude he wanted. He grabbed her face with one hand and moved close enough that their noses touched.

"Don't play with me, Mara," he said through clenched teeth. "You know I don't have the patience for it."

She nodded as much as she could in his grip, and he let her go.

"Come have another drink. Tell me about this angel."

She sat on the stool across the counter from him. He slid her a glass and waited.

Mara took several sips.

"I don't know that much. She was with that guy that I was messing with a couple of months ago. I decided to see if I could mess with him some more. I'm bored. That's the only reason I go to that place … to screw with humans."

The look he gave her didn't inspire more needless information.

"I didn't notice she was an angel at first," Mara continued, "because … well, *at first*, I didn't give a damn. But when Lucas gave me the cold shoulder and I finally looked at her, there was no mistaking she was a Yahuwah lover."

"Why couldn't you tell right away?"

"I don't know. Some kind of veil. I bet if she didn't have it, though, she'd be glowing like a Christmas tree. That human body of hers might hide the Divine light from a human, but I could see its shimmer. It wasn't constant, more like a faint pulse under her skin and in her eyes."

"That would be a pretty powerful veil, and a very powerful angel. Why would an angel pose as a high school student?"

"You got me, but that's all I know. I thought it was odd, too. So … here I am."

"Hmm …"

"I do know one more thing."

"I'm waiting."

"Where she *lives*. I followed her."

"You're telling me this angel actually has a place she stays in on Earth?"

"Yep. Curious, huh?"

"Yeah."

Javan sipped his drink as he considered the possibilities. How was he going to deal with an angel taking up residence so close to him? It might not pose a problem, but he couldn't be sure.

"So," Mara said, "what do you want me to do?"

Javan finished his drink and placed the glass on the counter, then made his way around to her. He touched her face, but this time, he caressed it. He wanted to take care of other things at that moment. The alcohol hadn't numbed his feelings enough.

"Eventually, I want you to show me where this angel lives." He took her hand and started walking her to his room. "Right now, I want you in my bed."

Chapter Nine

GABRIELLE ✝ SECOND IMPRESSIONS

Gabrielle woke to rays of sunlight barely beginning to sneak through her bedroom window to prod her awake and welcome her into the day. She tried to remember what she'd been dreaming of, but all she could recall was that Lucas was in it and whatever had happened left her feeling distressed. She couldn't revive the memory any more than that. It felt prophetic, though. Like one of her Knowings. But they happened when she was awake.

She wondered if there wasn't more to how deeply she was sleeping, if maybe Amaziah had been doing something to cause it. She knew he wanted her to rest, as did she, but she didn't like being unable to recall the images her mind created while she slept. It worried her that there was information she may need, knowledge she now wouldn't have.

Gabrielle looked at the glowing numbers of her digital clock—five forty-five.

Time for another day as a seventeen-year-old.

She found herself looking forward to her day, especially the parts that would have Lucas woven into them. After taking a shower, Gabrielle dressed and ran downstairs. She still hadn't branched out much when it came to food, so she made a piece of toast and topped it with peanut butter and honey—heavy on the honey. She took a bite of her breakfast and then chased it with chocolate milk, managing to somehow miss her mouth.

She laughed at her clumsiness and went back upstairs to change clothes. While she did, she pondered how much she'd already fretted that morning over what she should wear, laughing at herself for all the time she had spent considering whether or not Lucas would like her better in the blue or red shirt. She ended up choosing the blue one because she thought it would bring out the indigo that circled the green in her eyes. She pulled on the red shirt now—hoping that she could learn to eat more gracefully and not have to change again—checked her face and hair, and descended the stairs to finish eating.

Two months ago, Gabrielle was amused by the way the teenage girls were acting about boys. Now, she was one of them. The way she thought about things had changed so much since coming here, and she wondered what other changes awaited her in the time she had left.

Gabrielle looked at the time again—six thirty-five.

Time to go.

There was no need to wait around.

She maneuvered her car through the morning congestion as though she'd been driving for years. This was one thing she always allowed her angelic abilities to take over and control. There's no reason to risk an accident because of her lack of driving experience.

The closer she came to the school, the more unsettled Gabrielle became, feeling unwanted company was present on campus. She'd only seen Mara, but she only realized she was a demon once she saw her eyes. Gabrielle sensed the Fallen were there even more when she pulled into the school's parking lot, feeling the heaviness associated with them settling on her. Her discernment was terribly off. More than she counted on even though Amaziah had warned her, which concerned her more than she wanted to admit. She had to pay more attention today. The thought had crossed her mind that she may need to lift the Aegis Veil, but Amaziah would know immediately and yank her back to Heaven. Then, she had another idea and scolded herself for not thinking of it sooner.

Phalen.

Phalen would be more than happy to help her, and Gabrielle would love to have her company. Phalen would be able to see how many demons were in and near the school since her Divine discernment wouldn't be hindered the way hers was. Her presence wasn't nearly as attractive to the Fallen; they weren't gunning for Phalen's death like they were Gabrielle's.

I'll request Phalen's assistance when I see Amaziah today.

Gabrielle picked pretty much the same spot as the day before, put the car in park, lowered the windows, and turned the engine off. The morning wasn't as warm as yesterday. Swollen clouds, full of rain, hung low and ominous in the sky. She heard a rumble of thunder in the distance and felt something that made her heart jump. The same fluttery feeling in her stomach she'd had the day before returned.

Gabrielle closed her eyes and concentrated, releasing the Veil just a little, worried if she let it drop completely the Fallen would recognize her. She was beginning to feel like they would be around every corner she turned, behind every face she looked into.

Just as I thought ... Lucas.

She smiled, knowing he was approaching her car and she would soon see him. Gabrielle replaced the Veil and opened her eyes.

He was there.

"Good morning, sunshine!" Gabrielle said to Lucas as he took the last couple of steps to her passenger door.

"Good morning back." Lucas leaned down, resting his forearms on the door and smiling that amazing smile. "I thought it would be safer to approach your car from the passenger side from now on. Less opportunity for you to execute my demise."

"If I wanted to put you on a path for certain death, Lucas, I would find a much more creative way of doing it, I assure you." Gabrielle smiled and hoped she didn't sound too convincing. Just as she was about to try to say something witty, the clouds gave up their attempt to harness the rain, unleashing them in a sudden torrent.

"*Whoa!*" Lucas yelled and laughed.

"Get in, Lucas!"

Gabrielle turned the engine on and raised her windows as Lucas scrambled to get in the car.

Once his door was closed and he was settled, he cut his eyes at her playfully. "So, did you decide drowning me would be more fun today?" Lucas shot her a huge smile, running his hand through his now dampened hair. His eyes glistened from his burst of laughter, and Gabrielle thought it made them look even more brilliantly blue.

"Oh, just thinking back to how you told me you don't take a shower before you come to school because of first period gym class."

He smiled at her shyly.

There was a moment of quiet between them.

"Gabby," Lucas began, "I don't really know how to say this to you, I mean … without you thinking I'm strange, but I feel like I know you somehow. Like I need to be around you for some reason. *Crap!* I even sound strange to myself." Lucas paused. "Look. I know you don't know me, and I don't know you, and I promise I'm not some nut job. All I know is what I felt the moment I met you yesterday. And I know that pretty much every second of the day, and night, you were all I thought about. So, if that totally freaks you out, I get it. To be honest with you, it freaks me out. And now I'm rambling because I feel like a complete idiot spilling my guts to the most beautiful and intriguing girl I've ever met. So, I think I'll shut up, get out of the car, and go home and play sick. Just so I don't have to face you the rest of the day."

Instead, Lucas closed his eyes and let his head drop back onto the headrest.

Gabrielle's heart was beating so fast as she repeated his words to herself that she thought it was going to punch through her chest.

Gabrielle, what are you doing? You could be cast out if this goes too far.

Lucas opened his eyes when he felt Gabrielle put her hand on his. His gaze fell on their entwined fingers resting on his leg. His lips curved slightly with a smile.

"I'd like you to stay right where you are." Gabrielle said as he searched her eyes. In an attempt to reassure him further, she squeezed his hand even as she continued a mental war with herself about her decision. "I don't know why you feel what you do. I do know I feel … *something*. So, if you're a nut, maybe I am, too."

I've entered a human body and almost instantly lost my mind. That must be why people don't make any sense to us … they're all crazy.

Gabrielle watched Lucas relax and his smile fully return, but he lowered his eyes, clearly still embarrassed.

"Look," Gabrielle said, "this isn't something we are going to figure out right now. I'm just glad to know I'm not alone. Let's forget the whys and concentrate on the whos. I'd like to know more about you."

"Sounds good to me," Lucas responded, "I know I have at least a thousand questions for you."

Chapter Ten

LUCAS ✟ MISSTEP

Lucas did have at least a thousand questions for Gabby that had been wreaking havoc in his mind since he had first seen her.

He had spent so much time thinking about her, he was surprised he managed to get anything done at all. Sitting in her car with her, he had the same feeling he had before—that he was connected to her somehow. He'd asked Gran about her, specifically if she knew any Trayners, thinking maybe they had met when he was very young. If they had, maybe that would help to explain why he felt so drawn to her, but at the same time, he knew just meeting when they were children wouldn't justify the connection he felt.

For now, it didn't matter. Her hand was in his—her very warm, soft hand—and she told him she felt the same connection.

This is really nuts.

No way had he ever felt anything close to this; no way did he even think it was possible this quickly. He wanted to pull back, be more cautious, but the thought of not pursuing her wouldn't take hold in his mind. He decided last night, after lying in bed for hours as the Sandman abandoned him with nothing but whys running through his mind, that he was going to throw caution out concerning Gabby and dive right on into the deep end.

Nothing ventured, nothing gained.

As soon as he'd made the decision, he fell asleep, but she came to him in his dreams.

And, damn, they were good dreams.

He was able to touch her face, her hair, lean in as she was looking into his eyes, softly press his lips to hers, and wrap her safely in his arms.

He didn't know why he felt so protective of her, why he felt she was in danger. But he couldn't deny the threat he felt to her when Mara appeared. It was strange. Mara had proven she wasn't to be trusted and could be violent, and she had certainly creeped him out the last time he saw her prior to yesterday's encounter. But would she come after Gabby? It was a possibility after what she'd done to Gran. He didn't want Gabby to have anything to do with the girl.

Ever.

"So, how was the rest of your day yesterday?" Lucas asked. It was a lame question, especially with all the others rattling around in his head. But it wasn't the right time to ask those.

Gabrielle smiled as though she knew it wasn't what he really wanted to know, but she answered anyway.

"It was good."

She didn't say anything else for a few seconds, just let her eyes fall to their hands, still clasped together. She seemed to frown a little, but it was so slight and fleeting that he wasn't sure. It didn't make him feel very confident though when, as soon as the expression passed, she let go of his hand, acting like she needed to search something out in her purse, mumbling things to herself. He couldn't quite understand what she was saying.

She's speaking in a different language.

Languages had always come easily to him. He even spoke a few fluently, and whenever he tried to learn one, it came easy—too easy—just like so many other things in his life had. But this language, even though it tickled his ears with familiarity, was one he was sure he'd never heard before.

Then, she said a couple of words he thought he recognized.

"What's reckless and dangerous?" he asked.

Gabrielle stopped searching her purse abruptly and looked up at him, brows raised. Those amazing green eyes of hers were ablaze with curiosity. Lucas felt like she could look into his mind and find out everything she wanted to know, all of his secrets, if she desired to.

"What did you ask me?" Gabrielle's eyes questioned him as much as her words.

Man they're intense—intense and mesmerizing.

"I asked, what's reckless and dangerous? I thought I recognized some of what you were saying, but I'm not sure. I'm pretty good at languages … that's all." Lucas stopped talking. Now, those green eyes were framed by a scowl. He didn't like what he was seeing in them—distrust. He could see it in her expression, but he felt it, too. He could *feel* her.

But … how? And what did I say to make her look at me like that?

Everything outside of her car seemed to slow as she stared harder, deeper.

Students running to get out of the rain were now in some kind of a cross between barely moving and a walk. The rain that was coming down so hard that he could barely see more than the blur it caused was now almost frozen—he could clearly see each drop falling. Even the small splash each drop made when it hit something could easily be seen as it came up, then slowly descended to rest again. The tiniest ripples he'd ever seen were everywhere.

Everything is almost suspended.

Then Gabby looked away. Just like that, the spell was broken. Everything moved in real-time again. Things had gotten very strange, very fast.

Damn. I'm afraid to say anything after that. Did I imagine everything slowing down? If the world really did almost completely halt, how?

He ran through the conversation prior to her letting go of his hand in an attempt to figure out where his foot plowed into his mouth. But there was ...

Nothing.

Nothing that he could put his finger on, anyway.

Gabby was looking out the window, still silent, and he couldn't stand it any longer.

"Gabby, what's wrong? What did I say? Whatever it was, I didn't mean to offend you. If you were trying to keep your thoughts to yourself by speaking a different language, I didn't mean to intrude, and I promise I didn't understand anything else you said."

Gabby finally looked back at him; the same expression was on her face, but the intensity in her eyes had ratcheted back considerably.

Smiling slightly, still seeming confused about something, she finally answered.

"It's okay ... I'm sorry. It's just that, well, I *had* said those two words. I never expected you to understand them. I was speaking a *very* old form of Hebrew. You might be good at languages, Lucas, but very few hu—*people* would understand any of what I just spoke."

Lucas could tell she wasn't finished speaking. She looked at him closely for several seconds, and he worried she was about to do that intense thing again. Instead, she asked him a question.

"Where did you learn the words I spoke?"

Lucas scowled as he tried to think. He focused back on her face and gave her the only answer he had to give.

"I don't know, Gabby."

She stared at him a little longer, then seemed to let it go when the first bell for school sounded. He didn't know why she did, but he was glad. He was feeling a bit odd about it himself, now.

How did *I know?*

"Well," she said with a more familiar smile, "I guess we can talk more later. Looks like we're going to get a break in the rain."

Lucas looked out the window. The rain had all but stopped just as the world outside the car had minutes before, but now, the students continued to move as they normally would; rain fell as rain should fall; he was still sitting with the most beautiful, intriguing girl he'd ever met. Only he felt like maybe he should have just put a toe in first and tested the waters before diving into the deep end; he felt he may be in over his head.

Way over.

Chapter Eleven

Gabrielle ✝ Demons Among Us

"So," Phalen began, "you want me to scope out the demon scene, huh?"

Phalen took a seat at the kitchen counter's island. She'd arrived right after Gabrielle and Sheridan finished their work for the day, and her second in command left with Amaziah. Gabrielle was happy to see her friend and found herself, once again, entertained by how different she looked with each incarnation.

This time, Phalen chose long, straight, blue-black hair with the face of a young Asian woman. The one thing that was always constant, regardless of what appearance she took on, was the playful look in her eyes. That look was goading Gabrielle as Phalen waited for a response. Phalen blew a bubble from the gum she was chewing.

A purple one.

It made Gabrielle smile. The bubble fit Phalen's personality.

"Yeah," Gabrielle responded. "I'm having a really hard time seeing them. I feel like there is a strong presence at the school, but I can't raise the Aegis Veil or my own to discern whatever or whomever I'm sensing. Amaziah would make me leave for sure if I did. I know there's at least one there, but she wouldn't account for the intensity I'm feeling. Either there's a *lot* of the Fallen posing as students, possibly teachers, or there's one around that's exceedingly powerful."

Gabrielle was really hoping that the latter wasn't the case. She'd prefer that it would be numbers instead of power. Numbers would be easier for her to deal with.

"Who's the ol' she-demon?"

Gabrielle's mood shifted in the wrong direction as soon as she thought about Mara. Actually, it was more Mara *with Lucas* that made her blood feel like it was on fire in her veins. Apparently, Phalen caught the change in her demeanor, or maybe the Divine light her human body tried to conceal wasn't doing a very good job of containing her fiery color when she became angry. Whatever the reason, Phalen's brows were raised.

She's very perceptive, Gabrielle thought.

I can be, Phalen communicated back to her.

"Sorry, Phalen. I forget sometimes that an angel can still hear my thoughts when I'm in human form. Somehow, it seems like you shouldn't be able to."

"Coming through loud and clear, sister." Phalen smiled and relaxed as Gabrielle's intensity smoothed out a little. "So, back to the she-demon … what's what?"

"I ran into her yesterday, that's all. She doesn't seem to be all that powerful, though."

Phalen stared at Gabrielle for a minute, not backing down from Gabrielle's gaze, with clearly readable disbelief that she was getting the entire story. "Uh huh …"

Gabrielle liked Phalen. She had guts. She was one of the only angels Gabrielle had ever met that wasn't intimidated by her position. Phalen respected and admired her powers and abilities—that much she made clear—but she showed nothing of being timorous in her eyes or demeanor.

Phalen prodded further. "Are you going to tell me what's really up? Or am I going to have to figure it out on my own?" She waited for several seconds to tick off the clock, then continued. "Because as we just confirmed, I'm a *very perceptive* type of gal, and I *will* figure it out."

Gabrielle sighed, wondering how much to tell Phalen. *How much can I trust her?*

"You *can* trust me, Gabrielle."

Gabrielle looked at her and smiled.

"Stop doing that, Phalen."

"Can't. It's in my nature. Stop thinking without blocking what's going on in your noggin." Phalen replied with a smirk.

"Fine. I will." Gabrielle smirked back. After a long pause, and another long stare-off between the two friends, Gabrielle told Phalen what was going on. She started at the beginning and left nothing out, divulging her little secret that had turned into a huge dilemma.

She wanted to be with a human. At least, that was what her human body and emotions were making her believe she wanted. Which one it really was, her true desire or one created because of her human body, she didn't know for sure. She *did* know that if she made the choice to be with Lucas, if that was ever even something that would present itself as an option, it would mean joining the ranks of the Fallen. It was completely forbidden by the laws Yahuwah set in place for all angels. She would not be forgiven. He destroyed life on Earth once already because of the many angels who had disobeyed that law.

When Gabrielle finished, Phalen stared off into the distance as she let the implications sink in. When she spoke, she still focused on the same unseen thing she'd been looking at through the silence.

"Wow, Gabrielle ... I mean ... just ... *wow*."

"Yeah. *Wow*."

"You say something's different ... or, *off*, about Lucas. Like what?" Phalen finally focused her eyes back on Gabrielle.

Now Gabrielle fixated on something in the distance only she could see as she thought back to the conversation she and Lucas had as the rain pummeled her car. She'd seen him later at lunch and in the class they shared. He walked her as far as he could to her next class and later, after school, they'd chatted for a few minutes, but there seemed to be something between them now. Something unseen but definitely interfering with the ease they'd had together the day before and for the first part of the conversation that morning. There was a wall building, but was it hers or his?

Or are both of us piling on the stones?

She was sure at least part of it was her. She'd had a moment in the car, knowing that being with him was absolutely not the right thing to do, that it would have only one end—a heartbreaking one.

Gabrielle realized Phalen was still waiting for an answer. She took a breath, then began to explain.

"I was speaking Enochian to myself this morning when he was in the car with me, scolding myself in a *come to my senses* moment." She glanced at Phalen and saw a little relief in her eyes. "Don't get your hopes up. It didn't last … at least not completely. I am thinking more rationally about it now, though. Anyway, Lucas repeated a couple of the words."

"He understood the Divine language of angels? How can that be?"

"*Exactly*. How *can* that be? He shouldn't have been able to. And I don't believe for a second that he just got lucky. The words don't sound anything like the languages spoken on Earth—not even close."

"Yeah …" the word trailed as Phalen stared off into the distance again. She came back quickly this time, though. "Gabrielle, you asked me to come to help you because you are having a difficult time sensing demons with all the protection you're under." Phalen stopped as if she expected Gabrielle to know where she was going. "Is there any chance he could be one of the Fallen? That, for a moment, he let his guard down and slipped up?"

"It would explain some things … but I don't think that's what it is."

"You *don't* think … or don't *want* to? Because I wouldn't be so sure. I'm looking forward to getting a gander at this guy. Not only because he's somehow made one of the most powerful angels ever created desire him, but also to see if he has *black goo* for blood. What color are his eyes?"

Gabrielle smiled. "The bluest blue you've ever seen."

"No chartreuse around the edges anywhere?"

"Not a speck."

"Hmm ... maybe contacts ... but they've never been able to wear them. Their tears are too caustic."

Gabrielle didn't want to admit it, but Phalen raised a good possibility that she hadn't wanted to ponder or voice—good and terrible. It would clarify more than why he understood Enochian; it would also explain why she could sense him so strongly and why he was involved with Mara. Not that he'd have to be a demon to be involved with one, but it made the idea more reasonable in her mind.

But, if he is a demon, why *would he make me feel so at peace ... less broken?*

None of it made any sense.

"Gabrielle, are you sure he's not a demon?"

Gabrielle thought through everything she knew about him so far, which wasn't much really. But she knew how he made her feel. She couldn't believe a demon could give her the sense of peace he did.

"I don't think we have to worry about that."

"If you say so."

Gabrielle laughed. Phalen always said the same thing when she was going to take a leap of faith with her—Phalen's way of letting her know she had Gabrielle's back and was on her side.

"I say so."

Both Gabrielle and Phalen knew they would find out soon enough, anyway. When Phalen saw him, she should be able to tell if something wasn't right unless he had a very powerful veil in place, making him a very powerful demon if he did.

"Tomorrow," Gabrielle said in almost a whisper, "we should know."

Gabrielle didn't realize her brows were drawn until she felt them relax as Phalen lured her attention to her outstretched hand, holding something in purple wrapping.

"Gum?"

Gabrielle and Phalen rode to school the next morning with the intention of not only finding out what was making her feel so uncomfortable, but also if Lucas was one of the Fallen.

She still didn't feel like she was going to be disappointed with what Phalen told her about Lucas, but her confidence had waned a little after the dreams she'd had last night. Maybe it was the mere idea that he could be one of the Fallen in disguise, but her dreams about him weren't of the happy variety. As usual, she couldn't remember details, but the feelings she woke with several times during the night were ones she couldn't mistake—absolute trepidation and sadness.

"Hey, sister," Phalen said as she looked at Gabrielle from the seat next to her.

Phalen had changed her appearance, once again. She was back in the same one she had used the day they went to the beach to test out Amaziah's theory that Gabrielle would be spotted quickly—fair coloring, blue eyes.

"That's what I'm calling you from now on by the way," Phalen continued. "At least when we're not going through life-and-death stuff." She waited, as if to see if Gabrielle was going to protest. When Phalen got a smile and an amused shaking head back, she continued. "Anyway, *sister*, have you decided what my *role* is going to be in your life? I mean, you're suddenly showing up with a tall blond with legs for miles and an 'I dare you to mess with me' attitude and you're going to say what, exactly, when people ask you who I am?"

Gabrielle laughed. "I hadn't thought about it, really. I guess we can just make you my sister. My *adopted* sister. We certainly don't look like we came from the same gene pool."

"K ... that way it will make more sense when I call you *sistah*."

Gabrielle found herself laughing again. Phalen had a way of making her want to smile even when she didn't know if there was much reason to.

Phalen reached into her pocket and brought out a pack of grape bubble gum.

"Phalen, you may be addicted."

"Hey, I can't help it if this stuff is yum. I could be wanting worse things on Earth." Phalen moved forward in her seat so she was looking Gabrielle right in her eyes. "Like a romantic relationship with a human," she said with a wink, then sat back.

"We all have our vices, I guess. Even angels."

"Agreed, but mine won't get me booted from Heaven."

"I know ... but ... it *feels* right."

"How can a relationship between you and a human be *right*?" Phalen waited but got no answer. She tried again with a different question. "Are you sure you're not just trying to use him to forget about Javan?"

'Ouch.' Gabrielle thought, but this time, she expected Phalen's reply.

'Yeah,' Phalen responded, 'I thought that might sting a bit, but maybe you need to consider the possibility.'

"You have a point. I will."

"Hmm ... "

Gabrielle looked at Phalen quizzically. "What?"

Phalen watched Gabrielle while blowing one of her purple bubbles. This one ended up so big that Gabrielle worried she'd be helping Phalen get the grape stuff out of her hair. Instead, Phalen sucked it back in her mouth.

"I just expected more of a retort from you on that one. You getting soft?"

Gabrielle laughed. "Not hardly, Phalen. Since I try not to think about Javan, I just hadn't thought about that angle. I need to, though, before Lucas or I get in any deeper. Besides, you're always looking for a fight, so you're always waiting for a retort."

"Not with you, sister, not with you. I'd be a fool to ever want to go up against The Angel of Karma. And I'm no fool."

"No, Phalen, you're not," Gabrielle said with a wink. "We're here."

They arrived before most of the students so Phalen would have a chance to get accustomed to the surroundings. She would be able to discern the Fallen better if she already had a handle on the different energies in the area.

While Phalen studied the first prospects unloading from their cars and getting off busses, Gabrielle searched for Lucas. As the clock ticked off the minutes before the first bell, he was nowhere to be seen.

"Still no Romeo?" Phalen asked without looking at Gabrielle.

"No."

And that seemed strange.

She'd expected the morning to be like the last two had—with him arriving early like her and having a few moments together before school started.

"And we have our first sighting." Phalen pointed.

Gabrielle followed the direction of her finger and eyes toward the gym. She thought she'd stopped breathing, knowing that was where Lucas would be. With a relieved exhale, she began to breathe again.

"That's Mara."

"Pretty little demon, isn't she?"

"Yes, she is," Gabrielle agreed with a biting tone.

"Don't worry, you're much prettier. Lucas would be a fool if he ever got the choice and didn't pick you. And that's, of course, based on looks alone. Sometimes, your mood is worse than a demon's. If that info is thrown in, it might be more of a toss-up." Phalen laughed at herself, slapping her leg as she enjoyed the moment.

"You're really feeling full of yourself today, aren't you?"

"Yeah, well, someone has to lighten things up around here."

Gabrielle looked back at Mara. She was standing near the back of the building where a walkway led to the rest of the school, talking to someone who was shielded by the corner of the main building. More like flirting heavily. Mara tossed her head back in laughter, her long dark hair easing further down her back when she did. She brought her head forward again and stood on her tip-toes, moving forward slightly so that her head was mostly out of view. Whomever she was talking to remained completely out of sight, but Gabrielle saw two masculine hands settle on her shoulders.

Definitely flirting.

"She's not very powerful, Gabrielle. Not really. And I'm not seeing a lot of other activity. I'm not sure what's making you feel so out of whack here."

Gabrielle started scanning for Lucas again. She saw Nonie pull into the lot, and Nate came rolling in right after his sister. She watched as Nonie got out of her car and walked toward where Nate was still inside his.

Maybe Lucas rode with him.

Gabrielle waited, but the only person who exited was Nate. Gabrielle let out a frustrated sigh.

"What is it?" Phalen asked.

"Nothing. I was hoping Lucas rode with Nonie or Nate since I hadn't seen him yet, but he's not with them."

"Who are Nonie and Nate?"

"Close friends that live across the street from Lucas. They're right there."

Gabrielle pointed to the twins as they walked through the parking lot. Phalen followed her gaze and began to scowl.

"Hmm … that one's interesting."

"Who?"

"I guess it's Nate if he's the one with the pretty blond who's not so unpretty himself." Phalen pointed to make sure she was looking at the right teens.

"Yeah, that's Nate. What's so interesting about him?"

"Something's not right about his energy. It's … *fuzzy*. Wavy."

"Wavy? What does that mean?"

"I don't know how to explain it better than that. I've never seen energy like it. Very weird. It's like looking at something with the heat waves from Hell between you and whatever it is you're looking at." Phalen continued to scrutinize Nate as he began to take the steps two at a time to get to the front doors of the school. "Oh, wait a minute ... no, he's looking fine, now. Maybe my discernment was just protesting all this activity before I've had a proper breakfast."

"You could have eaten at my house if you wanted to."

"I *did* want to. No offense, sister, but you need a little variety and more abundance in your cart next time you go to the grocery."

"Whatever," Gabrielle said through laughter as the first bell rang.

"Wait a second," Phalen said, "what's with the heaviness? It's like the heavens just settled a little lower, right on top of me."

"That's exactly what I've been talking about. Do you see anything different?"

Phalen scanned the area again slowly. When her attention was back on the gym, she stopped.

"Nothing but another weird fuzziness over the gym and that flock of crows staring at us. I don't care for crows ... creepy little black-feathered things bringing dark omens and superstitions."

"Where?" Gabrielle asked as she looked. Phalen was right. The crows perched on the roof of the gym seemed to be looking right at them.

Like the ones I saw the first day of school ... maybe the same ones. Gabrielle thought. "Yeah ... but there's one superstition about them that's correct."

A chill shot through Gabrielle.

As she was about to say something to Phalen, movement caught her eye. Mara had thrown her arms around whomever she was talking to. This time, Gabrielle could see the face that belonged to the mystery guy along with the rest of him as he moved toward the gym doors. His arm was around Mara's waist, her arms draped around him, and her head rested on his shoulder.

Lucas.

Chapter Twelve

LUCAS ✝ LOVER

Lucas didn't have time to deal with Mara. But she had cornered him on his way to gym first thing in the morning, on a day when he didn't have enough fight in him to be the jerk he needed to be to get rid of her.

He hadn't slept at all the night before. All he could do was think about how, prior to yesterday morning in the car, everything he was experiencing with Gabby had felt so *right*, and now he felt like she'd drawn a line a mile wide between them that he had no hope of crossing. The most frustrating part of it was that he didn't know what he'd done to spook her. He'd run the conversation over in his head so many times it made his brain hurt. Her entire mood changed when he understood some of the words she was saying.

It just doesn't make sense.

Now he was tired, late, felt like a jerk because he'd parked on the other side of school so he could avoid Gabby, and he couldn't get away from Mara. He wanted to yell in her face and shove past her. But then he'd look like a real charmer to the students around him. They would have his brute theatrics spread through the entire school by second period.

He closed his eyes and took a breath for what must have been the tenth time since she stepped in front of him, trying to keep calm. He put his hands on her shoulders, hoping to make her listen to him more clearly.

"Look, Mara, I have to go. Sorry you don't like how things have turned out, but it is what it is."

No sooner had the words passed his lips when she threw her arms around him and seemed to almost melt into him, like she'd just been through something so incredibly emotional and physical that she had no energy left to support her own weight—and maybe not the will to, either.

"Lucas ... *help me*," Mara said in a frail whisper.

Mara sounding so fragile and feeling so limp in his arms worried Lucas, regardless of what he felt about how she'd acted lately. There was a time he had thought she was fun to be around, when she was kind and happy. That girl didn't stay around long, though. Mara turned into someone who was manipulative and dark. Now he felt that the girl he once enjoyed spending time with had just crashed back into his arms.

"Hey, let's get inside and sit down." Lucas said, walking her toward the gym doors. Mara placed her head on his shoulder. When her arms draped around his waist, he felt her body shudder. She was cold to the touch even after being in the warm morning sun.

He opened the door to the gym with his free hand and continued to escort Mara to the bleachers at the far end, away from as many eyes as possible, and they sat down. Luckily, most everyone was still in the locker rooms changing. He turned her toward him and raised her face so he could look at her.

His breath left him.

Mara looked as though she hadn't slept in weeks. Dark circles and blood-shot eyes told the tale, and her skin wasn't only cold, it was sallow. It was like he was looking at a completely different person than the one who flirted with him moments before.

A shiver rocked his own body.

"Mara ..." Lucas looked into the hazel eyes he'd not seen since she began to act so strange, so aggressive. He could swear they had been that weird yellow-green shade when they were outside. "Mara, what's going on?"

She looked into his eyes, worry etched in her face.

"I ... I don't know," she said, her brows furrowed. "I don't remember how I even *got* here!"

Panic slipped into her tone, and she looked around the gym frantically, then back at Lucas. Tears filled her eyes.

"Lucas ... what's going on? What's *happening* to me?"

She flung her arms around him again and held him tightly like she thought if she didn't, she would slip away somewhere—like he was her only lifeline.

Lucas slowly stroked the back of her hair while he tried to speak words that might help, though he wasn't sure exactly what would. What do you say when someone seemed to be two different people and one side, the softer one, was desperately trying to break free of the other?

"Shh ... take a breath."

Lucas said those words over and over to Mara as he stroked her hair. Slowly, she seemed to relax in his arms, and her breathing calmed. He didn't think she was crying anymore, either.

"Okay," he began, once he thought she could talk to him again. "What's the last thing you *do* remember?"

He felt her slowly drop one arm, bringing it up to wipe her face. She seemed to snuggle into him a little more, and he thought he saw the side of her face push into a smile.

Good, she's feeling better.

"Well, the last thing I remember that I actually *enjoyed* was the way it felt to have your tongue in my mouth and your hands searching my body in all the right ... *spots*. How 'bout you give me an even better memory to hold onto ... *lover*?"

Lucas's body went rigid, and he forced her face up so he could look at her. He shot to his feet and reeled back from her so fast that he stumbled and ended up on the gym's shiny wood floor.

Mara's complexion was back to normal, and her expression showed nothing of her worried, frantic state from moments before. But her eyes—they weren't hazel; they weren't even that crazy cat-yellow anymore. They were black—solid, shiny black.

"*What the hell?*"

Lucas blinked hard.

When he focused, Mara's eyes were back to the shade they'd been the last several weeks. The hazel and black ones were gone, and the eerie yellow ones had returned. Lucas stared, wondering if it had been his imagination. What he wasn't imagining was that the old, sweet Mara was gone again. The bitch was back. And he wanted nothing to do with her.

"What's wrong, Lucas?" Mara said with a smirk as she stood and sauntered over to him.

Lucas stood and met her halfway. He didn't care how freaky Mara was or how much of an ass he may look like to anyone watching. This time, she was going to get the message loud and clear.

He was inches from her. He lowered his face to hers in what could have looked like a kiss in the making, then stopped and glared into those evil, yellow eyes.

"Keep. Away. From. Me. *Got it?*"

Mara smiled like he'd invited her to dinner. "Why, Lucas, whatever did I do?" She batted her lashes at him.

He hated her at that moment. He hated himself, too, for allowing himself to get roped into her games again. He wanted a shower after having her hanging on him. He felt …

Unclean.

Unclean in a dark, evil way that Lucas had never experienced before. He could feel a darkness coming to life in him, clawing from his depths in an attempt to gain freedom. The feeling troubled him. He'd always felt he had to take the high road, be the nice guy, do the right thing—until now.

He moved even closer to Mara once he felt he regained control. "You haven't seen hostile, but you've deserved to. Just stay away from me and anyone that has to do with me. You and I have *nothing* left to talk about. Understand?"

Mara just held the same shit-eating grin. "You're breaking my heart, lover."

Lucas chose to walk away before she had him going down another path to Weirdsville. He didn't look back. Not while students looked back-and-forth between him and her. Not when he was approaching the locker room door. Not even when he put his hand out to open it and he heard her begin to cackle like some possessed witch—a cackle that replayed in his head all day.

Chapter Thirteen

GABRIELLE ✝ LOVE LOST

After Phalen left, Gabrielle went through the rest of her day at school in a daze that was occasionally interrupted by dueling feelings of sadness and anger. The competing emotions arose any time she recalled Lucas and Mara with their arms wrapped around each other. She told Nonie that she wouldn't be joining them for lunch, using an errand as an excuse, and managed to squeak into the class she shared with Lucas just as the last bell rang. Luckily, he was already there and seated on the far side, and there was an empty seat right by the door that would allow an easy and rapid exit.

She didn't want to talk to Lucas. Not today. Not tomorrow.

Possibly never.

She wanted to put the ridiculous feelings she thought she was developing for him behind her and focus on her task.

That's all I want.

Even as she thought it, she knew she wasn't being honest with herself, but she was going to keep saying it until she began to believe the words. Driving home from school, she gladly allowed her angelic ability take over. She was lost in repeating her new mantra until the car suddenly came to an abrupt halt, tires squealing in protest.

Gabrielle's hands gripped the steering wheel so hard her knuckles turned white.

What just happened?

She looked up to see if she'd hit something. Inside a black Mercedes, with side and rear windows tinted almost as dark as the paint, was a female demon. The car faced her own, blocking it almost head on.

Mara.

And she wasn't alone.

Gabrielle hadn't wrecked. She hadn't hit anyone. But she had a problem in her way.

A big one.

Sitting next to her was a face Gabrielle had never seen but knew immediately. Even with the Veil, there could be no mistaking the energy coming from the human form was Javan's. Javan and Gabrielle stared at each other for what seemed like a very long time but was only moments. The smile across his face was not an inviting one, and there was a look in his eyes Gabrielle wasn't accustomed to seeing. The love he once had for her seemed absent. She had often wondered if he still loved her or if there was even a remnant of what they once had shared. She felt she had her answer, and she felt the crushing realization that he was truly, thoroughly, lost to Light—and her. She didn't hold on to any ideas that he'd ever be able to be forgiven by Yahuwah, but she wasn't present when Javan was cast out; there had been no closure for her because she had never seen him again.

Until now.

She realized, at that moment, that she had been holding onto a small bit of hope that they could be together again, somehow. That foolish hope was now completely squashed—along with her heart.

What was I thinking? We could never be Reyahs again. I have to let him go ... completely.

Before either had a chance to do anything, the car sped off.

Gabrielle didn't attempt to move her own car for several more moments. Why had Javan appeared to her here—now? And who was Mara to him? How did she fit in to any of this? How did Lucas fit into any of this?

Gabrielle shuddered, shaken again by the knowledge that Lucas was, on some level, involved with Mara—possibly Javan. She was still going to have to find out more about what had happened to make Lucas so angry at Mara even though she'd made the decision there could be nothing between her and Lucas now—she had stopped kidding herself. The best-case scenario: her heart would be shattered. Again. The worst case: she'd become one of the Fallen.

A car horn jolted her out of her thoughts. She raised a hand in apology and drove the two blocks to her home. It made her uneasy that Javan must know exactly where she lived.

What could he want with me now?

She rushed in the house as fast as she could in front of the human eyes that might see her, not wanting to raise suspicion, dropped her things in the floor of her entry, and called to Amaziah.

It took much longer for him to arrive than Gabrielle had hoped. She spent the time waiting running through scenarios and possibilities. How deeply involved was Lucas with Javan and Mara? Ideas and images swam in different directions in her mind. They tossed and dove deep, then would resurface like a drowning victim. It left her mentally exhausted and confused—nothing made sense. When Amaziah finally did arrive, she felt like she had been trying to keep her head above water as those thoughts pulled at her legs, trying to drag her under, trying to kill some part of her she didn't want to let die. She fell into his arms when he manifested in her living room.

"I know, Gabrielle." Amaziah wrapped his arms around her as she wept. She tried to tell him what happened through her tears. "You don't have to tell me anything. I've been in tune with your thoughts from the moment I heard you. I am also surprised he showed himself to you. Especially in that manner. You have no idea who Mara is?"

Gabrielle shook her head. "I don't understand what he's doing, Amaziah … what he wants. The choice to rebel against Yahuwah was his and his alone. What could make him want to contact me in any way? I don't believe it's because he still loves me."

Gabrielle let go of Amaziah and frantically paced the room.

"That was *not* love in his eyes for me, Amaziah. It was more like contempt—maybe even loathing. What have I done to make him feel that for me? He knew when he chose the path he did that there would be nothing for us. Nothing at all. He abandoned and betrayed me at the same time he did Yahuwah. Is that not enough for him? Is he going to haunt me forever, making me always wonder when he's going to show up again, never letting me forget? Is that what he wants? To punish me? For *what*?" Gabrielle fell into the large, overstuffed leather chair and pulled her knees up to her chest, resting her chin on them. Her tears had stopped and were replaced with deep deliberation. She would have to protect her heart from Javan in the future. She cared too much for him, and that was dangerous. Her love for him could cause her to make the wrong decisions or worse.

It could make me want to join him.

Javan was a weakness. Something that could be used against her. She hadn't been truthful with herself about that until now. She hadn't counted on it being an issue for her here on Earth. The thoughts haunted Gabrielle. Amaziah made his way to her, knelt beside the chair she was sitting in, and placed his hands around one of hers.

"Gabrielle, Javan will strike out at anything, and anyone, who is still in Yahuwah's fold. You know that. You were together for a very long time, but a dark seed settled in his soul, and when it grew, it choked out any goodness or love he held within."

Gabrielle shut her eyes tightly in hopes that it would somehow make what she felt disappear—as if it never happened.

"Trust me," Amaziah continued, "in time, his intentions will be revealed to us. Either through his own desire to make it known to you or by an act of treason by one close to him. It may be something we can learn through our own contacts, but it isn't anything we can be enlightened to right now. I know seeing him was deeply unsettling, but don't allow it to distract you from your goal here. Be patient. And always remember, Gabrielle, a tortured soul can ultimately do no better than torture yours. He has embraced hate, Darkness. Nothing can break through a closed mind, not even love. If he doesn't accept love, he cannot give it."

Gabrielle pressed her fists to her eyes, trying to push away her thoughts. After failing to do so, she looked at her friend. His bright blue eyes searched hers to see if she was feeling better. She wasn't. Her heartache was not going to be pushed away so easily, but she needed to move forward regardless. She didn't have time to dwell on his betrayal.

Too much depends on what I do to let this get to me.

"Thank you, Amaziah, for being here." She smiled although it was listless.

"And I always will be. Now, go take one of those hot showers you always speak so favorably about. Sleep. Your work can wait for you to be better rested … and focused."

Sheridan's face flashed through her mind. Before she could say anything, Amaziah spoke.

"I'll deal with Sheridan. Go. Do as I've advised. I will wait here with Sheridan until you wake. Karma isn't going anywhere, either. Would you like me to Ease your thoughts so you can rest?"

"Please."

Amaziah placed his forehead against hers and closed his eyes. It only took as long as a breath, and she felt her muscles relax. Amaziah smiled his familiar, reassuring smile and disappeared into the kitchen where Sheridan was waiting. Gabrielle closed her eyes and tried, once again, to push thoughts of Javan from her mind without success. Amaziah's use of Ease helped, but unfortunately, it didn't take the thoughts completely away.

After a longer than normal shower, she crawled into bed and pulled the down comforter over her. The mental and emotional exhaustion seemed to settle into her human body's bones, weighing her down so much that it pulled her into a deep sleep. Lucas's face, as had become customary the last couple of days, was the last thing her mind saw as she gladly let dreams take her away into a world she hoped would be more peaceful than her day had been. But her dreams didn't allow her the rest she and Amaziah had hoped for. Instead, she woke more unsettled than when she lay down to begin with.

Chapter Fourteen

GABRIELLE ✟ AN EDGY ANGEL

"*NO, LUCAS!*" Gabrielle woke from her restless sleep, hearing the sound of her own voice calling out. She was sitting up, her hand pressing against her chest, her heart racing as fast as her mind.

What did I see?

Gabrielle pulled at the human strands of her memory, trying to manipulate them into something she could make sense of. She wished she could lift the Veil before she went to sleep. All she could remember was a jumble of images—an ancient book with a symbol of a two-headed snake coiled around a very long, curved sword that became a tree at the tip; Javan, laughing wickedly, his ominous glare falling on Gabrielle and Lucas; the wings of swarms of angels, Yahuwah's and the Fallen, fiercely fighting; Gabrielle and Javan in combat; Lucas, falling, landing on the ground far below them, lifeless.

Half premonitions were of little use to Gabrielle. She angrily went downstairs to confront Amaziah, thinking that he was the reason for her deep slumber that caused her to not remember her dreams. She found him with Sheridan, debating something again. Her voice reached them before she did.

"Amaziah! Please don't do whatever it is you're doing to put me into such a deep human sleep! I can't remember half of what I am supposed to see! Would you—"

Amaziah raised a hand to Hush Gabrielle, immediately blocking her ability to speak out loud and preventing her from communicating with him telepathically. It was a power he never used on her. It infuriated Gabrielle, but she had no choice but to wait.

"Gabrielle," Amaziah said calmly, "I have done no such thing to you. It may be an unforeseen, and unavoidable, consequence of taking human form. You know dreams are something angels never have. How can we when we never sleep? The difference in what you'll be able to recall compared to a vision, as you can see, is vast. If this continues to be a problem, consider transforming into your Divine form and allow your human body to rest on its own without you in it. But please … calm yourself. You know I would never do anything that might upset you in this way."

When he thought she had calmed, he raised his hand again, made a small gesture, and Gabrielle felt the restraint he'd placed on her lift.

Boy, would I like to have that trick.

"And one day, it may be given it to you. If Yahuwah sees its usefulness to do so," Amaziah said.

"Of course, Amaziah," Gabrielle replied, putting her hands together and resting them against the front of her body in a subtle show of respect.

Amaziah was her friend, and the closest thing she had to a human father, but she was still his subordinate. A fact she sometimes forgot. He had never told her exactly how high he ranked in the Choir of Angels, but she knew it was *very* high. When she'd asked him, he just said it was of little importance and went no further with the topic. He had Yahuwah's audience whenever he desired it, though. So, regardless of what he said, he was extremely important, and trusted, by Him.

Amaziah smiled, and the heaviness of her initial mood lifted. She shook her anger off and told him what she could remember of her dream.

Amaziah listened closely to the description of the images she was able to bring back to the waking world, the crease between his brow deepening with every detail. When she finished, he walked over to the glass door that led to the deck and a small yard that ended in a thick line of trees. He stood there, quietly thinking, for a long time. Finally, he turned to face them. Curiosity and concern mingled heavily in his eyes. There was something else he held in his gaze—a deep sadness, an emotional wound that had never quite healed beginning to open again. It made her stomach turn in sympathy.

"There was a book, ancient in appearance as you described. The Book of Barabbadon. It had a symbol of the two-headed snake twisting around the blade of a long sword as you also described. I saw it *thousands* of years ago. Long before Yahuwah had even breathed you into existence, Gabrielle. There was an attempt by Darkness to gain power over Yahuwah. The Book was the instrument used to wage a great war between Heaven and Hell, and all the beings within them. The angels in our eternal home who were witness to it don't speak of what happened. They would rather pretend as though the battle had never occurred at all.

"The number of casualties was terrible. So many lost those they were closest to, and their hearts still ache for them even without passing the reminders of our history down to the fledgling angels through stories. It was a somber time. A time I've hoped we'd never see again."

He paused, and Gabrielle could tell he didn't want to revisit the memory himself.

How many of those lost were angels he had been close to?

"It was ordered that the Book be destroyed. Without doubt, I have believed it had been. Now … I wonder. I have to go to Council with this information right away, Gabrielle. We'll talk more soon."

And he was gone.

"Gabrielle." Sheridan showed her displeasure with her commander loudly in her tone, which was unusual. It told how she didn't think Gabrielle deserved to hold the position she had and of her feelings about being put out by having to come here every day. Gabrielle was sure envy—jealousy—had hitched a cosmic ride tonight. "Don't you think this living as a human ... *thing* is a bit much? And you know how Amaziah worries over you, though I don't know why. Your decision to come here," Sheridan paused, "it seems a bit misguided. Some of the troops are starting to talk, and I—"

"Sheridan," Gabrielle's tone was flat and stern, the week's karma seeping deep into her mood past the point that she could shield anyone from it—especially Sheridan. "I don't concern myself with what others say. I know my decision isn't one many agreed with, including you. However, *your* opinion is one that I truly don't spend my time worrying over."

Sheridan stiffened. Even with her feeling particularly bold, she knew she had overstepped.

Gabrielle hadn't been entirely honest about not being concerned with what was being said. It did bother her, but what troubled her more was her willingness to be less than truthful. Other than keeping the visions she had of Lucas and her attraction to him to herself, she couldn't remember being anything but honorable with her brethren. Another side effect of her human body, she supposed.

She really did care less and less about what Sheridan thought of her, though. Gabrielle's trust in her had been slowly eroding.

"So, what are the instructions for today's lot?" Gabrielle asked with a bite in her tone and an upward glare at Sheridan. "Are the troops ready for their assignments?"

Even though Sheridan still held her stiff demeanor, she seemed to welcome the topic shift; she responded quickly. "Yes, the troops are ready."

"Then, let's get started."

Gabrielle hoped for the best. Her mood needed to lighten.

When they finished, she was relieved. She had been able to grant more good karma than bad. Tomorrow her mood would be better as long as she didn't have any surprises. She'd have to deal with Javan at some point, though, and that was something she wasn't looking forward to.

Starting tomorrow, she had an additional goal—one she realized as soon as she'd woken with the broken pieces of her dream. The piece she was most interested in right now concerned the Book.

Is it the same one the demon mentioned?

It could be a coincidence, but Gabrielle didn't believe in them. Between her dream about a book that looked just like the Book of Barabbadon—a book that could be used as a weapon to wage war on Heaven itself—and the look in Amaziah's eyes, finding out more about the ancient artifact just became a high priority.

And a convenient distraction from Lucas.

Chapter Fifteen

GABRIELLE ☨ NEW BONDS

The complexities of human desire were becoming more apparent. Wanting companionship, acceptance, success, and *things* were becoming more prominent in Gabrielle's mind. For an angel, wanting materialistic things was not an issue. Little was needed in Heaven.

With no use for a personal home, there was also no need for the things that would be required or wanted for one—no use for a vehicle, boat, money, makeup, designer clothing and shoes, jewelry, expensive vacations, or even food. Angels simply need the connection to, and love of, Yahuwah and each other. That was it. No sleep, no eating, no time off—life simplified.

She found herself with thoughts, even if they were fleeting, of wanting ... *things*. It had crossed her mind several times already that this is probably how it started for most of her comrades who had become one of the Fallen. They were assigned duties that involved a lot of contact with humans, in human bodies, and they began to feel their emotions and desires. When they returned to Heaven, those desires stayed with them, even in their true form. Then, the desires could take them over. Gabrielle knew she could keep herself in check, though.

At least I hope I can.

However, the situation with Lucas had surprised her, and until she saw him with Mara, she had certainly had a hard time keeping from toeing the line that separated what she was allowed to do with a human and what was forbidden. She needed to stay clear of that line if she wanted to remain an angel.

How could I ever have chanced my Divine life for him?

It wasn't an easy question to answer. No angel had ever spent as much time as she had in human form, not since Ramai, so no one really knew if the effect it had on him would be as profound in other angels.

She hadn't seen Javan again and had managed to avoid Lucas the rest of the week. It was now Saturday. She shouldn't have to see Lucas at all, and hopefully, not Javan either, which had her emotions battling between relief and sadness. She hated how it all made her feel, and to make matters worse, avoiding Lucas also meant avoiding Nonie. She was enjoying getting to know her and had hoped to learn a lot from their new friendship. It all added up to not wanting to be at the school, but she really had no choice. This is where she was told to be, so this is where she had to stay as long as she continued the task she took on.

Lucas had turned into a big complication, and the biggest was what was still unknown—why she was having visions and dreams of him. Whether she wanted to or not, she was going to have to find out the reason. Then, she could put it all behind her.

"No more Lucas," Gabrielle said in little more than a whisper

She pushed him out of her mind as she waited for Phalen at a local coffee house near one of the college campuses. It had a wonderful outside area dotted with tables and chairs to enjoy whatever beverage she chose. Mostly, it was coffee with what some might consider a mountain of sugar and a ladle of cream. A young woman laughed one day while waiting to use the cream and said that Gabrielle was drinking more of a dessert than a beverage.

The coffee house, once someone's bungalow home, was now one of many businesses that had taken over the houses nestled close to one another on a city side street. Gabrielle had loved spending warm summer days in the shade of towering oak trees as she observed and listened to the humans she was here to gain insight into.

She'd used the spot to better hone her teenage persona while figuring out *text speak*, cell phones, and the internet. She'd watch, trying to burn into her mind the gestures, speech, flirting, and mixture of uncertainty and boldness that seemed to be their demeanor, and then she'd go home and practice. It would be a comical scene to some if they could see her while she stood in front of the mirrored wall in her bathroom as she talked to herself.

There were older people who frequented the coffee shop: college students of varying ages, business people, writers and musicians; all were intriguing to her because they lived such different lives from each other. Angels, for the most part, lived very similar lives to their counterparts. The choices a human had—jobs, hobbies, clothes, make-up, hair, shoes, movies, books, museums, friends, lovers—seemed endless to Gabrielle. What makes them choose one thing or one person over another or change their mind after a choice has been made? It was a mystery that she still felt no closer to understanding.

Gabrielle took her seat on an outdoor chair, stretching her legs out to rest on another one across the table from her, then began to scan her surroundings. It was early in the morning, very early. The sun, now beginning its climb into the day, had only been fully visible for a little over an hour. The morning was already thick with humidity as the cicadas called to each other in the trees. The aroma of freshly brewed coffee and baking pastries were carried to her as people opened the door. Gabrielle smiled slightly, enjoying her human body on a morning that she knew was just one of a handful for her compared to what most humans would be given.

I wish I had more time here.

Her attention was drawn to a man and woman deep in conversation. They had their backs to her, but she could see their profiles as they spoke to each other. They seemed to be in their late twenties, dressed too casually for a business breakfast. There were no books or computers to indicate they were students, and their food and drinks seemed to be untouched. Gabrielle wasn't sure what they were doing, but she found oddities intriguing. No one else seemed to notice them, or if they did, it didn't garner their attention the way it had hers.

They seemed to sit a little too close to each other. Not that it was unusual for a man and woman to sit close together, but even with Gabrielle's limited experience in deciphering body language, their physical closeness didn't match the feeling she got from them. It was like they were sitting that way to be secretive. Her ability to hear far better than a human wasn't helping, either. She wasn't able to make out enough of what they were saying to understand their conversation—which was odd in itself. They were only thirty feet away.

As if they heard her thoughts, both glanced over their shoulders in her direction. She wasn't sure if they looked directly at her because she glanced away too fast in an attempt not to be caught staring, and both had on sunglasses with very dark lenses. Whether they caught her staring at them or not, they were now standing, leaving their uneaten food at the table.

Gabrielle watched them from the corner of her eye as they made their way to the sidewalk—a path that led past her own table. Unexpectedly, she felt the instinct to ready herself for confrontation. She fought off the impulse to call her Divine weapons as a tingling in her palms where they would appear grew intense—begging her to will them to her so they could be used again as if starved for battle. As the man and woman came closer, the desire became even more urgent. Two realizations hit her at once that made it clear why she was feeling the way she was.

They are not *human, and this is* not *a good place for a battle.*

There was no mistaking the sense of another with Divine blood now or the lurch of her insides that made her want to vomit. Gabrielle's muscles tensed and her heart raced with the anticipation of what was to come. She prepared to halt mortal time and create a shield to protect the humans, glancing at the demons as they continued their approach. They were definitely staring at her now. Both had lowered their sunglasses, allowing the chartreuse shade of their eyes to be seen. Her stomach did another complete turn and threatened to expel what filled it, this time with more force, but she pushed the bile back.

Standing, Gabrielle readied herself, intensely aware of their every movement—their pace, position to each other, every step, every twitch of a finger, blink of an eye, and rise and fall of their chest with each breath. They seemed to slow unnaturally as they closed the short distance between their table and hers. It was as though everything around them moved at regular pace except for them. Finally, they were upon Gabrielle, and she opened her hands at her side as she prepared to call for her Dither Swords.

"Hello, angel," the male demon said with a sliver of a smile, not stopping as they passed.

That was it.

Gabrielle was stunned that they didn't recognize or try to attack her, but then she remembered the Veil. It had been proven, several times, to not protect her completely from being shown as an angel, but she didn't think the demons realized who she was.

Gabrielle sat back down, adrenaline coursing through her human veins. Even if it was protecting her, the Aegis Veil was a problem. It dulled her Divine discernment even more than she was already admitting, dangerously so. Slowly, as more seconds passed with the demons out of sight, she felt the tension and nausea that had gripped her lose its edge. As she calmed, thoughts about the high amount of activity in the area from the Fallen began to race through her mind, and she felt her body shudder from an intense chill.

In all the times she had been to Earth before, in all of her observations in the past made while doing her job as The Angel of Karma, she had never noticed so many demons in one area. There were many everywhere, at all times, but not usually above ground and centralized in such large numbers. The Underworlders were easily blending in with humans. It was unsettling. She had no idea their presence would be so obvious. Were they here because of her?

This is becoming far too frequent of an occurrence.

Her presence must somehow be attracting them even if they didn't realize why they were coming here or who she was.

Or ... maybe they do.

They could be gathering in large numbers to attack her. For whatever reason they congregated in this area, the feeling of heaviness was a clear indicator that something was going on—something Gabrielle didn't understand.

She needed to tell Amaziah about the demonic activity and the unexplainable dread she felt, but she didn't want him to get more overprotective and call off this task. She needed the four months that remained to gain more insight. She had to stay even if something was coming—especially if something was coming.

"Hi, Gabrielle."

Gabrielle jumped at the sound of the female voice, her nerves apparently still piqued. Turning around, Gabrielle saw Phalen approaching. She'd almost forgotten Phalen was coming this morning.

Phalen still seemed to enjoy creating different bodies when she came to Earth in human form. Today she had the dark skin and butterscotch eyes of an African princess—tall and lean with feminine muscles that made her appear strong and proud, her hair cropped close to her head.

"Hi," Gabrielle said through a slightly forced smile as she tried to calm herself back down. It was nice to see a friend, especially after being in the company of enemies moments before.

"Did I just see what I think I saw leaving?"

"You did."

"I guess I didn't miss anything since the place is still standing." Phalen pulled out a chair and sat with Gabrielle, still looking in the direction of the exiting demons. "That surprises me."

"I don't think they even knew I was an angel until they were right up on me, much less who I am, because of the Aegis Veil."

"Yeah, that would do it." Phalen gazed at Gabrielle with curiosity. Gabrielle didn't like that look, at least when it was cast in her direction. It meant questions were flitting about in the gazer's mind—questions about things that made Gabrielle *special*.

"Do you feel as important as you are?" Phalen continued. "I mean, I was just wondering what it feels like to be so protected ... so looked after."

Gabrielle shifted in her chair—the only outward appearance of the unease she felt over Phalen's question and others she suspected were going unasked.

"I wish, sometimes, that I wasn't so unusual."

"Really?" An expression born of surprise crossed Phalen's face, pushing the curious one aside, to Gabrielle's relief.

With their friendship so new, Phalen didn't know how uncomfortable Gabrielle was with who she was—that Amaziah was one of the only angels more powerful than her in Heaven. Gabrielle would want no other position than the one she had, but she had never been at ease with all that came with it. It left her feeling isolated, and she craved the companionship that she saw other angels achieve easily.

It had been especially hard after Javan ...

Gabrielle met Phalen's gaze, then dropped her eyes before answering.

"Since I've been here, I've recognized something very familiar in human children concerning my own personality."

"What's that?"

"Small children, unlike how they tend to become once they are teenagers, don't seem to want to be different from the children around them. I don't know why, really. Maybe it's because when they have done things that are different in their short lives to bring unwanted attention on themselves, that made them uncomfortable. Maybe they are unable to process what to do with that feeling of the unknown." Gabrielle sighed. "For me ... *I* am the unknown to the majority of our brethren. That's what makes me different, and that makes it impossible for me to ever truly fit in. I am too different. Which is why I sometimes wish I was like you, Phalen. You aren't looked upon by any other angel as being unlike them. Even though I'm an angel just like the rest of you, I am still unusual—a curiosity. I'm on the fringe of our world, and all I really want is to fit in ... just like a human child—to feel I'm *a part* of my family instead of *apart* from you all."

Gabrielle and Phalen sat in the quiet that had become their moment. Gabrielle was glad. She could feel the human emotions contained in her body wanting to burst forth, and she wasn't ready to deal with it. The emotions, once again, were proving more difficult to control in this form than she had expected, and she fought to keep tears in place.

Ugh! They make me feel so weak and out of control!

Other than Amaziah and Javan, Phalen was the only angel whom she had ever told how she felt about her uniqueness, and sharing it left Gabrielle feeling vulnerable, particularly in her current form. The silence continued and was interrupted in Gabrielle's mind only when she closed her eyes and saw the face of the dark-haired, blue-eyed young man smiling back at her—the face she now knew belonged to Lucas. It made her heart ratchet. Thoughts about him never seemed to stop. She wanted them to, but didn't want them to. She was angry, though it was getting harder to tell if she was mad at him because of Mara or mad at herself for being so reckless with him. That, and not knowing what made him seem off, made her conflicted about the peace that came with his image. She wanted that peace but had to deny herself of it. Right now, there were more important things to pay attention to, and Lucas was getting in the way of her focus.

Her conflict of wanting to stay in her mind, looking into his eyes, and needing to focus on and her duties, was interrupted as Phalen broke the silence—and the vision.

"I get it, Gabrielle."

Gabrielle finally looked at Phalen again, and she was met with a warm grin that pushed her friend's cheeks into two brown peaks under her eyes. What Gabrielle saw in those eyes was acceptance. A sense of belonging filled her and chased away the vulnerability she had been feeling. She was becoming closer to Phalen than she ever would have imagined she could after being so betrayed by Javan. She never wanted to feel such a deep sense of loss again, and she truly wondered if she would ever be able to open up to another angel, but a feeling of deep kinship was forming. The realization that she was still capable of letting someone get close to her made her smile. She thought she and Phalen were going to be very good friends.

Hopefully for a very long time.

"So, Phalen," Gabrielle said, "since you haven't been to Earth much—well, not as a *tourist* anyway, do you want to see any of the city? See how the *other half* live?"

Gabrielle and Phalen had talked away most of the morning at the coffee house, and Gabrielle was getting the urge to do something else. It was nice to have a friend like Phalen, and she was surprised by how at ease she was with her already.

Phalen looked at her with a grin and a glint in her butterscotch eyes that spoke of something she definitely wanted to do,. She popped a piece of bubblegum into her mouth, offering some to Gabrielle without lowering her legs that were comfortably resting on a different chair. Gabrielle took the gum and smiled as she began chewing; the intensity of the grape flavor, both tart and sweet, caused her mouth to water.

Humans have such wonderful things to enjoy.

"They certainly do," Phalen responded to Gabrielle's quiet observation.

"I forgot, again, that there was someone who could *hear* what I was thinking," Gabrielle said and then blew a bubble the size of a grapefruit.

"Bet I can beat that bubble. I'm quite the expert on bubble blowing." Phalen smirked playfully.

Gabrielle smiled at Phalen's buoyant personality, wishing she could be as carefree.

"Anyway," Phalen began, "there *is* something I'd like to do. I've observed humans doing it, and it looks like everyone is having a spectacular time."

"I'm almost afraid to know, but spill it. What do you want to do?"

Phalen dropped her propped feet to the ground and leaned toward

Gabrielle with uncontained enthusiasm.

"Whitewater rafting!"

Gabrielle's eyes widened. This wasn't exactly what she had in mind.

"*Please*, Gabrielle! Let's do it! It would be so fun to know what it would feel like to do something ... *adventurous* in these bodies." Phalen's hands were drawn together in one large entwined fist pulled close to her chest as though she was pleading for her life instead of for an excursion.

Gabrielle laughed through her answer. "Sure, Phalen. That sounds like fun."

Phalen leapt from her seat and wrapped her arms around Gabrielle, stunning her. She slowly hugged Phalen back, careful of this new bond, but felt her muscles relaxing as she listened to Phalen's excited chatter about the fun they were about to have together. A smile stretched across Gabrielle's face as Phalen's verbal enthusiasm was randomly interrupted by the sound of popping gum.

Chapter Sixteen

GABRIELLE ☦ AN ADVENTURE

Gabrielle and Phalen descended on the Ocoee River that was nestled within the steep, lush peaks and valleys of Tennessee's Cherokee National Forest. It was narrow, rocks and boulders covering the banks on both sides. Everything else around them was dense with grass and trees. It looked as though Yahuwah had simply dropped a green carpet over the landscape. Gabrielle thought the scenery alone was worth coming for.

They stood next to a bright yellow raft belonging to one of many whitewater guides, not listening to the safety warnings he was sharing with their fellow rafters. Gabrielle and Phalen were more interested in the numerous energy signatures of demons that they'd seen since arriving because, for some reason, she could see them far easier than she had been able to for two months.

"How is it that I can see them clearer, now?" Gabrielle asked Phalen without looking at her. "Why the sudden change?"

"I don't know, sister. It's certainly intriguing though."

Gabrielle added it to her list of things to figure out. The list of mysteries seemed to grow every week she spent on Earth.

I'm supposed to be solving a mystery. Not discovering new ones.

Gabrielle wondered if the demons were able to sense her and Phalen or if the Aegis Veil would hide both of their energies. She hoped so.

Furrows between Phalen's brows created their own peaks and valleys on her face. "Who would have thought this would be some sort of demon pastime?" Phalen asked as she slowly scanned their surroundings. There were about three hundred people, either rafters or kayakers, waiting for their turn to become part of the roiling current of the river. Helmets and paddles, kayaks and rafts, humans and demons were scattered around the drop-off area and the bank of the river. "It's like a Fallen convention."

Gabrielle felt hot. Not from the early Sunday morning sun that was rapidly warming the day, but from the two dozen or so of the Fallen mingling with each other and with people—as though they belonged—causing adrenaline to rush through her body.

"Phalen, try not to look at any of them. They are far better practiced than us in how to act in a human body. And certainly don't stare if you do. I'm afraid it will give us away if we don't appear as natural as everyone else."

"That's easier said than done when we're this out-numbered."

"I'm not worried about their numbers. We can handle it. My concern is that there are so many of the Fallen rubbing elbows with humans ... like they are one of them."

"*You* can handle it, but I'm not so sure about me, Gabrielle. I'm not as powerful or as skilled as you."

Gabrielle attempted to hide a grin trying to escape onto her expression, not wanting to appear boastful. "But you're with me. You don't need to worry about what will happen if there's a confrontation."

Phalen raised her brows. "If you say so."

The smile fully formed across Gabrielle's face. "I say so."

Finally, it was their turn to put their raft into the water and begin their trip down the rapids. After everyone was situated, the guide pushed them into the current.

They had to maneuver a rapid almost immediately, and once they made it through and drifted further from the demons still waiting their turn to put in, Gabrielle found herself beginning to get caught up in her fellow paddlers hoots and laughter. Before she realized it, she had all but forgotten what she left on the riverbank. She was just as giddy as Phalen seemed to be, a smile splitting her face.

The guide instructed them about when and how to paddle to make the raft hit the rapids they approached so that there would be as much bucking, swaying, and air under them as possible. The river churned, crashing into large boulders that got in its way. At times, it forced the raft down river so fast Gabrielle thought they were almost flying. Other times, the river calmed somewhat, allowing everyone to laugh at each other for looking like drowned rats and to chat about the best rapid so far. After clearing one of the rapids, the guide instructed them to paddle to the bank. Once they stopped, he told them to watch the kayakers who had also stopped nearby and were in an eddy where the raging water of the river turned back on itself.

Gabrielle was glad they were going to take some time to watch the kayakers at play. She'd seen many on their way down and glimpsed things they were doing, but she was interested in really seeing what they were capable of.

"This is called Hell Hole," the guide told them as he sat on the edge of the raft with his feet planted on rocks just under the water to keep it in place.

"That's fitting after what we saw back up river," Phalen said quietly to Gabrielle.

Phalen was watching the kayakers, mesmerized, with the grin she'd been sporting since the first rapid still comfortably in place. Each kayaker took their turn in the churning water. They made their boats twist and turn, doing cartwheels and somersaults. Some would fly straight up into the air like a rocket launched from the depths, then surf as though they were on a wave in the ocean. It looked like they were having the time of their lives.

"You want to do that next?" Phalen asked as she glanced away from the humans playing in their kayaks, then back just as fast as she blew and popped another purple bubble.

"Maybe some time."

After watching for a few minutes more, the guide pushed the raft back into the current, and they were off once again. Hell Hole was apparently the last rapid on the river run, though, and all too soon, they were pulling the raft onto the riverbank—their adventure over.

Saying their good-byes to the others who'd paddled with them, Gabrielle and Phalen made their way to the far side of a building, then toward the trees where they would be out of sight enough to disappear without the attention of the humans around them.

They stepped into the cover of the forest and were about to depart when they heard something in the distance. It was the muffled sounds of a female crying. Phalen and Gabrielle stood rigid, then locked eyes.

"Come on." Gabrielle moved swiftly in the direction of the sound.

They burst past the foliage of the trees and undergrowth tangled on the forest floor into a small clearing full of yellow wildflowers bordering the river. Gabrielle heard Phalen gasp, then the sound of the snap and whoosh as she released her wings.

Two male demons held a young woman on the ground. She couldn't have been more than nineteen or twenty. One of the demons straddled her and had one hand covering her mouth as his other grappled with her clothing. The second demon sat on the ground above her head and pinned the girl's wrists to the earth in what Gabrielle knew would be an unbreakable grip.

Gabrielle put a hand on Phalen to keep her from attacking. Phalen looked sternly at Gabrielle as though she would fight her in order to help the girl. Gabrielle didn't explain. She raised her hand, and everything around them went still. Every bird and insect was frozen in flight. The breeze unmoving as if holding its breath. The water that was flowing near them now seemed more like a mural. The girl's terror and panic etched into her now unflinching expression—her struggling body quiet. Gabrielle's stomach did what felt like a complete revolution inside her as the energy of the demons focused on her.

The human bodies these demons had stolen would have been more than enough to draw the girl to them even without their ability to force attraction to them. It took a human with a strong mind to resist a demon who wanted their attention. Considering they could make the girl come to them willingly, what they were doing was simply out of their need for power and control—for domination. They wanted to completely destroy this girl's spirit until she was ruined. Gabrielle's stomach did another flip with the thought of how many women, *girls*, these two had violated.

How many have they destroyed?

She wasn't able to suppress the bile entirely as she felt the acid from her stomach burn her throat. She swallowed hard, sweeping the disturbing thoughts to the back of her mind at the same time.

The demons, now standing, turned their eerie, hungry eyes onto Gabrielle and Phalen.

"Well, what do we have here?" the taller, more muscular one asked.

He was extremely large, and Gabrielle was sure he was very powerful as her head began to feel as if it was tossing in the volatile currents of the river they had just rafted. The world around her fought to darken, pushing in on her as it tried to steal her consciousness. Gabrielle put her hand on Phalen's shoulder to steady herself. As she glanced at her friend, she was able to make out Phalen's face, riddled with concern.

Gabrielle began to sway.

"*Gabrielle!*" Phalen called out worriedly as she wrapped her arms around her.

Gabrielle shut her eyes tightly. This was certainly not the time to lose it. This demon, whoever he was, seemed to possess enough power to be more than a problem for Phalen. She had to pull herself together.

"*Gabrielle* ... *the* Gabrielle?" The large demon asked in a guttural, snide voice.

Gabrielle opened her eyes. The sneer on his face held the cold telling of malice without the words being spoken, but she could hear thoughts of revenge against Yahuwah forming in his mind. Veins in his neck and forearms bulged from muscles stiffening with his anticipation of that vengeance.

She knew their only chance was to be in her true form. It was too difficult for her to fight the powerful reaction of her human body this time. Just as she was about to change, she heard a loud clap, like thunder from a lightning strike hitting so near that its light would have been more blue than white. The sound seemed to reverberate off the rocky hills around them, and the earth beneath her feet trembled.

The next thing she heard was a familiar, welcome voice—Amaziah. He was saying something her jumbled human mind couldn't make out, but it was definitely her ally. A feeling of relief from the knowledge that Phalen wouldn't be fighting these particular Fallen by herself washed through her.

Gabrielle opened her eyes in time to see Amaziah face the two demons. Before they could open their mouths to take another breath, Amaziah's hands, held in a praying position, opened. The clapping sound had been his hands joining together.

The ground beneath the Fallen lurched. With a sound like hundreds of people ripping paper at once, the earth suddenly split open, swallowing the demons. Amaziah brought his hands together again, and the earth closed into a smooth, seamless surface once more—like nothing had happened. All that told of something occurring were the particles of dirt and small rocks still falling, settling back into place.

Gabrielle felt Phalen's arms loosen and another set pick her up.

"Close your eyes, my dear. You'll be home soon."

Gabrielle did as he requested and closed her eyes. A smile moved her lips, brought on by Lucas's face. Something stirred in her mind but also somewhere deep within—somewhere she had never felt such things. He was a distraction, and she didn't fully trust him. But she still had the nagging feeling that she needed to protect him ... she had to keep him safe.

The smile on her face faded as quickly as it appeared as the vision expanded to a scene that caused her brows to push firmly together.

Lucas was lying on the ground below her. It was a different scene than what little she remembered from her dreams. There was no one else around, just Lucas and Gabrielle and the energy of several others far off in the distance. She sensed where he was lying was close to sacred ground. More than that, the ground had been protected. She wasn't concerned with the other energies or why the ground was protected, though. Her concern was Lucas; he didn't seem to have life in him anymore. When she reached down to see if he was dead, Lucas disappeared, and all she touched was the hopelessness and pain of Darkness.

What happened?

She knew she wouldn't get the answer to that question, but she did understand the heaviness and stench of the Fallen, and of those who live in Shadows, was filling her senses—even though it was only a vision.

Why would they come after him?

She felt something grip her inside, wringing her heart. She pulled her hands to her chest and pressed hard against her bones in a useless attempt to make it stop as Amaziah moved her swiftly through the air.

"*No*," she whispered softly.

'*It's okay, Gabrielle. You are safe, now,*' Amaziah's voice echoed in her troubled mind.

She didn't respond.

Amaziah wouldn't understand. How could she make anyone understand when *she* couldn't grasp what this human was doing to her? Lucas was becoming a part of her in ways that were alarming. She would have to figure out how to keep an eye on him while still keeping her distance. He was in danger; of what, she still didn't know. It was a danger she could physically feel, though—and that was never good. Nothing could stop it. It wasn't just a possibility when she had this type of premonition—one that she experienced physically—it was a certainty.

A sense of well-being and love suddenly filled her completely. She was …

Home!

Although, it wasn't her dwelling on Earth. The joy and serenity of Heaven was all around her. Amaziah had brought her *home*. She looked at Amaziah, and he met her gaze with his brilliance.

'Why did you bring me here?'

'It's too dangerous for you, Gabrielle. You're staying here.'

'No.' Gabrielle struggled free of Amaziah's cradling arms. *'No, I'm not.'*

'Yes, you are. If I hadn't intervened, you and Phalen would have been in terrible trouble.'

'I was about to shed my human form just as you appeared, Amaziah. I would have been fine as soon as I was free of its frailty.'

'At least you admit to being more frail when you are incarnated.'

There was silence between them as Amaziah seemed to be picking his next words. He hated to argue, especially with her.

'Really, Gabrielle … they could have killed you. Don't you understand the risk? Do you actually have to have a Sundering Whip take off your head for reason to take hold of your thoughts?'

'I think you are being over dramatic and unduly protective.'

'Of course you do.'

'Amaziah, I have to go back. I am learning so much. I couldn't just let that girl be raped by them. I had to help her!' Panic over the girl's well-being gripped Gabrielle. *'What happened to her after we left?'*

'I know you couldn't leave her there to go through what they had planned, Gabrielle. I do not fault you for stepping in and interfering. It is expected. Nevertheless, you were at a huge disadvantage in your human body. It obviously can't handle the physicality of an encounter with the Fallen if they are powerful enough.'

Amaziah released a sigh. *'The girl is fine. I returned her to the moment before she crossed paths with the demons. She will never know.'*

'Good.'

Quiet settled between them. Gabrielle had to convince Amaziah to allow her return to Earth. How she was going to accomplish that was unclear.

'I will be better prepared for my body's reaction if it happens again.'

She didn't want to let him know how many opportunities to grow more accustomed to handling the effects she felt on her human form were possible. With all of the Fallen she'd seen in and around Nashville, there would be no hope for her continuing her task if he became aware.

'Amaziah—'

'Gabrielle ... you are too important to lose!'

'Yahuwah will make it without me, Amaziah! He's YAHUWAH! But he won't make it if Ramai and all the Darkness that lives in Hell and the Shadow World wins!'

Amaziah just looked at her for several moments before responding. When he finally did, there was a sadness in his tone that Gabrielle didn't expect.

'But ... maybe I won't.'

At that moment, she truly understood just how much he cared about her, and it touched her deeply. She had always looked at him as a father, but she wasn't sure if his own attachment to her was as deep.

'You are like a daughter to me, Gabrielle. I don't want to lose you.'

Gabrielle reached her hand out for his. He took it, then wrapped his arms around her, holding her tightly. They stood like that for a long time, and she let the soothing warmth of his energy seep into every part of her own. When he spoke again, it was soft, caring but almost defeated.

'You can go back. On one condition. If your human body even hiccups while near a demon, you will shed that form and take on your Divine one.'

'I will.'

Gabrielle wasn't about to argue. She'd expected a much longer debate. The quick resolution had her wondering again about Amaziah's lack of desire to assert his decision making power over her. However, it was a quick resolution she was going to be thankful for ... for now.

'Go, Gabrielle. Before I come to my senses and change my mind.'

'Yes, Amaziah. Thank you.' Gabrielle began to leave.

'One more thing. I will be trying to visit you more frequently to check on

you—to make sure you are well.'

He turned, and at once, he was gone.

Gabrielle exited her eternal home to return to her Earthly one.

On the descent, she found herself consumed with questions about Amaziah's willingness to go along with her wishes. First, when he said she'd been granted the ability to come to Earth at all and take on this task, and now ... *this.*

Why?

The answer, she knew, would come one day. She *felt* it.

Chapter Seventeen

GABRIELLE ✟ THE SHIFTER'S REALM

Searching for answers about the Book had been an incredible distraction. Gabrielle had been trying to track down information about it for a few weeks, but Amaziah had been right about there not being many angels who remembered it or the war that was waged with its power. Those that did had no more information to give than what she'd already been told by Amaziah, which hadn't been much. Since then, she'd seen him quite a few times. Once, when he came back briefly and told her that the information in her dream was still being looked into by the Council, telling her that they were considering the possibility that it hadn't been destroyed. And all the other times that he popped in were just to check on her.

It was almost smothering how concerned he had become after the incident at the Ocoee River. When she saw him two days ago, she asked him to give her space to collect the information she was on Earth to get and to continue to find out what she could about the Book. He agreed.

It had been nice not to have to worry about blocking thoughts concerning Lucas when she was with Phalen, as she did when Amaziah was near. Phalen knew her secret and had been there when she saw Lucas with Mara, so she didn't press her about it.

Phalen still wasn't able to tell if there was anything strange about Lucas's energy. Whatever caused the wavy effect that had settled around the gym that day was always there, but it would change locations. It made everyone's energy look off that was anywhere near it. Phalen told Gabrielle she wouldn't even be able to tell for sure that Mara was a demon if Mara was near it. Every time she'd come with her since, it had been the same thing. Neither one of them had been able to figure out an explanation.

But there was always that flock of crows.

Even with her suspicions about those birds, Gabrielle wasn't ready to get Amaziah involved. She may not want to stay anymore because of Lucas, but she still needed to accomplish what she came to do. It was easy to avoid him. Mostly because Gabrielle felt he was also trying to avoid her. This made her even more suspicious. Why would he want to stay clear of her?

Occasional words were spoken between them, but nothing that amounted to anything more than pleasantries, and only if they passed each other coming or going from the class they shared. The way Lucas looked at her sometimes, with varying mixtures of confusion, curiosity, suspicion, and desire, left Gabrielle more confused than before.

When she wasn't at school or taking care of karma, she and Phalen had been searching for information about the Book. But nothing seemed to prevent the thoughts of Lucas from coming altogether; the distractions only made it easier to push them aside.

Trying to find help to get leads on the Book was what they were doing now. They were meeting with Gabrielle's closest ally on Earth and leader of the oldest and most respected Shifter family, Grayson Torphine of the Turpin Clan. Grayson's family was like royalty among Shifters, and Gabrielle had called upon him countless times to assist in giving karma. The Shifters had long been Yahuwah's way of giving humans signs through animals—the Earth-bound messengers and protectors for humans that Yahuwah had put there for them. Now, she needed Grayson to help her with something else—finding information about the Book.

Gabrielle and Phalen appeared in their human forms on the human side of the Shifter's realm, and Gabrielle prepared herself to cross through the veil that protected it. She closed her eyes, stilled her mind, and thought of the image she needed while saying the name, Corstorphine. She reached out and took Phalen's hand as she began to step closer, then went through the veil to the other side.

"I never thought I'd get to see any of the realms of the Shifters," Phalen commented as they passed through the mirage that protected one of the places where shape shifters lived in safety and privacy. "Hanging out with you has its benefits, sister."

"This one is called Corstorphine. Remember it well, Phalen. If you don't, you will never be able to enter again unless you are with someone who does."

"Will do," was Phalen's response. No questions. Just, *will do*, then the sound of a popping bubble.

As they stepped through the blurry haze, the air around them became clear again, and she heard Phalen's breath catch.

"I guess I should have prepared you for how amazing it is here," Gabrielle said. "Yahuwah gives them abundant beauty to live among, and within, as reward and thanks."

'You're not kidding! *Amazing*." Phalen slowly turned in a circle with wide eyes and an even wider smile.

Phalen had chosen the same body that she had used on the day they first came to Earth together, again, and Gabrielle wondered if Phalen had settled on a favorite look of platinum blond hair and blue eyes. Gabrielle just grinned as Phalen took in her surroundings. Gabrielle had also been mesmerized, at first, with the grandeur of the Shifter's realms—especially Corstorphine.

"This place is *unbelievable* …" Phalen continued. "Simply unbelievable. It's *almost* as beautiful as our eternal home."

It seemed like forever since Gabrielle had looked upon Corstorphine. Since Grayson was her main contact with the Shifters and he seemed to be on the go and in other Shifter realms when she had called on him, it'd been quite a while since he was at his home base at the time they spoke. She threw herself into appreciating the scenery as much as Phalen was and tried to look at everything as though it was the first time she'd ever seen it, too.

It wasn't that the realm Shifters lived in was vastly different that the one humans lived in; it was just so much more colorful and just ... *more*. What was lush was more lush, vast more vast, grandiose was more grandiose, and the colors ... the colors were like you had an enhancement filter placed over your eyes. Shades never seen anywhere else were next to the brightest whites and truest blacks with lovely shades of grey that made the colors they sat next to contrast brilliantly.

There were flowers that, in all her thousands of years, Gabrielle had never seen anywhere else. And so many animals roamed free that posed no threat to each other, or any creature, that stepped into this glorious place.

"Yahuwah really out-did Himself, didn't He, Phalen?"

'Uh ... *yeah*. This is almost Heaven on Earth."

That's exactly what Gabrielle had always thought of the Shifter's realms. "Yes, yes it is. At least as close as it ever could be."

After taking in some more of Corstorphine's landscape, Gabrielle and Phalen made their way through the village to the castle where Grayson would be waiting to greet them. The Shifter's dwellings were made of wood and stone. Their closeness with nature influenced their desire for structure, clothing, furniture, or anything they used to be from the Earth. There were no artificial fibers or materials in this realm. And since the animals of this world had no fear of becoming a meal since the Shifters were strict vegetarians, Gabrielle and Phalen were stopped by curious ones along the way as if to welcome them to the neighborhood.

They were also cheerfully greeted by many Shifters as they made their way to Mareschall Castle, the home of the Torphine family and other members of the Turpin Clan. The castle was an impressive square structure built out of stone that sat on an equally impressive rise. It allowed those who dwelt in its great halls and rooms exquisite views of the surrounding hills that softly rolled toward distant crop and grazing fields, crystal clear lakes, dense forests, and the sometimes gentle, sometimes turbulent waters of the Brechin River that made up Corstorphine's diverse landscape.

The only thing lacking is snow-capped mountains and an ocean's beach.

In addition to the three levels that made up the castle main, four keeps were situated at each corner. A flag bearing the tartans and crests of each of the four clans that made up the Shifter society flew above each of the looming towers. The red and black tartan and crest of the Turpin Clan were displayed directly above the entrance to the castle grounds, as well.

As they were about to pass through that entrance, Grayson stepped out of the front doors of the castle to greet Gabrielle and Phalen. He was every bit as handsome and intense as the last time she'd seen him. He didn't have movie star looks. His brown hair, in long layers, was a normal shade; his blue eyes were not extraordinary in their color, but his heavy brows set at an angle made his gaze all that more intense when he wanted it to be. He was tall and muscular, but his muscles were long like a swimmers, and he was quite lean. As he drew closer, Gabrielle could see his face, unshaven for several days, and the feature that did make him exceptionally beautiful—his smile. She didn't know if she'd ever seen one she enjoyed as much, except …

Lucas's.

Gabrielle didn't have time to linger on the thought. Grayson swept her up into a combination hug and twirl, allowing Gabrielle to laugh the sad thought about Lucas right out of her mind—at least for now.

"Oh … m'lady. M'beautiful lady!" Grayson said and then put her down on the ground. With his arms around her, he beamed that smile at her that always lit up his eyes a few shades brighter. "Let me get a look at ye … yes, yer even more beautiful than last I saw ye. I believe I fancy this look you've chosen even better than the last."

She loved to hear him, or any of the Shifters, talk. They all spoke with a Scottish dialect, watered down from spending so much time in their other realms scattered around the world. There were four total: Corstorphine here in Scotland, and the other three in Jackson Hole,

Wyoming; Madrid, Spain; and Vancouver, British Columbia. So even though they had a strong leaning toward a Scottish brogue, it was layered with the Mid-Western accent of the U.S. and, at times, even some Spanish words and accent or Canadian flair. At times it was a challenge to understand them, particularly when they got ramped-up from happiness or anger. Then, unless you were of Divine blood, a linguist, or a Shifter, you could end up with such a mish-mash of languages and accents, it would leave your head spinning from trying to figure it out. And, chances were, unless you were one of those three, you never would.

"And you're still quite the charmer, aren't you, Grayson?"

"I aim to please, m'lady, I aim to please."

Grayson let Gabrielle go and looked at Phalen, continuing to smile. "And yer Gabrielle's comrade, Phalen." He stepped closer. Phalen held out her hand to shake his in greeting. Grayson took it, but then he gave her a less dizzying hug. "No way someone so close to m'lady gets just a gentleman's handshake fer a hello. Welcome to Corstorphine and Mareschall Castle, Lady Phalen. M'home is yers."

Phalen smiled back at him, doe-eyed, and glanced at Gabrielle. "You weren't kidding." She looked back at Grayson but still addressed Gabrielle. "He is a charmer."

Phalen did her best imitation of a curtsy and spoke to Grayson this time. "Thank you, sir."

Grayson laughed and ushered them both into his home, then into his private study. After getting them settled with hot cider and tea, he looked at Gabrielle. As was typical of Grayson, he got right down to business.

"So, m'lady, what is it I can help ye with?"

Gabrielle took a sip of tea, which wasn't quite sweet enough, and began to add more sugar. "There's a book, the Book of—"

"Barabbadon." Grayson finished with a smile. "I thought that might be why ye were payin' me a visit."

"You've already heard about it? How?" Gabrielle asked.

Grayson took a slow drink of his cider. "I only heard about it a few hours before ye sent the messenger that ye needed to see me. Kind of a *shifty* one, Lady Sheridan, fer an angel. Don't ye think?" He looked at Gabrielle who only gave a slightly raised brow in response, then he continued. "I had some things to take care of in the field fer our mutual boss, and I ran into an old … *friend*. He's one of the Fallen, but not yer average demon. If there's such a thing as a good demon, he's the one, and m'ancestors knew him before he fell.

"So, he told me of the flurry going on about this book ye want to know about. Says there isn't a demon that's not trying to find it. Says there's some lookin' on behalf of the de'il himself, Ramai. And he says others are lookin' fer someone else, but he hadn't found out who yet."

"Did he tell you if there are any clues to where it might be?"

Grayson stood and walked to the window behind his desk. He placed one hand high on the stones next to the glass, leaning into his palm. "Fraid not, m'lady. Far as I know, they aren't real clued in on it themselves, just lookin' here and there. He did tell me it's mighty powerful, this Book of Barabbadon, and he would like it to get into the *right* hands. Sad one, ol' Lek." Grayson was looking out of an oversized window that allowed him to see Lake Gormal, seeming to ponder his fallen friend. After only a few moments, he continued but spoke to the glass in front of him.

"Anyway, that's all I know. I was going to be contacting ye, but ye beat me to it. So, if there's anything I can do fer ye to help ye find the thing, all ye have to do is ask it of me, m'lady."

Gabrielle walked to the other side of the window and leaned her shoulder into the stones, placing her forehead on the glass.

"Unfortunately, it seems as if there isn't going to be much you *can* do other than keep your eyes and ears open. And ask the other Shifters to please do the same." Gabrielle let out a long, defeated sigh. "Seems like walls and obstacles are all I'm running into."

"M'lady." Grayson stepped toward her and turned her to face him. "I don't like seeing this sadness in those eyes of yers. I promise I'll do anything I can do to help ye, and so will my fellows. As fer whatever else is making yer heart heavy, I hope ye find yer way out of the shadows soon."

Gabrielle looked into Grayson's intense gaze. The intensity wasn't from anger; it was from concern and compassion. She felt the friendship of a hundred years in that moment and was wrapped in it as she let herself be pulled into his arms as he hugged her.

"Thank you, Grayson, for the help you always offer freely and the friendship you have given even more easily."

"Oh, m'lady, ye make that easy. Very, very easy."

Phalen cleared her throat as she walked up next to them and held out her closed hand. "I'm feeling a little left out, so I'm offering a token of friendship." Phalen grinned at them as she turned her hand over and opened it. "Grape bliss, anyone?"

Chapter Eighteen

Lucas ✞ Strange Ways

Lucas was at a loss.

It had been three weeks since the morning in Gabby's car when things had become weird between them. His feelings of caution were fading. All he wanted to do was talk to Gabby and try to make right whatever he'd done wrong. However, she was still avoiding him like he was a cockroach.

To top it off, she'd been a frequent visitor in his dreams. They were odd and disturbing, filled with red eyes and darkness and fear. When Gabby was present, he felt many things—safety, inferiority, love—stronger than he ever could have imagined.

But there was one dream …

In that one, he felt nothing but anger, hurt, and betrayal. All directed at her. He also felt strong with enhanced senses he had never known. It was exhilarating until he was unsettled by the way Gabby looked at him like he was a physical threat to her. None of it made sense. But he was sure Gabby held the key that would open the door to all the answers he sought.

"Hey, Gran!" Lucas yelled toward the kitchen as he was about to walk out the front door. "I'm going on over to the Daniels'."

"Okay," his grandmother, Emma, called back to him. "I'll be over in an hour or so. Tell Lizzie to let me know if I need to bring anything else."

"I will. See ya."

He closed the door behind him and made his way across the street to Nonie and Nate's house. He wondered how many times he'd walked this stretch of concrete and asphalt and how many more he'd add to that number by the time he and the twins set off into the real world, leaving these homes behind. Even then, there would be holidays and other visits when they'd all be together. How could they not? Sometimes family is chosen instead of given by only blood. The Daniels were definitely family.

As he jumped the three steps up to their porch, he didn't break stride as he opened the door and called out. "Yo! Where's the fam?"

"In here, Lucas." Lizzie, Nonie and Nate's mom, called back to him.

Lucas smelled yeast and smiled. "Oh, Lizzie, you must really love me. Are those your rolls I smell?" He walked toward the sound of her voice and the smell of food coming from the kitchen.

When he turned the corner into the farmhouse kitchen, Lizzie greeted him with a kiss on the cheek. "You know I love you. Kids are on the back porch. Here." She handed him a pitcher of sweet tea. "Take this. Glasses are already out there."

"No problem. By the way, Gran said call her if you need anything else."

Lizzie laughed and looked around the counters scattered with potatoes, ground beef, onion, cans of corn, and freshly shredded cheese. "Maybe an extra set of hands. I'm running a little late tonight."

"Call her. She's just piddling anyway. Hey, looks like shepherd's pie is on the menu."

"Yep."

"You definitely love me," Lucas said with a wink and pushed the door open with his free hand.

Nonie, Nate, and their little sister, Chloe, were playing Jenga on an oversized table that took up half of the screened porch. They looked up just as Nonie finished taking out a block. The sudden clattering of wood hitting wood startled everyone as the tower gave way and fell.

Nonie shot Nate the evil eye. "You hit the table, brother."

"Negative, sister."

"Can you ever play something, *anything*, without cheating or bending the rules?"

"Stop being a poor loser, Nee. It isn't very attractive," Nate said with a smirk and a wink.

Nonie smirked back and lobbed a Jenga piece at him playfully.

"What's up?" Nate said as Lucas sat the pitcher down.

"Hey, Lucas," Nonie said, already rebuilding the tower.

Chloe just smiled as she made Lucas's lap her seat.

"Wanna play?" Nonie asked as she continued to stack the pieces.

"Nah. I think I'll just watch you two duke it out this time."

"You running a fever, or something?" Nate asked. "For like, the past few weeks?"

Lucas shook his head and gave him a funny look.

"You just haven't been yourself for a while," Nate continued. "And I just wanted to make sure you're all right." Nate looked at Lucas with a hint of suspicion and something else that came to the surface from time to time that Lucas couldn't define. When it happened, Nate's demeanor would shift, just slightly, becoming a bit aggressive, and he'd get a darker shade to his eyes—a darkness that seemed to be only partially explained by the color difference. Whatever it was, it made Lucas clam up.

"I'm okay, man. Thanks." Lucas left it at that and began a thumb-wrestling match with Chloe. Nate seemed to get the hint and stood.

"Be right back, Nee."

"You're not getting scared are you, brother?"

Nate laughed as he opened the door to the kitchen. "Hardly. Just have a phone call to make."

After adding the last layer to the tower of blocks, Nonie poured herself a glass of tea and sat back in her chair, studying Lucas as she took a couple of sips. Lucas tried to ignore her, but Chloe wasn't as good at not saying something.

"Nee, why are you staring?"

Nonie and Lucas looked at each other.

"Hey, lil' sis, go see if mom needs some help."

"Okay ... " Chloe said, protest in her tone, as she slid off Lucas's lap and went to see her mom.

Lucas waited for Nonie to speak.

"This is about Gabrielle ... isn't it?"

Of course Nonie would know what was wrong. There was no use in denying it. Not to her, anyway. She always seemed to know exactly what was bothering people and why. Once, he asked her how she always knew, and she just said she was good at reading people. Lucas had never pushed further, feeling she wasn't so comfortable with the *how* of it, but always thought there was more to it.

Way more.

Lucas sighed heavily and began studying their large, fenced backyard so he didn't have to see Nonie's scrutiny for a moment. The yard was lined with mature trees and shrubs that lent themselves to privacy for the Daniels family, and it had a wooden swing set with a fort and slide attached. It had been there as long as Lucas could remember, and he had spent many hours playing on it with Nonie and Nate when they were kids.

That seems so long ago.

Lucas realized he had been lost in thought and responded to Nonie. "Yeah ... it's about Gabby."

"So, what happened? 'Cause there were some *major* vibes coming off you two, so I know you were both more than a little interested. Next thing I know, you're brooding, and she's distancing. She won't even spend time with me, and I know it's not because she's not charmed by my personality." Nonie stopped talking long enough for Lucas to glance at her, to which she gave him a smile. "So, it must be your fault."

Lucas continued to watch Nonie for a moment, then looked back to the trees. "I honestly don't know. It was like, at the same time, we both just got ... scared or cautious, or ... *something*. I was avoiding *her* for a while. But then whatever had spooked me started to fade, and I was drawn to her again. I've tried a few times to talk to her even if they were lame attempts. She wouldn't bite at all. She's avoiding being anywhere near me, which confuses the hell out of me because I know there's no way I've done anything wrong."

Silence lingered as they both seemed to consider what he said.

"Lucas, you need to talk to her."

"I *know* that, Nee. But how do I get her to talk when I can't even get her to stand with me for more than two seconds?"

"You just have to keep trying."

"I'm not a glutton for punishment, Nee. I've already looked like some lost puppy because of her ... and I haven't even taken her on a date!" Lucas stood and walked as far away from where he'd been sitting as he could and crossed his arms. "Maybe she's not so good for me." He spoke to the screen and thought back to the dreams, to the one that bothered him most. "*Maybe* ... she knows something I don't, and we would be terrible together."

Nonie chuckled as she joined Lucas. "Really, Lucas, you're just two people freaked out by the fireworks between you that anyone who was within a hundred yards would have noticed. Ya'll have the kind of chemistry books are written about, movies are made because of. It's what most people search their entire lives for.

"Lucas, if you let her go ... I swear I'll kick your ass myself. I would *love* to have someone like that come walking into my life, especially while I'm young. And I can tell you if they ever do, I won't let a little *fear* get in my, *our*, way."

Lucas wrapped Nonie up in a hug, giving her a kiss on her head.

"Thanks, Nee. You're pretty awesome. Any guy who gets your

heart will be a lucky, lucky man."

"Well, that's *very* true," she said through laughter. "But, he'd have to be one hell of a guy to get me to fall for him. Kind of a cross between a protector, a leader, a romantic, and a man's man all rolled up into one yummy looking gift just for me. And that's the clincher, he'd have to have eyes *only* for me. All that's a pretty tall order. Oh, yeah, tall is good, too, since I'm not so short."

Lucas squeezed her tighter. "You'll find him, Nee, or he'll find you. I know it."

"Your lips to God's ears, Lucas."

They turned at the sound of the door closing behind them.

"What'd I miss?" Nate asked as he put a bowl of chips on the table. "Mom says dinner's running behind, so here's some snackage."

When Nate looked up his eyes were his normal shade, his odd demeanor and whatever made him seem darker … gone. It was the Nate that Lucas was comfortable around, the one who had been a part of his life for his entire life.

My family.

While Lucas ate dinner with Gran and the Daniels, his mind was somewhere else. The conversation he'd had with Nonie kept replaying itself, and she was right. He had to try harder. She'd also been right about the fireworks between him and Gabby. There was no use in denying them.

He found his thoughts were jumping around a lot as he went from thinking about Gabby to Nate's odd moods, which seemed more frequent, and then to Nonie and her *feelings*. Thinking of Nonie and Nate, and how they had their own oddities, made him consider his own. Something he hadn't done much in several years. He'd almost forgotten about it until he understood some of the language Gabby had spoken. He'd *tried* to forget.

At first, he'd thought the things he seemed good at, way better than anyone else, were cool. But people started talking. Gran told him to play down his abilities. He began to wonder if there was something wrong with him. Something that would make people not like him or treat him badly. Whenever he asked her why he needed to play down what he could do, she just smiled and kissed him on the cheek. The one time she did give him an answer, her normally effortless smile became strained, and her eyes clouded with sadness. Then all she said was, "You're very special, Lucas. *Very special.*" And that was it.

He was ten.

In the seven years since, he'd given up sports. Because even when he tried not to stand out, it was obvious he was still out running, out hitting, out throwing, and flat out out-playing everyone else, regardless of the sport. It had been four years since he did anything that involved organized athletics.

School was easy for him, too. He still had to do the work, but he *got it* right away. It was similar with languages, but with them, there were times he could understand some he'd never heard before.

Just like that day with Gabby.

He cursed to himself as he realized she must have been freaking out because she'd noticed other things about him that weren't quite normal.

Feeling not quite normal was why he'd never truly let anyone other than the Daniels get close to him. He was popular at school, but not because he was great friends with everyone. It was only because he looked the part. It was like he had been given a pass into the popularity classification simply because he was tall, and others considered him good-looking, funny, and smart. And, even though he didn't play anymore, everyone had heard the stories of how unusually athletic he was. The track, football, wrestling, and soccer coaches always asked him—practically begged—to try out for their teams every year. He always said no. He always disappointed. Still, he knew, even though Gran never told him what she meant, that he was different.

Painfully so.

He'd never talked to anyone about it. How could he? There would be no way they could even begin to grasp what it was like to live inside a body that you didn't understand. To know that even if it looks normal, it isn't. He'd decided it was better to keep to himself until more made sense to him, protecting whatever it was that made him different from others, and even himself.

And ... maybe protect others from me.

Lucas sighed.

Gran was the only person who might have an explanation, and she was apparently unwilling to enlighten him. If he couldn't understand even a little of the *why*, he would remain alone with his uniqueness—and the loneliness.

"Lucas ... hey ... are you with us?" Nonie asked.

Lucas snapped back into the moment and laughed away his ponderings.

"Sorry ... yeah."

"We were talking about the touch football game this Saturday. I asked if you want to go grab something to eat before we go?"

His thoughts gunned toward Gabby. He'd asked her on a date, and she'd said yes. But that was *before*.

"Can I get back to you on that, Nee?"

She smiled a knowing kind of smile.

"No problem." She dropped it and changed the subject.

He would talk to Gabby tomorrow whether she liked it or not. Somehow, he was going to remove whatever it was that was in their way. He wanted to be near her again, hold her hand again, hear her voice and the sound of her laugh again—to have a first kiss.

I want that date.

Chapter Nineteen

GABRIELLE ✝ HEAR HEAR

Gabrielle and Phalen ended up staying the night at Mareschall Castle. It was fairly quiet. Most of Grayson's family was at their safe-haven in British Columbia or training young Shifters—which meant they were in the human realm.

There was little rest for Gabrielle, though, even with the marvelously overstuffed feather bed. As the sun teased at night's shadows, she took a shower and made her way to the kitchen.

She didn't expect anyone to be up at this hour, so she was surprised when she came through the archway separating the dining room from the kitchen to see Phalen staring out one of the castle's many oversized windows. Grayson's ancestors, who built Mareschall, certainly did so with the intention of being able to see the breathtaking scenery of Corstorphine even while indoors.

"Well, good morning," Gabrielle said. "What has you up so early?"

Phalen turned toward her.

And there it was, the purple bubble.

"Phalen, seriously, I'm going to have to take that stuff away from you. It's getting both scary and a bit annoying," she teased, then started to make coffee.

"I'll give up gum, if you give up sugar."

Gabrielle shot her a look that said *no way* and continued to make one of her favorite beverages.

"I didn't think so." Phalen turned her attention back to the scenery outside. "I had to see if the sunrise was as magnificent as the sunset. Look at it Gabrielle … it's unreal. Will you bring me back someday?"

"If you're sent to Earth and granted the time to do it, you can come without me if you've been here once. *If* you can manage to remember its name."

"*Really*? Fantastic." Phalen was still admiring the mix of purple, magenta, yellow, and pink painted across the sky. Not just the area where the sun was rising. The colors were showing the glory of the coming day over the entire expanse, completely erasing night. Phalen suddenly glanced at Gabrielle. "You keep referring to having to remember the name, Corstorphine. Why? Is there a reason I might not?"

"Yes." Gabrielle joined her at the window. It certainly was something to behold, Corstorphine invited into another day by the sun—by Yahuwah. She sighed happily. "Corstorphine, and all Shifter realms, are enchanted. When someone other than a Shifter enters, it remembers them. But if you don't remember *it*—its name and its beauty—it won't allow you to re-enter."

"Okay … but, why wouldn't I remember?"

"Because it makes those who aren't of Shifter blood work for it. Just as there's an enchantment that protects their realms from allowing someone unknown from gaining access to their lands, there's another that causes a non-shifter to forget it as soon as they leave. That includes us and any who have Divine blood. Because as we know … having Divine blood doesn't always equal good intentions."

"What do I have to do to remember it?"

"Take a special, vivid memory of the realm with you. Picture that image in your mind as you repeat the name continually when you leave to re-enter the human realm."

"Sounds easy enough."

Gabrielle laughed, catching Phalen off-guard.

"It does sound easy, doesn't it? Yahuwah wouldn't have created an easy enchantment, though. Especially if it's to safe-guard the protectors of, and messengers to, humans who have served him so loyally for more years than you have been alive."

"Gotcha." Phalen said.

Gabrielle turned and walked back to the coffee that smelled ready for her to make it a drinkable dessert. "As you're *trying* to remember the name and your picture of the realm, you'll be bombarded by other images and names. Many of our brethren have not been able to take one or both back with them to the other side. You have to have both to re-enter, repeating the name and seeing the memory in your mind, as you come through the veil. You'll be tested just as thoroughly, but once you've done it a few times, it gets easier. I have a suspicion your mind is searched for your intentions, but I've never had that confirmed." Gabrielle laughed lightly as they sat at the table. "It's like the realm is a jealous mistress who expects your loyalty and appreciation of her beauty, and once she feels she has it, she eases up on you but is forever suspicious of betrayal."

"Have you ever forgotten?" Phalen asked as they sat at the table.

"No, but it doesn't mean it still can't happen. I take the enchantment very seriously, and so should you. Even if you come for years like me, never take it lightly. You might really need to get here one day, but if you forget, you will never be able to get back unless someone brings you."

"Is that why I didn't have to know it coming in, because you knew it?"

"Yes."

"Tellin' Lady Phalen of our trickery, I see," Grayson said as he walked into the kitchen all smiles and full of energy, if his demeanor and gait told a true tale.

"Good morning, Grayson," Gabrielle said as she stood and greeted him with a hug. "Yes, I was."

"Good. I'd like the Lady to visit anytime she can. I quite enjoy a good opponent in archery. Ye'll come and compete with me again sometime, I hope." Grayson was now hugging Phalen who had also stood to meet their host.

After they'd had their meeting the day before, Phalen and Grayson took turns trying to outshoot the other one on the archery range while Gabrielle watched, keeping score and the peace. Those two needed a referee, for sure. They were closely matched although Phalen's full Divine abilities outshone Grayson's slightly less Divine ones. While Shifters had Divine blood, and therefore some Divine abilities and powers, they had human blood, too. Part Divine, part human, and part something Gabrielle wasn't sure about. From what Grayson had told her, the Shifters weren't absolutely sure either. Whatever it was made them what they were—shape shifters. Messengers for Yahuwah. Protectors of humans.

"It would be my pleasure, Grayson." Phalen responded.

Gabrielle brought an additional cup of coffee to the table. "I believe I remember from last night how you like your coffee, but I might be off a little on the sugar."

Grayson took a sip and smiled. "Perfect, m'lady. Thank ye. I could get accustomed to this kind of treatment."

"I'm sure you have scores of ladies vying for the opportunity to treat you better than *this*." Gabrielle teased.

"True, true. But none that will put up with me bein' away so much."

"The price of being your people's leader," Phalen commented.

"Yes, Lady Phalen, 'tis."

Sadness ghosted Grayson's face but vanished quickly. Gabrielle put her hand on his, silently praying that one day soon he would find a woman deserving of such a fine man, and that their hearts and lives would become so enmeshed they would never want to part.

Grayson looked at her as though he knew and gave a nod and a smile.

"So, m'lady, what will ye be doin' now? What's yer next move?" He asked Gabrielle.

"Keep trying to find out more about the Book. And if it *is* real and out there somewhere, get my hands on it before any of the Fallen do … especially Ramai." Gabrielle took a sip of her coffee. "That, and keep trying to win this war."

"Ahh, yes, the war. What will ye do when the war is over?"

"Assuming we win, I'll find a remote beach and take a *really* long vacation. Assuming we don't … well, that's something I don't even want to think about."

"Gabrielle," Phalen jumped in, "do you really think it's possible we'll lose?"

There was an edge of curiosity and fear in Phalen's voice that matched her expression. Gabrielle wished she had seen as little of the war as Phalen. Even though angels don't age, not like humans, what Gabrielle had seen humanity reduced to over the last thousand years, and the rate they'd declined in just the past hundred and fifty, made her feel so old—so tired.

"Yes, I do think it's possible. Frighteningly so."

"It seemed we were winning not so long ago. What happened?" Phalen asked.

"The Fallen."

"But they've been around, well, basically forever. Why are they such an issue now compared to, say, fifty years ago?"

"I think I can answer that one, Lady Phalen. Faith. Er, should I say the lack thereof? Humans don't care anymore. They don't pay attention to signs; they don't stop to see the miracles and beauty around them every day; they don't believe in anything but their computers, their money, and their instant gratification. They don't know what's truly important anymore, and they believe things are what brings them happiness. But it doesn't. It makes them step further away from what really will make them happy, and that kind of happiness can't be bought."

"He's right, Phalen. Add to that the influence the Fallen can have on the minds of those with weakened spirits, which is a rapidly growing number, and demons are having the time of their lives."

The conversation fell into quiet. There was no sound for a long time except for the birds doing their part to help wake the world, and an occasional sip from a cup and then that cup being placed back on the table.

"Well," Phalen said as she raised her drink to Gabrielle and Grayson, "here's to hoping they come to their senses."

"Hear, hear, Lady Phalen. Hear, hear."

"I'll toast to that." Gabrielle raised her cup to theirs.

"Now, would ye beautiful angels like to chase away these gloomy thoughts with a bit of fruit and cheese, as well as some homemade biscuits and jam? I've learned to make some excellent jam o'er the years."

"Sounds great. But then we'll have to leave your beautiful Corstorphine, I'm afraid," Gabrielle said as she freshened up everyone's coffee.

"Do we really, Gabrielle?"

"Don't make me feel worse than I already do about it. I don't want to go any more than you do."

She didn't.

She'd like to stay right where she was, with one old friend and one new one, in this beautiful place called Corstorphine, in wonderful Mareschall Castle that was somehow cozier with all its stone than most people's homes, and forget the realm of humans. She felt safer from stress and bad moods in that moment than she had in more years than she wanted to remember.

She wanted to stay for a while …

… she wanted to rest.

Chapter Twenty

GABRIELLE ✝ PERSISTENCE PAYS

Phalen was quite happy when she managed to make it out of Corstorphine with both its name and her memory of what was most special to her, which was the sunrise with its vibrant colors that spanned the entirety of the sky.

Gabrielle had so enjoyed seeing Grayson and hated leaving him and Corstorphine more than any other visit. Every day, things were getting more worrisome and much more dangerous for any on the side of Light. And, even though Shifters are well protected in their own realms, the human realm was becoming more treacherous all the time—and they spent a lot of time in it. She found herself increasingly concerned that she might not ever see him again.

She arrived after the last bell for first period sounded so she wouldn't run into Lucas. She was glad she did when she saw his Wrangler parked near the spot she usually took. He hadn't parked in that lot in three weeks. Today, because of being late, she was well away from it.

She spent first period in her own world that mingled Shifters and humans, angels and demons, happy and sad, safe and dangerous, beautiful and ugly, Light and Dark. The life she lived was complicated and full of contrasts—and getting more complex all the time.

When class let out, she was the last to leave, in no hurry for her next class either. At least until she stepped into the hallway and Lucas stepped into her path.

"*Oh*. Excuse me." Gabrielle tried to side-step him. He mirrored her movement. She tried the other direction, and he moved with her again.

"I guess you're going to make me go the long way around." She turned on her heel and tried to walk swiftly away from him. Swiftly ended up being a snail's pace, though, since she seemed to be going against the direction of every other student in the hall.

Ugh ... seriously!

"No, Gabby. I wasn't trying to make you go the long way around. I was *trying* to get you to talk to me," Lucas said to the back of her head, following her.

"Lucas, I don't think this is the time or place."

Lucas grabbed Gabrielle's arm to stop her, forcing her to look at him.

Gabrielle jerked free, shoving him back with her free hand in the process. Suddenly, the students gave her a wide berth. "Don't. Ever. Grab me like that again. Understand?" Gabrielle spoke as calmly as possible, trying to contain a very bad mood that was being made much worse at that moment. She glared at Lucas, but he didn't back down. He walked back toward her, but his expression was soft, apologetic.

"I'm sorry. I just want to talk with you."

"Trying to force me isn't something I'd recommend."

"Then tell me when it will be a good time, and name the place. We need to talk."

Gabrielle just stared into his unwavering eyes—those damn eyes that still made her want to get lost in them. In spite of her anger, she almost broke. But the memory of him and Mara hanging all over each other came roaring into her mind and brought any chance Lucas had of getting her to talk to him to a crashing end.

"Why don't you ask Mara what works for her schedule and get back to me? You two seem to have more to chat about than we do."

She didn't wait for a response, just turned and found a break in the crowd. As she reached the stairs, she couldn't help but look back at him. He stood where she'd left him, students flowing around him, with the strangest look on his face. She turned and raced to her next class—raced away from him.

And tried to race away from the tears now stinging the back of her human eyes.

Gabrielle managed to avoid Lucas at lunch, but the class they shared was another story. She'd arrived late, on purpose, hoping to have no communication with him. But Lucas had other plans. The only seat left was right behind him. Throughout class, he kept turning around whenever the teacher turned his back. And unfortunately for Gabrielle, said teacher was called to the office to take an emergency phone call.

Lucas was all over that opportunity. "What did you mean about Mara?"

"Lucas ... *really*. I don't want to talk to you about this."

"Tough, Gabby. I deserve to know why you're avoiding me. What did I do?"

Lucas looked genuinely confused, shaking Gabrielle's resolve. Again ... those eyes weren't helping matters at all.

"Not talking."

"You will. Eventually, I am going to get you to tell me what happened."

Gabrielle felt heat begin to flood through her body and her hands clench as anger began to rise to the surface again. Who was he to try to force her into a conversation?

"*Fine,*" Gabrielle said through clenched teeth as she began to gather her things. By this time, even though they were whispering, all eyes and ears were on them. It didn't help that she wasn't being quiet while putting her things in her backpack and made sure that the book, notebook, and pen made as much noise as was possible by fiercely stuffing them into place. "Three weeks ago, I saw you more than a little chummy with Mara walking into the gym. *Happy?*"

She couldn't say more, no matter how mad she was. She couldn't tell him that what was even worse was that she didn't know if he was a demon.

Lucas sat back a little, then brought his body forward again as he spoke. "Gabby, you've got that all wrong. I know what it must have looked like to you, but you *are* wrong."

Gabrielle didn't respond. She didn't even look to see if there was any sincerity in his eyes to match his tone. She just left. She didn't care about the class or that she wasn't supposed to leave.

What could they do, anyway, call my parents?

After making it into the hallway, thinking she made it to freedom, she heard the door to the class open again and Lucas calling to her.

"Gabby, wait!"

She didn't

"Gabby!"

She walked faster.

"*Gabrielle!*"

That got her attention.

His voice—the tone—it was melodic again, much more melodic than she'd ever heard it sound before. His voice was like …

Like an angel's.

She turned to face him, scrutinizing him, raising the veil in her mind, careful to leave the Aegis in place. She wasn't willing to test Amaziah's patience by removing his protection. Lucas's tone wouldn't have any effect on her; she was an angel. She simply recognized it. But it could have a profound effect on a human, allowing the one speaking the ability to induce strong persuasion if it was used for that purpose.

"Who are you, Lucas? *What* are you?"

He looked stunned but kept moving toward her—more slowly now.

"What do you mean?"

"*I mean, what are you*? The sound of your voice. Knowing a language you should never have known." Gabrielle must have looked like she was peeling back his layers to find the answer herself. "*Who are you?*"

He was less than a foot away. Lord help her she wanted to touch him so badly. He just stared at her. She could almost see his mind searching for a response, desperately trying to find the answer. He couldn't find one, she could see that.

Whatever, whoever, *he is … he* honestly *doesn't know what I'm talking about.*

Now … *she* was stunned.

"Gabby, I'm clueless. The language thing … I've always been a natural at foreign languages. What makes that *one* so special? Why couldn't I have known it or have heard it somewhere before?"

Realizing she couldn't tell him the answer unless she told him who and what *she* was, she turned and ran from him. For the second time that day.

As Gabrielle made her way to her car at the end of the school day, she was lost in thought about her exchange with Lucas. She was now sure that there was something very unusual about him. But she was also convinced he was at a loss as to whatever it was.

Looking up from the ground, she stopped. Lucas was leaning against her car. She'd left her last class early specifically so this wouldn't happen, but there he was anyway. Now that he was there, she realized her resolve had weakened. She started walking again, shaking her head.

"Boy, you don't give up, do you?"

"Nope."

She reached him and leaned against his Wrangler, now conveniently parked next to hers.

"What's left to say, Lucas?"

"For starters, I should have a chance to tell you what really happened that morning you saw me with Mara. And I think there's a little something to talk about now concerning what you were asking me a couple of hours ago."

He had her on the last one at least. She'd opened that can of worms right up, and she needed to buy some time to figure out how to put the lid back on. If he really didn't know what he was, there was no need to freak him out more than he probably already was. Now there was also the little problem of not being able to tell him who and what she was so she could explain further about his voice and language.

"Okay, Lucas. But not here."

Lucas looked relieved, even smiled a little. "Sure … where do you want to go?"

Good question.

After thinking on it a few seconds, Gabrielle decided it would be safe enough to go to her house. An angel would notice a human's energy, so there wouldn't be surprise manifestations.

"How about my house?"

"I'll follow you."

As they pulled out of the school lot and made their way toward her house, all she could think about was Lucas and what he might be and how she could explain away her concerns about it without telling him everything.

Chapter Twenty-one

Lucas † Chances

"Finally." Lucas said to no one but himself as he pulled out of the school's parking lot behind Gabby. He had thought it would take longer to convince her to talk to him after he'd learned she saw him with Mara draped all over him.

A chill ran through him with just the thought, but at least Mara had been staying away from him since. He wasn't planning on telling Gabby the whole story about what had happened that morning, though. If she thought he was strange now, it'd be worse if he told her he thought Mara's eyes not only changed colors, but that her entire eye went completely black, and that she's not the same person he'd originally met.

Yeah ... I think I'll keep that little tidbit to myself.

After about five minutes, Gabrielle pulled into the driveway of a brick townhouse. He turned off his Jeep and slid out, and they both silently climbed the steps and went in.

Lucas tried to take in everything he saw. The townhouse was larger than he thought, but its exterior was deceptive; it was built deep instead of wide. From the large entry where he stood, stairs hugged the left side of a curved three-story wall; a large contemporary chandelier hung from the ceiling directly above a round entry table in the center of what was really a room in itself. A beautiful arrangement of the most unusual flowers he'd ever seen were on the table. He was borderline captivated by it, actually. The colors of the unusual petals and buds were like they were from another world. Gabby stepped in front of them as she placed her things on the table and gave him his mind back as he continued to take in what he could from where he stood.

A music room or a study—maybe both—was immediately to the right and showcased a white baby grand piano, a large ornately carved wooden desk, and shelves of books that lined every wall he could see—most looked aged. He loved books and hoped he would have the chance, one day, to spend a lot of time in there looking them over. The only other thing in the room was a very large dark brown leather couch that looked like the most comfortable thing he'd ever seen.

Gabby turned and motioned at him to follow her. "Are you thirsty or hungry?"

Lucas followed, but both his feet and mouth responded slowly as he continued deeper into her home.

"Yeah ... sure." He walked through a long, wide hallway with nooks and crannies holding paintings and sculptures. Eye-candy was everywhere, capturing his attention like a five year-old walking through the gates of Disney World for the first time.

"Are you coming?"

Lucas managed to just glance at the remaining art as he left the hall that led into a massive room that held the kitchen, family room, and dining room. He had already thought the hall was full of interesting and beautiful effects, but after a quick scan of this room, he realized it had been simple in comparison to the one he was now in. Beautiful things were everywhere.

Not at all in a cluttered way, just ... *interesting*. He'd never seen a home with so many styles of furniture, art, and nick-nacks. And *somehow,* it all worked together perfectly. Nothing looked out of place or like it wasn't meant to be among all the other things on the walls or in the room. And everything was anchored by more of the same oversized, comfortable looking, dark leather furniture that was in the library. Only in here, there were two couches and one chair with a matching ottoman that was easily big enough for two people.

A large flat screen was situated over a fireplace with more shelves on either side of them, full of CD's and ... more *things*. Quite a few unframed black and white photos had been left on the ottoman, making him wonder if Gabby had taken them.

What does she fill her time with outside of school?

The dining room was about what he would have expected, furnished with a large wooden table and chairs and a buffet server. There was more eclectic art hanging on the walls and a larger arrangement of those unusual flowers on the table.

The kitchen was a gourmet chef's dream with dark stained cabinetry and tiles that were as current as the high-end stainless steel appliances. A large island in the middle held a six-burner gas range and a bar that curved around one corner with six stools nestled around it. The back wall of the townhouse was almost completely glass, bathing the room in light.

He glanced around the room again. There were no pictures of Gabby or her family—or anyone else for that matter—anywhere.

Absolutely none. Odd.

"Do you want some sweet tea or a Coke?" Gabby called from the fridge she just opened.

"Coke's great ... thanks," he said as he walked through the family room into the kitchen, pulling out one of the stools to sit.

"This is a *really* great place, Gabby."

Gabby turned and looked at him, a smile parting her lips as if she was pleased he liked it.

Man ... I miss that smile.

"Thanks." She slid a can of Coke across the counter to him and popped the top on her own, picking up a notebook that he'd glimpsed a few lines of poetry in before she closed it to conceal its contents. "It's kinda ... *different*, I know. But I really like it. Chips or pretzels?" She asked as she made her way to the pantry.

"Chips." She grabbed a bag and opened it, handing it to him as he continued to talk. "You and your family must have done a lot of traveling to have found all of these things," he said as he put a chip into his mouth and opened his can to take a drink.

Gabby chuckled lightly. "Yeah, you could say we've been around."

There was an awkward silence as he ate chips and she randomly looked at different objects. Lucas took another drink and then cleared his throat nervously. "So, about the Mara thing."

Gabby's attention was solely on him, and the intensity in her gaze made him wish she would keep looking at her things as he talked.

"There was something wrong with her that morning. Something is *wrong* with her, period. And what you saw was me trying to help her get somewhere so she could sit down." Lucas paused to see if she might possibly, *hopefully*, believe him. Her expression gave nothing away. "Gabby ... she *literally* collapsed into my arms. What should I have done? Let her hit the ground and walk away? I couldn't do that. Not *then*, anyway." He stopped and waited for her response.

"Say I believe you ... I still want to know why you're so angry with her. Are you going to tell me now?"

Oh, boy ... here we go. How do I bring her back to me without telling her everything?

"That's complicated."

"Complicated, huh?"

Then, the staring at each other began and continued for several tense moments.

"Gabby, she means nothing to me. She never really did. Can't we just leave it at that?"

More staring.

"I don't know, Lucas."

Green eyes ... dissecting him.

"Can you think about it while we talk about the thing in the hall today?"

Finally, she blinked.

"Sure, Lucas."

Back to staring.

"Okay ... I guess I'll start. What was so strange about my voice? And why shouldn't I have known that language? If you know it, why is it such a stretch that I could have heard it before?"

Gabby shifted in her chair and took a chip for the first time, chewing it slowly. Lucas thought it was a delaying tactic. Especially as she took another one, chewing it just as slowly, and then a sip of her drink.

Why doesn't she want to talk about it? Am I that strange to her?

"Gabby ... "

She cleared her throat this time. "Yeah," she said and took another drink. "It's just hard to explain some things."

Tell me about it.

"Maybe it's nothing. I've been taught to be overly cautious by my ... parents, so maybe I'm just being paranoid."

"Why do you have to be overly cautious?"

Gabby seemed to ponder this question a little too long.

"They spend most of their time at the island resort they own in Florida, which leaves me alone quite a lot. They just want me to be safe, I guess."

"Oh." He didn't believe her for some reason. But he didn't care, either. What he did care about was keeping her talking, to spend as much time with her as possible, to figure out how to get them back on track. At least they were communicating.

"So, you're being over-cautious because you think I might be a danger to you?" His mind flashed to his dream where she seemed threatened by him.

Gabby actually smiled at that suggestion.

Maybe she's not afraid of me after all? He thought with more than a little relief.

"Cautious, yes. Because of you being a danger to me, no. I can handle myself pretty well," she said with a lot of confidence.

"Okay. Then why did you pull away from me?"

More silence, more of those green eyes that seemed capable of penetrating his soul.

"I became worried that things were moving too fast, and that I was more interested in you than I should be."

That seemed honest. "Why shouldn't you be interested in me?"

"Because, Lucas ... I don't usually stay in one place very long. Like I said ... we get around."

She's not afraid of me; she's afraid of getting hurt. That's *easy to relate to.* "I'm willing to take the chance if you are, Gabby. I have just as much chance of getting hurt here as you do, you know."

She seemed to feel the honesty in his statement. Her brows softened, and a smile played at the corners of her full, red lips. Something in her eyes made her look happy ... a *glow* seemed to be coming from them now. Though it was so subtle, it was probably just his imagination or a trick of the light in the room. But damn ... it made them even more beautiful.

"Yeah ... you do."

Lucas took a chance and reached out to take her hands. The strong, warm energy he'd gotten when they'd touched before still happened, and it made him smile. Something about it made him feel connected to her in a way he had never felt with anyone else before.

And that's just from touching her hands. To his relief, she didn't pull away. "Will you take the chance with me, Gabby?" He asked with his eyes even more than with the words he'd spoken. Every ounce of him wanted to be with her. He couldn't explain it, but it was what it was. He felt she was the answer to questions about things he did not yet understand and of things he had wondered about for years. Her response took so long that he began to think he might be willing to get on his knees and beg when, thankfully, she smiled. Before she opened her mouth to say the words, he knew that she was going to say yes.

"Okay, Lucas. I'll take that chance, too."

Those are the most beautiful words I've ever heard ... in any language.

Chapter Twenty-two

Gabrielle ✝ Sisters and Demons

Since returning from Corstorphine with Phalen, the amount of time Gabrielle spent worrying about completing her original task and needing to find the Book had worsened. The days were fewer to do either, but the Book was the main cause of her concern. It was on her mind more and more as though something was prodding her to find it—like a silent, invisible creature harassing her to hurry up and get her hands on the artifact.

While making her way to New Orleans to meet Phalen, Gabrielle reflected on how the week had gone quite unexpectedly.

The conversation with Lucas and their decision to move forward with whatever it was that they were doing had lifted her mood dramatically. She felt like she gave in too easily, but something in his eyes—and the way he made her feel—caused her to push the screaming voice of reason behind the door it came out of and shut it tightly, muffling its disapproval.

That was Monday.

For the rest of the week, she and Lucas spent as much time together as they could. Both arrived early to school, and they spent lunch with Nonie and Nate. Gabrielle was growing fond of Nonie and Nate and found she looked forward to seeing them each day, too. They always made her feel at ease, with the exception of a few times when Nate would watch her intensely. Something about him made her leery of him, but most often, he was enjoyable to be around.

The twins were always laughing and poking fun at each other, themselves, and any innocent or not so innocent person they chose. More times than not, that other person was Lucas, and he seemed to enjoy the banter as much as they did. Gabrielle felt a real bond between them—like Lucas was their brother. With what she'd learned about Lucas's past and family history, she was glad he had the twins and their family in his life.

Lucas confided in Gabrielle that his mother and father died when he was just a baby. She could tell by the pain in his eyes when he spoke of it that, even though it had happened a very long time ago, he hadn't come to terms with the loss. From what he'd been told by his grandmother, Emma, who had raised him, they'd died with his grandfather in a home burglary gone wrong. No one had ever been charged. Gabrielle knew she could find out who was responsible and bring them to justice if it hadn't already been taken care of. However, she shouldn't. It was for Yahuwah alone to decide when it was time to make someone reap what they'd sown, who would be rewarded or punished.

Gabrielle just decided how the karma would be given, not how severe the punishment or high the reward. She brought happiness, or woe, in thousands of different ways. Sometimes simple, sometimes intricate, sometimes mild, sometimes severe. Then she waited for her next lot from Yahuwah.

Lucas told Gabrielle his grandmother was wonderful to him, but if it hadn't been for Nonie and Nate and the rest of the Daniels family, he would have been lonely. They were, as Gabrielle had already begun to suspect, his family. Nonie and Nate had a little sister, Chloe, who was seven. And apparently, a very happy and unexpected surprise for their parents, Lizzie and Ben.

Ben was the pastor of a large church just around the corner from where the Daniels family and Lucas lived, and Lizzie was a semi-retired surgeon. Holidays and special occasions always found the two families together, and they frequently ate dinner under the same roof. Really, the two families weren't separate at all except for the space the pavement and grass placed between their two homes.

Gabrielle enjoyed hearing about the festive times they shared. The funny, and not so funny, stories of escapades the three teens and the rest of the family would find themselves in. She found she wanted to be part of that family somehow, in some way, and was looking forward to meeting the rest of the Daniels crew and Lucas's grandmother.

Her fourth week of high school had just ended, and tomorrow was Nonie and Nate's first touch-football game—a weekly event until Christmas. She would get to spend even more time with all of them and was particularly happy that Lucas would be picking her up. Right before leaving school, he said he'd see her at about eleven the next day so they could grab something to eat before the game.

Reminiscing made her mood light, and she began to feel even happier as she neared New Orleans and sensed Phalen. She hadn't seen her since they crossed over from Corstorphine, back into the human realm, and she'd missed her.

Gabrielle appeared in front of Phalen's smiling, bubble-blowing face. She still seemed content with the appearance of the fair-haired, blue-eyed beauty that she created the first day they came to Earth together.

"Hey, sister! Ready for a little treasure hunting?" Phalen asked as she gave Gabrielle a hug.

"You bet!" Gabrielle answered in an unusually jovial tone and then started walking down one of the city's now darkened, deserted alleys, whistling as she did.

"Whoa, sister ... what's with the merriment? Did I miss the news flash that we've won the war, or what?"

Gabrielle just looked over her shoulder and smiled, then resumed whistling.

Phalen materialized right in front of her. "Gabrielle ... this is about the *human*, Lucas. Isn't it?"

Gabrielle stopped whistling. The concern in Phalen's voice had opened up that door and let the damn voice of reason out. It told her that the worry in Phalen's voice was warranted, which she knew without the reminder.

"Yeah ..." she responded, "and don't do that again. This alley might look deserted, but it's still New Orleans with a lot of humans. All those humans have a set of eyes." Gabrielle dematerialized and rematerialized deeper within the shadows between the buildings. It was a humid late September night, and there was electricity in the air, warning of an approaching storm. Phalen's concern is what dampened her mood, though. And Gabrielle was sure, if she could have seen her own expression being reflected back, she would have looked as if she'd been defeated in some major battle, waiting to find out if her life was going to be spared. It was a quick shift from the happiness she was feeling moments before.

Phalen manifested in front of her again.

"I thought I just told you not to do that!"

"Well ... *you* just did it!"

"I made sure to put up a veil before I did it so no one could see."

"Then they wouldn't have just seen me, either, because so did I."

"When did you receive the ability to veil yourself so thoroughly? And why didn't you tell me so I wouldn't worry about needing to do it?"

"Amaziah bestowed it on me right before I came to meet you. I haven't had the chance to tell you, yet."

The two angels stared at each other, Phalen's brows pinched, apparently from concern and irritation. Again, Gabrielle thought of how much she liked and respected Phalen for not being intimidated by her. Phalen eyed Gabrielle, but her eyes and brow gradually relaxed.

"Hey, I'm not going to go blab about your thing with Lucas, you know. I just don't want to see you end up down here permanently ... if you know what I mean. Partially because I'd miss you too much, but mostly because I don't want to fight you. Especially since, even in that weakened form, I'm pretty sure you'd still school me in combat."

"I could never hurt you, Phalen."

"Hmm ... that's both a relief, *and* very scary."

"What do you mean?"

"Well, you said you wouldn't hurt me which is, of course, a huge relief. Because you and I both know that, even stripped of most of your powers, you'd still make easy work of me. But the very scary part is that you didn't say you weren't willing to be cast from Heaven for this human." Phalen paused. "Gabrielle ... you're not willing to fall for him ... are you? And I mean the end of you being *you* kind of fall."

"I know what you mean, Phalen, and I want to say no. But ... I am having a more difficult time keeping that line in view every moment I spend with him."

Phalen began to aggressively pace back and forth across the width of the alley. "You're starting to make me mad, Gabrielle. And what makes me even angrier is that I can't fight you about it! I *should* tell Amaziah about this. Then, he could *force* you back to Heaven. But ... that wouldn't do any good, because you have to come back to Earth as The Angel of Karma." She stopped pacing and glared at Gabrielle with narrowed eyes. "And both of us know you'd be able to find plenty of reasons to *have* to come back. Wouldn't you?"

Gabrielle didn't answer. Phalen was right about everything. But what really got to her was that Phalen cared that much about her. She'd grown fond of Phalen but had no idea that she felt so strongly about their friendship, too. Phalen's habit of calling her sister suddenly took on new meaning and importance to Gabrielle.

Phalen leaned against the brick wall of one of the buildings, looking defeated.

"Hey ..." Gabrielle said, "I promise to be careful. Okay?"

"Can you promise to leave him alone?"

"No ... that's something I can't promise. At least, not right now."

They looked at each other for several long moments. Gabrielle couldn't take the sadness and concern etched into Phalen's expression anymore.

"Hey, where's that offer of gum you're becoming famous for when you want to lighten up a situation?"

Phalen looked at her a little longer before answering. "Sorry … I'm not feeling very bubbly right now."

After walking the rest of the way through the alley, across a street, and into another alley in silence, Phalen finally spoke.

"So, tell me who, or *what*, are we meeting down here again?" Phalen handed Gabrielle a piece of gum as she popped a piece into her own mouth.

"Guess not feeling bubbly didn't last very long," Gabrielle commented. Phalen responded by sticking out her tongue. "We are here to talk to Ka'awa."

"Yeah … that's right," Phalen commented sarcastically. "A *demon*. Or at least, a *half-demon*. What kind of evil little sprite is he mixed with? And can you tell me *why* we are talking to a demon about this?"

"Because this particular *demon* has an interesting ability. Concerning which of the Gentry he is mixed with, I don't know. I don't particularly care. He's just someone who might be able to help."

"How so?"

"There are things he may know, *if* we can actually get it out of him, that Yahuwah won't because of the deal Yahuwah made with Ramai. Ka'awa seems to have inherited a talent from one of his parents … an extremely powerful one. He's a very proficient Seer. Though, he still may not know anything about the Book."

A look of understanding washed over Phalen's face. "Gotcha."

"Ahh … Gabrielle, so nice to finally meet you."

The voice came before Ka'awa's physical body appeared in front of them, blocking their way.

"Ka'awa," Gabrielle came to a stop.

Gabrielle and Phalen stood across from the rather menacing, smiling figure. Ka'awa was tall, thickly built, and definitely looked like a demon even with the glamour concealing his appearance. His hair was black and slicked back; his eyes were a strange mustard color that seemed to glow faintly. She wondered if the strangeness of his eyes had anything to do with him being a proficient Seer of the world and what happens in it.

Lightning briefly illuminated the darkness of the alley but had done so just long enough for Gabrielle to notice the light reflect off a black stone pendant hanging from a leather strap around his neck. Something about the piece of jewelry sent off alarms in her mind.

Is it an amulet?

Her concern worsened when he noticed her focus on it and then quickly moved it under his shirt.

"I have heard so much about you, Gabrielle," he stated. "Your incredible powers are spoken of in the Underworld and Shadow World in great detail. I have often wondered, *hoped* really, that I would one day have the opportunity to address you personally." Ka'awa's smile took on a harder edge. "It would entertain me to find out who between the two of us has more power."

Phalen's posture immediately switched into a fighting position. Ka'awa simply winked at her, which Gabrielle could tell didn't faze Phalen as she blew and then sucked back in a bubble. Gabrielle wondered why he thought he might be a match for her. His hand absently moved to the pendant as if he was reassuring himself it was still there. The motion sent a fresh wave of concern through her, furthering her interest in the stone.

Gabrielle smiled and put her hand on Phalen's shoulder without taking her eyes off the half-demon. She suddenly wanted to know more about his parents, sensing he was more of a threat than anyone thought.

"Yes, Ka'awa, I would be quite entertained by that, myself." Gabrielle felt Phalen's body return to a more relaxed position under her hand. "This is not the time for games, however."

"Of course, Gabrielle. How, exactly, can I be of assistance to The

Angel of Karma?"

"I bet you already have that answer, Ka'awa."

He smiled larger and chuckled. Both were unfriendly.

"Ahh ... I see my reputation reaches even the loftiness of Heaven."

"It is known."

"Well, I will try to stay out of my normal habit of riddles and games ... for *you*," Ka'awa stated in the most believable tone that Gabrielle thought he was capable of, though she knew it was far from the reality of his true intentions. Seeming to know he hadn't fooled her, he chuckled and winked again, this time at her. "I believe you are looking for a certain book. Is that correct?"

"It is."

"Yes, the Book of Barabbadon. It seems it's a very popular artifact as of late. Many have come to me to find out the location of its resting place."

"And what have you told the others?"

"The same thing I will tell you."

Ka'awa paused for what Gabrielle suspected was dramatic effect, though she wondered if he was accustomed to some form of payment at this point in return for the information he was about to divulge. Gabrielle simply raised her brow. She had no patience for his games, and even if Ka'awa thought he could defeat her, he seemed to think twice about testing his theory.

What stories had he heard about my powers and abilities?

He nodded his head once and continued. "I've told everyone that if I knew where it was, I would have already retrieved it myself."

She had figured as much, but there was something in his eyes, a quick flicker, that he was holding back.

Why had he remained in this city for hundreds of years? It's near one of the Gates of Hell, but there are many of those.

Ka'awa's attention was diverted toward the sound of jumbled conversations and laughter that spilled into the alley when a back door to a bar opened. Gabrielle followed his gaze. As the door closed, Gabrielle recognized the female demon who stood in the doorway and locked eyes with her.

"Mara …" Gabrielle said absently. "Interesting."

"Yes," Ka'awa responded without looking away from Mara. "*Interesting*. It would seem that I am a popular … *artifact* this evening. If we are done here, Gabrielle, I have other matters to attend."

"Thank you for seeing me."

"Oh, it was my … *pleasure*, Gabrielle." He kept his attention on Mara but continued to speak. "Sorry I wasn't able to spend more time getting to know you, Phalen. But there will be *other* times for that in the future."

"*Great*," Phalen said under her breath. "I can't wait, creepy dude."

Gabrielle smiled but continued to watch Mara.

Phalen seemed just as interested in the female demon. 'What do you suppose she's up to, sister?'

'Hmm?' Gabrielle pulled herself back from her wonderings. "I don't know, but I sure would like to.'

"I'm sure you would," Ka'awa responded, even though she hadn't been speaking aloud, "and, I could tell you, but I won't."

Gabrielle felt jealousy creep into her as she remembered Mara pawing Lucas, wondering how far their relationship had actually gone. She didn't like to think about him being intimate with her.

"I need to talk to you," Mara said to Ka'awa, keeping her eyes on Gabrielle.

"I know. I've known for quite some time that you were trying to find me. It certainly took you long enough. You're not very resourceful, are you?" he asked with a cruel smirk.

Gabrielle wondered what he knew about Mara.

"Unless, *of course*," Ka'awa continued, "you have someone else helping you. Can't you do anything without your *friend*?"

Gabrielle could see Mara's jaw clench as she glared at Ka'awa.

"Aww … did the truth sting, Mara?" he asked smugly.

"Maybe," Mara said, "that's what I want you," Mara looked back at Gabrielle, "and others to think."

There was little doubt, even with the limited time she had to observe them, that there were no warm fuzzies between these two. *No loyalty among the Fallen, I guess.*

"No, Gabrielle," he responded to her thought. "There isn't."

Gabrielle looked at Ka'awa and made a note to block her thoughts better around him. Apparently, being a Seer wasn't the only thing he'd inherited from his parents. He also had quite a knack for mind-reading.

He smiled as though he heard that, too.

Gabrielle continued to study Mara. She hadn't been around her long enough to really look at her, to read her for a sense of something—anything—that might give her a clue about why Mara seemed so interested in Lucas. As the seconds passed, the tension grew. Mara seemed over-reactive, her eyes flicking at even the slightest movement from Gabrielle or Phalen.

She's ready for a confrontation; that much is clear. And I would love to give it to her.

"*That* would be entertaining," Ka'awa chimed in.

It isn't likely to happen here, Ka'awa, so don't get your hopes up.

After that, Gabrielle ignored him. But he gave an exaggerated pout to show he heard her anyway. She wasn't worried for herself if a fight broke out, but she wanted to make sure that Phalen wouldn't be harmed if the edgy demon misread a movement and decided to attack. And she didn't want Ka'awa to jump in, either.

She was about to try to ease Mara's mind and leave when Phalen made a move toward Mara. In response, Mara immediately called up a Dither Sword.

"*Whoa!* Easy, little she-demon. I come in peace … well, with a piece of gum, that is."

Gabrielle had a hard time keeping her laughter contained.

Mara looked at Gabrielle with a confused expression and must have seen the amusement that she was trying to keep in. She straightened her body, and the Dither Sword vanished. She scowled at Phalen for a long moment, head slightly cocked.

"You mean I have to introduce yet another poor soul—well, not in your case, *you're soulless*—to grape bliss?"

Mara's expression turned to a mixture of agitation and confusion.

Phalen cracked a broad smile and handed a piece to her.

"Seriously, try it. It will make you feel better. And you look like you need to feel better."

Mara looked at both Ka'awa and Gabrielle before she cautiously took the gum from Phalen's hand, chewing it slowly as she scrutinized Phalen.

"Anyway," Gabrielle interrupted the lingering silence, "we have things to do." Gabrielle nodded to Ka'awa. "Mara," she said as both a hello and goodbye in a particularly unfriendly tone.

Mara nodded once in response, returning her gaze to Phalen as soon as she did. Gabrielle saw Phalen blow a bubble, then suck it into her mouth. One of the biggest smiles moved across her face as soon as the gum was back behind her lips and she could resume chewing. Again, Gabrielle had to keep her laughter contained. As they made their way back out of the alley, Phalen looked over her shoulder at the two demons.

"I think Mara liked me, sister. This bubblegum is a great icebreaker, don't you think?"

"Yeah, sure. Just don't try to use it as a peace offering in any actual battles."

"I'll be too busy kicking demon butt to offer gum."

"I would love to know what Mara is up to, and what it has to do with Lucas."

"You sure it *does* have something to do with him?

Gabrielle thought before answering. "No, I'm not, and I'm not going to find out tonight. So," Gabrielle hooked her arm around Phalen's, "let's get back. I want to get tonight's work over with so we can get to the next stop of the evening."

Phalen's eyes lit up with anticipation. "Fantastic! Where are we going after you finish the karma bit, anyway?" She blew a purple mass out of her mouth.

Gabrielle poked it with her finger, popping it. It covered the entire bottom half of Phalen's face. Gabrielle received a smile and a hard thump on her arm in return.

"Okay." Phalen began pulling gum off her chin. "Seriously, where we going?"

Gabrielle was looking forward to what she had planned. She had a surprise waiting for Phalen. One that Gabrielle felt the young angel would be particularly happy about.

"You'll see."

Chapter Twenty-three

GABRIELLE ✝ CHANGES

"Sheridan," Gabrielle said when arriving with Phalen from New Orleans and their visit with Ka'awa.

"Gabrielle," Sheridan said in an icy tone.

"Do you have the orders from Yahuwah ready for me?" Gabrielle asked with indifference.

Phalen was quick to escape while she could by picking up Gabrielle's iPod. Gabrielle didn't need exceptional hearing to notice the volume going as high as it could. She smiled as Phalen made her way toward the library—dancing and singing.

"Of course," Sheridan responded after Phalen was out of sight and handed Gabrielle one simple piece of blank paper. As soon as Gabrielle's energy was recognized, names and instructions began to appear, as well as notable past actions that should be taken into account. It was as if the words were just shy at someone's touch who wasn't its master. Only The Angel of Karma was allowed to see the details before giving the orders to her troops—a way of making sure that no one could be warned or protected by those in Darkness and Shadows, should the document fall into the wrong hands.

The punishments or rewards were meant to encourage humans to want to do—to be—good. Darkness, of course, would love to stop them from being carried out which was the reason for the secrecy and the reason decisions were made, and instructions given, quickly.

As soon as Gabrielle gave orders for the first page of names, the writing disappeared in ghostly wisps as more names and details replaced them. Gabrielle went through all the names and gave her orders, then dismissed Sheridan.

Before Sheridan left, though, she turned and faced her superior with a defiant posture.

"Gabrielle."

"Yes."

"You say you don't care what is said about your decision to be here. But I feel you should know that there are rumors being spread that concern your ... *activities* here," Contempt edged into Sheridan's icy tone.

"Do you?" Gabrielle maintained indifference.

"Yes, I do."

Gabrielle rematerialized closer to Sheridan. Sheridan tensed, but it didn't stop her from continuing to speak her mind.

"I don't want to see you do something that might jeopardize your position. And—"

"Oh—" Gabrielle couldn't help but laugh, "on the contrary, Sheridan, I believe you would *love* to see that happen."

Sheridan's hands almost smacked together as she clasped them, resting them against her body, then bowed her head slightly.

The reaction was surely from the change in Gabrielle's color that she allowed to come through her human form. Anger showed quickly on her if she let it, and she was in no mood for Sheridan tonight.

"Sheridan, I have far more important things to do than deal with an angel who has been waiting for her chance to step into my position for as long as she's been the second in command *to* that position. And, don't lie to me. You and I both know that you would be the first to offer my wings up to Council. You would probably volunteer to strip them from my back."

Sheridan's energy trembled. Gabrielle's color was almost aflame in red now, matching her words and tone. In all the years they'd worked together, Gabrielle had never talked to Sheridan that way or shown an indication of the power she was capable of around her. Sheridan was clearly not anticipating the show of supremacy she'd just witnessed. There were few angels with the power and energy to create the amount of color Gabrielle just showed, far fewer with the courage to turn it on their brethren.

"Are you finished?" Gabrielle asked, adopting a tone of indifference. Though, she knew her hue completely contradicted it.

"Yes," Sheridan responded in a much quieter, more subordinate manner.

"I'll see you tomorrow."

Gabrielle watched as Sheridan vanished, taking a deep breath and sighing loudly when she was gone. She shouldn't have trouble from her again anytime soon, at least not directly. Now, there was a bigger problem that could result from their confrontation.

The trouble Sheridan may want to cause indirectly.

"Are you ready, Phalen?" Gabrielle asked as she entered the library. Phalen sat on the sofa reading a book, her foot keeping time with the beat of the song she was listening to.

"Sure." Phalen stood and turned, stopping as her gaze landed on Gabrielle. "*Wow* ... what got *that* color all pumped up?"

Gabrielle hadn't given herself time to calm down. She was still mad as hell. "Just some long overdue words for Sheridan."

"*Oh, Gabrielle!* Couldn't you have let me know so I could see her crumble?" she asked with a huge grin. "I agree with Grayson; she's shifty."

Gabrielle felt her mood lighten although she didn't think her normal color would be returning for a while. "Sorry, but that wasn't something I would have wanted you to see."

"That intense, huh?"

"Yeah, at least I think Sheridan would say so. But let's change the subject, okay?"

"No problem."

"Let's go, then. I'm ready to lighten my mood."

Gabrielle and Phalen manifested at the top of the eastern edge of El Capitan in Yosemite National Park. Grayson and Rissie immediately greeted them.

"*Grayson!*" Phalen yelled in happy surprise as she flung her arms around him.

Gabrielle laughed happily that she'd gotten the reaction out of Phalen she'd hoped for.

"Hello, Lady Phalen! What a nice greeting ye gave me." He smiled at her as he put her down, then made his way to Gabrielle. "M'lady … what a pleasure to see ye again so soon. I'm so glad I was able to give ye somethin' toward yer search." Grayson paused, studying her. His smile grew. "But I'm even happier that whatever made yer heart heavy seems to have taken its leave of ye in just a few short weeks." He gave her a massive hug.

If I could pick a true brother, Grayson, it would be you.

"Aw," Phalen said from where Grayson had put her down. "That was so sweet, sister."

"What was, Lady Phalen?" Grayson asked as he released Gabrielle.

"Should I tell him, or do you want to?"

Gabrielle laughed. "I was thinking that if I could pick a brother, the kind a human has, it would be you, and Phalen heard me."

"Oh, m'lady, ye should just consider me picked, then." He hugged her again even tighter.

As he did, her color returned to normal. Her heart was so full that her eyes began to tear up. "Okay," she said as she pulled back from Grayson and popped him playfully on his arm. "Enough of that. I have a reputation to keep up." Gabrielle walked over to Rissie and hugged her, too. "Rissie, it's so nice to see you again. How have you been?"

"Lovely, m'lady. And ye? Have ye been well?"

"Yes. I am well," Gabrielle responded warmly. She motioned to Phalen, "Rissie, this is Phalen."

Phalen greeted her with a handshake, but just as Grayson had done when she first met him, she ended up with a hug although it was not the lift someone up off the ground kind that he liked to give.

"Nice to meet ye, Lady Phalen," Rissie said, then stepped back. "And, if ye haven't noticed yet, Shifters are a huggin' lot. As long as we like ye, anyway."

Gabrielle had always been fond of Rissie. She was slightly younger than Grayson and also his cousin. Rissie acted as his third in command. His second in command was Rissie's brother, Trygg. She was almost a foot shorter than Grayson with chocolate, shoulder length hair and smoldering, brown eyes. Although she wouldn't stand out in a crowd, she had a definite effect on men.

"So," Gabrielle addressed Phalen, "are you ready to go treasure hunting?"

"Absolutely. Where?"

"A cave just over the lip of Horsetail Fall. You and I are going to look for the Book while Grayson and Rissie keep an eye out up here."

"That's right," Grayson said. "We'll let ye know if anyone decides to do a little huntin' of their own."

"Let's go, then," Gabrielle said to Phalen. "If you see anything troublesome, Grayson, you know what to do."

"Yes, m'lady."

Gabrielle disappeared and Phalen followed. They manifested behind the falls in a narrow opening to a cave. Gabrielle said a few words in Enochian, and a ball of light appeared in each of her hands. She said a few more and the lights began to float—one in front of Gabrielle and the other in front of Phalen. When they moved, the orbs of light moved; when they stopped, the lights obeyed.

"Cool, sister. I'm going to have to remember that trick."

"My trick is now yours, Phalen. I just taught you the words."

Gabrielle moved deeper into the cave, which became wider and higher.

"Okay … well," Gabrielle began, "Grayson said his informant heard the Book may have been hidden here."

"Who's the informant?"

"One of the Fallen. The one he called Lek."

"Grayson really thinks he can trust him, huh?"

"Apparently. And Grayson isn't someone who gives his trust easily to those outside of us angels and his own fellows. If he trusts this demon, I have to at least give him the demon the benefit of the doubt because I trust Grayson."

"Yeah, I have to say, I've only known him a few weeks, and I'd pretty much trust him with my life."

"That trust is well placed, Phalen," Gabrielle replied.

She and Phalen continued to search the cave for any signs of something out of the ordinary.

"So what is it that Grayson and Rissie are looking out for?" Phalen asked.

"The Fallen, of course."

"Why? Do you think there might be trouble?"

Gabrielle said a few more words in the language of angels, and the cave trembled in a rolling wave from one side of the floor to the other, then did the same over the sides and ceiling until every inch had been covered. All the while, the rocks that made up the floor and sides of the cave behaved as if they were pliable instead of rigid. They could hear the rolling move deeper into the cave, and as it moved further away from them, the trembling lessened.

"Because if Lek knew about this, then there are others who do, too. If any show up, I'd rather we were up there instead of down here when they come, *if* they come."

"Smart."

"Yeah. I guess I have my moments,"

"Unless you're around Lucas or thinking about him. Then ... you don't seem to have those moments." Phalen bent over laughing at her own joke.

She just received a raised brow and smirk from Gabrielle.

"What?" she asked, full of innocence. "You know it's true."

Gabrielle didn't have a retort. Phalen had a point, even if it was meant in fun.

Gabrielle closed her eyes and said her last words in Enochian once again, only in reverse order, calling the rolling motion back toward them. The energy she'd sent out continued seeking what she was looking for. When it finished the second sweep, Gabrielle opened her eyes.

"Nothing." Gabrielle sighed from frustration. "Well ... I guess it was worth a try. Let's get out of here."

"Okay. Hey ... what was that you just did? And why can't we just do it everywhere and find the Book that way? If it actually exists, anyway."

"Don't worry about it. It was just something I wanted to try. And we could do it everywhere if there was enough magic at our disposal."

"Magic?" Phalen stopped, putting a hand on Gabrielle's arm to stop her. When Gabrielle looked at her, disapproval was in her eyes. "Sister ... did you get that from one of the Gentry?"

"I did."

"But we aren't supposed to deal with them or their magic!"

"You and the rest of our brethren aren't, but I can *if* I feel it's necessary."

Phalen dropped her hand from Gabrielle's arm. "I don't care, Gabrielle. They are way too sneaky. You wouldn't know which of them too trust any more than I."

"I needed to try. I don't think it will be that effective of a tool, anyway. It's new magic that I asked one of my allies in the Shadow World to conjure, and I think it's too weak."

"Maybe they liked your idea and made it too weak on purpose so they could use it to find the Book themselves."

"Oh, Phalen ... stop being so dramatic!" Gabrielle snapped. Calming herself, she continued. "I had to try. I need to find that book before it gets into the wrong hands."

Phalen studied Gabrielle for a long time before speaking, then took a deep breath and sighed. "If you say so."

"I say so ... now, let's get out of here. I don't like caves. They make me think about Hell, and that's something I think about enough as it is."

As they were about to dematerialize, they both heard a sound that made them stop. It was the long melodic call of a wolf joined in mid-chorus by a second one. It was Grayson and Rissie.

"Trouble's here," Gabrielle said. With that, she and Phalen were back above ground.

Grayson and Rissie were nowhere to be seen, but eight of the Fallen were only a quarter mile away.

"Gabrielle ... where are Grayson and Rissie? Are they okay?"

Gabrielle smiled to reassure Phalen. "They're near, and they're quite well ... as you'll soon see."

She could see Phalen scan their surroundings for the two Shifters, but all she would have seen were a couple hawks perched in one of the scraggly pines scattered around the rocky mountaintop. Gabrielle could tell Phalen was concerned that she couldn't see them and that she should have been able to on the top of the mountain; there wasn't much up there to take cover behind.

"If you say so."

"I say so," Gabrielle responded absently. The Fallen drew near.

As usual, her stomach began to protest. They were approaching aggressively, and Gabrielle suspected there wouldn't be much talk when they arrived. As they drew closer, a female in front began to speak.

"If you found what you came here to get, you might as well know I'm about to take it from you."

Gabrielle took all of the demons' energies into account—three weren't particularly powerful, three seemed moderately so, and two had Gabrielle concerned. Those two, the female speaking and a male to her right, were clearly going to be a problem. Gabrielle wondered how Phalen, Grayson, and Rissie would do with the other six if she concentrated her efforts on the strongest.

'Phalen, I'm going to try to keep the female that spoke and the male to her right engaged with me. I need you, Grayson, and Rissie to handle the others until I put an end to the ones I'll be dealing with.' She glanced at Phalen. *'Can you handle it?'*

Phalen smiled and nodded. *'I think we can keep them busy.'*

The demons continued to advance, and so did the stench that accompanied them. Gabrielle's insides lurched again as her opponents came within striking range. She hated waiting for them to make the first move and fought back her resentment of the law she had to abide by. If she could attack first, she could almost guarantee that she could keep the more powerful demons attention directed at her. Just before they advanced on her and Phalen, a vision flashed.

Her breath stopped, and it felt as though a vice had clamped down on her heart.

"NO!" Gabrielle yelled as she felt the impact of emotions the vision brought with it. "Phalen, Grayson, Rissie! Go! Leave!"

"What?"

"LEAVE!"

"*Why* would I—" Phalen's question was cut short as the demons attacked her.

The evening was instantly brighter from Dither Swords clashing. Grayson's form didn't allow him to answer, but the call of two hawks approaching told her that he and Rissie weren't heeding her warning, either.

Gabrielle raised her hands as her bow appeared in one and several arrows with Holy Fire burning on their tips manifested in the other. She released them as soon as they appeared. In the fraction of a second it took for more arrows to become solid in her hand, she watched the others hit their targets. Two hit the male; one hit the female. The demons simply pulled them out of their bodies and gave her mocking smiles.

How can they not be affected?

Gabrielle released the next three arrows, and again, they hit their targets. This time, they seemed to do some damage. Both staggered but began to advance on her again.

They should be ash!

As Gabrielle continued to feel the dread from the vision, from what it showed the outcome of this fight being, she let the demons get closer so she could take time to assess how her friends were faring. She was relieved to see that Phalen was holding her own with three of the demons.

A quick glance toward the other fight showed the remaining three against two of the largest mountain lions Gabrielle had ever seen. That was the confrontation she was most concerned with. Only one minor demon stood against her friends. The other two would not be easy for Grayson and Rissie to handle.

Gabrielle focused her attention back on her targets. *I have to finish these two.*

She let the bow vanish to make way for Sundering Whips. The Fallen froze, knowing the fatal damage they could do—regardless of whatever was protecting them. Gabrielle began to crack the whips. All she had to do was allow them to feel they were out of range, then she'd strike with a third, twelve feet longer than the ones she was currently wielding and the only one of its kind.

"*Grayson!*" Phalen called out.

Gabrielle heard the fear in Phalen's voice, and a split second later, she heard the cry of a mountain lion—of Grayson. Then, the sound of another and Gabrielle guessed Rissie had also been struck.

As Gabrielle advanced, she cracked the third Sundering Whip above the demons' heads and then sent it gunning toward them. It found one target's neck, removing his head, then immediately the other's, ending the lives of the Fallen in front of her. The light of the Dither Swords being used by Phalen and the demons increased as their fight intensified, illuminating their surroundings more and reflecting off identical pendants—exactly like the one Ka'awa had tried to keep her from getting a good look at—lying on the ground next to the demon's headless bodies.

An angel's shrill scream caused Gabrielle to turn. Phalen was battling three demons on her own, trying to protect Grayson and Rissie who were on the ground behind her, badly injured. The sight in front of Gabrielle caused a reaction she'd never had before. She'd been angry in battle, but the anger that coursed through her now could not be contained. It caused the ground to tremble and trees to shudder. Rocks and boulders lost their grip on the mountain-side and began to cascade to the earth below. Her Divine light turned crimson, making the air look as though it was bleeding.

All of this was enough to get the remaining demons' attention. They all stopped what they were doing and glared incredulously.

Grayson was on his side, turned away from Gabrielle. She couldn't see how badly he was injured, but she could hear his heart beating weakly.

He's still alive.

Rissie pulled herself across the ground to get to him, her left leg useless. Phalen was next to him, turning him gently onto his back, her own blood falling from her arm onto the rocks.

The shock was quickly wearing off the Fallen. Two attackers began to flee, but the remaining four advanced on Gabrielle and her friends.

Power she was unaware she possessed surged through her body. The rocky earth trembled again, so hard that trees lost their roots and fell, and a crack began to split the mountain top. Gabrielle was evoking the energy of the Earth, and she was ready to unleash that energy on the unholy creatures that had caused her friends pain.

"Now the pain will be yours." She spoke with such ferocity that the demons stopped abruptly.

She opened her mouth and screamed—the battle cry of one of the most powerful angels ever created. For the first time in Gabrielle's existence, she wanted every creature that could see her to bear full witness to her abilities. The power of that scream caused a concussion that forced the remaining demons to meet the ground hard with their backs. Gabrielle wasted no time as she called her weapons and beheaded all four of them with two cracks of the Sundering Whips. She allowed the other two to flee to tell the tale of what they had seen. The Fallen needed to know she was more powerful than they knew—more than even she had known. But more than that, she wanted to get to her friends.

"Phalen, move aside," Gabrielle said as she neared her friends. She looked down at Grayson as she knelt next to him. Putting a hand on each side of his face, she began to murmur in Enochian as her tears fell onto his face. She closed her eyes.

"What's wrong with him?" Rissie asked. "Is he going to be okay?"

Gabrielle heard Phalen move to Rissie, then speak quietly. "Gabrielle is calling on Yahuwah to help him."

Gabrielle continued to speak, begging the Creator to help her friend. Grayson was badly wounded. Her chest tightened from the thought of him dying. "Please live, Grayson … please live." That was the only break she took from her pleas to Yahuwah. As she prayed, she listened to the conversation taking place on the other side of Grayson. Rissie asked questions so fast it was difficult to keep up.

"She's asking Yahuwah to save Grayson? It's that bad? Is he going to make it? Is Yahuwah going to help him?"

"Yes, Rissie, that's what she's doing. And yes, if she's asking for His help … it is that bad."

"Will He help Grayson?"

"I don't know. We'll have to wait for Gabrielle to finish and ask her."

The conversation ended when Gabrielle's prayers stopped, replaced with her quiet sobs as she rocked Grayson in her arms. She removed her hands from his face so she could shift her legs under his upper body. She hugged and rocked him for several minutes as she spoke in words that Rissie could understand, assuring her that Grayson was going to make it.

"Thank you, thank you. Thank you, Yahuwah."

She listened to his heart beat steady and strong as tears continued to fall slowly down her face. Tears from the fear that she would lose him, joy that she wouldn't, and guilt because it was her fault he was there. When she finally looked at Phalen and Rissie, her remorse multiplied. It crushed in on her, her stomach threatening once more to let loose as she looked upon her friends and their wounds.

While there was little blood on Grayson except for a bad gash over his right eye, blood flowed from deep wounds on Phalen's arm and face, and Rissie's leg was broken badly enough that the bone had pierced her skin.

Fresh tears blurred Gabrielle's vision, making Phalen and Rissie look as if they were the wavy creations of an impressionist's painting. She blinked to see more clearly, and when she could, she noticed Phalen had moved in front of her.

Phalen looked at her with concern. "Gabrielle, isn't Grayson going to be okay?"

It took several seconds for Gabrielle to answer her as she looked at Phalen and Rissie's wounds. "Yahuwah has helped him, but he will need time to heal and recover completely. He was bleeding internally." She placed her hand on Phalen's arm near her wound. "You're badly hurt. You should ascend and see our healers."

Phalen looked at her arm as if she hadn't noticed she was injured at all. "What, this little thing? I've been left with worse from sparring sessions. Don't worry about it." She studied Gabrielle for a moment. "Look, I'm going to be fine." She looked at Rissie's leg, then back at Gabrielle. "So is Rissie. And you just said that Grayson will make it, too. We're all okay."

Gabrielle used the hand that had been on Phalen's arm to dry her tears. She wasn't going to continue to put her friends in danger for something she may never find—that may not even exist. She would look for it by herself from now on. At least as long as she could before Amaziah found out.

"Phalen." Gabrielle moved her legs out from under Grayson and picked him up off the ground. "I need you to help me get Rissie and Grayson back to Corstorphine so they can be tended to." Phalen nodded as she picked Rissie up off the ground. Rissie flinched when she did, sending fresh waves of sorrow through Gabrielle. "I want you to stay there for a while and make sure they are recovering. You can report back to me every day about their progress."

"Okay ... if that's what you want," Phalen said in a reserved manner. "What about the Book?"

Gabrielle sighed. "I'm not going to need any more help looking for the Book right now."

"Why? We have to find it first, if it exists."

"I will keep trying to find out what I can through my sources and allies and follow the leads I think are promising. I want ... I *need* you to be in Corstorphine to take care of Grayson and Rissie. I can't do it myself, or I would. I have to finish what I came here to do, and I'm running out of time to do it in. But I know you'll take good care of them, Phalen. I want you there in my stead." Gabrielle tried to smile. She was sure it looked as half-hearted as it felt.

Phalen watched Gabrielle a little longer, and just when Gabrielle was sure that she was about to say something in protest, Phalen simply nodded and smiled.

"Good," Gabrielle said. "Then that's settled."

Grayson lay unconscious in Gabrielle's arms. She felt the weight of what could have happened settle on her. She could have lost three close allies, two who were more than comrades to her. She wondered how the Fallen could take the punishment of the Holy Fire Arrows as though they were no more than mortal weapons—those sting, but Divine weapons kill. It might have something to do with what she now felt sure were amulets that they and Ka'awa wore.

The Fallen have to be getting assistance from someone. Probably the Gentry.

Things were changing. Too many things. And demons were more powerful than they had ever been before.

And more dangerous.

Chapter Twenty-four

LUCAS ✝ DARK FAMILY

"Yo!" Lucas called out as he walked into the Daniels' home. "Where's my breakfast?"

"We're in here, Lucas," Nonie called from the kitchen.

Lucas made his way toward the scents of bacon, biscuits, cinnamon rolls, coffee, and eggs and was greeted with good mornings. Gran smiled broadly at him and gave him a peck on the cheek as she made her way to the table with cinnamon rolls. Lizzie also headed that direction with a pitcher of orange juice in one hand and a gallon of milk in the other.

"Smells great." Lucas grabbed a bowl of scrambled eggs and a platter that held at least two pounds of bacon. "Looks great, too."

"Kissin' up to the cooks?" Nate asked with a grin.

Lucas smiled as he replied, "If that's what it takes to keep getting fed like this."

"Well," Nate continued, "you're going to need all the help you can get today if you think you're going to win."

"Ahh, Nate, I don't need help. Just my talent to whip you in anything we do."

"In your dreams, Lucas ... in your dreams."

Lucas was looking forward to today's game more than usual. This would be the first opportunity to spend any real time with Gabby outside of school. He was lost in thought about her through most of breakfast unless someone addressed him directly. Then, he would give a quick answer so he could get back to his ponderings. He'd never felt a pull to someone like he did to her. It wasn't just an attraction or a crush—or even lust—though he was more than attracted to her in that way, too. What male wouldn't be? It was something more.

Much more.

After breakfast was over, Lucas passed the time with the twins before picking up Gabby. Nonie and Nate brought out a deck of cards and a bag of coins, and the three of them began to play penny poker.

As Nate shuffled, Lucas felt his eyes on him and sensed the shift that forewarned that Nate was about to act odd again. When he looked at him, Lucas's concerns were validated by the darker color of his friend's eyes. Lucas shivered.

"What's with the stare, Nate?"

Nate continued to shuffle the deck methodically, his eyes remaining fixed on Lucas.

Lucas shivered again. *What gives?*

Nonie adjusted in her seat and leaned forward on her elbows, squinting at Nate. "Yeah, brother ... what's with the visual probe?"

Nate stopped shuffling and leaned forward to put them in the middle of the table. He slapped the cards down loudly, and Lucas and Nonie jumped. Then he sat back slowly as he looked first at Nonie and then to Lucas. A strange smile pulled up on one side of his mouth.

"Nate, man, you're acting a little odd." Lucas looked at Nonie quizzically. "Is it just me, Nee?" He hadn't ever voiced his concerns about Nate's behavior before. But it was occurring so frequently now. This time, it seemed even more intense. He had to know if it was just his imagination or if someone else noticed something wasn't right, too.

Nonie didn't look at Lucas. She had her eyes set steadfast on her brother. Lucas waited for her to answer. When she didn't, he stood up to leave. He was tired of this mood Nate got into, and he wasn't about to stay around for a three-way stare down.

"Where ya goin', my man?" Nate asked just as Lucas was about to put his hand on the door and escape.

Lucas let his hand rest on the knob as he half turned to respond. "What's it look like, Nate? I'm leaving." He turned back, but Nate spoke again.

"Why? I thought we were about to have a friendly game of cards."

Lucas turned his back to his escape. "Nate, I don't know what your problem is, especially in the last couple of weeks, but either tell me what it is or cut out this creepy act you keep pulling." Lucas felt he was boring holes into Nate instead of just waiting for a response. When several moments passed, he added, "Seriously. I'm over it."

"Yeah," Nonie chimed in. "I've noticed you're being a little weird sometimes, too. So it's not just Lucas seeing it."

Lucas glanced at her and noticed her expression still hadn't changed. He focused his attention back on his friend's face. Although, he didn't feel friendship coming from Nate. He felt something else—something cold and dark. Something Lucas didn't understand.

Something he didn't like.

"Have I?" Nate asked tone of innocence. "Sorry 'bout that. I guess I'm just a little worried about you."

"Worried?" Lucas started back toward the table. "Why?"

So much for my escape.

Lucas wanted to hear an explanation, hoping for something that might let him know Nate wasn't turning into some ... *dark* person.

That's what it is.

Lucas was glad for the few moments of quiet that came after that realization. That was exactly what Lucas saw in his eyes and demeanor when this happened—something sinister and something very unlike the Nate he was used to.

Nate kinda smiled again, but it still wasn't particularly friendly. "I just wonder why you're so wrapped up in Gabrielle. She gave you the brush-off for weeks, you know."

"Yeah, I know." Lucas adopted a similar expression to Nonie's. "What's your point?"

Nate huffed out what was some kind of laugh, then replied, "I don't think she's good for you, my man. She's ... I don't know ... *different*."

Lucas let out a similar huff of laughter. *What does Nate think of me? I've shown more strange quirks than Gabby.*

"Different? And what's with the *my mans*?" Nate just smirked. Lucas wanted to pick up the chair his hands rested on and hurl it at Nate for being such a jackass. He felt like that *thing* that tried to creep out of him a few weeks ago was trying to escape again. He didn't remember ever feeling this much aggression toward anyone.

Except for Mara that day with Gran.

Then, it hit him. That was the first time he'd felt this other side of himself, but he'd brushed it off as just a reaction to Mara hurting Gran. He didn't want to think of Nate being in the same category as Mara, but he was beginning to think that the two of them were remarkably similar in that way. Like there were two completely different people within their bodies, and you were never sure which one you're going to get from day to day or even minute to minute.

He was beginning to wonder about himself a little, too. What bothered Lucas more than that comparison was the look in Nate's eyes and the smile that spread across his face—like Nate knew that Lucas was thinking about throwing the chair.

'*Go ahead, my man... do it. Hit me with the fucking chair.*'

The voice in his head wasn't his own; it was Nate's. At least a strange, distorted voice that sounded like his. But it was deeper—more menacing—and it held a hatred he would never expect to hear out of his friend. If Lucas wasn't paralyzed by the questions racing through his head and the fear that flowed over him like a shower from Hell, he would have bolted out the door.

He suddenly felt cold, all the way to his bones cold.

"What are you talking about, Nate?" Nonie asked.

Lucas was glad she said something because Nate's gaze diverted to his sister.

That was so not cool. What the hell just happened? Could I have actually heard someone else's voice in his head?

"She's weird." Nate focused back on Lucas. "She doesn't seem to bring out the best in you, my man. Unless you consider your *softer* side the best in you."

"Really? *She's* weird?" Nonie asked, then scrutinized Nate. "Who are you, and what did you do with my brother?"

Did she actually wonder if this wasn't Nate?

He was seriously considering the possibility, himself.

That just seems crazy.

As Lucas watched his friend, he saw his eyes slowly shift back to their normal shade. Nate began to look slightly uncomfortable with the two sets of eyes staring at him. They belonged to faces holding expressions like they thought he was nuts. He laughed uncomfortably as though he didn't really know what to say.

Or maybe even what had just happened.

"Oh … forget I even said anything." Nate picked up the deck of cards and started shuffling them again.

Suddenly, Lucas felt sorry for him. In an instant, he was back to the Nate he'd known his whole life—only shaken and maybe confused.

Kinda like Mara had.

The similarities made his insides turn, like his stomach was trying to make his mind understand something about the situation—something that should be taken more seriously.

"Okay, Nate. Consider it forgotten." Lucas tried to give Nate a reassuring smile when he looked up briefly from the deck in his hands.

"So," Nate said, "are you two ready for me to whoop you in cards or what?"

Lucas pulled the seat out and made himself comfortable as Nate began to deal the first hand. His personality seemed to become more his own with every card he tossed in front of them.

"We'll see about that, brother," Nonie said as she settled back in her chair, too. Lucas thought she also sensed the shift in Nate.

Her brother was back again.

But for how long?

Chapter Twenty-Five

Gabrielle + Human Emotions

Gabrielle chose to let her human body rest without her after she made sure Grayson, Rissie, and Phalen were taken care of in Corstorphine. The guilt she carried grew heavier after seeing the reaction of the other Shifters when they saw the state Grayson and Rissie were in. She hoped by staying in her true form she would receive a premonition or Knowing without losing any of the information it contained, but nothing new was shown to her.

It was nine o'clock on Saturday morning when she returned to get ready for Lucas to pick her up. After what had happened the night before, when she almost lost more of those she cared for, her need to be with him was stronger than ever.

There had been a time, for a very long time, when Javan was the only one I ever thought I'd desire to be with. Things change. Even what we think is unchangeable.

But was it her human body's emotions making her feel she was falling for Lucas? Or was it real? Gabrielle wasn't sure, and she didn't know how to find out. She'd been drawn to him with just the visions, and the feeling of peace and happiness was a definite whether in her Divine form or her human one. That feeling of peace would end at some point; there was no escape from it. She would have to deal with the loss just like she had with Javan. The only difference was that she knew the end was coming with Lucas, and it was coming in about three months. She hadn't had that knowledge with Javan.

What are you doing, Gabrielle?

The question lingered as she showered and dressed, and it continued as she wasted time flipping through channels on her television, not really noticing anything on the screen as the images took turns trying to capture her attention. None did.

She looked at the clock on the mantle again. Ten forty-eight.

Any time now.

Several *very long* minutes passed, and she looked at the clock again. Ten fifty-seven. More minutes trudged through human time.

Come on, Lucas.

The knock on her door finally came, and Gabrielle made her way to the entry as calmly as she could. Her desire to see Lucas was almost overwhelming. As she opened the door, she tried to slow the bounce of her heart.

Lucas was there. He was safe. Smiling. Standing in front of her in long khaki cargo shorts and a blue, unbuttoned shirt, the long sleeves rolled up like there was nothing to be concerned about— no demons around every corner, no creatures lurking in the shadows of his world, no epic war on the horizon. He was unaware of it all. The thought made Gabrielle a little mad though she didn't know where the anger was actually coming from. And she didn't want to dwell on it. She quickly diverted her thoughts back to what she saw in front of her—back to Lucas.

He wore a white t-shirt under the button-down that was snug enough that she could begin to make out the muscles it tried to conceal. A terrible urge came over her to kiss him, but she pushed it back to where it had come from. There was more intensity between them the more time they spent together. She worried it wouldn't be long before she'd be unable to hide her growing feelings for Lucas from Amaziah. For all she knew, he was already aware. He could easily have someone watching her, not to spy but to ensure her safety, especially since Javan made his appearance.

"Hi, Gabby."

"Hi back." She resisted the urge to wrap her arms around his neck and let her lips softly touch his, knowing her desire could quickly escalate into a much more risky embrace, but she couldn't help wondering what it would feel like.

"Are you ready?" he asked.

"I think so," Gabrielle responded, looking down at her clothes as if to ask him if what she was wearing would be appropriate.

How can I go wrong with sweat pants and a t-shirt for touch football?

"Gabby." Lucas slowly looked her over. "Only you could make *that* outfit … look *that* good. Really, is there anything you can put on to make me want to look at you less? On second thought, don't do that. You wouldn't be able to, and I'm certainly *not* bored with the view."

Smiling, she stepped aside so he could come in, closing the door after him. She turned around, expecting him to be further inside the foyer. Instead, he had stopped and turned toward her. He was so close she almost ran into him. Without saying a word, he slowly brought one of his hands toward her face, stopping briefly as though second guessing himself. Gabrielle felt her pulse begin to quicken as his hand moved toward her cheek and rested on her face; his thumb slowly stroked her skin. Lucas never stopped looking into her eyes, and she felt pulled into them. The heat from his skin touching hers caused a chill, making her shudder. He smiled slightly. It felt like he was searching her mind and wanted to look even deeper, into her soul, making her feel he could pull her own to his. Her insides melted, and she loved it. She wanted to swim in that feeling—drown in it. She had never known sensations like this, not even with Javan.

His face coming toward hers was almost a blur, and before she could stop him, his lips pressed against hers. A chill moved through her again, but she didn't shudder. She pulled him closer, letting him push his body harder against hers. The combination of heat and chill crashing against each other in her body made her mind spin. Somehow, a rational thought broke through the chaos in her mind, through the yearning to have him even closer to her—to have him completely.

I have to stop this!

She felt her hands slip into his hair as she pushed herself even closer to him, denying the prompt to stop. His body reacted to hers as he kissed her more intensely. His hands began to search her body, and she felt their caress as they moved down her back, kindling more heat—more exquisite chills. She could tell by the urgency of his movement and breathlessness that he was feeling the same.

All at once, an image flooded into Gabrielle's mind. It was Javan glaring at her and Lucas, a remnant of her dream. It was swift and offered no additional information, but it was enough to force her to release Lucas. With her eyes still closed, she stumbled back slightly, catching herself on the entry table.

"*Whoa!*" Lucas said, breathing as heavily as Gabrielle. "That was ... *intense.*"

Gabrielle heard him take several breaths before his breathing began to calm. All the while, she was internally yelling at herself about how completely reckless and dangerous that was for them. Particularly for her.

"Gabby," Lucas stepped toward her, "are you okay? I'm sorry. I ... I didn't mean for that to go so far, really. I've wanted to kiss you since I saw you in the parking lot that first day. It's kinda like I was more, and more, unable to resist it. To resist ... *you.*" He paused, waiting for her response. "Gabrielle, please look at me." Lucas gently put his hand under her chin and lifted her head.

Gabrielle opened her eyes. He was frantically looking at her. She reached up and softly, slowly traced the side of his face with her fingertips. "Lucas, you only did what I wanted to do. I'm not mad, not at all. I just need a minute to think. I wasn't really expecting that. Not yet anyway."

"To be honest," Lucas said, "I don't know how it got out of hand. I was just going to steal a first kiss and *wammo!* I'm off in another world and, quite honestly, out of control. Are you an enchantress?"

Gabrielle could tell he was trying to lighten up the situation, but he didn't know he wasn't far off the mark. All she could do was smile although she could imagine the trouble she was going to find herself in for this and the trouble it may cause. Her head was spinning with thoughts, coming at her so fast all they did was get tangled. The *I shoulds* and *I wants* were competing so vehemently, it was almost painful.

"Lucas, can you wait for me out in the car? I need to pull myself together, and I think I can accomplish that quicker alone."

Lucas studied her face. She was sure it was an attempt to confirm it was really the reason why she wanted him to leave her alone. His expression told her he didn't buy it.

"*Really*, Lucas. Everything is fine. I'd kiss you right now to prove it to you, but I don't think that would be the smartest thing ... for either of us." After another moment, Lucas turned and opened the door.

"Take your time, Gabby." He looked back as he spoke, showing a flirty grin, "I could use a few to calm down, myself." Lucas walked toward his car, leaving Gabrielle with her warring thoughts. Thoughts about feeling so drawn to Lucas, a human whom she could be putting into terrible danger because of who she was, about the repercussions if she let things go too far—about becoming one of the Fallen.

After several minutes staring at her reflection in the entry's mirror, scolding herself, reiterating all of the bad outcomes that could result from the relationship between her and Lucas advancing, she made the decision to tell him she wouldn't be able to continue seeing him. Again.

"We're both going to get hurt when I have to end my time here, anyway," she told her reflection and sighed. The face looking back at her held sadness in its eyes.

It was what she should do. It was what Amaziah would certainly tell her to do. And then he wouldn't speak to her for at least a decade because he would be so angry about the line she'd crossed. Her time on Earth was too short, anyway. Three months would be gone before she knew it, and then she'd have to leave.

Her plan to end things with Lucas came to an end itself as soon as their eyes met again. The moment he looked at her, happiness and peace began to move through her just because he was close.

By just knowing he is here to be with me. Why shouldn't I have happiness even if it is only temporary?

She told him she'd forgotten her keys and ran back inside to grab them off the entry table, caught a glimpse of herself in the mirror again, told her reflection she was an idiot, and headed back out the door to spend the day with Lucas—a seventeen-year-old human she was apparently willing, for reasons she couldn't begin to explain, to risk everything for.

Even my life.

And with that realization she had another—this wasn't just her human body feeling something for Lucas. *She*, The Angel of Karma, was falling for this human. Hard. Her mind raced, and her stomach fluttered as she reached for the car's door handle.

"I'd ask if you're ready," Lucas said as she sat in the car and closed the door, "but last time I asked, you almost molested me ... *again!*"

"Whatever!" Gabrielle said through a laugh that slightly calmed her. She took a deep, quiet breath. "Just drive, I'm hungry. Where are you taking me anyway?"

"How do you feel about the meal of champions ... pizza? I may be a little superstitious, but I haven't lost a game yet if I eat an Italian pie before I play."

"Sounds yummy to me!"

Gabrielle liked pizza, but she would have tried pickled frog brains if it was while she sat across from him. Lucas had his hand on hers before he'd even pulled out of the driveway.

"This should be pretty safe?" He said it more as a question than a statement. Gabrielle put her other hand on top of his as a response.

"Are your parents home from Florida yet?" he asked.

Gabrielle smiled and shook her head. "No, they'll be there a bit longer."

Anyone who might wonder was told her parents were at their

resort for an extended stay as a way of explaining her continued lack of parental supervision. Gabrielle didn't think a seventeen-year-old living mostly on her own would cause any alarm, and so far, she'd been right. No one ever acted as if they gave it a second thought. Part of that was probably due to people's perception that she was remarkably mature for her age.

If they only knew ...

Chapter Twenty-Six

Gabrielle † Watchers

Lunch with Lucas was incident free. No unwanted appearances from the Fallen, no crazed teenage make-out sessions, no strange or worrisome Knowings. Just the two of them enjoying being together, laughing and holding hands while leaning toward each other as close as the table would allow. Gabrielle appreciated the piece of furniture acting as an obstacle since the urge to kiss him again escalated with every moment she was near him.

Before she knew it, they needed to leave to meet the others. Lucas drove through side streets to the church where Nonie and Nate's father was a pastor, parked his car away from the others, and faced Gabrielle.

"Hey," Lucas began, "I know we need to slow down, and I don't want to push things—at least, not on purpose. I want to be with you more, but I don't want to mess anything up. I feel that you're going to be very important to me." He waited for Gabrielle to answer.

"Thanks, Lucas. I—"

Tapping was coming on the window next to her. It was Nonie, smiling from ear to ear. Lucas lowered the window.

"Hey ya'll!" she chirped. "I hate to break up your party for two, but everyone else is here, so let's get movin'!" She bounded off toward the other teens waiting in the large grassy field next to the church.

Gabrielle saw Nate wave to them from the waiting group. She waved back and opened the door to get out. There were about twelve other kids—a mix of boys and girls—not counting herself, Lucas, Nonie, and Nate, who looked as though they were going to play. Another twenty or so were sitting on the invisible sideline. Lucas lifted her hand to his lips and softly kissed it, then turned it over to kiss her wrist. He breathed in deeply. "I love the way you smell ... like an angel."

A laugh escaped Gabrielle. Once again, the irony was lost to him. She kissed his hand and closed her door. As they made their way to the group of friends, Gabrielle noted how beautiful the day had turned out. The sun was high in the sky, and the air was cool with an almost constant breeze. She loved the way she felt at that moment—young and carefree, happy to be where she was, and especially, enjoying her company. She thought it was close to how happy she felt in Heaven. Only there was so much more to experience here.

Humans don't have it so bad, really, if they'd just learn to appreciate it.

She wasn't going to let her worries hinder her fun. Not today.

If she had taken the time to look closely at her surroundings, her mood would have been quite different. She may have spotted the black Mercedes she'd almost hit days before parked far back in the lot, far enough away that Gabrielle wouldn't notice it or its occupants. Inside appeared to be two average teenagers. Sitting. Watching. Listening. If Gabrielle had looked even closer, she would have recognized Mara and Javan. Javan was glaring at her and Lucas—with a look on his face that could kill.

"Run Gabby! Yessss! Touchdown!" Lucas yelled, running toward her, arms in the air victoriously signaling his winning touchdown throw to Gabrielle. The teammates converged on her in a celebratory group tackle; everyone piled on top of each other, shouting the lyrics to the obligatory *We Are the Champions* chorus. Gabrielle and Lucas found themselves on the bottom of the pile, pressed against each other once again.

Quietly, so no one else could hear, Lucas whispered to her. "They don't have any idea how dangerous this is for us." They stared at each other as the warm, tingling sensation ricocheted through Gabrielle until everyone peeled themselves off the pile. Lucas stood up and pulled Gabrielle up by her hands with so much force she landed in his arms.

Whoa! He's stronger than I thought he'd be.

He smiled and took her hand, breaking their embrace, and the two exchanged high-fives with their teammates, Lucas shooting Nonie and Nate playful "loser" comments. Before the exhausted and dusty group of teenagers departed, they scheduled the following Saturday's rematch.

Gabrielle was glad to have another game to look forward to. She was tired but invigorated. She, Lucas, Nonie, and Nate made their way back toward their cars, poking fun at each other the whole way—laughing as though all four had been friends for many years. Gabrielle felt very close to all of them and didn't want to dwell on the reality that her stay here was for such a short time, though she found herself doing so anyway.

Nonie's voice forced her thoughts back to them.

"Gabrielle—*hello*. You still with us? I asked you if you'd like to join us for dinner at our house. What do you say? It'll be fun. Mom's making her famous spaghetti, and I think she made chocolate cake."

"Sorry ... I went back to my home planet for a minute," Gabrielle said laughing. "Sure! I'd never turn down pasta, especially if it's famous. And I *absolutely* would be a fool to walk away from chocolate cake." Gabrielle smiled at her, and the smile Nonie returned showed she was pleased she was coming.

"Lucas," Nonie said, "make sure my mom remembered to ask

Emma. I think she's getting forgetful in her old age, but don't you *dare* tell her that I said so." She winked at him and grinned.

"I will. And, I won't."

Lucas still hadn't let go of Gabrielle's hand, not that she wanted him to, but she noticed that Nate glanced down at their entwined fingers several times, and she sensed something. Maybe jealousy. She wasn't sure, but she could tell he wasn't thrilled about the pairing.

I wonder why?

"That was a great game, Nate," Gabrielle said in an attempt to break the ice that seemed to randomly thicken between them. There were moments he was relaxed and talkative around her; other times, he wouldn't say much of anything. Occasionally, she would catch him studying her as if he knew what she was or was aware of more than he needed to be. She felt like she had to try harder to convince him that she was just like them.

"Yeah, thanks. But not good enough to kick your butts," he responded. A grin stretched across his face. "But don't get used to the feeling of victory, pretty lady," Nate continued. "Next time will be different."

"You flirting with my girl, Daniels?" Lucas let go of Gabrielle's hand and quickly had Nate bent over, his arm firmly around Nate's neck as he threw fake punches. Nate was overacting, twisting his body like he felt each blow down to his core. Repositioning, Nate picked Lucas up by the knees and threw him off balance, and the two were wrestling in the grass.

"There they go." Nonie laughed and leaned against the car next to Gabrielle. "There's no telling how long they're going to be wrestling like that. They really are just like brothers."

"It's nice to see him close to you all. I mean, with what happened to his parents and grandfather. He needs your family. Each of you means a lot to him. Maybe more than you know," Gabrielle kept her eyes on the theatrics in front of her as she spoke.

"*Sooo*—" Nonie began with the kind of tone that made you look at someone when they spoke because you knew they were about to say something that might make you, them, or both of you a little uncomfortable. "*My* girl, huh? I could tell the two of you were hitting it off, but I'm a little surprised at how fast it's progressing." Gabrielle and Nonie were looking at each other now. Nonie's hazel eyes searched hers, trying to read something in them. "Lucas doesn't fall this quickly, and really, I've never seen him this into anyone—*ever*."

"Yeah, it's caught us both a little off-guard. As over-dramatic as it sounds, it almost seems out of our control." Gabrielle sighed. "It's like our relationship has a purpose of its own. It's leading us, and we have to follow. What scares me is *what* is it leading us to? What *is* its purpose? I know it sounds crazy."

Gabrielle was looking at her feet now, watching her foot as she nervously pushed a rock back and forth with it. It did sound crazy, but it was the conclusion she was coming to; she normally had more control than she'd been executing.

"Don't get me wrong. He's happier than I've ever seen him. But you know he hasn't had a lot to be happy for, really. And I just don't want to see him get hurt." Nonie paused and rolled her eyes. "*Jeez!* I sound like my mom. But you get the point, right?" Nonie was looking at her inquisitively. "He's just as important to us as he's told you we are to him. So, even if I don't think I absolutely need to, I'm going to say it anyway. Back off if you're not completely into him, if you're only going to hurt him. Please."

Gabrielle glanced back to Nonie with her brows raised and smiled.

"Wow … I'm glad he knows how lucky he is to have you. I don't want to hurt him, Nonie. And I'm *definitely* really into him."

Gabrielle looked at Nate and Lucas who now stood, laughing as they dusted themselves off. Lucas smiled a crooked, flirty smile as he walked to her.

"Definitely," she said again.

Even as the word escaped her lips, Gabrielle knew it wasn't going to be that easy. That wanting him, and being able to be with him romantically, were two drastically different things in her world. She had absolutely no idea what the future held for her and Lucas. She was in dangerous territory for an angel, and she knew the price could be very steep for her.

"Definitely what?" Lucas asked, out of breath from the wrestling match.

"Definitely time to get cleaned up," Nonie replied. "'Cause Mom won't let us close to the dinner table if we don't."

"Yeah." Nate looked at his watch. "It's getting to be about that time. If we leave right now, I can even catch a nap!"

"Like you don't already sleep *enough!*" His sister kidded. "If it's the whole *beauty sleep* thing you're going for, you might want to try another angle, brother. I don't think that mug would improve if you snoozed right through the rest of high school."

It was the twins turn to wrestle as Nate picked Nonie up, slung her over his shoulder like a sand bag, and toted her in the direction of the grass. Nonie tried to wiggle out of his hold the whole way.

"Did you have fun today, Gabby?" Lucas asked through light laughter as he watched the twins. His laughter quieted. "I did," he said in a kind of sheepish voice, making him sound boyish and vulnerable, causing Gabrielle to take her gaze away from the tussling in front of her. When she looked at Lucas, he heart skipped ahead several beats.

"I think it's safe to say I enjoyed myself."

"Good. Now ... unless you can't see the trend that's presenting itself to you, the only person here who hasn't ended up in the grass being wrangled by Nate would be *you*. So maybe we should take off before he realizes his chance to torture you is about to be gone. That way, you'll have plenty of time to freshen up and rest before I come back to get you for dinner. Unless you'd rather drive yourself. I can take you around the corner to show you where we live."

"Let's go."

They headed to his car and yelled good-bye to the siblings. Nate had Nonie pinned in some kind of wrestling hold, and she was yelling for mercy although she was hard to understand through her giggles. Gabrielle smiled but was glad she hadn't stayed long enough to become Nate's next victim.

"See ya 'bout six!" Nate said without looking up.

Lucas started the car and turned it toward the exit. Out of nowhere, a large black blur passed inches in front of the windshield.

"*Whoa!*" Lucas slammed on the brakes.

They followed the path of the object to its stopping point on the asphalt. The black blur turned out to be a crow joining the rest of its flock. Gabrielle was feeling more uncomfortable about seeing them so frequently. She counted them.

Ten.

Very uncomfortable.

"Is it normal to have so many crows around?" she asked.

Lucas shrugged while continuing to observe the murder of crows, which was staring back at them.

"I don't know … I've noticed them kinda hanging around from time to time for most of my life, so I guess it is. Seems like I see them more lately, though."

He started moving the car forward again, and as he looked away from the flock and back to Gabrielle, she watched them take off in unison as if they were one creature.

Gabrielle shivered.

She felt the threat growing around her, and she was more aware of it when she was near Lucas. It was something she didn't like or understand. She could be putting him in so much danger just by being with him. She wondered if her relationship with Lucas was the reason he was in danger in the dreams she'd been having.

"So what would you like to do, have me pick you up or drive?" Lucas asked.

"In order for me to find my way around better, maybe I should drive myself. If you don't care?" Gabrielle tried to banish the images that she'd conjured up from her dreams. She had a strange feeling—like she was being watched or that something was coming for her. She figured it would be better for her, and safer for him, if she had some time to use her discernment on the way to the Daniels' house. Just in case. If she was with him, she wouldn't be able to use its full effect. It would be too dangerous if a demon noticed her.

His smile showed he wasn't upset.

Lucas made a right out of the parking lot and then another right at the next street. The sign read: Haber Drive.

Houses with perfectly manicured lawns lined both sides of the street, each with their own distinct character. Some were older, but quite a few had been through what appeared to be significant renovations and additions. Lucas stopped at the sixth house on the right and pointed across the street.

"The white house there, the one with the ivy growing up the trellis on the side, that's Nonie and Nate's house."

Gabrielle liked it. It had an inviting appearance. She had a flash of how it would be decorated at Christmas. Lots of wreaths and lights hung on the house, and she could hear Christmas music playing inside, even through the closed windows and doors. She smiled at how festive it was.

"Boy … they sure know how to do it up with the Christmas decorations, don't they?" She said without thinking.

"Well … *yes*. But, how would you know what their house looks like at Christmas?"

Gabrielle felt her insides turn cold, realizing what she'd said, and that there was no way she *should* know.

"Oh, I just meant that I bet they do it up. The house would look great with lights hanging from the eaves. In all the windows, if it were mine, I would put lit wreaths with just a red bow on every one of them. With Mr. Daniels being a pastor, I figure they really get into the spirit of things."

Gabrielle held her breath as the seconds passed. She could tell by his expression that her explanation didn't work, but after a few more moments, he let it go.

"Yeah, they do it pretty much the way you just described."

Gabrielle didn't like the look on his face. Why wasn't she on her game when she was with him? She was so at ease when he was around. Lucas turned his attention toward the houses opposite of the Daniels' home and pointed to the one they parked in front of.

It was smaller than the Daniels' house but every bit as inviting. It was a brick bungalow with a nice big front porch and two rocking chairs waiting to be sat on. Three large ferns hung above the railing. Like all the others she'd seen on the street, the lawn was neatly trimmed and edged.

"This is my house."

"I love it!" She genuinely did. She wondered what the inside looked like and where his room was, but she stopped her imaginings from following that thought through any further.

"So, you think you can find us all right tonight?"

"Yeah, I do." Gabrielle hoped he wouldn't bring the Christmas decoration thing back up as he turned in the street to take her home. She was relieved when he pulled into her drive and the subject seemed forgotten.

He kissed her hand before she got out of the car, seemingly as afraid as she was that things would get out of control if their lips touched.

"I'll see you about six," he said.

Gabrielle nodded and left. As she made her way into her house, she began to tense, already sensing Amaziah. She had just closed the door behind her when she heard his voice from his usual spot in the kitchen calling out to her.

"Gabrielle—we need to talk." There was distinct concern in his voice.

Damn ... this isn't going to be good.

Chapter Twenty-seven

GABRIELLE ✝ REALITY CHECK

Gabrielle wasn't ready for a conversation about her and Lucas. It didn't matter, though—it was coming anyway. She paused time, anticipating a long discussion.

"Coming, Amaziah."

How was she going to explain the relationship developing between her and Lucas? She didn't want to think about it, hoping Amaziah didn't have all the details. She let her mind wander to other matters and sat on the stool across the counter from him, but couldn't calm her racing heart. The muscles in Amaziah's face were tense with a deep furrow between his brows, indicating his worries.

"Gabrielle, there is information you need to be made aware of concerning your dream, as well as other matters I have been sent to take care of."

She was surprised and relieved it wasn't about Lucas but couldn't recall ever seeing Amaziah so worried, making her wonder if she wanted to know what he'd learned, realizing that his intensity scared her more than anything she could ever remember. Amaziah wasn't one to show concern outwardly.

"What did you find out?"

"The Book you saw in your vision—The Book of Barabbadon—it seems it was not destroyed. Yahuwah was betrayed." Amaziah spoke in a hurried, ragged breath. "He has called on the Angels of the Thrones to help Him find who deceived Him and search for the Book."

Gabrielle felt her stomach drop to the floor. The Thrones was her Choir. She would have to return—for good, she guessed. "But I haven't accomplished what needs to be done." She couldn't tell him how she wasn't only frustrated because she hadn't finished what she started, but that she also was saddened that things were going to end far sooner for her and Lucas than she had expected.

"He has excused you, only because you are the only one who can enforce karma. But Gabrielle, these are dangerous times for all of us, and I am asking you to leave and come back with me to Heaven, now, where you'll be safe. You are vulnerable here."

Gabrielle let out a soft, slow sigh of relief, hoping he wouldn't notice.

She was relieved she wasn't going to have to explain about her and Lucas. But there were even bigger concerns growing about what her visions were warning of. She could sense the disquiet within Amaziah, making her wish the concern in his voice *had* been what she first suspected—a relationship she had no business having. It was selfish of her to be relieved when so much was going on that was far more important.

I need to get my head straight.

"If I'm not being ordered back, Amaziah, I'm going to stay. I have to. We can't lose this war."

Amaziah looked down at his clenched hands on the counter in front of him, slowly shaking his head. She knew it wasn't what he wanted to hear, and she hated upsetting him. She walked to where he sat and hugged him. He put an arm around her and hugged her back.

"I knew that was what you would say. But I had to try. I know what you are doing here is valuable and will aid us immensely. I am very proud of you, Gabrielle. You have lived up to everything I thought you would—and more. So that you know, Yahuwah is happy when your name is spoken. Your efforts are noticed—and appreciated."

"Thank you. Thank you for your concern and for your praise. It means so much to know that you and Yahuwah are pleased with me. And thank you for understanding I have to stay."

He smiled and let go of her as he stood and slowly walked to the door to the porch. "Gabrielle, I have been instructed to inform you that you are being given more powers and abilities to help keep you safe while you are here. This isn't done often, so you can imagine how much faith Yahuwah must have in you." He looked over his shoulder.

Gabrielle nodded her head in understanding although she was stunned. Amaziah continued.

"You will no longer lose constant communication with any of your brethren while in your human form, and you can do so without ascending. You are granted control over the four elements—air, water, earth, and fire. You now have the ability to make people forget whatever you choose, as long as it's in their best interest or to keep them from exposing you as an angel. And, as I understand you discovered on the mountain top last night before I had the chance to tell you, you can summon the Earth's energy to you in order to increase your powers. You can use these additional abilities at your discretion just as the others you have always had."

So ... that's why I was able to evoke more power.

Gabrielle was floored. She was already one of the most powerful of Yahuwah's angels, but now, she was entrusted on a level she never imagined she'd reach. She was humbled and gave thanks even before Amaziah finished.

"There's one more ability I can bestow on you—the ability to Hush. It has been fun for me to tease you about how much you wanted this ability, but it was decided it may serve you well while you are here. Now my ability is yours as well."

Gabrielle almost laughed as she looked up to catch her friend's playful gaze. She would have been more playful towards Amaziah, maybe even Hushing him for a moment, but this wasn't a playful occasion. She found her mood too heavy to tease him right now. This was serious. And the times she found herself in were dangerous. More than she'd already suspected if Yahuwah felt this was necessary.

Amaziah took her hands in his. "I need to be going now. I won't be stopping in for a while unless some of this is resolved quickly. I'll send reports if I learn anything new, and you know you can simply call to me through thought, and I will hear you. Just as I always have. Your abilities to communicate are almost as high now as any can obtain. Remember to use them and the others He added to your arsenal. It's a huge responsibility to be entrusted with so much. Other than me, there has only been one other angel He made this powerful, and we know what happened to him. Use them with clarity and forethought, and if you always put Yahuwah and His ways first in your use of them, you will be fine."

Gabrielle nodded in understanding. Ramai was the only other angel granted this amount of ability and power ... and he became the Dark Lord. Now, Gabrielle knew Amaziah's rank, and she had a difficult time perceiving that she was now his equal. At least she was in this way. She hugged Amaziah, sorry he had to leave so soon. Just as he was about to ascend, he stopped. Without turning around, he addressed her again.

"As far as Lucas and you are concerned ... of course I know."

Gabrielle tensed.

"I make it my job to know how you are doing. You know that. Please ... be *very* careful. You are being allowed extra privileges with this relationship, but only because He thinks it will help you learn what is needed faster so you can return home sooner. Don't go too far, Gabrielle. You know what I mean ... and you know the ending won't be happy if you do—for him *or* you."

"I will, Amaziah. I'm sorry I didn't tell you about it right away."

"I know why you didn't, and I know how close you have already let the two of you become. Again, please think of where this will leave you both when your time here has ended, and of the danger you are exposing both of you to. I trust you to always keep that in mind as you go forward, and to do what you need to with the new abilities you now have ... *when* the time comes."

And he was gone.

She understood what he meant about using her abilities when the time came. He was advising her to make Lucas forget her when she had to leave, but that still left a problem.

I won't be able to forget him.

She should have known he knew about Lucas and the relationship developing between them. How could she ever believe Yahuwah wouldn't know of it even if Amaziah didn't?

That was foolish. This body makes me think and do foolish things.

Being in human form was making her a little *too* human in ways she hadn't expected.

But ... this is what I am here for, to figure out what makes humans do the things they do.

Gabrielle called Sheridan so she could get her work done. She showed up immediately, and the two angels got busy taking care of the day's tasks. Sheridan was particularly quiet, but Gabrielle had too many other things on her mind to worry about it if she didn't want to bring it up herself. She was sure Sheridan had heard about the honor that had been bestowed on her today, and she imagined her silence was due to her continued lack of confidence in Gabrielle. It would not surprise her if Sheridan was still shaken by what happened between the two of them. Sheridan had thought she'd kept her feelings about her from being known, but now she knew Gabrielle had been aware of how she felt for quite some time. She'd never brought it up to Sheridan before because she'd always remained committed to their job and loyal to her as far as she knew. Regardless of Sheridan's feelings, she was an outstanding second in command. She went too far last night, though.

Enough was enough.

When the work had been completed, Sheridan left.

Gabrielle let herself fall listlessly onto the couch. *Tomorrow ... my mood will be a challenge, at best.*

Chapter Twenty-eight

Gabrielle + More Surprises

Gabrielle set mortal time in motion again. She still had an hour and a half to get ready for dinner. It was going to be hard to keep her mind off all that had unfolded since she left her human friends, even with Lucas there.

She tried to replay the vague images from the dreams—the Book, the battle between Divine angels and the Fallen, fighting Javan, and Lucas's lifeless body lying below her—hoping to understand what it all meant.

How is it all connected?

She still wondered what role she was supposed to play in Lucas's life. She was beginning to believe it had something to do with the Book. *Everything seems to come back to the Book of Barabbadon.*

She hadn't asked Amaziah what was in the Book, but she wasn't going to call on him for it now. She'd have to wait until she saw him again. After taking a long, cold shower in hopes of shocking the troublesome thoughts out of her mind, Gabrielle stood in her closet trying to figure out what to wear.

After several minutes, she realized she was focusing on something trivial and snatched a black dress off a hanger. She was annoyed with herself for worrying about what to wear when so much was going on that threads snapped as she yanked it over her head. She ran a brush through her hair, applied mascara and some lip gloss, and started downstairs. She knew she wasn't trying very hard to look nice, but she didn't care right now.

She turned on Haber Drive at five fifty-five just as Lucas was crossing the road. He recognized her car and waited for her to pull up.

"Hi," Gabrielle said as Lucas opened her door.

"Hi back." Gabrielle tried to push the earlier events out of her mind without much success.

Lucas whistled and stepped back when Gabrielle got out of the car, looking her up and down with a smile. Gabrielle was a bit self-conscious as the flutters he always gave her cranked up their activity.

"Are you *trying* to be the death of me?" he asked jokingly.

Gabrielle didn't find it at all funny. It brought a flood of images that she was trying to block of battles and blood, of those she cared for most injured, possibly dying. The tone accompanying her response clearly conveyed her feelings.

"Don't *ever* say anything like that, Lucas." She scowled at him and slammed the car door. "It *isn't* funny."

"Hey ..." Lucas came toward her, and Gabrielle could tell he was concerned. "I only meant because you look ... well ... *amazing*. After what happened this morning, I don't know how much more I can take. I was only trying to compliment you. You're even more breathtaking than usual." Lucas put his hands on her arms, and Gabrielle felt heat begin to flow through her body, soothing her.

"I'm sorry. I didn't mean to snap. Any reference to you and death is off limits, though. Okay? Even if it is a joke."

Lucas still looked concerned, "Sure, I'll remember that." He softly kissed her forehead. Gabrielle closed her eyes and was surprised as a tear slipped down her cheek. She turned to open the door to her car to get her purse, taking the opportunity to wipe it away before he could see it. She didn't need him to know how upset she was. He wouldn't understand how much more was involved. That it wasn't only his death comment, but that she had premonitions and dreams of him in which she thought he *had* died, and how close she'd come to losing Grayson, Phalen, and Rissie the night before.

Gabrielle turned and smiled at him the best she could without it looking forced.

"Are you nervous?" he asked.

Gabrielle took his misread and ran with it. "Yeah, I guess I am a little."

"There's nothing to be concerned about. Ben and Lizzie are fantastic people; Chloe is an absolute doll; and Gran … well, she's related to me, so you know she could be no less than amazing."

Gabrielle couldn't help but laugh.

"*There* it is. That's what I wanted to hear. The sound of your laughter." He kissed her forehead again and took her hand to lead her across the street. "Come on, let's go."

"Okay." Gabrielle wasn't surprised being near him made her feel better even with the heavy burden of her knowledge and thoughts.

Lucas didn't knock on the Daniels' door. Gabrielle guessed he never had. The entry opened directly into a large open family room where she could see the back of Nonie's and Nate's head. They sat on one of two crimson couches, watching a football game. The furnishings were casual and oversized, the kind that seemed to invite you to get in and get cozy. As Gabrielle looked at her surroundings, she caught impressions of other rooms and could tell right away the Daniels family wasn't afraid to use color. She breathed in deeply through her nose, enjoying the smells of garlic and herbs coming from the kitchen.

"Sup!" Lucas called out to announce their arrival.

The twins turned around and smiled. A little blond-haired head popped up to say hi, too. She took one look at Lucas and scurried over the back of the couch to get to him. "Lucas!"

Apparently, this was Chloe, and she clearly adored Lucas as much as the twins. Chloe jumped into Lucas's open arms and slung her little ones around his neck.

"Hey, Chloe!" Lucas was grinning from ear to ear. "Why aren't you cooking my dinner?" Chloe started giggling and squirming as Lucas tickled her sides.

"I don't know how to cook, *silly*!" she said, giggling through every word.

Lucas put her back on the ground, and Chloe looked up inquisitively at Gabrielle, still smiling.

"Are you Gabrielle?"

Gabrielle smiled and nodded.

"You *are* pretty. Nate said you were."

Gabrielle wasn't sure how to take knowing that Nate thought she was pretty. She wasn't even sure that Nate liked her being with Lucas. "Thank you! I think you're very pretty, too." Gabrielle couldn't help but smile even bigger at the youngest of the Daniels clan.

Chloe skipped toward what looked to be the kitchen and yelled into it. "*Mommy! Daddy!* Lucas and his pretty *g-i-r-l-f-r-i-e-n-d* are here!" She spelled out the word with dramatic little girl over-emphasis.

Gabrielle looked at Lucas who had a faint red hue rising in his cheeks. Nate and Nonie were laughing and high-fiving each other. Apparently, they were the ones who'd put Chloe up to the girlfriend reference.

"Nothing like a seven-year-old to put you on the spot," Nate yelled to Lucas without turning around.

An average height, slender woman with shoulder-length light brown hair came out of the kitchen, followed by a tall man who must have been at least six foot three. His hair was darker blond, like Nate's. They both seemed to be in their late thirties.

"You must be Gabrielle," Nate and Nonie's mom said, smiling as she and her husband approached. She had her hand outstretched.

Gabrielle walked toward them to meet their greeting.

"I'm Lizzie, and this is Ben," Lizzie said while glancing at her husband.

Gabrielle smiled back and shook their hands. "Nice to meet you. I'm Gabrielle Trayner. Thank you for having me to dinner. It smells wonderful, Mrs. Daniels."

"We're glad you came, and please, call us Lizzie and Ben. We're not much for formalities around here. I hope you like spaghetti."

"Very much, especially if it's famous, which I hear yours is."

"Zee doesn't fix anything that isn't good." Ben flashed a smile at his wife and kissed her on the cheek. "Come on in and get comfortable," he continued, motioning to the seating in the family room. "We aren't formal, but we are sports nuts, so I hope you enjoy watching them. Do you like football?"

Gabrielle shot Nate and Nonie a playful look. "Well, after the beating I was able to inflict today, I'm quickly becoming a fan."

Nate groaned, and Nonie threw a pillow at Gabrielle as she stuck out her tongue for added effect.

"We'll see how much you like it after next Saturday's re-match, girlie," Nonie said.

"Well, it looks like you're going to fit in just fine around here, Gabrielle," Lizzie said. "I'm going to finish getting dinner ready. Lucas, I sent Emma to get some more milk, in case you're wondering where she is. She should be back anytime." Lizzie's gaze returned to Gabrielle. "She's really looking forward to meeting you," she stated softly and smiled.

Ben and Lizzie returned to the kitchen, and Gabrielle and Lucas sat on the couch opposite the twins and their sister. Gabrielle didn't know what teams were playing, but Nonie and Nate were glued to what was going on.

"Tennessee and Alabama," Lucas whispered as if he knew what she was thinking.

"Thanks," she whispered back. She wasn't paying attention to the TV, though. There was something bothering her. She felt the way she had earlier in the day when they were at the church—as if she was being watched.

The front door opened, catching Gabrielle's attention.

"I'm back!"

She saw a lovely woman walking in the front door, noticing she hadn't knocked, either. Emma made her way to where they were now standing by the couch. Gabrielle could see, even from a distance, how blue Emma's eyes were. She placed her in her mid-fifties although her face didn't have many wrinkles to show her age. Her hair was cut in a choppy pixie and was as white as snow. Her red lipstick contrasted her hair and rounded off a sophisticated look. She was quite striking, very un-grandmotherly in appearance, with a peaceful demeanor.

"Gabrielle," she said as she approached. "What a pleasure it is to meet the girl who's made my grandson beam." Emma hugged Gabrielle. She immediately liked Emma—very much. She felt an immediate kinship between them.

"It's so nice to meet you, too."

"Hi, Gran." Lucas leaned and gave Emma a kiss on the cheek. "I would've gone to get this for you." He took the milk from her and started toward the kitchen.

"Oh, I didn't want Gabrielle to be waiting for you." Emma smiled at her again.

There was something about Emma that Gabrielle couldn't quite figure out that made her want to talk to her. Not about Lucas, TV, movies, or news—she wanted to sit with her and tell her about her visions, Javan, the Book, demons somehow becoming more powerful, and the war. Things Gabrielle knew she couldn't speak of to her.

"Time for dinner!" Lizzie called.

They went into the kitchen and sat at a long wooden table. Lizzie had already set large bowls of spaghetti, salad, and a basket almost overflowing with garlic bread on the table. It smelled and looked wonderful. Ben said grace, and after all the food had been passed around, the family and their guest settled into comfortable conversation.

Gabrielle quickly found out that the twins got their bantering lessons straight from their parents and that she wasn't immune as a target. By the end of dinner and dessert, everyone was laughing and poking fun at each other. Ben even praised Gabrielle for a few of the zingers she'd thrown out.

The time passed quickly, and before she knew it, it was almost eight. The twins, Lucas, and Gabrielle cleaned up the kitchen while Emma, Lizzie, and Ben took their coffee to the family room, and Chloe went to her room.

Lucas whispered in her ear as they stood next to each other drying the dishes Nonie was washing and Nate was putting away, "They *really* like you. I can tell. Especially Gran."

His mouth being so close to her ear, him speaking so breathy and warm into it, made Gabrielle's eyes close as a sensational chill ran through her body. She forced her eyes to open again.

"I like them, too," she whispered back as she regained control over her body.

She did like them. It had been a pleasant evening full of smiles and laughter. But the good feeling she had with the two families had been interrupted repeatedly throughout dinner by a worrisome one. She continued to feel watched ... stalked. She was sure someone, or something, was lurking just on the fringes of her awareness. It disturbed her, but she couldn't raise her veils to try to discern who or what it might be without putting everyone at risk. Trying to figure it out would have to wait.

After the dishes were done, they joined the rest of the family to watch another game. Ben, Lizzie, and Emma were on the couch Nonie and Nate had been on earlier, so the teens sat together on the other one. The conversation and laughter continued for the rest of the evening, and Gabrielle was surprised when it was time to leave. She said her goodbyes and thanked Ben and Lizzie, then walked to her car with Lucas.

"It's been a really great day, Lucas," Gabrielle said.

She leaned against her car, and Lucas stood in front of her, reaching for her hands.

"Yeah." He kissed one hand. "It was." Then the other. "You really do look amazing tonight. I could barely keep my eyes off of you."

Gabrielle leaned forward and whispered in his ear. "So ... are you ever going to kiss me somewhere closer to my lips again?"

She barely finished speaking before his mouth was on hers. The kiss was soft but long. Her mind spun, and the warmth flowing through her found very specific places to burn. Gabrielle pulled away, placing her forehead to his chest when she felt herself beginning to lose control as she had that morning. Amaziah's words of caution repeated in her head.

"I better go." She sighed.

"I guess so." He was running his fingers gently through her hair, giving her the same raised bumps on her arms she had the first day of her incarnation; this time, it wasn't from mint chocolate chip ice cream.

As much as she hated to leave him, she did need to go. Tomorrow was Sunday, the only day of the entire week she would have to herself. She planned to put out more feelers about the Book, and maybe see if she could find out what Javan was up to.

Thinking of Javan reminded her that she needed to see if she could get more information from Lucas about Mara, but it was too late to do it now. Gabrielle ran her hands slowly up and down his chest, feeling how solid with muscles he was and his heart beating steady and smooth. She wondered what it would feel like to do the same thing without his shirt, which sent a fresh flash of heat through her. She shook the thought out of her mind. Once again, being in human form was proving to be a challenge for her self-control.

"You okay?" Lucas asked.

"Yeah," she laughed, "I'm great, actually."

"See you Monday?" Lucas kissed her hands again and then her forehead.

"Definitely."

He kissed her gently again before she got into her car and pulled away.

Gabrielle made it only a couple of houses down before she lifted the veil in her mind and felt the full intensity of being watched. There was no mistaking someone was out there. When she looked in her rear view mirror, she knew why.

Chapter Twenty-nine

GABRIELLE ✟ OLD FLAME

A couple of houses down from the Daniels' home sat a black Mercedes. Javan must have been using a glamour, or she would have visually seen him.

Great ... more surprises.

Gabrielle reached the top of the street and turned the corner, parking as fast as she could. Before Lucas had even closed the door to his house, Gabrielle was manifesting near the Mercedes. Everything around her was unmoving, except for Mara and Javan, as mortal time was suspended.

They stepped out of the car at the same time. Javan's black clothes matched his hair, his bad-boy demeanor enhanced by a faint scar that ran jaggedly from his left ear across part of his jaw line and faded at his Adam's apple. Gabrielle was sure his striking looks, added to the attitude, would have human girls falling all over him. She was also sure he enjoyed it excessively, and she hated thinking of what he might be doing to them.

"Intimate little evening you had tonight, *babe*. Not to mention the fun you had today. Who knew you would enjoy ... *playing* with the likes of humans. Really, Gabrielle, I expected much more from you." Javan slowly, deliberately, walked toward Gabrielle.

"Then I guess that gets us closer to even since you more than let me down decades ago, Javan. What do you want?" Gabrielle motioned for him not to come any closer to her. He smiled and complied.

"There was a time you couldn't wait for me to be near you. To caress and kiss you similar to how that *boy* was moments ago. Only, I must say, you seemed to derive much more enjoyment when I was doing the touching." He shot her a knowing, evil grin.

Gabrielle's heart sank from seeing what Javan had become. She had a hard time accepting that the demon she saw before her was the angel she had cherished for so long. She didn't understand what had happened to him, but it didn't matter. He was her enemy now.

And I am his.

Gabrielle hardened herself. "I wouldn't be so sure of that, Javan. What do you want?" She was already beginning to feel the effects of the bad karma she had handed out earlier, and if things escalated with Javan, it would soon be a bigger problem. She needed to put an end to this quickly. She wasn't ready to do battle with him, not yet. She needed time to let what he had become sink in so she could handle what she would possibly have to do to him.

Mara remained behind the open passenger door. She was beautiful, her chartreuse eyes emphasized by the black hood of her sweatshirt resting just above her brows. The effect drew attention to the intensity of her glare. She didn't make any movement toward Gabrielle, but the demon didn't take her eyes off her, either.

Mara looks like an evil version of me.

Javan began to pace slowly in front of Gabrielle.

"What do I want? I want a lot of things, Gabrielle. Or should I call you *Gabby*, too?" He cut his eyes at her. "I want to rule over humans. I want dominion over Heaven, Earth, and Hell. I want *Yahuwah*, and Ramai to fall on their knees before me." He stopped pacing and stood in front of Gabrielle. She thought she saw the harshness of his eyes soften slightly. "I want you, Gabrielle."

His tone was kind, and she thought she heard sincerity in it. The pain of no longer having the love they once shared closed in around her, making it hard to breathe. Gabrielle noticed Mara flinch at his last statement, and she wondered how close the two demons were.

"You *can't* have me, Javan. We can't be together, now. You knew that when you made the decision to rebel, to fall."

"Unless you join me." Javan moved closer to Gabrielle and put his hands on her arms.

The dark feeling it caused surged through her body and made her stomach churn. She felt sick.

"*Imagine*, Gabrielle, how it would feel to be together again. You could live without all the rules that restrain you. I could still be your Reyah ... and you could still be mine."

"Get your hands off me, Javan. Unless you want things to get *really* messy." Gabrielle glared at him. If he didn't take his hands off her quickly, Lizzie's dinner was going to revisit her for sure. "*Seriously* ... your touch isn't pleasurable anymore, Javan. It makes me feel vile."

She saw his eyes harden again, and he let her go. He took a few steps back and stopped.

"If you joined with me, Gabrielle, I assure you my touch would bring you deeper ecstasy than you ever imagined possible." He smiled and glanced back at the demon behind him. "Just ask Mara."

She heard Mara snicker.

Guess that answers that question, she thought with disgust.

Gabrielle felt her stomach toss again as it threatened to unleash its contents.

"You basically have two choices ... *Gabby*. Stay on the side you're on, and die. Or take your place with me, and *live*. I'll give you some time to think about it, my sweet—*angel*. But not too much. Time is running out for your God—and your kind."

Javan made his way back to his car, and both he and Mara disappeared behind the dark tinted glass.

Gabrielle didn't know how long she stood in the street, but when she finally moved, she realized she was trembling. She turned to walk to her car, needing the time it would take to get back to it on two human feet. She glanced at Lucas standing perfectly still in his doorway, mid-turn, about to close the door behind him, and worried about the danger he was now in.

And it's because of me.

As she turned her attention back to the road in front of her, she thought she saw a shadow move past the window next to Lucas. Gabrielle stopped abruptly. Her mind sprinted through possibilities of who, or what, could be moving in Lucas's house.

Nothing should be.

Gabrielle made her way up the sidewalk to the brick bungalow and cautiously walked up the porch steps. Carefully, she inched around Lucas and stepped into the family room. The decor was cozy and in deep, rich colors. It reminded her of the way an English manor would be decorated, only more relaxed. It felt very comfortable even though she was tense.

"Hello, dear."

Chapter Thirty

GABRIELLE ✝ THE NEPHILIM

Gabrielle jumped at the sound of the voice. She looked over to see Emma, sitting in an overstuffed chair located in the far front corner of the room, smiling at Gabrielle.

"Emma, is there something you need to tell me?" Gabrielle's mind swiftly jumped from one possibility to the next. There could be only one answer to explain this though. Gabrielle was wide-eyed, stunned.

"Isn't it obvious?" Emma got up, walked to Gabrielle, and touched her cheek with her hand. "I have Divine blood. There would be no other way I could be talking to you like this." Emma gestured to everything suspended in time. "Is there?"

Gabrielle was really getting tired of surprises.

"Of course not," she said through an exasperated sigh and walked to the closest chair, one at the dining room table, and plopped down on it. "You're not one of the Fallen. I can tell that much." She studied Emma, realizing little things that she should have noticed earlier. Like the way her eyes sparkled with a light not quite human, or how warm her touch was, or—more than everything else and completely obvious to her now—the melodic tone to her voice. She finally relaxed and smiled at Emma, ready to ask the question she wanted and needed to know. "So what happened? How did you come to live as a human?"

"No, Gabrielle. I wasn't cast out of Heaven by Yahuwah or sent here as a punishment. I was an angel, though. I *chose* to live as a human, but I still have my memories of my time as an angel. A few other things stayed with me, as well."

"Well, I guess that explains why I wanted to bare my soul to you back at the Daniels' home. I felt the kinship between us. Why did you give up living as an angel with Yahuwah to be here?"

"Oh ... I think you're closer to understanding my reason than you realize." Emma motioned to Lucas and sat in the chair across the table. "I fell in love with a human. Much like I expect you are with my Lucas." She smiled at Gabrielle, reached across the table, and took her hands in her own.

Gabrielle nodded her head.

"If you're the Gabrielle I'm thinking you are, I'm honored to be in your presence and frightened by the things I imagine could have brought you to the decision to be here. *Are* you Gabrielle, The Angel of Karma?"

Gabrielle nodded again, then filled Emma in on the reasons she decided to live as she was and all she knew of the Book of Barabbadon. When she finished, Emma looked tired and worried. She stood and walked over to Lucas, looking back at her once she reached him.

"Who was the demon you spoke to outside?"

Gabrielle smiled weakly, not wanting to dwell on thoughts of Javan any longer. "That was Javan. My former Reyah."

Emma knew what it would mean to lose a Reyah and let the subject drop, changing it quickly to a new one. "I have to tell you, Gabrielle, I liked you already as Lucas's friend, very much." She smiled, then turned her attention back to Lucas, studying his face as if it was the first time she'd ever seen him. "Even though we've just met, I had a good feeling about you. I'm sure that was me sensing our kinship, too. But now I'm very concerned about his safety. You know the danger he's in because of you." She turned her full attention to Gabrielle. Her expression clearly showed her fears and that she had more to say. "But he already was … because of who *he* is." A tear spilled free of her eye and fell down her cheek.

"What do you mean?" Gabrielle waited as Emma regained control of her emotions.

"I've already told you how I made the decision to become a human because I fell in love with one, but there's more to it." Emma paused, seemingly trying to decide where to begin. "There's a prophecy. You, and every person who believes in Yahuwah, know of it. Most of the rest of the world does, as well. The prophecy of the coming of the Destroyer and the Great War coming to an end." She sat back down at the table with Gabrielle, her expression stoic as she continued.

"As an angel, I'd just risen in rank within the Choir of the Powers and was sent to protect Mason, Lucas's grandfather, who was just a child at the time. I wasn't told much at first, except his bloodline would play a role in the coming of the Destroyer. I didn't know if that meant his lineage would be positive, or negative, toward this prophecy. And it didn't matter. It was what Yahuwah requested of me, so it's what I did.

"Over time, after Mason grew into a man and I had some interaction with him as a human myself …" Emma paused. "I'm sure you've come to realize when you choose to take human form, you also take on their emotions, desires, and tendencies."

Gabrielle nodded.

"Well," she continued, "to get to the point, it was while I would visit him in human form that I fell in love with him and he with me. After that happened, it was impossible to deny what my heart wanted, and I asked Yahuwah to grant me life as a human so I could be with Mason. He did as I asked, but only if I agreed to retain my memories of my life as an angel so I could remember Mason's importance. That way, even though I no longer had most of the abilities I once enjoyed, I could still do what I was able to in order to continue to protect Mason, along with the new guardian assigned to him. I agreed, of course, and began my life with him."

Emma excused herself and returned a few moments later with two glasses of sweet tea. "I was getting thirsty and thought you might be, too." She handed Gabrielle the glass. After taking a long drink, Emma continued her story.

"For a while, everything was just as I'd imagined it would be. Mason was nineteen, almost twenty, when I started my permanent human life with him. He had no idea about my origins, and I had no intention of telling him. Even though he was a believer in Yahuwah, the human mind finds a great deal of difficulty wrapping itself around the reality of Heavenly creatures or anything else they may consider fantastical. I didn't want him to be driven away from me because of his possible inability to believe me. So I kept it from him." A distant look came over her. She smiled, losing herself in thoughts. Gabrielle didn't cut into her attention to the past.

Memories are all she has of him now.

Several minutes passed, and Emma came back to the present.

"I'm sorry, Gabrielle. Where was I? Oh, yes." She cleared her throat in preparation to continue. "We were married just after he turned twenty. Almost a year later, Lucas's mom, Hannah, was born. She was the most beautiful baby; her eyes were *so* blue. The color of Lucas's, actually. We *loved* having a child and would have had many more, but it wasn't in Yahuwah's plan. We watched Hannah grow into a beautiful young woman and had many happy years, but I was always watching for something else—the danger I knew we were all still in. The problem was that I didn't ever know what I was protecting Mason, and Hannah, *from* to begin with. Was it another human or group of humans? Was it demons? Or was it the Dark Lord, himself? It was very tiring, always being suspicious of the people who came into our lives, constantly looking over my shoulder, reading too much into *coincidences*. But having Mason and Hannah made it all worth it." She smiled at Gabrielle. "I wouldn't change a second of it. At least until ..." Darkness washed over her expression. "Until they were taken from me."

Gabrielle waited for her to continue. She was paying close attention to what Emma was telling her, sensing it would all tie together, somehow, with what was currently happening—and what she'd seen fragments of in her dreams.

"Lucas," Emma continued, "was only three months old when it happened. My Hannah and her husband, Stephen—Lucas's father—were only twenty. The same age I was when I had her. It was in this very room that I found them. There was no blood … only death. I don't know how he took their lives. He could have done it in many ways because, although he was in human form, he was certainly not one. His speed and strength would have given him away even if I hadn't sensed he was once brethren. He must have sensed the Divine blood in me and thought we would be many against him at any time if he didn't leave, so he did. He thought he'd accomplished what he'd set out to do when he came here—destroy Mason Hunt and any of his descendants. But he didn't leave before I was able to strike him, and I left him with an ugly reminder of his supposed victory.

"What he didn't know was that the child he killed, also three months of age, wasn't Hannah and Stephen's baby. He was a neighbor's child, left with us for a few hours while they went out. Lucas had been safe, all along, with me. An hour earlier, I left with Lucas to have his pediatrician look at a nasty rash that covered his back. A rash that had disappeared completely by the time he was examined. I've often wondered if it was a Divine way of getting him to safety."

Gabrielle felt tears beginning to burn her eyes. The sadness was for Emma but also from the realization of the danger Lucas was in.

And he doesn't even know.

"I fell on my knees that night and prayed harder than I'd ever prayed. Pleading with Yahuwah to guide me in how to keep Lucas safe, to prevent that … *thing* from finding out that, ultimately, he'd failed. I didn't know if I should stay here and believe Lucas would be safe or if I should flee with him. My answer came the next day. A new family moved in across the street, and a man came over, concerned by all the police cars and news vans that had converged on our street. All of them were coming and going from our house or yard. He was let through the police line after explaining he was a pastor and offered his assistance to anyone who may need it. The policeman informed him of what had happened and told him about me and the state I was in—which, as you can imagine, wasn't very good.

"When he walked in and looked at me with little Lucas in my arms, I saw what I thought was recognition in his expression. But I knew I'd never seen him before. He came to me and held out his hand, which I felt compelled to take. He walked me into my bedroom and closed the door behind him so no one would be able to hear. He told me that he had a dream the night before, but it was unlike any dream he'd ever had. It seemed very much real. In this dream, an angel told him he would need to help Lucas and me. He was shown our images and charged with being there for us in any way he could—to guide Lucas as he grew."

Emma stood and began pacing the room.

"So, I got my answer. Obviously, if I was meant to leave, this man, who had just moved in across the street, wouldn't have been told to take care of us. I told him all I knew. He knows my origins and has kept it a secret all these years. Lizzie is the only other person who knows. Even Lucas has no idea."

Gabrielle tensed with a sudden, horrible realization.

"Wait a second, Emma. Lucas has *your* blood in him, too. He's also your *blood* descendent." Gabrielle was standing now, walking cautiously over to Lucas.

"Of course." Emma responded, confusion in her tone.

Oh ... all of this makes so much sense, now.

"Emma ... don't you *see*? When I pause time ... it *doesn't* affect angels."

"But Lucas isn't an angel, Gabrielle. He's—"

"A human, with *Divine* blood," Gabrielle interrupted. "He's a quarter angel ...essentially ... he's Nephilim."

Chapter Thirty-One

MARA ✜ TEMPER, TEMPER

Javan and Mara left Gabrielle standing on the street and went back to his loft. He was visibly agitated, so Mara waited to say what was on her mind as long as she could. When the door to the loft closed behind them, she turned to Javan.

"What did you mean back there when you told Gabrielle you wanted her? If you think I'm going to play second to her, if you *manage* to get her to join you, you're wrong. I'll—"

It was startling how fast he moved even for a demon. Before Mara could react, Javan pushed her up against the wall, his hands clasped dangerously tight around her neck. She could barely breathe, but she knew better than to fight back—he was far stronger than she was.

"You'll what?" he asked through his teeth. "What, exactly, is it that you think you can do to me? You have no power, or authority, over *me*. It's the other way around. Do you need a reminder of that?"

Mara felt Javan's grip tightening; her vision was disappearing. She was about to pass out when he released her. She sucked in several sharp breaths, struggling to get air into her aching lungs. Javan walked to the kitchen and poured himself some whiskey. Mara weighed her options for her next move, knowing she was in dangerous territory. If he kept drinking tonight, she would need to find somewhere else to be. He was testy and mean enough without liquor coursing through his veins. Alcohol only made him all that much more intense.

Intensity isn't something Javan needs more of.

She decided to play it safe and walked over to one of the large chairs flanking the couch in the sitting area. She fell into it sideways and threw one of her legs over the armrest. Javan was still glaring at her as he poured his second drink.

I'm going to have to get out of his way and go somewhere else, for sure.

Mara broke the chilly silence. "You can't blame me for not wanting to share you, you know. It's your own fault for being such an *amazing* lover." She stood and walked seductively over to him, slowly pulling her arms out of her sweatshirt, then over her head. Her hair cascaded out of it, brushing the skin on her bare arms and back as it fell.

Javan put his glass down and met her the rest of the way, grabbing her and pressing his lips hard against hers. She relinquished herself to him completely as he picked her up and placed her on the counter. Javan closed his eyes and smiled. Mara was sure he was imagining Gabrielle was in his arms.

Chapter Thirty-two

JAVAN † THE DESTROYER

When Javan woke from a deep sleep several hours later, he found himself alone in his bed. Mara had left while he slept, and he hoped she wouldn't return anytime soon.

It was hard for him to act as if he wanted her company. All he actually wanted was her loyalty and assistance for a while—then, of course, her blood. At least she satisfied some of his other desires.

Not as well as Gabrielle, but she will do until I have my Reyah at my side again.

Javan willed himself out of bed, pulled on a pair of sweat pants that hung low on his waist, and went to the kitchen. After pouring himself another glass of whiskey and taking a long drink, he sat down on the couch and turned on the TV. The news was a poor replacement for the steady stream of information he had access to when he was an angel, but its coverage of human war and scandals provided some insight into how the Fallen were faring. He hoped for some sign of the prophecy or a clue to where the Book was hidden. Anything.

But he was never appeased. His followers, although growing in numbers, were proving to only be moderately helpful in keeping him informed of the things he needed to know. If there were any signs of the Destroyer's arrival, he wasn't hearing about it.

Javan knew he was the one the prophecy spoke of—the Destroyer. He *felt* it. Even if he wasn't the intended, he would kill the one who was and use the Book to achieve his goals. However, his patience was waning. He needed the Book, and he would do what he had to in order to speed up the inevitable.

He closed his eyes again, and an image of Gabrielle filled his mind—only she wasn't alone. The human, Lucas, was there, too. And Lucas was the one embracing *his* love.

My Reyah.

Javan seethed and sat up suddenly, hurling the glass of whiskey across the room, shattering it against the brick wall that got in its way. Shards of glass flew in every direction as if protesting its demise.

"I'll take care of him," he said out loud to the empty room. "*Soon.*"

Chapter Thirty-three

Gabrielle † Family Secrets

"Oh, no!" Emma whispered through the fingers of her hand that now covered her mouth, understanding the problem that Lucas being Nephilim could pose.

Gabrielle stared at Lucas, taking in every angle and curve of his face while he stood—motionless. She couldn't see any signs that he was aware of his surroundings in any way. He wasn't blinking. He wasn't twitching. There was nothing she could see that indicated he wasn't fully frozen in time as any other human would be. But she couldn't be sure if he could hear what was being said.

Gabrielle turned to Emma. "I can still take care of this if he can hear us, Emma." Gabrielle approached Emma. "*Emma!* I *can* fix this," she said as convincingly as she could.

Emma finally looked up and met her eyes. "But … should you, Gabrielle? Maybe it's time for him to know everything. It is his life at stake. I think he's old enough now to know."

Gabrielle could tell she was trying to figure out the right thing to do and was looking for her to help in the decision. Gabrielle walked back over to Lucas. Emma continued to talk from behind her.

"He looks so much like Mason did at his age. A little taller than his grandfather, but his features are *so* similar. I've even called him Mason before." Emma walked over to the window where she'd been sitting when Gabrielle first came in. "What should I do, Gabrielle?" She lowered her head, and Gabrielle knew she'd started crying even though she made no sound.

She let Emma's tears flow for a few uninterrupted moments, using the time to do some thinking herself. It was a dilemma. If Lucas was kept in the dark about his past, *and* his present, his future could be at even more risk than it already was. He wouldn't know to be cautious. On the other hand, if he did find out, would he even believe them? If he hadn't been able to hear her and Emma, and they told him later, he'd probably think they were crazy, talking about being angels and some dark being who wanted to end his life that it thought it had already taken. She knew she could make him believe, though—if she had to. She could show him. There could be no doubt in his mind if she let him see her true form. Gabrielle wasn't sure what to do. She would call Amaziah. Maybe even seek counsel with Yahuwah.

"Emma, will you be okay like this for a little longer? I don't want to begin time again until we have an idea how we're going to move forward with Lucas. I'm going to go outside and get guidance from Amaziah."

"Yes," Emma replied through sniffles. "Yes, I'll be fine. Do anything you can. *Please*."

As Gabrielle started to walk past Lucas, she wished he'd put his arms around her and kiss her gently as he'd done earlier when she said goodbye. She paused, put her hand around his, and squeezed lightly. As she was about to let go, he squeezed back.

Gabrielle froze. Had it only been a reflex? She squeezed his hand again, twice, slowly, and waited for Lucas to respond.

He squeezed.

Twice.

Slowly.

"Emma." Gabrielle spoke in a tone that demanded more attention than it normally would. Emma looked up at her, fast and quizzically. "Emma, he definitely heard us." Lucas squeezed long and hard this time. "I think he's trying to tell me that he wants to know." Another squeeze came.

"How do you know?"

"He's telling me." Gabrielle gestured to their hands with her head and eyes. "I don't think we need to wonder or ask anyone else what should be done. It's his will, his desire."

Taking her hand out of his, she motioned for Emma to come to her. She placed Emma's hand in Lucas's, and before she could even ask her if he squeezed it, she gasped.

"You're right, Gabrielle."

"Well, I guess I'll get him out of this state I put him in."

Gabrielle closed her eyes and raised her hand. She said nothing, but immediately, everything came back to life including Lucas, who proceeded to finish what he was doing when she'd frozen everything—closing the door behind him.

When he pushed the door shut, he didn't make any attempt to turn around. Instead, he put his forearm up on the door and placed his head on it—like he was about to count to twenty for a game of hide-and-seek.

Emma walked to him and put her hands on his shoulders. "Lucas, dear ... please look at me." Her voice was shaky.

Lucas turned slowly to face Emma, then pulled her firmly against him as he squeezed his eyelids together tightly, trying to force his tears to stand their ground. They did not obey.

Gabrielle couldn't imagine how difficult it must have been, listening to everything the two angels talked about, not able to let them know he was there, too—hearing every word. A flood of guilt consumed her, and she ran into the kitchen and began to weep.

What would he think of her now? The thought was selfish, but she couldn't help but think it anyway. They'd been in each other's lives for a little less than a month; nevertheless, their bond was already strong. She understood why she'd initially been so drawn to him, and him to her. Angels always tuned into each other. They would've been pulled together even if she hadn't almost knocked him down with her door that first day. Somehow, some way, it would have happened. Now, he might tell her to stay away from him.

She supposed she could just pick a different city, a different school. But she knew that wouldn't make it easier—just further away. Distance might even make it worse. Of course, she could just ascend back to her home and let her human identity fade away until Gabrielle the human became less than a memory for the people she'd met.

Humans forget.

But if he let her, she could help him with his new knowledge. She knew she'd do whatever she could even if he told her to go away. She would still work for his happiness and safety as much as was in her power to do.

Gabrielle stopped crying. She could hear the muffled conversation between Lucas and Emma in the next room. She didn't want to listen. It was private. She really shouldn't be there at all, but she wanted to stay, to answer any questions Lucas had.

She felt like an intruder. And that's exactly what she was. Angels weren't intended to have such close and constant interaction with humans, especially for such a sustained period of time. It opened the door up to too many problems. This situation was a prime example. Gabrielle was falling for a human, and he was falling for her. Because of that connection and her status, he was in a great deal of danger from the Fallen—and from Javan especially, simply because of jealousy.

Maybe Amaziah was right. Maybe she shouldn't stay. Maybe the result of this research would be that she'd somehow make things worse. She certainly wasn't making a positive impact on Lucas's and Emma's life. Gabrielle sighed, laid her head on the table, and tried to shut out the conversation in the next room. She closed her eyes, and without intending to, she drifted into a dreamless, visionless sleep.

Chapter Thirty-four

GABRIELLE ✝ MOVING FORWARD

Something stirred Gabrielle from her sleep. She raised her head and saw a familiar face sitting across from her. She wondered how long Lucas had been there. They looked at each other for several seconds, neither seeming to want to be the one to speak first. Lucas broke the silence.

"So ... an angel." Lucas still had no expression.

"I'm sorry I couldn't let you know before, Lucas. But there was no way. Would you have believed me?"

Lucas took some time to answer.

"No. I wouldn't have. The only reason I do now is because I was held hostage for who knows how long, listening not only to *you*, but to my grandmother, talk about being angels and having powers and living with God before here. I know Gran's sane. But if it had been you, alone, just coming out with, *Hey, by the way, Lucas, I have wings and can fly. Is there a message you want me to give God for you tonight when I check in with Him?*' No. No way." He paused again and studied her more.

I really wish he would smile. Or scowl. Or yell. Something. *Almost anything would be better than this.*

"So, I have an angel for a girlfriend. A really *powerful* angel for a girlfriend."

"If you still want me to be." Gabrielle let her eyes fall away from his.

Lucas put his open hand on the table in front of her, and she placed her hand in his. Was he reaching out to let her know he did want her, or was it a kind gesture before breaking her heart?

"Gabby ... *Gabrielle*. Look at me."

Reluctantly, she met his gaze.

"I'm not going to lie and say this is easy for me. *Especially* to the angel that's in charge of handing out karma. I just found out two people I know are *angels*, for crying out loud! One is someone I've loved all my life. The other is someone I care about *a lot* even though I've only known you for a short amount of time. There's a demon who will be after my blood if he finds out he didn't finish the job seventeen years ago. And let's not forget, *I'm* not altogether human myself. I feel like I'm getting punked, and at any time, someone is going to jump out and show me the hidden cameras. So please, have a little patience with me. I have to let this sink in."

Gabrielle relaxed just a little, feeling she wasn't going to be shut out. "You'll have all the time you need from me, Lucas. If, after all this sinks in, you still want me in your life on any level, I'll be here for you. If you decide you can't handle who, or *what*, I am, I'll understand. Even though I won't be happy about it."

"Gabby, I don't think I can make it through all this without you. I want you in my life more than ever. But what happens when it's time for you to go? Where will that leave us? Do you know?"

"To be honest, I don't. I didn't expect to fall for a human. I'm sorry it happened, *only* because the last thing I want is to hurt you. But the fact is, I couldn't seem to help myself. It felt like it was supposed to happen, that you and I were meant to be ... maybe we are. Even if it doesn't make sense.

"I don't know everything, but I know who does, and He doesn't do anything without a purpose. That's part of what my job is about, after all. I do want you to think about the possible outcomes for us. The good *and* the bad. In a way, I'm glad this happened tonight. I know it's rocked your world, but it's better for the truth to come out sooner than later. I don't know how I would've brought it up and convinced you without freaking you out more by showing you my true form. Now you can really think about this before you get in any deeper."

"Did you completely miss what I just said to you, Gabby? I know I want you in my life, and I know I don't want it to be in a way that's less than you already are. I'm moving *forward* with you—with us. I'm concerned with the outcome, and I know we could come to an end, but it's worth the risk. At least it is for me. Is it for you?"

Gabrielle felt relief creep through her. She'd been prepared for him to take quite a bit of time to think about this, but she wouldn't have to wait. She smiled and finally saw his smile return.

"Yes, if you're absolutely sure." She searched his face for any trace of uncertainty.

Lucas stood and walked over to her. He pulled her up to him, put his arms around her, and whispered in her ear.

"Without a doubt."

Gabrielle let herself ease into the warmth of his body as he held her, enjoying the heat it awakened within her. She loved how happy he made her and wondered if she made him feel as happy. They held each other, silently, for a long time—just listening to each other breathe, feeling the pulse in the body they pressed themselves against. For a while, she wasn't sure if she would ever know that warmth from him again—not after what he'd just found out about himself. About her. Gabrielle didn't want it to end ... not yet. She would enjoy every moment with him for as long as Yahuwah would allow.

Chapter Thirty-five

LUCAS ✝ NEW SECRETS

Lucas kissed Gabby on the forehead as he released her. All he had just learned about himself, his family, and her swam around in his head. He had a lot to think about and was already reflecting on things that had happened in his life. Now, he understood why Gran couldn't give him the answers he'd wanted when he was younger. At the time, he wouldn't have been able to deal with it as well as he could now. Everything made more sense—his strength, his speed, and why languages and learning came easy. There was a reason for all of it. For the first time in his life, he had some answers to why he seemed so different from everyone.

I am different.

Gran came into the kitchen to say she was going to bed. All three showed their exhaustion with heavy eyes and a contagious round of yawns that began with Lucas.

"I should be going, too." Gabby said, then said bye to Emma, who gave her a hug.

Lucas walked her outside. With every step he took, he made sure he wasn't dreaming by biting his lip.

"Will I see you tomorrow—I mean, later today?" He asked Gabby as they made their way down the steps of the front porch.

"That may not be the best idea."

"Why not? I thought I made it clear to you that I don't need time to think about whether or not I want to be with you." He paused, concerned she was having second thoughts. "Or are *you* the one who needs time?"

Gabby laughed and stretched to kiss his nose. With that smile and kiss, he felt confident that things were okay.

"No, it's nothing like that. There's a lot you still don't know about me and my job. More so, what effect my job has on me."

Lucas must have looked as confused as he felt at that moment because Gabby explained further.

"The thing is, my mood is directly affected by how much good karma I enforce, compared to bad. If I'm able to give out more good karma, my mood reflects that. And the reverse is true as well. Do you understand?"

"Yeah, sure. I'll just add it to your quirks." He smiled. "But what does that have to do with seeing you or not?"

"I dealt with some *pretty* bad people yesterday, and it more than outweighed the good. I'm expecting a *very* bad mood. I don't think you'll want to be around to see that side of me."

"What? Are you going to turn all green and grow biceps the size of tree trunks? Because if that's the case, then yeah, I'll see you at school on Monday. Otherwise, I think I can handle it—unless you plan on freezing me again." He raised his brows for a dramatic expression of contemplation, and Gabrielle shook her head to appease his question. "Besides, if I'm really going to be with you, I want to see and know everything about you. Plus … I just found out you're only here for a few more months … I'm going be a part of every second of that time I can." He kissed her hand. "Deal?"

"If that's what you want. Just don't say I didn't warn you."

"I stand warned. There's a secondary motive anyway. I have a *lot* of questions I would love to get answers to."

"Okay," she said. "I don't think you have any idea just how bad my mood may be, though. I've got quite a bit to do tomorrow, so I'll need to stick around my place. Why don't you come over whenever you're ready and bring school work if you have any. That way you can escape into your chemistry, or whatever, if I get too intense."

"Sounds good. Do *you* have to do school work?"

Gabrielle laughed. "No—no. I take care of that in a snap, if you know what I mean." She grinned.

"How 'bout working that magic for me so I have more time just to look at you?"

"Not a chance, Lucas!"

"Well, it was worth a try. Now go home so I can hurry up and see you again. I'll walk you to your car." He scanned the street. "Where is it?"

Gabby motioned. "It's just around the corner. I had to make it look like I was leaving before I could come back and confront Javan so you would go into your house."

"I'll walk you to it."

He took her hand and started toward the sidewalk.

Gabrielle laughed. "I wasn't planning to walk to it, Lucas. I don't have to act like I'm human anymore. You know my secret now."

He raised his brows in understanding.

"Since you brought up Javan, can we talk more about him?"

"Sure, but we have plenty of time to do that. I need to know about what happened with you and Mara, too."

"Mara? Why?"

"Mara's palling around with Javan."

"Oh!" He scowled. "That would explain things."

"What do you mean?"

"Like you said—plenty of time for that."

He kissed her gently, and she turned to leave.

"Hey!" She spun back around. "I guess you already know not to say anything about all this to anyone, right?"

"Yeah," he laughed, "I think I'll keep this information *all* to myself. By the way … did this angel stuff have anything to do with the language you spoke in the car that day when I recognized some of what you said I shouldn't know?"

Gabby nodded. "I was speaking Enochian, the language of angels. You recognized it, well, a little of it. It's the language you would have spoken as soon as you were created if you were a full-blood. It's not learned, it's *known*. It's on our tongues and in our minds from the moment we begin our lives. I guess it hitched a ride in your DNA."

"Oh. Makes sense, I guess."

They smiled at each other, and then both turned to continue to their homes. Lucas glanced back from the steps, wanting to see her one more time, but she was already gone. He smiled and shook his head.

"Having an angel for a girlfriend is going to take some getting used to."

Chapter Thirty-six

JAVAN ✝ UNEXPECTED COMPANY

Javan went back to bed after he drank his latest temper tantrum away. It had become a routine for him over the last decade. He was growing tired of how long it was taking him to gather the information he needed. The longer it took, the angrier and more intoxicated he became. His alcohol-laden slumber lasted far longer than normal. He opened his eyes to late afternoon light coming through his window, cursing the painful throbbing in his head.

Mara still hadn't come back since she slipped out of his loft. He knew she was trying to smooth things over with the seduction routine. She'd over-stepped when she confronted him after Gabrielle had her fun-filled Saturday with Lucas.

That worthless *human*.

He didn't care. It suited his needs at the time, and not wanting Mara's company wasn't wavering. He was glad for the solitude. The only one he wished to be with had looked at him the night before with pain in her eyes that he'd never seen in her, and he knew he was responsible. Guilt began to slip into his mood, which he angrily pushed away. He had no time or patience for regret.

She'll come around. He told himself as his feet hit the cold hardwood floor.

Stumbling into the shower, he turned on the water and stepped in without waiting for the hot water to make its way through the pipes of the old warehouse. His was one of ten lofts in the converted building, and based on the inadequate plumbing and wiring, they had spared as much money as they could. The space was large and would perfectly serve his purposes later, though—and later was all he focused on.

After he had dried off, he stood in the full-length mirror admiring his human physique. He'd chosen well. The body he took was tall and muscular with just enough mass to intimidate. He had dark hair and eyes, olive skin, and an intensity to his features that gave him a dangerous air, which he found was particularly appealing to females. Anyone guessing his nationality would likely suspect Spanish or South American.

He pulled his sweatpants back on and decided to search the internet for more clues about the location of the Book. This type of research was mind numbing, but until he found a high-ranking demon who would follow and assist him, he was stuck finding information through the followers he had recruited and by means of human knowledge.

"Gaining information was so much easier before I became one of the Fallen," he said through a sigh.

He hated to use the word demon for himself even though that was what he'd become. He felt it was beneath whom he was destined to be.

Before he was able to begin his research, he sensed someone was waiting for him outside the door to his loft. Even those who had joined the ranks of demons were still able to sense the presence of Divine blood or those from the Shadow World. It was one ability Yahuwah didn't remove from his banished troops. Javan thought it was his way of reminding them of where they'd come from.

As if any of us need reminding.

Javan stood and cautiously made his way to the door, trying his best not to make noise. Being in a human body didn't afford him the stealth he would have had as an angel. He continued through the large room, shadowed heavily from dusk settling outside his windows. When he reached the door, he quietly pressed his ear to its cold metal, listening for something that would give him a clue to who was waiting for him on the other side. At first, he heard nothing, but then, within his own mind was the voice of a female, speaking softly to him—requesting to enter.

Javan opened the door to find a beauty. Black eyes, heavily spiked with red, looked back. She wasn't tall; his six foot frame loomed over hers. Her skin was creamy white and contrasted her long auburn hair. By his estimation, she was flawless and one of the Damned. Immediately he desired her, an effect he knew she would have on any man. What would it be like to couple with a Qalal? He'd never considered it. It would be nearly impossible for a human to survive what may happen.

But I'm not human.

A smile played at the corners of his mouth as he felt his body responding to his thoughts. She smiled back.

"Javan, I'm Cecily. I understand you need help finding a certain ... *something*."

Her voice was enchanting. A smile completely reshaped his normally stern expression as he addressed her.

"Yes." He continued to covet her body. "I do."

"If you invite me in, I think I can make your day ... possibly your night." Her expression became provocative. "Depending how long you'd like me to stay."

Javan stepped aside with a wide welcoming motion. In his most charming voice, he invited her into his loft. "In that case, *please* ... make yourself at home." Cecily sauntered in as Javan closed the door behind her, clicking the lock into place.

"Trying to keep me in, or someone else ... *out*?" Cecily slowly turned on her heel as she spoke, stopping once she was facing Javan.

"I know better than to think a locked door would hold you captive. It's safe to say you know the answer."

Javan held Cecily's gaze. Neither spoke for several moments. In that time, Javan continued with only two trains of thought—what one of the Damned wanted with him, and what it would be like to have her in his bed. He gave most of his mental energy to the latter, and he felt one side of his mouth curve up in response.

"What is it you think you can help me with, Cecily?"

"There's word traveling through the Shadow World that you're seeking the location of a certain book."

"The rumors are correct." Javan moved closer to Cecily. "*And?*"

Cecily turned on her heel again to continue further into the loft, looking at him over her shoulder—luring him to accompany her deeper into his home.

Javan followed.

"And the book you seek is the same as the book Ramai intended to use against ... well, I don't really care to even utter the name, but you know who I speak of ... *personally*. Don't you?"

Javan didn't respond right away. He continued to follow her without taking his eyes off his captivating, dangerous guest. His desire increased with every step, almost to the point of being uncontrollable.

"That's the one ... yes. And *you* think you know how I can find it?"

Cecily turned back around to face Javan, who didn't stop walking until he was as close as he could get to her without actually touching. Cecily slowly traced the muscles on his bare chest with her cold fingers, keeping her eyes on what she was doing instead of his face. He felt a chill run through his body—more a result of his desire than her frigid body temperature.

"Oh, sweetie ... I can take you to it myself. But it's going to cost you."

The cost didn't matter to him. The reason for everything he had done to this point, for everything he would still do, was to retrieve the

Book and gain its power.

"What's your price?"

"First things first, Javan. What do you say we get something out of the way, so it won't be such a ... *distraction* when we start talking business?" She propositioned him as she cut her eyes to various parts of his body. Cecily confidently turned her gaze to his eyes. He'd never seen eyes that could summon someone to them the way hers were.

Calling to me—welcoming me to take her.

Javan went after Cecily with a hunger to possess, greedily kissing her, searching her body with the hand that was free from the task of forcing her to him. He felt her respond. He moved his hands low to lift her up to him, then carried her to his room. Her legs wrapped around him, the strength in them evident as she squeezed. What was he doing? This was no mortal woman. She could crush this human body if she wanted to. He didn't care, though. If he had to abandon it and find another to use, he would. All he wanted was her. He wanted to relish in the sensations of being with her. Hopefully, through the rest of the night.

He fell on top of her on his bed and removed her clothes, and any thought of danger slipped away—into her.

Javan stirred from a deep sleep. As he tried to move his normally nimble frame out of bed, he had to slow abruptly, wincing from the pain he felt almost everywhere. He cautiously made his way to the bathroom and flicked on the light, squinting until they adjusted to the brilliance he'd unleashed, then walked to the mirror. Once he was able to open his eyes, he gasped.

He knew he was looking at the same body and face he had admired after his shower earlier, but the reflection now showed hideous bruises in shades of purple, blue, and black splattered around his torso. Trickles of blood seeped from small puncture marks, one on the inside of his upper thigh—that one made him wince from the sheer sight of what it was located next to. Except for light purple bruising around his mouth, his face was unscathed.

He smiled and chuckled; pain shot from his mouth and ribs. His human body survived the escapade. It was more than worth the risk he'd taken. Cecily was divine.

"What's so funny?"

He heard Cecily's voice behind him, making him jump. He hadn't heard her approach.

He turned to see an unclothed and physically unmarked Cecily—still looking irresistibly alluring. Javan let his gaze fall wantonly over every inch of her body, enjoying looking at what he'd just conquered. He hadn't been able to see her like this while she lay under, or on top of, him. Her curves and angles were perfectly balanced and symmetrical. Her skin snugly fit her frame, leaving nothing but a toned body beneath. Time no longer affected her beauty; she would never age or sicken, and she would always be this exquisite.

Even with all she could physically and visually offer him, he knew she could never stop the pain he felt from losing Gabrielle—the one thing that caused him to regret his decision to challenge Yahuwah. The one thing, if he was given the chance to change what he'd done, he would stay for.

Gabrielle would be worth the aggravation of bowing to Him.

That chance would never be offered. Of that, he was sure. There was no way he could turn back time; there was only one who could. And there was no way Yahuwah would ever forgive him. Javan would just have to believe Gabrielle's love for him would return her to his side.

Some day.

Javan's attention was drawn away from thoughts of reconciling with Gabrielle when Cecily dramatically shifted her stance as if her body was getting tired in the position she was standing in. The idea was ridiculous because it was impossible—the Qalal didn't tire in mind or body except in sunlight. She achieved the desired result, which was letting him know that the staring and silence between them had become boring.

Javan finally spoke, smiling a mischievous smile as he did.

"I just didn't know if this body would survive our fun. I'm happy I don't have to vacate it to find another one that isn't broken."

Cecily glided toward him. "I was on my best behavior." She used her fingers to trace the muscles and curves of his chest again. She continued speaking between lingering kisses that went from one side of his neck to the other. "I was—really—*very*—gentle."

"*That* was gentle? I'd hate to see what rough is like."

Cecily moved her lips down his chest. She stopped to look up at him. "On the contrary, if you were in a body that could handle it, a Qalal's body, I assure you, you wouldn't hate it."

As she continued on her previous path, Javan closed his eyes, smiling and sucking in a sharp breath through his teeth when she reached her destination.

Chapter Thirty-Seven

Gabrielle ✟ Puzzle Pieces

Gabrielle decided she would go to sleep when she got home. No work, no hunting for news about the Book, no trying to figure out what would happen with her and Lucas or what Javan was doing—which she was certain involved the Book.

Just sleep.

The clock on her bedside table showed a quarter after three in the morning. She didn't bother to change clothes, just slipped her sandals off and curled up under the covers. As soon as she fell asleep, the dreams came.

Gabrielle sat upright with a jolt, sweating and breathing heavily. The dreams were more detailed; information was no longer impaired when she was in her human body. She was shown the same five scenes, but this time, they were connected. The Book was mere steps from where Gabrielle and Javan fought; the swarms of angels weren't fighting separately or at different times; they were all around them. Their numbers were so vast that the sounds of their swords clashing and screams of pain were almost deafening. Then she was looking up at Javan as she held Lucas in her arms. She'd descended to him after watching him fall to the ground, while Javan laughed wickedly. The entire time, Light and Dark angels continued their bloody combat. The Divine blood of angels and the almost black fluid that coursed through demon's veins intermingled on the ground around where she and Lucas landed. The stench of Darkness was heavy in the air, making her want to vomit.

I have to tell Amaziah.

This time, she wasn't shown the vision of just her and Lucas as he was lying on the ground—energies from unknown beings were fleeing in the distance. That one … she still hadn't had again.

At least, not yet.

She didn't waste time and called Amaziah. When he responded, she told him what was revealed in her dream. Then she told him about her encounter with Javan and Mara. She went on to fill him in on what she'd discovered about Lucas, Emma, and his family's death. And reluctantly, informed him that Lucas now knew everything about her.

Amaziah wouldn't be happy about Lucas learning who, and what, she was, but he gave no indication of it. He let her know he understood. She couldn't worry about him being angry, though. Especially with the mood she already felt.

It was five fifteen.

She was still tired but had too much on her mind to go back to sleep. Instead, she took a quick shower, brushed her teeth, and threw on a comfortable pair of lounge pants and an oversized sweatshirt. She glanced at herself in the mirror and went downstairs to make a pot of coffee and her standard breakfast of toast with peanut butter and honey. After eating, she went to the great room and curled up in her oversized chair and just sat and thought. She thought about her decision to live among humans, Javan being cast from Heaven and what he'd become, what Javan had planned, her visions and what they meant, what could be done to prevent them from coming to pass, the trouble she could be getting herself into because of the relationship with Lucas—and a lot about Lucas, in general—the war, her friends who were now injured because of her and had almost lost their lives, the Book, Amaziah's strange compliance with her wishes, creepy crows hanging around in a particular number she didn't care for, and demons becoming more powerful.

Ugh ... I don't know if I can take much more.

The one thing she tried not to think about, and had to continually evict from her mind, was the last thing she always saw in her visions—Lucas's lifeless body. But the merciless image was slipping through again at that moment, creating a feeling of dread that settled heavily on her.

She needed to find out what was in the Book. But with no history passed down about the Great Battle Amaziah had told her about, she had absolutely no reference to figure out what it could be used for. Knowing what was in it might make Javan's intentions clear. If he intended on obtaining and using the Book himself, she had to find out if he had a real chance to succeed.

The morning passed quickly, and when Gabrielle looked up at the clock again, it was twelve ten. The only reason she even thought to look was her stomach grumbling about being empty. She made her way to the kitchen.

She'd had no epiphanies that morning and found herself irritated, having accomplished nothing.

What did I expect to happen? I can't put a puzzle together with only a fraction of the pieces.

Yet she just spent hours trying to do just that.

Frustrated, Gabrielle slammed the door to the refrigerator she'd been standing in front of; glass bottles clanged together inside in protest. Regardless of her stomach, she had no appetite. She went to get more coffee but found the pot almost empty.

After spending more time harassed by questions she wouldn't find answers to at the moment, she decided to call on Sheridan to take care of her work before Lucas came over. She hoped karma would have a better day. She'd hate to try and get through school with a mood resulting from two back to back days of mostly negative karma.

Sheridan showed up promptly.

They got to work and finished quickly. The day's lot came out to be pretty even, so at least tomorrow would be no worse than today. Instead of dismissing Sheridan, as she typically would, Gabrielle asked her to stay. She needed information.

The two sat opposite each other at the kitchen counter's bar. Sheridan looked perplexed and a little apprehensive about Gabrielle's request. She'd never asked her to stay before, and after what had happened between them, Gabrielle guessed Sheridan wasn't sure why she was now.

"I need to know what's been learned about the Book, Sheridan. I don't want to bother anyone who's helping to search for it if you can tell me."

"There was a Cherubim speaking of it before I came to you. He was telling the story to a troop of angels. There's a tremendous amount of interest since it is one that's been lost to most of us, and many of our brethren are mourning as if it just happened. It must have been terrible, Gabrielle.

"The battle happened after Lucifer fell and became the Dark Lord, Ramai. It's believed the that the Book everyone is searching for is his creation and, in fact, Yahuwah was not betrayed at all. But instead, that there was a copy made.

"Lucifer, blessed and granted by Yahuwah with knowledge, wisdom, power, and authority that was far superior to all other angels, eliminates all others with the ability to have brought such a book into existence. The Cherubim said it's basically a blueprint of our eternal home and everything Yahuwah created. Only it's a *word* blueprint. Those same words that breathed life into this world and ours can be reversed and used to destroy any of His creations. Whoever wields the power of the Book will hold *everything* created at their mercy. No one seems to know how the holy information came to be known by Lucifer before his falling, or how the copy of the book was lost to him, but it's crucial one of us finds it before any other being gets a chance to use its power." Sheridan stopped as though she was trying to decide where to continue.

"The Cherubim also said the words have to be spoken from the Throne of Yahuwah to work. That was what the fierce battle Amaziah spoke of was fought for, to protect the Throne, and why the Seraphim were involved. Michael and Raphael managed to gain possession of the original Book before the Throne was reached, and so the battle was won. However, the book in your vision is still being sought. Of course, we aren't the only ones searching for it. Ramai and other fallen angels want it badly because they know ultimate power could be gained."

Sheridan stopped speaking, seeming not to want to continue for some reason.

"Is there more, Sheridan?"

Sheridan took her time to answer before continuing cautiously.

"There is more, Gabrielle, but you should know it won't be easy for you to hear." She hesitated. "As you know, the reason Javan was cast from our home was known to few."

Gabrielle nodded, now understanding Sheridan's hesitation. Javan was a touchy subject when she was in the best of moods, and Sheridan knew she was dealing with an already edgy angel.

"The reason has been shared now because of the circumstances. Yahuwah wants all to be known to us so we can look for the Book with full knowledge of everyone we may encounter in its retrieval.

"Javan went to Yahuwah and challenged His authority. He demanded to be granted powers to do as he chose. He was removed and was to be punished by taking away his rank in the Cherubim and placed in Choir Three of the Third Triad. Javan was infuriated he would be put into the lowest of the Angelic Orders. He vowed he'd find the Book and destroy all Yahuwah created and loved, unless Javan deemed it worthy of surviving. It isn't known why Javan thought it existed, but he was convinced he would be able to have its power. Even though it wasn't Yahuwah's desire to do initially, He cast out Javan after Javan's threat."

Silence held the space between them for a long moment.

Gabrielle let everything she'd been told settle into her mind. Studying each new puzzle piece, deciding how it fit. So much more made sense now. Javan actually believed he was going to be able to control Yahuwah along with everything and everyone He created—including Ramai and his legions of demons. It all seemed surreal. How had she not seen the Darkness in Javan? How long had they been together while those thoughts consumed him?

Could I have stopped him?

Sheridan spoke again, interrupting the stillness between them.

"There's one other thing you should be aware of, Gabrielle."

"Yes?"

"Information was given to Ramai by a human Seer. For some reason, Ramai intended to kill the Seer and his family. The Seer offered to tell him the full prophecy concerning the Destroyer coming into power, which he had received the night before, *if* Ramai spared their lives. We are trying to find out exactly what Ramai was told because it will make what we already know of the prophecy more clear. That's all I know, but I'll keep you informed about anything else I learn."

"Thank you, Sheridan. You may go."

Gabrielle was immediately alone again. Her thoughts were swirling in her mind. Things would become dire if the Book was found by anyone other than those still in Yahuwah's fold. With all the new information in her head, she found it difficult to keep her mind on one thing. Sheridan was right; it had been very hard to hear about Javan. Gabrielle was devastated by what he'd become, and she knew it would never be any easier for her. He would always be a part of her, and she would always miss him.

What had become of their relationship didn't matter, though. The last pieces of the puzzle were still out there, and she had to find them.

And I need to know exactly what the prophecy predicts.

Chapter Thirty-eight

JAVAN ✢ A SEER

Javan went to the kitchen and poured another glass of whiskey as Cecily walked a few steps behind him, softly purring to show her satisfaction.

"I'd ask if you want some," he said as he poured his drink, "but I know what the answer will be."

Cecily smirked. "Not my cup of tea. Thanks bunches, though." She slowly meandered through the large room, stopping to study various pieces of art and to run her finger over the bindings of books scattered around the room.

Javan walked over to one of several windows that stretched almost the entire height of the loft and stared out into the darkness, wondering if Cecily could really take him to the Book. The night was slipping away. He knew he needed to wrap up the evening's fun and have the conversation they'd put off. There would be no hope of getting rid of her once daylight reached into shadows. Not that he minded her company. He was enjoying it thoroughly, but Mara could be back any time. Even though he didn't have to answer to her, he imagined she wouldn't take the situation well if she discovered Cecily there. He didn't want to alienate Mara. Not when she will be so useful later.

Cecily came to the window and wrapped her arms around him from behind. Her hands began to wander again. Javan stopped her and turned to meet her gaze. It was terribly difficult to resist her.

"Now that we've had our pleasure," he said as he fought the urge to give in, "it's time for business."

Cecily's expression cooled. "You're no fun," she said flatly as she walked away and sank into the corner of the leather couch.

"If you say so." Javan flashed a knowing glance. "You say you can take me to the Book. How do you know it's the right one? How do I know you aren't wasting my time?" He sat down on the couch next to her. "And what's the price you referred to earlier?"

She waited to answer him as if heavily considering the words she was about to speak.

"I know this book is the one you seek because I've seen it."

"Just because you've seen a book doesn't mean it's the *right* book."

"No, *sweetie*." She looked at him with disgust. The annoyance in her tone matched her expression. "You're not getting it. I've *seen* it in a vision. I'm a *Seer*."

Javan didn't concern himself with her sudden shift in the charm department. He found it intriguing. She was similar to him in many ways—the fallen angel and the Qalal—they were both damned. They just acquired the status in different ways. He laughed to himself at the comparison.

"As far as if I'm wasting your time ... I don't care about your time, Javan. I care about mine." She laughed humorlessly. "You should try to have a little *faith*."

"I have *faith* I will get the Book with or without you. Can we get on with this? Your price?"

"Mmmm ... I guess the honeymoon's over," she said with a wink. "My price isn't monetary. I have more than enough money. I have eternal life, so I'm good there. I can have any man I want. Or woman, for that matter. What I don't have, what I want, is power."

Javan felt a smile tug on one side of his mouth again. *I like her more and more.*

"I'm a young Qalal by our standards. I've only been turned for a little over three hundred years. It would take me hundreds, and hundreds, of years to be considered an Elder. Even then, I have to try to put myself into the position to become one, and that could take hundreds more years. After all that effort and time … it still might never happen. I want the power the Elders have, and patience isn't a virtue I've ever possessed."

Javan had to admit he was intrigued. "How, *exactly*, do I assist you in your endeavor?"

"You see, Javan, I have a little faith, too. In you."

Javan half-smiled at that statement. He liked having fans—especially ones as desirable as Cecily. His own smile prompted one from her that seemed Knowing. He wasn't sure how to interpret it, but it made him wonder how much she knew about him and what she might be up to. Before he could ponder the questions for very long, she continued.

"To be more precise … I have faith in you becoming the Destroyer."

"Why do you think I'll become the Destroyer?" he asked as nonchalantly as possible. Her assumption made him wary. He'd never verbalized his belief to her.

"I've *seen* that your reason for wanting the Book is to bring the prophecy to pass."

He studied her intently.

"That is what you want the Book for, Javan. Don't deny it."

"Yes, it is," he said, still cautious.

Cecily sighed and rolled her eyes. "Javan, I'm growing weary of you. Let me get to the point, and then I'll leave you to consider my offer. I want you to grant me power over the Elders when you become the Destroyer. It's that simple."

Cecily stood and made her way toward the door. She had less than an hour before the sun came up and obviously had no more desire of keeping his company during the coming day than he did hers. At the door, she turned to face Javan who was still sitting on the couch surveying her. "I'll be back in a few nights. You can give me your decision then."

"I'll be looking forward to it."

"Oh … *I know* you will be," she responded.

He heard her purr playfully, then she was gone.

Chapter Thirty-nine

Gabrielle ✟ Differences

Gabrielle moved time forward again and heard a knock at the door. She could feel it was Lucas. He must have been about to knock just as she and Sheridan started working. She hurried to the door, realizing he would have been unable to move and fully aware, once again. Like the night before, guilt washed over her. She had the same lurch in her stomach and pain in her heart. Gabrielle opened the door to the face she yearned to see whenever he was away.

Lucas pulled her to him and held her snugly in his arms. "Haven't you heard it's rude to keep a guest waiting at the door?" he asked with a smile and pressed his lips to hers.

"I'm sorry, Lucas," she said when they released each other. "I'll figure out what I can do to keep that from happening to you again."

"Yes, *please* do that."

They continued to talk as they walked to the kitchen. Gabrielle was still hungry even though she didn't feel like eating.

"What did you think was happening over the last couple of

months when I paused time and you didn't know anything about why you were suddenly, randomly, unable to move?" She asked.

Lucas laughed.

"I actually thought I was slipping into a trance or something. It only happened a few times, but I have to admit, I was getting pretty concerned. If I hadn't learned that you were pausing time to explain it, I would've ended up at the hospital getting brain scans."

"It would've been scary when they didn't find a brain." Gabrielle stopped in the living room and faced him, then winced playfully like she was going to be attacked.

Lucas raised a brow and smirked. He had her on the floor before she knew it. She had never been tickled before, and it made her laugh so hard that tears began to trickle out of her eyes, landing warmly in her ears. It was torturous, in a strange, fabulous way. When he finally stopped, he gave her a quick kiss and then sprung back to his feet. She lay there smiling and catching her breath, drying the path on her face that her tears had taken.

"That'll teach ya!" Lucas said as he learned over and offered his hand.

She reflected on the day they had first met when he offered it to help her out of her car. She had blamed her response on her unfamiliar human body. Now ... she knew it meant much more; this human was significant to her.

Life is funny, she thought as she reached for his hand. Before he could pull her up, she put her feet against his torso and pulled. His smirk quickly rearranged to a slack jaw and his eyes widened in surprise as he sailed over her and landed with a thud on the floor behind her.

"Ow!" he said through a laugh.

Gabrielle stood over him with a smirk, her hands on her hips. "Let that teach *you*!"

Lucas smiled as he got up, then wrapped his arms around her waist. She loved the way he made her feel—warm, peaceful, content, *safe*. Safe to be herself—safe to let her burdens go, to relax. Lucas leaned toward her, pausing before kissing her to look in her eyes, then his lips met hers.

"Lesson learned," he whispered through a light kiss.

They held onto each other for a while before finally moving to the kitchen, still holding hands.

"So, it only happened a few times—feeling suspended in time?" Gabrielle asked, puzzled he noticed it so rarely.

"Yeah, as far as I know. I had dreams sometimes where I felt like I was awake but couldn't move. I remember how *quiet* it was when I had that feeling."

"That makes more sense," she said. "I start my work late in the evening most of the time. So, if you were asleep when I paused time, you wouldn't have even noticed."

Gabrielle grabbed things from the refrigerator to make a sandwich and then bread from the pantry.

"Are you hungry?" she asked.

"I'm not much of one to turn down food even when I'm not. Want some help?"

"Sure."

After making their lunch, they sat on the floor in the living room between the couch and the coffee table. Gabrielle turned on a football game.

Lucas grinned. "You know, you don't have to watch this for my sake."

"Who says I put it on for you? I have a lot to learn before next Saturday's rematch."

"I love the way you think, *angel*," he replied, a mischievous look crossing his face.

"I love the way you look at me, *Nephilim*," she said in return.

"Even when I look at you like this?" He moved his face dangerously close and slowly examined every inch of her face. His gaze lingered on her mouth, teasing her by moving closer every few seconds as though to kiss her. His hand moved to her neck, partially cradling her head.

"*Especially* when you look at me like this," Gabrielle said, so breathless from anticipation she barely could get the words out of her mouth. She closed her eyes so the rest of her senses could take in the moment. She felt his breath hitch as he neared; desire filtered into every part of her body as she warmed from within. She crossed the short distance remaining between them. He immediately responded to her kiss, and his hand moved to the back of her head, weaving his fingers into her hair—gently pushing her head toward his.

Gabrielle's mind began to spin, and she wondered if he would ever lose the power to make her feel this way. She hoped not. She paid close attention to every sensation his touch sent racing through her, to the smell of his skin that mingled with cologne—taking in the scent as she moved her lips down the curve of his neck—and to the sound of their breath as they became increasingly lost in each other.

His hand began to wander over her body like the first time he kissed her. He made her feel wanted—beautiful. It filled her with unfamiliar desire. They were lying down, slightly away from where they'd been sitting—where they had more room to move. Lucas's body pressed against hers, and Gabrielle felt his craving for her becoming more intense as each second passed. His hand moved under her shirt. It was warm and soft on her skin, yet it sent chills racing through her body.

Gabrielle put her hand on his, bringing herself slowly back to the reality she needed to stay in. He didn't protest but continued to kiss her softly as he relaxed.

"You know, I'm old enough to be your grandmother multiplied by something *obscene* … like … a thousand times."

"Cougars are the in thing right now," he said between kisses.

"Well, that would make me more of a Saber Tooth. I don't think society's ready to accept *that* kind of an age difference." She sat up as he remained on the floor lying on his back, his hands behind his head. The definition in his arms distracted Gabrielle for a moment.

"No one but us even knows. You look like you're my age."

"Lucas, we need to speak seriously about this for a minute."

Lucas sat up with over-dramatic seriousness, and Gabrielle

popped his shoulder with the back of her hand.

"*Okay!* I'll be serious, but only for a minute, like you said."

"A minute will be enough," Gabrielle said. "Everyone sees me as a seventeen-year-old, but you and I know I'm not. Lucas, I'm thousands of years old by human time."

"I don't care, Gabby."

Gabrielle shook her head and waved her hand in an effort to show him that wasn't what she meant. Let me just say what I need to say, okay?"

"YUP!" he said, popping the P.

Gabrielle felt herself becoming agitated. She wasn't sure if she felt that way because he was taking this conversation so lightly or if it was negativity from her job. She decided it was probably some of both. She stood up in a huff, showing her disapproval, taking a more severe tone as she continued.

"Lucas, you are not my equal when it comes to physical experience. I can't be with you in the way I think you want me to be. In the way I know I want to be with you." Gabrielle saw the shocked look on his face, and even though she'd warned him how she could be, she made an effort to reign in her irritation. "Look," she continued, "I just want to make sure you understand, *really* understand, our limits—or at least mine. I operate under more stringent rules than you do as a human. Not only because I'm an angel, but because of the job I have *as* an angel."

Lucas's expression was smooth, telling her nothing.

Gabrielle turned, one hand on her hip, slowly running the other through her hair, stopping at the nape of her neck. She sighed heavily. "You don't understand *how* different things are for us, Lucas. This is so much more complicated for me than for you." Gabrielle lowered her head.

She was still turned away from Lucas, not sure if she could look at him. Sometimes human emotions were so difficult to understand. She wasn't accustomed to feeling unsure of herself. She heard fabric moving against skin as Lucas stood, then his footsteps as he approached.

He wrapped his arms snuggly around her from behind. There was silence for several minutes, but Gabrielle was relieved it wasn't awkward. It was comforting. All he seemed to want to do was hold her tightly as if assuring her he would always be there. Gabrielle rested the back of her head against his shoulder.

"You're right," he said.

She felt the warmth of his breath on her ear, causing a tingling sensation to run through her.

"I don't know how different things are for us. Maybe you should explain some more to me so you don't feel alone. You know about humans, for the most part. I still don't know very much about angels."

Gabrielle turned to face him. "What do you want to know?"

"Can we start with Javan? I know he was important to you, but I don't know what a romantic relationship is like for angels."

Gabrielle flinched at Javan's name, as the combination of loss, anger, and love she felt for him came to the surface. "Okay." She took a deep breath. "Angels have many relationships similar to the ones you have here. For example, my superior, Amaziah, is more to me than my overseer. He is my teacher, my friend; he's as close to a father as I can get. I love him very much. Our relationship is probably closest to the one I imagine you have with Ben." Lucas nodded in understanding.

"There are many angels I consider friends. Others are my brethren who I have a kinship with but don't know personally. We're there for each other for whatever is needed, and we offer our assistance with no hesitation, expectations, or questions. We simply need to ask, or be asked, and it is done. In this way, the way we relate to each other contrasts humans. Humans tend to need a motivation of some kind even if it's subconscious." Gabrielle waited to see if he had any questions. None came, so she continued.

"We are also capable of having a very close relationship, if we choose to, with a Reyah—a companion. Like a husband or wife. We couple, which is like your sexual relationships; however, when we do, it's … *different*. It's far less physical than emotional and spiritual. The opposite of what humans experience. A human can achieve satisfaction from a purely physical exchange. This wouldn't interest most angels at all. We crave the deep emotional connection physicality alone can't begin to offer. It's basically a waste of our time, so we either have what we desire or nothing else."

Gabrielle motioned for him to follow her. Her stomach was becoming insistent on her filling it. She picked up her sandwich and took a bite, chewing and swallowing quickly. Lucas was hungry too, judging by his almost half-eaten sandwich. It made her smile. He didn't notice her amusement, concentrating on his next mouthful.

Gabrielle took a sip of her drink and continued. "The way we choose a Reyah is similar to how you would choose a mate. We're drawn to each other, but not because of chemical or physical attraction or ulterior motives that can often guide humans. We're drawn to our mate through Divine guidance; Yahuwah leads us to them. He chooses for us because He knows our match. He guides humans in the same way, but people tend not to pay much attention. You know, free will and all. The biggest difference is we have only one Reyah for our entire existence. If something happens to one of the pair, we can never have another. When one of us loses our Reyah, it's a greater loss than what a human would experience. When a human loses someone, they can choose another love when they are ready and at least ease their pain and fill the void. We feel the pain and void of our loss like it has just happened—forever."

"That seems so cruel of God. To make you feel the loss forever like that, I mean."

"The way we live in my home, as it relates to this subject, is nothing like how humans live. I guess it would be cruel if we lived as you do, but we don't. We don't lie to, or cheat on, each other. We don't get bored and decide to find someone better. Occasionally, there are exceptions, but for the most part, my kind are exceptionally faithful.

"In my home, there's no death from illness or old age. We *can* be killed, but only by another with Divine blood. All we have to fear is an attack by one of the Fallen—a demon. The only other way we are separated forever is if Yahuwah casts one of us out—like with Javan."

"How long has it been since Javan fell?"

"Over a century ago, as your time passes."

Lucas gently reached down to take her hand and kiss it. "You talk about time being different for us. What do you mean?"

"We don't really have time-keeping. If we need to measure it for some reason, for the purpose of our interaction or duties with people, we use the method you do—seconds, minutes, hours, days, months, and so on. Time is infinite for us, though. When we're ascended, it's useless to keep up with it."

"How do you do your job and have it work within our time?"

"The simple answer is I don't have to work within your time, so I don't. I make your time work for me." Lucas looked confused. Gabrielle tried to clarify. "Really, it's a moot point unless I'm in human form. When I'm here, I pause time so I'm not missed, and I don't miss anything I need to be a part of. In mortal time, my job would take much, much longer than a full day. I mean, *every time* I take Yahuwah's orders and hand out karma. So my time moves very swiftly when I'm in my home, while yours, in comparison, moves incredibly slow for me." Lucas still seemed to be having a hard time understanding.

"The full answer is really too hard for you to understand. Try to keep in mind that anything is possible for Yahuwah even if something seems impossible to you. You don't have to have answers for *everything*. Life would lose so much magic, all its wonder, if you had all the answers to every question you ask. It's nice to have unknowns, sometimes. It allows for imagination. It's a shame people don't use theirs much, anymore."

Gabrielle adjusted to face him, still holding his hand as she did. It seemed they always had to be touching if they were near each other, like some invisible power pulled their bodies closer. Lucas smiled as if he read her thoughts.

"Does that help?" she asked.

"Some, but I still have more questions. Why do you call God, Yahuwah and Satan, Ramai?"

Gabrielle laughed.

"Because Yahuwah is His name, and Ramai … it's what Angels began calling him after he fell. It means deceiver."

He smiled, then drifted into his own thoughts. The break allowed things to enter her mind that she didn't want to dwell on.

She kissed him on his hand to get his attention. "How about we take a break from this and get some fresh air? Want to take a walk? I need a little more distraction and a little less reality."

"Fresh air sounds good."

The last thing she wanted to think about right now were the laws she was supposed to conduct herself by when it came to relationships with humans, or that being allowed romantic interaction was pretty much unheard of. She had plenty of time to think about it later when he wasn't with her. She planned on enjoying the happiness and peace being with him brought her while she could, knowing, at any moment, it could end.

Chapter Forty

GABRIELLE ✝ A VISION

After Gabrielle had changed clothes, she and Lucas slowly made their way to the park a few blocks from her townhouse. She had spent a lot of time there over the summer months, watching mothers pushing strollers and joggers pushing themselves to their limits. Almost everyone had ear buds in, drowning out the sounds of birds singing, insects buzzing, and wind blowing through the leaves, causing the trees to sound as if they were giggling as the breeze tickled them. It made her sad that all the simplicity and beauty surrounding people was lost to them. So many pleasures and miracles went without notice.

It was a perfect early fall day, and Gabrielle was glad to enjoy it before it passed. The leaves were showing hints of the colors they would be turning, becoming trimmed or dappled with the reds, yellows, and oranges that spoke of fall's approach.

By an unspoken decision, Gabrielle and Lucas stopped at the playground, and each took an available swing. After several minutes of silence, Gabrielle slowed hers until it was barely moving. She slipped off her flip-flops and played in the sand with the tips of her toes, drawing formless squiggles and unidentifiable shapes.

"So, how about I get a round of questions?" Gabrielle's mood was still edgy, and she worried her request sounded more like a demand. Lucas didn't seem to notice or mind.

"My book is open to you, sweets."

"*Sweets?*"

"I thought it would be a little premature to call you love ... love."

Lucas was flirting, and Gabrielle was enjoying it.

"Sweets doesn't always describe my mood, so it may not be an appropriate pet name. And *love* may be a little pre—"

"But ... I *am* falling in love with you, Gabby. I don't see a reason to deny it. Facts are facts. Love is love—*love*."

Lucas smiled his crooked smile, making him irresistible. She abandoned her swing and made her way to the human she too felt she was completely, recklessly, falling in love with.

"You shouldn't interrupt your elder," she said. "Or a lady. I was going to say, a pet name of *love* may be a little premature, but I like the sound of it anyway."

"Oh." Lucas stood. He placed a hand on each side of her face and caressed her cheeks with his thumbs. He didn't make a move to kiss her, and she was glad. There was something very important about the moment Gabrielle didn't quite understand. She felt the connection between them growing, stitching them together as they looked into each other's eyes. This was one of those moments, a little miracle, she felt people didn't thoroughly absorb. She was glad he seemed to want to linger in it as long as she did.

A Frisbee that had lost its way landed at Gabrielle's feet, moving them back into the world they'd removed themselves from. As Lucas threw it back, Gabrielle looked up and smiled, wondering if it was Yahuwah's way of getting her back on track.

"What's that smile for?"

She took her gaze off the heavens and let it fall back on Lucas, still smiling. "Oh, nothing ... so, back to you being in the hot-seat."

"Ahh ... yes," he responded a little apprehensively.

"I need to know what happened between you and Mara. I want all the details. How you met, things she said, maybe something that happened you thought was *off*." Gabrielle didn't want to come right out and tell him Mara was a demon.

Finding out a demon was in his life first ... then me. That's a lot to accept.

She wondered how he'd take the news that he'd ... been involved ... with one of the Fallen.

Lucas laughed, but there was no humor accompanying it. "*Hmm* ... I'm not sure where to even begin. The whole thing was trippy, *off*, like you said." He took her hand, and they started to walk again. "I met her after school let out for the summer. She'd just moved here from some little town up in Kentucky. I can't recall the name. She was really cool, at first. And with her being easy on the eyes and possibly fun to hang with, I thought what the heck? Then, after about three weeks of some *really* hot times together ..." Lucas looked at Gabrielle, seeming to realize what he'd just said.

"Don't worry. I won't say I *want* to hear everything, but I need to. I can handle it." She smiled at him for encouragement though she hated hearing about him with Mara.

"Well, I'm sure you get the gist without those details. Long story short, she became strange. She started showing this unusual mean streak, seemed to get pleasure from other people's pain—emotional and physical. She just generally became—well—evil, or something. She went from wearing bright colors and girly clothes to wearing dark, mostly black clothes. There's nothing wrong with black, but when it matches the person's mood, it isn't quite the same thing as a simple color preference. And her eyes, they were this pretty shade of hazel, but they turned more yellowish-green. When I asked, she said she had contacts, but I didn't believe her. I sensed something was very wrong, so I made a break from her."

Lucas stopped at a bench, and they sat down.

"But why were you so angry with her when you saw her at school last week? What was that about?"

"Patience ... love." He said the last word as if he was testing the waters. "I didn't hear anything from her for a couple of weeks, and then she shows up at my front door. I caught a glimpse of her when I was coming to open it and asked Gran to tell her I wasn't there. Now that I think about it, Gran seemed leery about answering it herself. I guess she sensed there was something wrong with her before she even saw her. When she opened the door and told Mara I wasn't there, she shoved Gran across the room and screamed, *'You lying bitch!'* She just went psycho, like a switch flipped inside her. I think the only reason I got Mara out of the house so easily was because I caught her off-guard. She had to be extraordinarily strong to send Gran flying across the room like that. I guess I should have thought it was stranger at the time, but it still freaked me out.

"Anyway, I tackled her with so much force that it sent both of us back through the open door. We ended up on the porch and almost down the stairs. I got up and told her to leave and not to come back, or I'd call the police. Then, I went back in and closed the door. She laughed this wicked laugh. Seriously, Gabby, it was more like a cackle. It gave me chills. I heard her outside talking to herself and laughing that laugh for several minutes until she finally left. That first day of school was the first time I had seen her since."

"That certainly explains your hostility."

"There's more. That day you saw her with me and got upset, *that* was the creepiest. I didn't tell you about it before because I thought you would think I was a loon." Lucas paused to consider his words. "It's hard to explain. And it might all just be in my head."

Lucas went on to tell her what had happened, and Gabrielle listened carefully. By the time he'd finished, she determined he hadn't made the connection that Mara was more than *off*.

"I bet the Mara you met originally is still in there, just pushed so far down she can't get out. Possession is more common than people think, and it's very powerful. A demon can be sneaky in its possession, only come out from time to time, or it can be all-consuming and just take full control abruptly. It sounds to me that, for Mara, it's the latter. I can help her, if it's Yahuwah's will."

"Why wouldn't it be? Why would He want someone to be

possessed?" Lucas asked in a baffled, almost angry tone.

"Lucas, you have to have faith He has a plan even when you don't think His hand is in a situation at all. He knows *everything* that's happening. Well, with the exception of some things He agreed with Ramai to be in the dark about, but that's a story for another time. But if it isn't His will, He intervenes or uses it to His advantage. It all works out in the end, as long as the person has faith."

"I get the faith thing. Really, I do. But if you're right and she is possessed by a demon, it just doesn't seem to be fair. She seemed like a decent girl—a little loose, maybe, but who am I to judge? She wasn't alone in fooling around while we were together. But other than that, she seemed really decent. What made me any better? Why'd she get possessed and not me?"

"Lucas, you didn't know her long, and I don't know her at all. We don't have enough information about her to understand if she was somehow inviting a demon into her life. Even if she didn't know what she was doing. A lot of times, that doesn't even matter. If a demon wants to possess a human, there isn't always a way to avoid it."

"I'd still like to see her okay again—to be a normal teenager."

"I believe the use of normal and teenager together in the same sentence is what is called an oxymoron—*isn't it?*"

Lucas shot her a playful warning glance. Before Gabrielle could get two steps away, she was lying on the ground with Lucas on top of her, tickling her sides as she laughed and begged for mercy.

Mercy came as his warm lips pressed firmly against hers, and she surrendered to him without protest. She didn't know if she could resist if she wanted to.

As the sun reached its rays out to touch their skin one last time before it fell asleep for the night, Gabrielle felt Lucas press his body hard against hers like he was trying to melt into her. She was glad it was getting dark. There was nothing except how he made her feel and how she made him feel in return.

The images flashed so quickly she almost didn't pay attention. When they came the second time, they weren't as fleeting. She sucked in a sharp breath as the vision, full of screams and terror and death, played out in her mind. Gabrielle sat up so quickly she nearly threw Lucas to the side, leaving him scrambling the rest of the way off her. He knelt next to her with a stunned expression.

"Gabby! What's wrong?"

She didn't answer. She couldn't. The vision was vivid, playing in front of her like it was on a movie screen.

"Gabrielle! Please! You're scaring me!"

The panic in his voice broke through her concentration as she tried to figure out how she might be able to stop the vision from happening. As the images in her mind faded away, she focused on Lucas. He looked at her with wide, expectant eyes—desperation dominating his expression.

"Lucas … I'm sorry. I just had a powerful vision, and it took me by surprise. I saw …" She wasn't sure how to tell him or even if she should.

"What, Gabby? *What* did you see?"

"It was you. You, Nate, and Nonie. You were being attacked."

"What? By who?"

Lucas began to calm slightly. Maybe he didn't think what she saw was as alarming as he'd thought, but it was. He just wasn't thinking about the right kind of attacker or, in this case, predator.

"The appropriate question is *by what*, Lucas."

He looked at her, puzzled. She could tell he was losing patience with her as she began to get lost in the vision again when he let out a huff. She looked at him for a moment longer and hoped he would be as accepting of this information as he had been about her.

"Lucas, you're *really* going to have to have an open mind about this and trust me when I say there are things that people don't believe exist but are quite real."

His head moved quickly in an exasperated nod.

"You were being attacked by the Damned, Lucas—by the Qalal."

Lucas's expression was one of confusion. She realized he didn't know them by the name she gave.

"Humans call them vampires."

Chapter Forty-one

GABRIELLE ✝ THE FANTASTICAL WORLD

"Vampires?" Lucas asked in disbelief.

Gabrielle nodded, knowing he'd have a hard time wrapping his mind around this. It was enough for him to accept angels and demons, but now, he was faced with something he probably never considered possible.

They had barely spoken as they walked back to her townhouse, both deep in thought about her vision. Once inside, they went straight into the kitchen and sat at the counter bar. When Lucas spoke, he seemed to be in a trance, his tone flat and distant.

"Blood sucking, red eyed, incredibly strong and fast, burst into flames in sunlight, stake through the heart, sleeps in a coffin—*vampires*."

"I've never known any who actually sleep in a coffin, and they don't burst into flames in the sunlight, but other than that, yes. However, they are called Qalal, and they don't exist for the reasons Hollywood would have you believe."

"I hope you're going to enlighten me, then. If I'm going to be scrapping with them, I need all the information I can get."

"Qalal exist for one reason; they don't value human life. They are those of your society who choose to murder or commit suicide. Hollywood has one thing right—they are damned. Their punishment isn't turning into a monster with an insatiable urge for blood for eternity, though. It's living that eternity with the absence of Yahuwah's love and Light. It might not sound bad, but it leaves them an empty shell. Nothing, not even the blood they crave, ever satisfies them. The longer they go without Grace, the more they realize what they have forsaken. If they choose to take human lives, it becomes harder to deny their thirst the longer they live by that choice. As their craving worsens, the absence of Yahuwah's love and Light is felt more profoundly. It becomes a miserable existence, but they don't realize how bad it will get until it's too late."

Lucas went to the refrigerator and got them Cokes, handing one to Gabrielle as he asked a question. "What happens if they don't kill people?"

"Unlike the Fallen, they have the opportunity to earn redemption. If they prove they value human life by *not* killing or turning humans, they can regain their soul. It takes a very long time to convince Yahuwah of their sincerity, though. Most give into their urges. But some attain redemption. If they do, they become Guardians—protecting and guiding humans. They aren't quite angels, and it isn't how humans typically exist in Heaven, but it allows them to ascend, and it beats Hell or remaining Qalal."

"How do they survive if they don't drink blood?"

"There isn't anything they can't eat; they just don't *want* anything else. Animal blood helps dull their desire for what they really want, but the craving for human blood is severe. To refrain is agonizing, especially at first. Eventually, if they are able to keep from giving in to their wantings, it gets easier."

"So, why can't they go into sunlight if it doesn't kill them?"

"They can but usually don't. The sun represents the Divine light of Yahuwah, hence something they are not allowed to enjoy. It drains their energy. Pretty quickly, actually. It leaves them in a drug-like stupor for days, and it takes a long time to regain their strength. When they do go outside in the day, it's usually only so for short periods of time."

Gabrielle stopped talking, letting the information find its place in Lucas's mind. He didn't say anything for several minutes, and she imagined he was trying to get a handle on his ever-changing reality.

"What else exists that most people don't believe in?"

"Do you really want to know, Lucas? I'm not sure you'll believe me if I tell you."

Lucas didn't answer right away, then nodded reluctantly.

"There are all kinds of fantastical creatures people don't think literally exist. There is what *you* call werewolves, but they aren't what you think. Then, you have fairies, dwarves, goblins, and numerous nature spirits. The—"

"I think that's enough for now," Lucas interrupted. Gabrielle wasn't surprised. He seemed to grow paler with every word she spoke. "Go back to the werewolves. You said they aren't what I think, so what are they?"

"Werewolves are actually shape shifters. They can shift into any animal form they want, but wolves are the traditional choice. Shifters are a very old variation of humans, but they live far longer. In their case, the dog years comparison you use for how fast a dog ages compared to a human would be reversed. *You* age at a much faster rate than they do. I know one shifter, Grayson, who looks like he's about your age, but he's actually one hundred and eight."

"You actually *know* a werewolf? Have had *conversations* with it?"

"Not it, *him*. I interact with many Shifters. I have relationships with many who live in Enchantment and Shadows. There are times I call on them to assist me in my work, and I have close relationships with some because I've worked with them for so long."

Lucas slumped into the counter more, looking tired and worried, but Gabrielle could tell he wasn't ready to stop the conversation. She could almost hear his mind racing through the information, trying to seek answers to all the questions he had.

"Back to the vampire attack you saw in your vision—what do you make of it?"

"That's perplexing, because out of all the Shadow creatures, I have the least amount of contact with them. But usually Qalal operate very discretely. As a whole, they stick to a few strict rules. An attack like I saw in my vision would be surprising."

"What can we do?" Lucas's concern was written deeply in the furrows between his brows and the frantic look in his eyes.

"Well, first I'll meet with their Elders and confront them with my vision to see what I can find out. It could be they, or a rogue coven, are planning something. I may not find out, though. They can be deceitful, but they know it would be a *very* bad idea to lie to me. It might turn out that they have no knowledge of anything concerning the vision. If the latter is the case, I should have their assistance in my search for who these particular Qalal are."

Lucas squinted at her. "Why would they want to help you?"

"Refraining from killing or turning humans isn't the only way to help themselves regain their souls. You could say they score additional points if they assist me when I need them. They've helped countless times in my work. That, and they're aware of my abilities, so they'll be wary of crossing me."

"In your work?" Lucas raised his brows. "How?"

"I've been given the power to use those that live in Shadows and Enchantment at my discretion in order to deal with—*certain*—situations."

"That doesn't sound pleasant."

Gabrielle smiled. "It's not. But that's the point." She paused. "We need to begin preparing for the attack."

"When will it be?" There was a frantic edge to his tone.

"I don't have the specific date, but we should have some time."

"How do you know?"

"The attack was outside, and I saw heavy snow falling. So, unless everyone goes on a ski trip, or there's some crazy weather in Tennessee at the end of September, we have time to prepare. And to hopefully get more information."

"You're sure about the snow?"

"Yes. But premonitions and Knowings aren't absolute. The result is usually unavoidable, but how it happens, and even when, can change."

Lucas focused past Gabrielle to the kitchen cabinets, but she knew he saw nothing except the scenarios he was creating in his mind. After some time had passed, he turned his head slightly. He looked into Gabrielle's eyes, his own pleading with her before any words escaped his lips. When they did, they came out in a faint whisper.

"Gabby, you *have* to help us. Please."

She took his hand between hers and moved as close to him as she could with the counter still between them.

"I will, Lucas. I promise."

Lucas lowered his head, and Gabrielle wondered if he was trying to hide tears, but when he looked up, his expression was stony.

"When are you going to see their Elders?"

"Immediately after you leave."

"How long will you be gone?"

"Maybe half a day. I know where to find them, but once I do, it will take time to discuss everything."

"Can't you just pause time?"

Gabrielle got the feeling he didn't want her to be away from him. After all he'd become aware of in just a matter of hours, she didn't blame him. She wasn't crazy about leaving him, either.

"Sure, but I don't need to. I can be there now if I want to be, but I'll still have to speak with them in human time."

Lucas looked a little confused.

"Only those with Divine blood are functioning and aware when I pause time—angels, demons, Shifters, Nephilim, and the Gentry. Trust me, there isn't anything Divine in a Qalal. I have to talk to them in mortal time."

"Oh." He looked distant again. "Can I come with you?"

Gabrielle pressed her normally full lips into a thin line.

"Gabby, this concerns me and people I love."

There were so many reasons it was a bad idea for him to go. She understood why he wanted to though, and she would ask the same if she were in his position. As she thought about the pros and cons—mostly cons—his stony expression held.

"I don't know, Lucas." Gabrielle stood. "It's dangerous for you to be in the company of Qalal. You *are* their preferred food source."

"I don't believe they'll hurt me with you there. You seem confident they regard you with quite a bit of respect in the 'Don't screw with me' department." Lucas stood, as if to punctuate his comment.

"To be sure! But Lucas, there's a lot you don't understand about Qalal or any of the other creatures you can get into trouble with."

Gabrielle placed her palms on her forehead out of frustration and as a reminder to keep her temper in check. She could feel her agitation rising, and Lucas seemed to sense the need to give her some time.

After quite a few deep, calming breaths, she continued. "Here's the thing. Once they're aware you know about them, you're fair game. You become *available* for them to take care of, *if* they decide to, with no repercussions."

"Why?"

"They, and the other creatures, see any human who knows they exist as a direct threat to their survival, and they're right. I'm sure you can imagine how they would be hunted if people knew about them. Yahuwah allows Qalal to protect themselves, without punishment, if a person knows of them through no fault of the Qalal. When you add the intense urge they have for the blood in your body, and that they can have it without hurting their chances of reclaiming their soul, you're in big trouble."

Lucas didn't acknowledge if he understood the consequences except with his body language. His face remained stony, but he put his hands in his front pockets, letting his shoulders drop forward as his body fell back against the counter.

Unmoving, they stared at each other for a long time.

Breaking the silence, Lucas spoke. His voice was quiet, but deliberate, and there was complete determination in his eyes. "Gabby … *I'm going.*"

Chapter Forty-two

LUCAS ✛ DARK THOUGHTS

The rest of Lucas's evening was a blur of packing bags, making travel arrangements, and explaining to Gran why he and Gabrielle were running off in the middle of the night and would be gone for a couple of days. Luckily, Gabby was able to get them a red-eye flight to New York and then another to Europe early the next morning.

For obvious reasons, Gran wasn't happy about the decision he had made, but because he still had the same look of determination, she didn't put up much of an argument. She was well aware of his stubbornness and that there was no changing his mind once he made a decision, but it also helped that she knew he was in the safest hands possible.

He and Gabby didn't say much on the way to the airport. The lengthiest conversation was when Lucas brought up needing to stop to get money for the trip, which mildly amused Gabby. She explained that when money was needed, she would simply have it. He shook his head and decided to just go with it.

Money appearing out of nowhere was something else to add to the list of what was an impossibility for Lucas a day and a half ago. Circumstances were forcing him to become an open-minded and fast learner.

He still hadn't been able to get the look on Gabby's face during her vision out of his thoughts. Her eyes were wide with panic and horror while the rest of her face held no expression, frozen from the onslaught of images. She had seemed so far away that he hadn't known if she would hear him calling her name at all. How bad had the scene playing in her mind been?

Maybe it's better if I don't know.

In the short amount of time that had passed since he had learned of the fantastical side of the world, especially that he was a part of that mystical side, he had wondered if he was better off not knowing. It would mean remaining in the dark about whom he was, though. He would continue to have unanswered questions about himself, probably for the rest of his life, and that wasn't comforting, either.

It would mean that I wouldn't know that there is someone out there who tried to kill me, who will probably try to kill me, again. Someone I want to find. Someone I will find.

Fresh adrenaline surged through him from his anger and need for revenge. His hands formed tight fists. He wanted to cause the demon who murdered his family as much pain as a human could, dragging it out as long as possible. He wanted to see its black eyes plead with him for its existence as he watched its life fade away to nothing.

The way he enjoyed watching the lives drain out of my family's eyes, and the child's—the one he thought was me.

He wanted that more than anything he had ever wanted in his life.

He hadn't mentioned to Gabby or Gran that while he stood there in the living room that night, frozen and unable to speak, listening to the horrific end of most of his family, he was already planning an agonizing end for the demon. With every word spoken about the murders and the murderer, more power and life was breathed into that dark creature that he was beginning to accept lived within him—a creature that would remain silent no longer now that it yearned for blood. Lucas smiled tightly at the thought. Whether anyone thought it was right or not, he would enjoy the moment he ended the life that had caused him so much loss—so much pain.

He just had to figure out how to find him. Lucas knew it was going to take a tremendous amount of planning and patience. He hoped accompanying Gabby would teach him more about what he needed to know of the Underworld and Shadow World and all its inhabitants.

Lucas closed his eyes and focused on calming himself. He didn't want Gabby to see, or somehow sense, his intentions. If he were honest, the level of hate it brought out of him was unnerving. He had never felt the hunger to end someone else's life. He didn't even know he had it in him *to* feel it, but he wanted to watch as the demon's blood spilled, and know he was the one responsible the demon's death.

He focused on how it felt to hold and kiss Gabby, trying to recreate the feelings of warmth and desire, hoping it would be stronger than the anger as he tried to push the dark thoughts away. It seemed to work. He felt his pulse slow, his hands relax. Lucas shook off the obsessive thoughts as he brought his focus back on their journey and the angel who sat next to him. He took her hand in his as they continued their drive to the airport, but it wasn't until they were seated on the plane, taxying down the runway, that he began to truly feel better.

Lucas turned to Gabby who was peering out the window next to her, looking into the black night surrounding them. The color seemed to be deeper than normal. Was it because the thick ceiling of clouds blocked what little light the moon and stars offered, or was it his new knowledge of the real Darkness of the world? He wasn't going to think any more about creatures lurking, though. He was going to be content just looking at her, and he had a feeling she was somewhere in her mind where nothing in her human vision would garner her attention.

Butterflies stirred his stomach. They had hitched a ride as soon as they left his house but were more active as he considered what could be in her thoughts. Was she thinking about the vision? His safety? What the Qalal may do to him later? If he was worth all this trouble? If God would strike them both down for their relationship? It was all a part of the unknown craziness he was venturing into. He sighed quietly and tried to let his thoughts drift further toward Gabrielle—away from questions he had no answers for.

Lucas could have never imagined someone would have the ability to possess his heart so completely—so quickly. A lock of hair slipped out of her messy ponytail, and he gently tucked it behind her ear, feeling a familiar rush of warmth.

Gabby turned her head toward him, then her body. She reached out to put a hand on his cheek. When her fingertips touched his skin, more tendrils of heat meandered through him—dwelling in every inch of his body. He wished they were alone so he could kiss her the way he wanted. Instead, he closed his eyes, took her hand, and slowly brought it to his lips. Starting at her fingertips and ending at the bend of her elbow, he tenderly kissed her skin. When he raised his head and opened his eyes, she was smiling her brilliant, perfect smile, causing his stomach to flip.

"Thank you, love," he whispered, "for letting me come. At least this makes me feel like I'm not just waiting around to be a victim. I couldn't sit by and do nothing. It would have made me crazy."

"I think you're pretty much ready for the straight-jacket *now* for doing this," she whispered, laughing as she did. "But, I would have insisted too, if I were you." She paused, seeming to get caught up in studying his face; he was only inches away from her. She reached to touch his cheek again.

"I do understand, Lucas."

After a few moments, they closed their eyes and drifted into restless sleep. Both had similar, unsettling dreams full of blood, violence, pain, and heart-wrenching loss.

Dreams they both kept to themselves, hoping that was all they would ever be.

Chapter Forty-three

GABRIELLE † THREE WORDS

Gabrielle and Lucas awoke at the same time as the captain's voice alerted their descent into New York City. The flight had been smooth, and both slept the entire time, but neither felt rested due to the vivid, violent scenes that played out in their minds.

They made their way through the wide walkways of the airport until they found a quiet spot to wait until their flight boarded for London. Gabrielle sat and propped her feet up on her carry-on. Lucas lay down on the seats next to her, placing his head in her lap. She switched back and forth between running her fingers through his hair and gently stroking his temple with her thumb.

Images of the dreams and visions took turns in her mind. It was frustrating to have so many unanswered questions, to know something horrible was coming in Lucas's future—maybe *several* things based on all she'd been shown—and any one of them could end his life.

And I can't do a damn thing about it because I still *don't know what* any *of it really means!*

"I've always liked to fly just so I can people watch. But there isn't much opportunity to do that in the wee hours, huh?" Lucas asked, pulling Gabrielle back from her ponderings.

"What?" she asked through a laugh. Lucas had asked his question with a straight face, and the outburst of laughter from Gabrielle startled him. Gabrielle had to give herself a second to reign in her amusement. "You're flying to another continent to see the Damned, and your thoughts are about having no people to watch. I'm both impressed and concerned you're not asking many questions." She became more serious. "Don't you have more questions? We've covered a little about angels and other things, but not enough to satisfy what I would think would be natural human curiosity."

Lucas smiled and shook his head. "Oh, love."

Her heart skipped when he called her that.

He sat up slowly, scooting his body into the seat next to her. "I have a million questions in my head. I just don't know where to start."

"How about with something easy, and we can go from there? If you're up to it?"

"Sure. The only other thing to do is sleep. I don't think I'll be getting much of that on these incredibly wonderful, sleep inviting, cushy, *comfy* plastic seats," he said with more than a hint of sarcasm. "What did you think of your first flight? Well, on a *plane*."

Gabrielle laughed lightly. "That I could have been at our final destination now instead of taking over half a day like we're doing." She saw Lucas flinch and realized how she must have sounded. Her mood still wasn't that good. She quickly tried to make up for her choice of words and delivery. "But if I had traveled the way I'm accustomed to, I wouldn't be here with you. For that reason alone, I would happily trek across the world and back if you were my companion on the journey."

Lucas made a dramatic gagging noise. It was her turn to be caught off-guard.

"What?" Gabrielle asked, confused as to what brought on the dramatics.

"It's a really good thing there was no one around to hear you because, as much as I believe you mean it, that sounded disgustingly sappy. I think anyone within earshot would have hurled." He could barely contain his laughter, sending Gabrielle into a playful attack mode as she proceeded to pinch him anywhere he wasn't constantly trying to move to protect.

After several seconds of wrestling and laughter, they calmed down. A few moments more and they were snuggled up again, Gabrielle's head resting on his shoulder, easily picking up the conversation where they'd left off.

"I did mean it, you know. Even if it did sound sappy. You make me sappy, Lucas. One big sappy, dopey, teenagery, mushy, mess of a powerful—I should know better than to be doing this—angel."

"I'm happy I have that effect on you, love. I don't feel so ridiculous now about the things I think about you." He kissed the top of her head, then moved the conversation back toward his questions.

"Why does it make you feel ridiculous?" she asked.

"We haven't known each other very long."

Gabrielle could hear a smile in his tone even if she wasn't looking at him to see it, but he seemed hesitant to voice the rest of what he wanted to say. After she felt his shoulders rise with a deep breath, he continued.

"Most people would say that it's too soon to have feelings as deep as I already have for you. I ... uh ..." Lucas let out a soft chuckle but never finished his statement.

Gabrielle realized what he was trying to tell her, though. The idea of hearing the words *I love you*, and not just *I'm falling in love with you*, coming from his lips terrified her. This relationship was turning out to be so much more than she ever bargained for. She'd hoped for it, though, even if she hadn't easily admitted that to herself.

But ... wow ...

Gabrielle let that conversation drift off to a quiet and possibly premature end. She just wasn't ready to deal with those three words at the moment. Luckily, Lucas filled the silence with another question.

"So … will you tell me what all of your powers and abilities are?"

Gabrielle smiled. "I wondered when you would get around to the *superhero* powers. I have quite a few. Some I've just received and haven't used … *yet*. I know we've talked about a couple of them, but I'm just going to go down the list."

Lucas grinned and nodded.

"There's, of course, pausing time—"

"*That* one I won't ever forget," he said.

Both snickered, but Gabrielle felt the bite of guilt return for a moment. She quickly shook it off and continued, not wanting to let the emotion take over her mood.

"There's telepathy with other angels, but that's one all angels have. So is reading a human's mind, but we rarely do that. It's considered too intrusive unless it's a necessity. If we use that ability, we have to answer for it to the Council."

"Why?"

"We aren't supposed to interfere with a human's free will. Unless we plan to in some way, there's not much of a reason to use that ability."

Lucas made an exaggerated *of course* gesture, which brought on a much shorter version of their earlier wrestling match. Gabrielle continued after he pleaded for mercy.

"I obviously have the ability to take human form and have human interaction."

"My personal favorite, I must say," Lucas piped in and flashed that wonderful crooked grin.

Gabrielle couldn't resist returning it with her own. "I can Hush, now. Which I'm considering trying out for the first time on you," she said jokingly.

"What's that?"

"With a small gesture and thought, I can make any creature, whether of Divine blood or human, be quiet. It takes away the ability to verbalize, and in the case of those with Divine blood and Qalal, ceases their ability to communicate telepathically. Then, I just lift the Hush, and they can communicate normally once again.

"I can make people forget whatever I feel they need to, with only the thought to make it so, be where I want to be within moments; I have tremendous strength and speed, and I have power to command any creature, except demons and the Gentry, to do what I ask when it relates to my job, but *only* then." Gabrielle took in a deep breath and let it out slowly. "And I now have the ability to control the four elements."

"Whoa! Really?" Lucas nearly sprang to his feet. He turned and looked at her with wide eyes and probably the biggest grin she'd ever seen on his face. "You can control the four elements?"

"I'm not surprised you like that one." Gabrielle smiled, wondering what was going through his mind. She'd bet he was thinking of all the ways he would use her powers.

Lucas made an exaggerated *of course* face and gesture again, then played like he was protecting himself from the pinching he was sure would be coming from Gabrielle. When he stopped, he smiled and kissed her, resituating himself closer to her.

"I would take *any* of the powers and abilities you have, but if I had to pick just one, it'd be a toss-up between controlling the elements and making money appear like magic—whenever. Push come to shove ... money would win."

"Oh yeah, I guess I forgot to mention the money ... and stuff."

"And stuff? What others are you *forgetting*?"

"Wouldn't *you* like to know? I have to leave some surprises for you."

Lucas was getting a kick out of all the things Gabrielle could do, and it made her happy to feel he accepted her for who she was. The nagging voice in the back of her mind returned though, still trying to get her attention. Asking if she really thought it was going to work out between them—pointing out she could never have a future with him.

Unless ...

She pushed the voice away, not wanting to give it the opportunity to take root and grow. It would take over her reasoning if it did, and she'd have to abandon Lucas and this feeling she had with him—*forever*. The only other option she could see was if she made the decision, as Emma had, to live life completely as a human—to die as one. That wasn't an option she wanted to consider. Leaving her brethren's, and particularly Yahuwah's, presence was the last thing she desired to do. With neither choice, giving up Lucas or her Divine home and life, being appealing, she'd continue to push the voice away—and would keep doing so whenever it returned—until she was forced to make a decision.

The day will come when I have to.

"Gabby, are you ok? You look upset."

"I'm fine." She smiled, trying to wipe her thoughts clean again. "Any more questions right now?"

He smiled a very sexy smile and nodded. "Do you know what God thinks about one of His most powerful angels and little ol' me hooking up?"

She really didn't want to stay on this subject. It would prompt the voice to chime in again.

"He knows, and all I can tell you at this point is He believes our relationship is beneficial. He thinks I'll obtain important insight about people's motivations pertaining to a romantic relationship." Gabrielle paused as she felt the full weight of what she was trying to do to help win the war rest on her, dragging her mood and expression down with its heaviness. She knew that thinking about the burden of it would cause her to quickly become grim and intense, but this was reality. Lives—*everything*—was at stake. "We're fighting a war, Lucas. A war for the souls residing in the bodies that walk and will walk Earth. There isn't one of Yahuwah's children He doesn't want to see come home to Him when their time here is over. But Darkness is becoming stronger, and it's causing us to lose more and more of you every day. I *have* to figure out how to get through to people so they'll *want* to do, to *be*, better—to make the right decisions." Gabrielle paused. "For now, He's allowing this; I don't know for how long. That's why I wanted you to think about if you want to continue with our relationship. We have no guarantees. Other than that, I've been cautioned to not go too far."

Lucas looked at Gabrielle and spoke thoughtfully. "I guess I'll just have to let out little bits of information at a time, then. Maybe that'll keep you around longer." He smiled, but she saw the sadness behind it. "I can always play hard to get."

They both laughed at the suggestion.

"What? Little late?" he asked playfully, raising one brow as if the thought surprised him.

"Yeah." She chuckled. "I'd say so."

The next three months would pass far too quickly. She wished she could slow time, make it last longer. But that was beyond even her power.

Chapter Forty-four

GABRIELLE † CHILDREN ARE THE BEST

The serious, and not so serious, conversations helped make their layover pass quickly. The questioning had ended without either one deciding it was time to move on, but Gabrielle knew he would need more answers later.

When they boarded the plane, Gabrielle took the window seat again. She was going to have to work and didn't want any more disturbance of her human body than necessary when she began her communication with Sheridan.

As everyone settled in for the long flight, she explained to Lucas that outwardly she would look as if she was sleeping. And if he needed her, all he had to do was shake her, stressing not to do it unless he had to. Again, she was surprised how easily he accepted the information.

Gabrielle closed her eyes and called to Sheridan, and the two got to work. Sheridan had nothing new to report concerning the Book and reassured Gabrielle she would alert her when there was. When Gabrielle came back to Lucas, there was a little more than half an hour before their descent. He was sleeping, apparently well judging by his open mouth and slight snore. She couldn't help but laugh.

Her amusement caught the attention of a little girl sitting in front of her who stood up in her seat and turned around to look at Gabrielle. Her blue eyes sparkled with the wonder only a child can possess. She was about five years old with hair the color of white sand and perfectly smooth skin. She moved the fingers on her right hand to say hello, and when Gabrielle waved back and smiled, she stood up further in her seat, revealing her wide smile with one missing front tooth.

Children are the best.

She rarely had to give out bad karma to them unless they were particularly cruel. She did reward the good things they did when Yahuwah felt it was needed to give them positive reinforcement. Other than that, He allowed them to learn through the results of their choices until they were older. She caught herself wondering what it would be like to have children of her own—not that it was possible.

Lucas woke to see Gabrielle playing peek-a-boo with the girl and just watched her—seeming to enjoy their interaction. When the girl noticed Lucas was awake, she immediately ducked behind the seat. Gabrielle and Lucas laughed as the girl slowly peeked over the top of the seat. Once she decided she wanted to flirt with Lucas, she turned on her little-kid charm and entertained them until the captain announced they were beginning their descent to London. The girl turned around and gave verbal protest to her mom. She wasn't ready to abandon her fun with the strangers behind her.

Lucas took Gabrielle's hand and squeezed. She returned the gesture and laid her head on his shoulder, leaving it there until it was time to stand and leave the plane. As they approached the baggage claim, Lucas told her to wait while he grabbed their things.

Gabrielle decided to do some of her own people watching while she waited. She wondered where everyone was coming from—where they were going. She was caught up in thought about the people moving around her when the little girl from the plane moved into her line of vision. Gabrielle focused on her, ready to say bye to their new friend. When her eyes settled on the child, Gabrielle's shock sent her stumbling back a couple of steps, struggling to catch the breath she felt had been knocked out of her.

The little girl with sparkling blue eyes and big, friendly grin had stopped. The sea of people that had been flowing around her were no longer there—only the little girl and Gabrielle remained. She was turned slightly to face Gabrielle—*glaring*.

Her once blue eyes were solid black and so shiny that the bright lights of the terminal glinted off them. Her smile was the furthest from friendly as it could be; it was a sneer and abnormally wide for her, or anyone else's, face—showing brown, gnarly teeth. She flicked a long red serpents tongue at Gabrielle, and she could swear she heard the little girl hiss.

As soon as Gabrielle felt the shock subsiding, the little girl's face and eyes returned to normal, and she turned to continue walking as her mom and the tide of people returned.

Gabrielle watched her. *Did that really just happen? Is my human mind's imagination getting the best of me?*

As if the girl heard her, she turned again and shot Gabrielle a wicked smile, releasing an unnerving, evil giggle as she did—a giggle Gabrielle was sure only she could hear. Then she turned around again and vanished in the crowded airport.

A wave of nausea overtook Gabrielle, and she felt light-headed. The walls around her began to sway, and the ground beneath her joined their dance. She felt her body go limp. Blackness closed in from all directions. Just before she lost consciousness, she felt two arms wrap around her and heard Lucas's voice in her ear saying her name—desperation edging into his normally melodic tone.

Another voice overpowered Lucas's, making his seem distant.

'You may be powerful, Gabrielle, but Yahuwah created me even more powerful long before you existed. I am the power of His power, mind of His mind—the first angel He showed true favor toward, and the one who still haunts every moment of His existence. He knows what I will do.' There was another laugh, but this one was not a little girl's. It was sinister. *'I know His secrets, Gabrielle, so you'll never be a match for me ... and one day soon, you'll find out exactly what I mean ... the hard, painful way.'*

As she drifted further away from the conscious world, she heard the caw of a crow. Then everything was quiet.

❦

Gabrielle opened her eyes to see a crowd of unfamiliar faces staring down at her, an even split of curiosity and concern in their expressions. Her mind was foggy from what had just happened with the little girl—the demon—but she began to sit up slowly.

"Easy, love."

She turned in the direction of Lucas's voice but did so a little too fast, sending her mind spinning. Thankfully, she was still on the ground, or she would have ended up there again—bringing even more unwanted attention to her than she already had.

"Are you okay? What happened?"

"I'm fine, just a little embarrassed," she whispered so only he could hear. "I'll have to tell you what happened when we have less of an audience."

Lucas helped her to her feet and politely told everyone she was all right so they'd continue on their way. It took a little more convincing for the airport security, and after several tries to set their minds at ease, Lucas finally told them that she was pregnant. Gabrielle looked at him with wide eyes—wishing he was a full-blood so she could say several very choice words to him telepathically. When the security officers were appeased and carried on with their duties, Lucas looked at her with a hint of playfulness in his eyes.

"Well … what did you want me to do?" he asked through a little laugh. "They weren't letting it be. I had to get rid of them somehow!"

She quickly let her irritation go because of what she saw replace the playful expression he had shown a moment before. Lucas looked at her expectantly, concern now dominating his expression. Gabrielle knew what he wanted, but she didn't want to tell him until she was sure they had privacy. She also needed time to gather her thoughts.

"Let's get our car first, Lucas. When we start driving, we'll talk."

After getting the keys to their rental, which required a little more of her angelic charm since they were too young to rent a car, they made their way to the lot and found their vehicle. It was simple and small, but it didn't matter as long as it got them where they needed to go.

"You want me to drive so you can concentrate on telling me what happened?" Lucas asked.

"I'll be fine driving. It's probably better if I'm behind the wheel. We can get to where we need to go easier that way."

"Whatever you say."

"I hate to push it," Lucas said once they settled in the rental and were on their way to the hotel, "but are you going to tell me what happened back there? I'm a little concerned over here, you know."

Gabrielle was expecting Lucas's question, but it sent her back into her deepest thoughts about the encounter with the little girl and the affect it had on her. It was not an average, every day, demon in the child—it was incredibly powerful, and she was sure who it was. She had never been so affected when encountering one of the Fallen, and the overwhelming sensation was alarming. She was pensive, already planning how to handle the next time they crossed paths—and there would be a next time.

"Love …"

"I'm sorry, Lucas. Of course."

She told him everything she'd seen and felt and saw it visibly shook him, as well.

"Why do you think it affected you so strongly?"

"It was an exceptionally powerful demon, more powerful than any I've ever encountered. I'll talk to Amaziah about it when I speak with him again."

"How often do you talk to him?"

"Normally, frequently, but there's a lot going on right now. I don't know when the next time will be. I can contact him if it's necessary, but I'm not going to distract him from his duties for this. He's looking for something that's important."

"I'd say what just happened is pretty important, Gabby. You may be in danger. You said another with Divine blood could kill you. Unless I misunderstood what you told me, that includes demons." There was urgency in his voice again. "It sounds like it was trying to let you know it's watching you."

"Yes, it includes demons, and I'm glad it showed itself to me because now I do know. Lucas, my job leaves me open to revenge seekers. It's in their nature to go after me if given the opportunity. I've had to deal with demons in the past, and I'll have to in the future. It goes with the territory, you know." She reached for his hand to reassure him. "I can't call to Amaziah every time I bump into one of the Fallen. I can handle myself just fine. But I love how concerned you are for me." She raised his hand to her lips and kissed it.

He clearly wasn't at ease. His body was rigid, his expression still agitated.

"I guess I can't do anything to change your mind. Just know I'm not happy about it. I don't care if you are an angel. Demons scare the crap out of me, and I would die if anything happened to you."

The thought of him dying brought the images in the grim dreams back. "I told you I don't want to hear you talk about dying."

Lucas studied her, contemplating his response. His expression was stoic. "You'll have to be unhappy with me mentioning dying, just as I'm unhappy with you for not taking the danger you could be in seriously."

She studied his face and realized they were at an impasse. She felt a smile curve the corners of her mouth. "Touché."

Chapter Forty-five

LUCAS ✝ INFURIATING

It wasn't long before Lucas realized having a small car was good in London. The roads were thick with cars and buses. The way people drove made him nervous, and he was glad Gabrielle was behind the wheel. He glanced over at her, still concerned about how she was after the incident at the airport, but all he noticed was how completely at ease she was with the chaos around them.

The streets of London, with its amazing old buildings and sidewalks that were as full of people as the streets were of cars, were even more lively and interesting than he'd imagined. He was amazed by the variety of nationalities represented in the faces he saw and wondered if London deserved the title of the Melting Pot of the world more than New York City. The people and architecture intrigued him, and he rolled down his window to smell the scents and hear the noises of the city. The scents he smelled—mixtures of the river's inhabitants, food, horses, and car exhaust—took turns dancing with the wind. Sometimes, the smell of the river would dominate; other times, it was the aroma of something enticing cooking in one of the many restaurants they passed. A thick ceiling of grey clouds hung over the city, releasing a constant drizzle. The damp, cold weather that London was famous for chilled him. He pulled his jacket around him a little tighter and rolled up his window.

"You drive like you've lived here all your life," he said.

"Don't be too impressed. I get quite a bit of help."

"What do you mean?"

"I've got skills. Angel skills," she said, attempting a James Bond imitation, then smiled. "I have ..." She paused. "I guess the best way to describe it is that I have an internal GPS. All I have to do is think of where I want to go, and I'm led there."

"Cooler and cooler." He shook his head in disbelief.

Lucas opened the door to their hotel room and they stepped in. Both took a moment to take in their surroundings. It was simple, which was a polite way to describe the sparsely decorated room. The colors were neutral. Two chairs and a small table were in one corner, and a small chest with an old television sitting on top was against the wall across from the bed. And then, there was the bed—a double.

Tonight's going to be interesting.

Lucas glanced at Gabby and watched her eyes pause when they reached the bed, her eyebrows slightly raised, and she quickly cast her eyes at him.

They burst into laughter.

"We'll figure it out later," she said.

Lucas moved his mouth into his crooked grin. "You're not afraid of me are you?" he asked sarcastically.

"Only if you try to molest me."

"I promise to be on my best behavior," he said, holding up the scout's honor sign.

"You will if you know what's good for you." She gave him a peck on the cheek as she passed him. "Me first!" She shouted.

He realized where she was headed and tried to get to the bathroom before her. She bounded into the small closet-like room and shut the door behind her. He laughed into the door that separated them. "Girls take *so* long in the bathroom!" He heard her giggle and wished they were there for a different reason. He closed his eyes and hoped they'd have the opportunity another time. "Don't forget there's someone else out here who would like a turn at some point in the near future!"

"I could never forget about you!"

Lucas smiled as he lay down on the bed, tucking both hands behind his head. He stared at the ceiling that had several brown stains from old water leaks.

Or stains from vampires spilling their very *Bloody Marys before they go out on the town for some fresh food.* Lucas chuckled humorlessly, knowing the thought was silly, but it led to a more serious one.

"Gabby," Lucas began, loud enough for her to hear through the closed door. "What do I need to know about the Elders? What should, or shouldn't, I do to avoid getting sucked dry or turned into a vamp myself?"

He heard the knob turn and looked to see Gabby standing in the doorway. She leaned against the frame, her arms crossed loosely in front of her, her expression borderline morose. After standing silently for a moment, she spoke to him in a voice so faint it was barely a whisper.

"*Please* ... just wait on me here. You don't have to be a hero. You don't have to put yourself in more danger." Her eyes pleaded with him.

He didn't want to upset or worry her. Even though he knew what he was doing was dangerous, he felt he had to go. Maybe it was morbid fascination drawing him here—maybe it was something else. He had a strong sense from the moment he met Gabrielle that destiny was at work with them. It could be this was all part of it. He walked to her and kissed her forehead, then bent down to level their eyes, placing his hands on her cheeks. He spoke as softly as she had.

"Love ... I *promise* this isn't some lame attempt at playing the hero. It's just something I have to do. I know you're worried, but I'm going." Now, his eyes pleaded with her to understand.

She gave him a forced smile and nodded her head so slightly he may not have even known she'd moved it at all if he hadn't had his hands on her face.

<hr />

They were back in the car and pulling away from the hotel before much more was said, and Lucas was becoming more anxious now that the time he had to prepare himself for the meeting with the Elders was running out.

"So, do the Elders even know we're coming?"

Gabrielle smiled at his question. "Of course."

"How? I've been with you from the time you told me about the vision 'til now, and I haven't seen you call them. Do you call them on the phone, or what? I don't know what the appropriate, The Angel of Karma wants to speak with The Elder Qalals, protocol is."

Gabrielle stifled her laughter and pressed her lips together to try to keep from smiling.

"Well, I did notify them, but I didn't do it *personally*. I had my second in command tell them. They're expecting us. *Both* of us." She glanced at Lucas. "If I was communicating telepathically, Lucas, you wouldn't know. I could be speaking to you audibly and sending thoughts to one of my brethren at the same time." She chuckled. "I'm pretty good at multitasking."

"I'm beginning to see that." He smiled and shook his head as he usually did when trying to comprehend her world—a world he was finding himself more enmeshed within. He became more serious. "You know, I may be crazy for going with you to this vampire meeting, but I'm not stupid. I really do want to know how to handle myself and learn whatever you think I need to know about them."

"Sure," she responded, smiling. "I was about to get to that. The drive will take about an hour. We have plenty of time."

"I thought they were here in London."

"Oxford."

"Why not stay there?"

"To be honest," Gabrielle glanced at him and took his hand, "I didn't want it to be easy for them to find us when we're done. They might try to get to you right away if we stay that close. It's a long shot that they would, but I want to be as safe as possible." She deliberated on her next words. "Since you'll be fair game, they might find the hunt for you hard to resist even with me around. I still don't think you comprehend the amount of danger you're putting yourself in. Basically, for the rest of your life. This is a *really* bad idea."

She looked at Lucas, and he wondered if she did it to see if he was willing to think twice about his decision, but she would have only have seen resolve.

"You know ..." Gabrielle started. Lucas noticed a shift in her tone that captured his attention more securely. She looked alarmed. "I can't believe I didn't consider this possibility sooner!"

She stared intently at the road before her, deep in thought. Lucas wanted to know what she was so taken aback by, but it was obvious she was considering something important, so he fought the urge to press.

Several minutes crept by, and he was about to interrupt her thoughts when she abruptly pulled over to the side of the road. She turned to him with an intensity in her eyes he hadn't seen before and looked at him as though she was going to change his mind simply by using the force of her gaze. It was the first time he had truly sensed her power, and it made him feel small. When she spoke, her voice was ominous and as distant as her mind seemed to be seconds earlier.

"Lucas, how do we know the reason for the Qalal attack isn't simply because they are after you and everyone else was in the wrong place at the wrong time? As I already told you, my vision didn't show me *why*. If they are acting within their rights to kill a human who knows about them in order to maintain their anonymity, it does make sense."

"I don't think that's it, Gabby. I know you know more about vampires than I do, but you said they can kill only those who know. From what you described, they were going after everyone, not just me. I know *I* have no plans to tell my friends and family, so why were they going to that extreme? It seems to me like me knowing has nothing to do with it."

"Even so, it *is* a possibility. This adds to the reasons why you shouldn't go in there with me."

He could tell she was getting frustrated that he wouldn't be more sensible.

"I'm going."

Gabby sighed heavily and jerked the car back into motion. She fixed her eyes on the road, but now she wore a deep scowl, mumbling something Lucas couldn't make out. It was probably something he didn't want to hear, anyway—about how foolish, or what an idiot, he was.

He let her mumble, permitting his own thoughts to explore the possibility deeper, wondering if the trip would garner him any additional insight into his new world. It had to, on some level. He just hoped it would be enough to help him to make plans for a certain demon. He didn't let his mind stay there long, needing to be as clear-minded as possible about the subject around Gabby.

Especially now that I realize she has the ability to know what I'm thinking ... if she wants to.

He turned his attention back to her, smiling as he saw how her brows seemed even more pinched than just moments before. She was terribly annoyed with him.

"You know you can't stay mad at me forever, love."

When Gabby answered, her words came fast. "Oh really? And why not? Maybe I will, but I won't get a chance to let you know I'm mad at you forever because you got yourself killed by Qalal because you won't listen to reason!" She was looking at him more than the road, making him thankful for angel GPS. "So yes I can!"

Lucas's playful smirk made an inappropriate appearance, which made her glare at him. "You're an angel, love. It's not in your nature."

Gabby turned her attention back to the road and let several

moments pass before she responded. She mumbled something again when she did, but this time, it was loud enough to hear. Though he couldn't understand the words, he could tell it was Enochian because it tickled his mind more than any language he had ever heard, making him long to speak and understand the words himself. He found himself silently trying to mouth some of the words she spoke. The last two, he understood. They were in English.

"You're *infuriating*," she said under her breath.

Lucas chuckled. He put his hand on her leg, leaning to kiss her neck. He raised his mouth to her ear and spoke into it slow and breathy. "And you don't play fair, speaking a language you know I won't understand."

He kissed her ear and moved his lips back to her neck, smelling her scent and wondering what it was about it that he recognized. Sometimes, he thought she smelled like a field of wildflowers after a light summer shower. Other times, she smelled of exotic spices that he was probably never going to be able to place. He wasn't going to try now. He just wanted to enjoy smelling it, the feeling of her warm skin against his lips, and seeing the goose bumps his touch caused.

Chapter Forty-six

GABRIELLE ✝ ABOUT THE QALAL

Gabrielle fought back an almost uncontrollable urge to close her eyes and let her head fall back so she could just enjoy how magnificent it felt to have him kiss her the way he was. She knew he was right; she wouldn't be able to stay mad at him forever. But it was pathetic that she couldn't seem to last even five minutes without turning into mush.

"I pray you're right this time," she whispered. "Now, stop that before you make me wreck."

"I thought you had angelic car control or something," he said, continuing to kiss her neck.

"I do. But you're making me feel a little too human, and it throws my instinct off."

"That's a bad thing?" He was slowly making his way back to her ear, and she felt the heat rise in her body with the anticipation of how it would feel when his lips arrived there. Before he did, he stopped and playfully bit her neck, drawing a surprised shriek from her as she placed her hand where his mouth had just been.

Lucas bent forward in his seat in a fit of amusement, his arm across his stomach like it hurt. Little noise was coming out of him, but his body heaved as if he was laughing heartily. She saw tears welling up in his eyes when he looked over at her.

"Are you turning hysterical on me?"

His apparent fit continued for at least a minute before he was able to speak, though still trying to catch his breath.

"Oh … love!" He paused to take a breath, and she injected more verbal protest.

"Talk about a mood killer!"

"I'm sorry …" He wiped tears from his eyes. "I just got the sudden urge to practice a little."

"For *what*? Because if that is some mating ritual of yours, count me out," she teased, letting a coy smile curve her lips.

"No. I thought I'd practice in case they turn me," he responded as he shot her a flirty look.

"That's not even funny!"

"It is a little."

"*Honestly*!" Gabrielle said with a sigh and then took his hand and put it back on her leg as Lucas situated himself comfortably in his seat.

"We've got about forty-five minutes before we get to Oxford, so let's get back to what you need to know before we get distracted again. There's other information you'll need, but it can wait until later."

"Shoot."

"You have to remember, at all times, they will be just as diverse in appearance as humans, because they *were* once human. Some will be more attractive than others. But Qalal are the most alluring, charming, and intriguing creatures you'll ever encounter, *if* they choose to be. Don't—"

"I would disagree with that, love," Lucas interrupted.

Gabrielle glanced at him and saw him looking at her more lovingly than he ever had, making her forget to breathe for a moment.

How does he have that effect on me?

She smiled back and continued. "Anyway, don't let your guard down. They're also proficient predators. They have a profound effect on humans. You *will* be drawn to them, Lucas. Count on it."

"What if I can't stop myself?"

"I'll be there to stop you. Don't worry." She gave his hand a reassuring squeeze. "It's best not to look at any vampire for too long. Just good practice. Trust me." Lucas nodded. She was glad he seemed to be taking this part seriously.

"Anything else?"

"*Plenty*. But that's all you need to know for now. I'll give you a crash course on the way back home. They'll know they can't get to you as long as I'm with you, so I'm not as concerned about tonight as my precautions would indicate. Really, it never was tonight that concerned me. But ... better safe than sorry." She shot him a bleak smile. "I think they'll wait until you're alone ... unprotected. So, just know I'm going to be your shadow, basically, for a very long time."

"I think I can handle that," he said, then whispered to himself. "My personal angel bodyguard—*hot* angel bodyguard."

Gabrielle kept her amusement to herself, not wanting him to know how good her hearing was yet. It might come in handy in the future.

They pulled into Oxford just after two in the afternoon. Gabrielle could tell Lucas liked the look of it. She'd always been fond of it herself, especially the architecture. It was beautiful and old. So much history moved quietly, invisibly around the streets. The medieval stonemasons' handiwork showed their skill, and the city possessed some of the most spectacular stained glass windows she'd ever seen. She could walk the streets and tour the buildings of Oxford for days and not get bored, especially if she had the camera she'd bought.

Gabrielle turned onto another road. Lucas noticed the signs to Oxford University.

"You're not going to tell me that they're professors at Oxford, are you?"

Gabrielle smiled. "No, but they have been here since around the thirteenth century, so their home is near the University."

"Why'd they choose Oxford?"

"Maybe because they could get to a more populated area at the time—London—to prey on people if they chose to and still be far enough away not to draw suspicion. Plus, there would be a large amount of wildlife to feed on without leaving carcasses where they would be easily discovered. Beyond that, I don't know. I've never asked."

"Why not?"

Gabrielle laughed softly. "It never mattered, and I haven't really sat around with the Elders making small talk at afternoon tea."

Lucas laughed, too. "I just got the mental image of The Angel of Karma and vampires sitting on settees and armchairs around a coffee table while having a proper English tea." Lucas absently shook his head. "Yeah ... I can't see that happening."

Chapter Forty-seven

JAVAN ✚ THE DEVIL'S OWN SELF

Javan lay on the couch for an undetermined amount of time—his thoughts far away. He supposed he had nothing to lose by trusting Cecily, and he didn't have any other leads on the Book right now, anyway. He would have to deal with Mara, though. She'd already demonstrated her jealousy. Having Cecily help him would involve a lot of contact between him and the Qalal. It would take only moments for Mara to notice the attraction he had for the vampire.

I need a shower, he thought, pushing his deliberations to another time. After allowing the hot water to soothe the aches in his body, Javan dressed and left his loft. He didn't know where he was going, just that he needed to get out for a while.

Although he was enjoying the time away from Mara, he wondered where she had gone for so long. They hadn't been apart much since she'd joined him, when they met in Santiago, Chile.

He'd been wandering the world, hunting down leads about the Book. It was after another dead end and his efforts to find a new lead when they crossed paths. At the time, Mara was using another body. She had chosen one belonging to a woman married to a powerful Chilean politician and was having quite a good time with it—sleeping with politicians and foreign dignitaries, then blackmailing them for her, or the husband's, benefit. She probably would have insured his being elected president had she stayed. Javan chuckled quietly. The politician's wife must have seemed quite different after Mara left her body if she'd survived the departure. A human body so thoroughly taken by a demon for such a long period of time rarely did. If she had survived, she would've been clueless about what had happened.

Javan and Mara sensed their shared origins, and he told her what he was searching for. He was surprised when she told him she wanted to join with him. Mara never told him why, but they'd looked for the Book together ever since. All he knew was as soon as he told her *why* he was looking for it and who he felt he was destined to become, she asked if she could assist him. He would be extremely powerful one day. Surely Mara sensed that and wanted to rule by his side.

That place will be Gabrielle's.

After searching for years with no luck, Javan felt drawn to Nashville. Since seeing Gabrielle, there was no doubt why he was being pulled here. He would always want her near. She was a craving.

Javan had been surprised to see Gabrielle's energy coming from the other car that day. Part of that surprise was from knowing Yahuwah had allowed her to be incarnated for more than the few moments her duties might call for. But mostly, it was because he never imagined Gabrielle could be the angel Mara had run into. He could tell when Gabrielle saw him that she was also surprised. But then, sadness took over her expression; there was no delight in her eyes when she recognized him. Instead, he saw confusion and pain that quickly washed away her shock. He couldn't show her how glad he was to see her. His hatred for Yahuwah, who took him from her, dominated his expression. The entire experience, and thinking about the jeopardy his love was in every moment she was in that human body, made Javan angrier at Him, reinforcing his desire for vengeance. Gabrielle was his.

Fallen or not.

He'd hoped, even if it was foolish, she would want to be with him if they ever crossed paths again. He hadn't expected both of them to be in human form for their first encounter since he'd fallen. He longed to see her as she was created. She was beautiful in her human body, but she was glorious as she was meant to be—a Divine angel.

What could have prompted Gabrielle to leave Heaven to be here—with humans? Her job? He knew things had been getting increasingly difficult for her before he fell, but what she could hope to accomplish escaped him. Javan felt a flood of anger and jealousy as he considered the next possibility.

Lucas.

The new thought interrupted the direction of the other, and he felt his scowl deepen. He shook his head to remove the image accompanying the human's name—the one with Gabrielle in Lucas's embrace.

He's just a human. What pleasure could she derive from him?

Javan considered the possible explanations why Gabrielle would come here because of Lucas. He couldn't come to any satisfying conclusions. She hadn't been cast out of Heaven. That was made clear two nights before when she paused time outside Lucas's house.

Something tugged at the fringes of Javan's memory.

There is something about that street—that house.

It was a feeling he hadn't been able to shake since he and Mara waited for Gabrielle that night. Something his gut was trying to tell him. The unfailing memory of an angel was one of the casualties of his fall, and now there was an annoying blank chasm in his mind. Sometimes, Javan wondered if there was a block in his mind that was put there intentionally. There were—*certain*—angels, Fallen and Divine, who could do something like that.

But for what purpose?

His attention that night had continually strayed to the house Lucas later entered. Whatever his mind wanted him to remember wasn't ready to step out of the darkness it hid within. Javan sighed. He rubbed his temple with his finger, trying to will the images forward—beckoning to them to step into the light of his consciousness.

Again, they disobeyed.

But the teasing memory did assist him with one thing—it gave him a direction for the moment, and a direction had been evading him since he left his loft. He turned his car around in the middle of the road, ignoring the oncoming traffic, almost causing an accident. Car horns blared in protest, and he caught more than a couple of middle fingers. Javan chuckled humorlessly as he accelerated, screeching the car's tires.

Almost instantly, he heard the siren. He looked into his rearview mirror to see flashing lights. Javan let out another sigh. He would have to take care of this in his own way. He didn't have a license or any other form of identification, for that matter.

He looked around for somewhere that would allow the least amount of eyes to witness what would happen. The sun was falling deeper into the horizon, so the world of shadows would gain its stronghold quickly.

The time of day is on my side.

He let his eyes linger on the car behind him for just a moment. There was only one person in the patrol car. He grinned as he spotted a suitable location and made a right turn down an industrial road. It was almost barren of people as their commute to get back home from work had begun long ago. Javan pulled into an empty parking lot behind the building.

The patrol car pulled in behind him. The officer began to gather his things and opened his door. As he crouched slightly behind it to use as a shield, he put his hand on the gun at his waist. Javan felt another arrogant chuckle.

The door isn't going to help you ... either is the gun.

"Step out of the car with your hands in the air!"

Javan did as he was instructed, allowing the officer to feel he had the situation under control. The officer slipped out from behind the door of his police cruiser and continued toward him, barking another demand.

"Slowly walk to the back of your car and place your hands on the trunk with your legs spread."

Once again, he complied, smirking at thoughts of the fun he was about to have.

Javan couldn't see, but felt the officer getting closer. He shut his eyes and concentrated—feeling the features of his face begin to distort and move into beastly contours and angles while he released his glamour just enough to get the result he wanted.

This was Javan's preferred method of dealing with humans—terrify them to the point that he sent them to a place in their mind that made it basically shut down. Javan thought of the fragility of the human behind him—so sure of himself with his training and gun under his hand. Guns couldn't do anything to Javan except force him to find a new body. But the officer would never get the chance to use his weapon.

Depending on the individual's fortitude, what Javan was about to do could leave the person who witnessed it in a state ranging from severe shock to complete detachment from the world around them. They might recover from it and think it was just an awful dream, or it could drive them over the mental edges of sanity.

Death is another possible outcome.

A cruel smirk reshaped his mouth.

The hands of the officer began to pat him down. When he was satisfied Javan had no weapons, or anything of interest, he stepped back.

The sound of his voice was more relaxed as he spoke again. "Sir, I need to see your driver's license and insurance."

"Of course. It's in my car. Is it okay if I get it now, officer?" Javan used his most soothing, sincere voice.

A completely unguarded human mind is the most fun to fuck with.

"Just move slowly."

"Yes, officer."

Javan did as he was instructed and carefully moved his body off the trunk of his car. As he made his way around the bumper, he slowed his movements.

"Officer, what am I being pulled over for, anyway?" Javan began to turn his body slightly toward the man, his head following slowly so his face was the last thing to be seen.

"You're kidding, *right*?" The officer asked and then continued, not waiting for an answer. "Sir, you almost caused at least three accidents back there when y—" he was unable to finish.

The officer now saw the face of the man he was addressing—realizing it was no man at all. Javan saw terror swell in his eyes, the color draining from his face. The officer was trying to say something as his lips moved reluctantly, but he appeared to be unable create a coherent thought to form the words. Javan wondered if the human even had breath in his lungs to push words out of his mouth.

Javan glared menacingly into the man's eyes, speaking to him in his mind, creating images of the monsters of his childhood and adult nightmares. He could almost see the man's mind trying to make sense of what he saw in front of him, trying to figure out why he heard a voice echoing in his head that was not his own. Javan smiled enough to let him see darkened, jagged teeth. The man flinched but couldn't seem to will any other movement from his body, his hand still on his gun. As Javan had suspected, he wouldn't have to defend himself from the threat it posed—this man was far too stunned to do anything. The officer, still staring, growing increasingly distant from what he thought was reality, fell to his knees.

A feeling of triumph rushed through Javan from the power he had over this human. He'd take so much pleasure in the moment every living thing, including his former brethren, fell to their knees before him.

What will be most satisfying is Yahuwah bowing to me.

He was pulled from his musing by the sound of the officer hyperventilating. Javan scoffed and turned to get back into his car, leaving the man on his knees. Just before he pulled away, he looked to see if he had attempted to move at all. Javan smiled.

The man *had* moved—he had placed his gun under his chin. Javan heard the shot as he turned back onto the main road and huffed out a snide laugh in satisfaction.

"Guess you were one of the weaker ones."

Javan sat in his car in the same spot on Haber Drive as he had two nights before while waiting for Gabrielle. He'd been fixated on the bungalow house Lucas entered for at least thirty minutes. Still nothing broke through his subconscious.

What the hell *is it about that place?*

He heard voices across the street and let his attention divert toward the sound. The people Gabrielle had been to see last weekend were coming outside. Two of them, who Javan guessed were the mother and father, carried out trays with food as a small child dragged a large quilt behind her. Two more, the teens, carried out a full pitcher, plastic cups, and plates.

After spreading the quilt on the grass under the sprawling branches of a big oak, they sat in a semicircle and began to eat. The sound of the door opening at the house Lucas lived in pulled Javan's attention back to where it needed to be. An older woman with white hair turned to pull the door closed behind her.

Javan watched as she crossed the street and joined the others under the tree but became distracted with a feeling he knew all too well—someone with Divine blood was close. Carefully, he looked around at his surroundings, then up toward the sky. When he couldn't find the source for what he was feeling, he directed his attention back to the oak. Everyone seemed to be truly happy. Javan shook his head and smirked.

"Ignorance is bliss."

He never understood how people could be so stupid not to notice those of the Underworld and Shadow World they shared space with.

Although he thought he checked thoroughly, he was distracted once again, still sensing there was someone near. He shifted and looked around again—nothing. His real concern was Gabrielle. If she were going to join the festivities, he would move on. He wasn't powerful enough for a confrontation with her, not yet. But more than that, he was hoping not to cross paths with her again until he figured out how to make her want to be with him again. Judging by her response the other night, she would more likely kill him right now than take him back.

I don't ever want to see that look of sadness and disgust on her face again and know it's because of me.

The feeling remained steady even after fifteen more minutes had passed. Whoever was causing it wasn't moving around, making him wonder if he was being watched. He would have let it go if it weren't for a new feeling. *I've crossed paths with whoever this is before, and it's definitely not Gabrielle.*

The white-haired woman began laughing, tossing her head back as she did. Javan studied her as the group conversed. The tugs on his memory were more urgent. There was clearly something he needed to remember about that house and the woman living in it.

He watched them finish their meal, and then the older woman cut and served her pie. The two teens and child began a game of tag. Now that they were out of earshot of the younger ones, the adults shifted the conversation to something more serious. At least, that was what their expressions and body language indicated.

They moved themselves into a tighter circle, leaning in toward each other. Javan guessed it was so they could speak privately. He was only able to see the older woman's expression sporadically and only from just below her eyes up. He saw something in her eyes he recognized, and a memory from seventeen years ago burst forth.

His breath caught in his chest as images flooded back to him. Instinctively, his hand went to the left side of his face and traced the scar that ran jaggedly from his ear, down his jaw line and to the front and middle of his throat. He could almost hear the sizzle of his skin as the Sundering Whip grazed it and feel the awful, burning pain it caused. A growl rumbled in his throat as he replayed the image of the whip as it split his flesh.

Now he knew why the street, the house, and that woman were familiar to him. She was the one who came into the house when he killed Mason Hunt and his family.

"Bitch!"

He hissed the word as though it was as a weapon that could strike her down. The desire for revenge surged inside him, seeping into every part of his body, causing a rage of ideas for retribution to flood his mind.

"Your turn at the receiving end of a Sundering Whip is coming."

He wanted his revenge on this angel to be slow and painful. He wanted her to experience the pain her strike had caused him on her own skin. He wanted her to suffer in ways she never imagined. He wanted to enjoy seeing her in agony in a place she could never be found.

I want the human living in your home who thinks he deserves to be with Gabrielle to join you in that eternal misery.

And once he became the Destroyer, he could ensure it *would* be eternal.

As he sat in his car, tossing early ideas for vengeance around in his mind, a crow passed his car and landed on a limb of the oak. He watched as it turned and looked directly at him—cawing once as if to say hello.

"Ahh … the messenger of the gods," he said and laughed snidely. Then he repeated a counting rhyme he'd heard many, many years ago.

One crow for sorrow,

Two Crows for mirth,

Three Crows for a wedding,

Four Crows for a birth,

Five Crows for silver,

Six Crows for gold,

Seven Crows for a secret, not to be told,

Eight Crows for heaven,

Nine Crows for hell,

And ten Crows for the devil's own self.

Before he finished the rhyme, more crows joined the first one in the large oak. They were all turned toward his car, their eyes fixed on him. Javan counted the birds. When he finished, he said the number aloud.

"Nine."

Another crow landed on the driver's side windshield wiper of Javan's car. It studied Javan, then spread its wings as it lowered its head and cawed.

"Ten." Javan smirked. "Hello back."

Chapter Forty-eight

LUCAS ☩ NO ESCAPE

Lucas took in the scenery as Gabby pulled onto a small side street flanked by large, two and three story brick and stone homes. Some looked as if they were small hotels, and others were lined with hedges so high he was barely able to see the houses as they passed. The driveways became further apart as the property sizes grew larger.

After driving several more blocks, she finally turned into a driveway between some of those high hedges. The towering shrubs weren't able to hide the structure behind them anymore.

"Wow ..."

The house was massive. Americans would have classified it as a mansion. The grounds were perfectly groomed, and he saw a sizeable garden behind it. From what he could tell, there was a maze hedge, as well.

Gabby pulled around the circular driveway until she stopped at the steps to the front door, ignoring the spaces right next to them for parking. Lucas looked at them with a puzzled expression.

Gabby glanced at Lucas. "It doesn't matter," she said in response to his unspoken question. "They aren't accustomed to day visitors, and I assure you, we'll be half way back to London before the sun even gets close to the horizon. I'm not taking any more chances than needed." She shot him a perturbed look. "Unlike some of us."

They got out of the car and Lucas waited for Gabby before continuing up the steps. The butterflies he had in his stomach when they were leaving Nashville were now more like full-grown condors. It didn't help his apprehensive feelings or nervous stomach when a crow drifted down and landed on the roof above the entry, then another did the same with every step they took.

"Seriously," Lucas began, "I'm beginning to get completely freaked out by the crows. Does it mean something?" He looked at her, then back to the crows. As usual, they were staring back.

Gabby's expression was troubled. She didn't take her eyes off the birds as she responded, looking at each of them as if she were counting. When she finished her assessment her brows drew closer together.

"You don't want to know, Lucas."

Yeah ... I probably don't.

The front door opened before they climbed the last step, and Lucas found himself even more apprehensive about looking at who—*what*—opened it. Gabby put her hand on his shoulder as she leaned in to whisper in his ear.

"She's human."

He looked up and saw an attractive blond holding the door open for them. With her hazel eyes, full, red lips, and model looks, she would have turned most men's heads.

She would have turned mine, too, over a month ago.

Though now that he'd met Gabby and fallen for her, he couldn't imagine anyone holding a candle to her in any way. Now the most he thought of this woman was that she was attractive. The blond looked at Gabby and then him, moving her eyes slowly over his body. When she found his eyes, a flirtatious smile spread across her face.

"Welcome." Her eyes stayed on Lucas as they entered the house. "The Elders are expecting you." The Elders' greeter stayed several steps behind Gabby and him, but he could feel her eyes on him, anyway. They paused at the end of the long entry until the woman could move ahead to guide them.

Gabby seemed oblivious to the opulent surroundings. Lucas could only imagine how this must pale in comparison to the things she'd experienced. As they continued walking in silence, Lucas wondered what it must be like to live the life she had, thinking back to their conversation about how different things were for them when he was at her home in Nashville.

Right before her vision about the attack. From vampires like I am about to meet. Vampires, *for crying out loud.*

Lucas shook his head slightly as he thought about what he was doing and how the differences between the lives he and Gabby had lived—would continue to live—were becoming more apparent with every day they spent together.

More distinct than Lucas wanted to face.

Unlike Gabby, he was impressed with the Elders' home, to say the least. Paintings, some he recognized from his fine arts class, adorned the walls in both rooms that flanked either side of the entry. He guessed that at least some of them were authentic. The room to the right must have been intended for a sitting room, but the velvet covered couches and chairs didn't show signs of wear. He wondered if they had ever been used at all.

Heavy burgundy drapes hung from windows at least ten feet high, the fabric pulled back and pooled on the floor. Lucas studied the floor for several seconds. He'd never seen wood like that and wondered what exotic place it had been shipped in from. He was about to turn his attention to the room on the left when their escort interrupted his pondering.

"This way."

She led them down a hall to the right, but it was more like a large, long room.

He laughed to himself. *This* hall *is bigger than my entire house.*

She stopped at two massive wooden doors stained a rich mahogany that were intricately carved with what seemed to be Biblical scenes. It wasn't what Lucas expected. Then again, he'd never been in a vampire's house, so he shouldn't be expecting anything at all.

With noticeable effort, she pushed the doors open, exposing another very large room. This one was much darker than the ones he'd just seen. The walls were paneled in the same shade of mahogany as the doors, and the wood floor was stained almost black. The lights in the room were covered by large, thick, maroon shades that bathed the room in a deep red hue, and the seating was dark brown leather. There were four oversized sofas, two facing each other on each side of an enormous stone fireplace that he could easily walk into with height to spare.

A generous fire burned lazily, lighting the area in a golden light, teasing the red hue the lamps cast as the flames licked at the surrounding air, making its light dance further in and out of the room. It mesmerized Lucas until a loud pop came from the burning wood, breaking the spell. He laughed at himself quietly, trying to calm his nerves, and continued to take in the layout of the room as though it would help if he needed a fast escape.

Between the sofas were three large round tables, again in an exotic dark stained wood, with wide flower arrangements on them that were low enough that they wouldn't interfere with people's—*vampire's*—ability to see the other side. The walls displayed several oversized paintings of people from a long ago era.

Hmm.

He looked around the walls of the room again.

No windows. So much for escape options.

"Make yourselves comfortable." The greeter remained focused only on Lucas, making him uncomfortable. "I'll let them know you're here." Before she left, she turned and motioned to a small bar area. "There are some fine Brandy and Scotch choices if you'd care for anything to drink." She shut the heavy doors behind her.

"Jeez!" Lucas said in a slightly exasperated tone.

Gabby put her finger to her lips. He did as she wanted and said nothing else while they waited in silence for the Elders.

They didn't have to wait long. Lucas heard the doors begin to open again and then saw Gabby stand to face them. Lucas mimicked her and stood, as well—prepared to meet creatures he'd once thought were only of peoples' imaginings.

As the first Elder entered the room, the light from the fireplace seemed to reach further toward the doors as if to greet her. Although the fire's golden light was what reflected off the vampire's eyes, all Lucas could see was red.

Chapter Forty-nine

JAVAN ✝ AN OBSTACLE

Javan left the cozy scene on Haber Drive as soon as they all went into the house. Now that he remembered what happened in Lucas's home, he couldn't block the memory from his mind. It was like the replay button was stuck. Back in his loft, sitting comfortably on his patio with nothing to concern him except the cool breeze carried to him through the dark of night and the glass of whiskey in his hand, he allowed the images to consume his thoughts—letting his mind drift back seventeen years.

He'd been following the family around for a couple of weeks, waiting for his chance to eliminate Mason Hunt and his bloodline. It was Mara who told Javan about Mason's lineage being related to either the arrival, or destruction, of the Destroyer. The angel who'd been sent to protect Mason was a Cherubim, just as Mara had been before she was cast from Heaven.

As soon as he heard the reason the man was being protected, Javan made the decision to kill Mason. But finding him had proved to be more difficult than Javan had originally thought. It took almost two decades to find him. When he did, he realized he would have to eliminate Mason's daughter and grandson, too.

It took several more weeks of constant snooping, eavesdropping, and spying by him and Mara before he was satisfied that Mason had no other descendants. It was just the three of them. His opportunity to kill all three at once came when Mason's daughter, Hannah, brought her child to Mason's home.

He'd arrived at the house, simply walked up to the door, and knocked. Mason answered the door himself, but before he could speak, Javan thrust him into the wall fifteen feet behind him. Mason hit hard enough to shake the walls of the house, then landed on the floor. Instinctively, Javan knew death would consume Mason quickly and diverted his attention to the stunned audience.

Hannah's husband, Stephen, was next. Javan hadn't planned on killing Stephen, but he lunged at him. If he'd just sat and continued staring blankly, Javan would have let him live.

Maybe.

But he had to try and be the hero. He died from a broken neck.

Hannah died a little slower. Javan smirked at the memory. She'd started screaming that he would be punished by God, that he was going to go to Hell.

Blah, blah, blah.

Javan suffocated her, covering her mouth and nose with his hand. But he didn't let her die until she watched the life drain out of her infant son's face first—tears had streamed out of her eyes faster than Javan knew was possible.

Then the angel came.

He knew as soon as she walked through the door what she was and that others would be coming. As he turned to the back door to exit, he felt the whip hit his face, then the burning of its scorching fibers as it sliced easily through his flesh. He was able to flee before he found himself out-numbered. As he vanished into the night, the angel in the house released a shrill scream.

It had taken nine months for his face to heal. The jagged scar often burned as though still fresh. But that's what happens when a weapon designed for an angel is wielded. Not many angels could use the Sundering Whip. It took a great deal of practice and skill to use one with desired results. Javan knew the angel was talented in its use. If he'd been even slightly closer to her, the whip would have made quick work of removing his head from his body.

Recalling the incident made the scar burn again, feeding his desire for revenge. Javan could have acquired a new body, one without the scar, but he rather liked the visual reminder of his first accomplishment on his path to becoming the most powerful and worshiped being in the universe. He never expected to find that angel again. He never imagined he might be able to settle the score. He now entertained the many ways he wanted her to suffer, but he knew he'd have to be careful.

Javan began to wonder more about her, why she was not one of the Fallen, but also clearly not an active angel. She was aging.

Why is she hanging around?

Regardless, he had to keep in mind *he* was one of the Fallen, and because of that, he was weakened. Since she wasn't damned, he didn't know how much of her power Yahuwah had allowed her to keep. She kept at least one of her weapons, and there was no telling how many others she could use against him.

It was getting dark. He wondered where Lucas had been all day. Gabrielle's car hadn't been in her driveway when he drove by on his way from, or back, to his loft. They were together—he knew they were. He felt the familiar mixture of rage and jealousy that sprang to life inside him anytime he thought of that *boy* with Gabrielle. His blood felt like it expanded in his veins, his pulse echoing in his head. It was maddening.

Who was Lucas to the angel on Haber Drive?

He'd have to do some digging himself, and through the use of others, to get his answers.

He parked his car in the loft's garage and entered the elevator. When the doors opened on the fourth floor, he saw Mara sitting by his door.

"Where've you been?" she asked.

"I could ask the same of you." He smiled. An added glare showed it wasn't friendly. "But since we aren't each other's keeper, fuck off."

Javan opened the door and walked in, leaving Mara behind to close it.

"Lock it, Mara."

He felt her eyes on him as he walked away—studying him.

"Since when do you lock the door?"

Javan sighed in an exaggerated fashion and threw his keys on the kitchen counter.

"Since *when*, Mara, do you find it necessary to play twenty questions with me? I want the door locked from now on. Period."

Javan poured them both a drink. He needed her loosened up and tipsy so she didn't have her radar scanning him or his loft so thoroughly. "Drink up. We have a long night ahead of us."

Mara took the drink hesitantly from Javan, who smiled at her over the top of his glass, and drank his in one big swallow. Mara followed suit. He was sure she could tell he planned on getting her drunk right along with him.

She set her glass back down, and he poured them both another large shot, then took his glass and the bottle of tequila to the couch, flipping on the TV. The news was reporting the sad discovery of a police officer who had apparently committed suicide. A smile moved across Javan's face and he turned the volume down.

"I already know how that story ends." He focused his scowl back on her.

He had so much on his mind, and the last thing he needed to concern himself with was the local news. All he wanted to do right now was tell Mara what he needed from her, and then have her get the hell out of his way.

And out of my loft.

"Mara, I'm going to need you to be out a lot this week gathering information."

There was another reason he needed her to be as scarce as possible for at least the next week, but she didn't need to know about the impending visit from Cecily. Especially since he was looking forward to spending some more time with his new Qalal friend.

"Sure. What do you need me to find out?"

"I need you to do some research into the background of Lucas and that woman he lives with. I don't know what her name is, but I'd venture a guess you know Lucas's full name, so start there."

"Sure, it's Watkins. Why?"

He shot Mara a look, causing her to flinch.

This can't be happening.

"Mara ... how *old* is Lucas?" The name, Watkins, was Mason's daughter's last name.

He could see Mara trying to figure out why it triggered such a hostile response and maybe wondering what her next answer might bring out of him. Cautiously, she responded.

"Seventeen. He'll be eighteen sometime in April. I can't remember the date."

Javan stared at the TV, but he didn't see its images. All he saw was the scene from seventeen years ago, the baby Hannah held in her arms—the one she cried over as she watched him die.

Time seemed to stop as he realized he may not have succeeded in destroying Mason Hunt's bloodline, after all. He could see Mara trying to say something to him, but he didn't hear her. Instead, he heard his pulse echoing in his head again, thrumming loudly past his ears. As he contemplated his probable failure, he felt an inhuman growl begin deep inside him, coming from depths he didn't know his hate and anger could reach. As the reality of who Lucas most likely was took root in his mind, added to Gabrielle's relationship with him, Javan's heart raced. Darkness caused by rage closed in around his vision. All he could see was that worthless *boy*. Lucas had just been in the way of him getting his love back. Now, he was a huge obstacle on his path to becoming the Destroyer.

An obstacle I am going to take immense *pleasure in eliminating.*

With a guttural sound escaping his body, unleashed into the freedom of his loft, a second glass in as many days shattered—destroyed in the hand of the demon imagining Lucas's death.

Chapter Fifty

LUCAS ✝ NEW TRUTHS

Lucas watched as eight Elders walked, almost glided, into the room. They dressed in expensive suits and carried themselves purposely—refined in appearance and demeanor.

All except one—the female Elder—the first to enter and whose eyes the firelight danced off. As Lucas considered her beauty, he found he only could describe her as … dazzling.

She was svelte, dark hair styled in a sharply angled bob, and elegantly dressed in a fitted, full-length black gown that was slightly longer than the stretch of her long legs. A high slit beginning in the front and angling to the left caused the extra fabric to sway back and forth on the floor behind her as she walked, as though its purpose was to remove any trace of her footsteps. The neckline plunged deeply, and as she turned slightly, Lucas saw that the back plunged even deeper.

They all looked to be in their twenties except for two, and they appeared to be no older than thirty-five.

Lucas found it interesting that the physical appearance of most of the male Elders wouldn't have drawn attention to them in any part of the world. Only two were exceptionally good-looking. But every one of them were exceptionally alluring. They all garnered his attention so strongly that it left him almost stunned. Or maybe the feeling was caused by one of their abilities. A way to make it easier to get their victim to do what they want.

The Elders bowed their heads slightly to Gabby in greeting as each walked by her and took a seat across from them. If she was tense, it didn't show. But he knew his own body language was bound to be transparent. Still, he was glad he came.

At least, I will leave knowing the effect they can have on me.

He felt his heart begin to betray him as it skipped a couple of beats, then sped up. The Qalal seemed to notice. Eight sets of eyes looked in his direction, staring at him incredulously—eyes belonging to bodies that also had a set of fangs each. He felt their eyes search him. Maybe they were trying to figure out why he was there.

Or wondering how I will taste.

Lucas felt a shiver begin to creep down his spine, and he suppressed it the best he could. The silence seemed to drag on for an unbearable amount of time. It was so quiet even he could hear his heartbeat. Just like the vampires seemed to be able to.

How hard was it for them to resist their urge to pounce on him at that moment? To puncture his veins and release the warm, fresh nourishment he held beneath his frail skin?

Finally, the first male to walk in the room spoke, never withdrawing his gaze from Lucas. Lucas tried to do as he was instructed by not returning the look for long. He was sure it made him look like terrified prey, but he didn't care. This was far more intense than he'd imagined it would be.

"To what do we owe the pleasure of your visit, Gabrielle?" the vampire asked in a flat tone, soaked with disinterest.

Lucas wondered if this was the leader among leaders since he was the one who spoke. He appeared to be in his late twenties, brown hair, perfect skin, and looks that would make any woman fall at his feet—*or fangs*. He was tall but not overwhelmingly. What was overwhelming was his allure. Gabrielle had been spot on; Lucas was drawn to him—frightfully so. He was very glad she was here. There was no way he would make it out of this room, otherwise.

"I'll get to the point, Phillip," she said in a calm, imposing voice.

Lucas couldn't fathom being able to form words and push them out of his mouth in their company. He was completely incapacitated.

"Please." Phillip smiled, but it didn't alter his smug expression.

"I had a vision. It involved an attack on a group of humans by Qalal."

Lucas finally felt them take their eyes off him, their interest piqued by Gabby's statement—releasing him from their mental snare.

Phillip seemed to ponder her words. When he answered, his tone remained the same, as did his expression. "Was it a provoked attack?"

Lucas knew he was asking if the humans knew of the vampire's existence. His thoughts flashed back to Gabby's concern that he might be the cause of the attack. He still didn't think his being here would turn out to be the reason.

"I don't believe so, but it was unclear. I wanted to meet with you in case you know of any rogue covens that might try something this brazen, and to make you aware it's coming so you can assist me in hindering the occurrence all together. *If* it's your desire to do so."

Lucas thought her last statement was wrought with a subtle warning. Based on the momentary shift in Phillip's expression from arrogant to fearful and then back again, he would bet he was on target.

"Gabrielle, you know it's always our desire to assist you as much as we can. Have we not always done so in the past?" Phillip's tone didn't convey the fast shift Lucas noticed in his expression. It remained as flat as when he first spoke.

"Yes, Phillip, you have. And it hasn't gone without notice, I assure you."

With her reassurance, Lucas thought he noticed Phillip and the other Elders relax a little.

"But," Gabrielle continued, "difficult and dangerous times are approaching, as I'm sure your Seers have told you. I don't know where some hearts are at this time. I'd like to believe your desire to be forgiven is still intact and not overcome by the Darkness that taunts you with the misery of your relentless, unquenched thirst. But how am I to be sure?"

"There is no reason for us to falter, especially now. Our Seers, in fact, have brought to our attention many ... *differing* scenarios. None of us knows which will come to pass. But we do know the fabric that makes up what humans *think* their world consists of is going to be altered," he replied, making a point to glance at Lucas with a fleeting smirk when he said the word humans—like they were insignificant. "Or, maybe a better choice of words would be ... shredded."

Lucas noticed eyes on him again, and he began to feel a desire come over him to stay longer in the manor with the Elders.

Why would it matter? We could still catch our flight in plenty of time tomorrow if we stayed here instead of going back to London this afternoon.

He shut his eyes tightly against the thought. Why would he think such a thing? He opened them, and they immediately focused on the female Elder. He had been trying to avoid looking at her in particular. As soon as his eyes met hers, he knew he had been right to do so. Penetrating, red eyes—the eyes of a predator—soothed him. Lucas felt the room recede and the vampire draw closer to him. Lucas didn't think what his mind thought he was seeing was really possible but then questioned how sure he was that the Qalal was, in fact, still sitting with the others.

Is she getting closer to me ... or am I going to her?

He wanted to look at Gabby for reassurance, but he couldn't move.

It seemed to Lucas that the conversation was growing faint. The words spoken between Gabby and Phillip became muffled, like he was hearing them through an unseen wall.

Like it's taking place in another room entirely.

He could still see Gabby in his periphery, though. Time seemed to have slowed, but he couldn't reconcile why he thought so.

Lucas's thoughts about the strange feelings began to lessen as his mind drifted further away from Gabby and the male Elders. He had become almost entirely oblivious to everyone and everything but the female vampire when he thought he heard his name spoken. It was the voice of his angel—a voice that, even with the intense power the vampire had over him, he was unable to ignore.

"Lucas!" she said again in a tone somehow urgent and controlled at the same time. "Tessa ..." Gabby said in a much deeper, imposing tone than he'd ever heard, "this *will be* the only warning you'll receive from me—I assure you."

Lucas felt control return to him instantly. As the room and everyone in it crashed into place, he gulped in air, realizing he hadn't taken a breath for some time. Lucas snapped a bewildered, terrified look in Gabby's direction.

The Elders simply sat, just as they had been, with the same pompous expressions they'd had for the entirety of the meeting.

"I've taken up enough of your time. Thank you for your information and for any you can supply me with in the future." Gabby began to stand, and as she did, she placed her hand behind Lucas's elbow to signal him to do the same. Lucas did as she wanted but thought the gesture was also to help steady him as he stood. He was grateful. His mind was still thick with fog, and he felt almost drunk as they walked back toward the huge wood doors they'd entered through.

He could have sworn he heard the Elders snicker darkly, but when he turned to look at them one more time, he saw only faces carved in snobbery. As Lucas looked back, he noticed Phillip walking close behind them. Phillip closed his eyes, made an exaggerated sniffing motion with his head, and smiled—showing his perfect human white teeth.

How do their fangs come out?

"Gabrielle ..." Phillip said, "it's puzzling. I know your scent well. Even in this form you've taken, I would have known it was you. Lucas's is new but distinct. Unlike any ... *human's* I've ever encountered." He was walking next to Gabby, now. "Why is it I smell his scent so ... *heavily* on you?" he asked as he moved his hand next to her neck, wafting her scent through the air toward his nose—his focus was where Lucas had been kissing her prior to arriving. Phillip's nostrils flared as he drew in a deep breath. He turned and smiled a knowing smile at Lucas, who felt his cheeks warm.

"*I see*," he said, with a great deal of self-satisfaction, knowing his presumptions were correct by the scarlet color Lucas knew was rising in his face. The Angel of Karma was involved with a human—a human he could kill freely if he chose. He continued to speak; however, he turned his attention back to Gabby. "You … *like* this human, Gabrielle," he said with more than a little innuendo in his tone. Gabby remained unaffected by his insinuation. "This *is* unexpected. And *very* intriguing, I must say."

"*Must* you?" she retorted. "*I* must say that it's really none of your concern. Phillip, I have been more than patient and understanding of your condition since I am the one who brought a human here. I know what I've done tests you. But after what Tessa just did," Gabrielle paused as she glared in Tessa's direction, "don't push me. I've had a really annoying streak of bad karma to deal with lately." She met Phillip's gaze. "I'm sure you can imagine what that means for all of you if you cross me."

Gabby's response shut down Phillip thoroughly, and they all walked quietly until they reached the large entry area. The Elders stopped, decidedly, as if they'd rehearsed it a hundred times.

"As I'm sure you'll understand, Gabrielle." Phillip's eyes shifted quickly to the front door and back to Gabby. "We won't be accompanying you the rest of the way to the door."

Lucas looked toward the massive windows on either side of the front doors, mostly to keep from looking at any of *them* again. The front of the house faced westward, and bars of sunlight now stretched deep into the room. He hadn't noticed the sun's rays penetrating the rooms earlier.

We must have been here much longer than I thought.

This added to the confusion he already felt and to the overwhelming sense of being completely defenseless. If it hadn't been for Gabby …

How am I ever going to protect myself, or *my family, against them in an attack?*

"Of course." She stopped and turned to their hosts. "I will see you again."

"Very well. Until then," he heard Phillip say in response.

The Elders all bowed their heads to Gabby, once again at the same time, as if she was royalty. The way Lucas had seen her handle the Elders, and their obvious respectful fear of her, had affected him. He was falling in love with her; of that, he knew. But now, he was in awe of her. This angel, who looked like a teenage girl, was absolute.

And absolutely *out of my league.*

What could she see in him? What would make her want him? There was nothing his mind could come up with.

Gabby's hand was still gently, but firmly, holding his elbow to make sure he was close to her. As they made their way to the door, all Lucas could focus on were his new truths …

His mortality had never been so glaringly real.

His weakness had never been more painfully obvious.

And his new reality was filled with dangerous creatures and a Darkness he didn't know if he'd ever understand.

Or survive.

Lucas thought he heard a faint whisper, a hiss, as they were about to step into the fresh air—into freedom, knowing true freedom was something he would never feel again. His world had changed. His life would never be the same. What time was left of his life would be spent with the knowledge that he was hunted—that he had fallen a notch on the food chain.

As thoughts about the future he faced became more worrisome, the hissing whisper grew and was joined by other voices, all male except for one. They spoke to him of hunger and pain, of a thirst for blood that was an agonizing craving. The whispers became so frantic they ran together, a jumble of sounds he couldn't decipher, until the noise stopped and his mind went abruptly silent. The respite was a brief one, though, as Tessa's voice broke through—lone, and chillingly clear.

'I'll enjoy seeing you again, Lucas. One day when you are alone. One day very, very *soon.'*

Then the sound of maniacal snickers filled his head.

Chapter Fifty-one

Lucas ✝ Anything That Helps

Gabrielle and Lucas remained silent, and neither made a motion to touch the other until well after they'd left the city limits of Oxford. Lucas found no need to take in the scenery this time as he looked out his window—seeing nothing more than a blur of colors racing into his past. His former reality. His enthusiasm for the beautiful place they'd driven into had faded. Now, it was foreboding.

Lucas felt so safe because of Gabby before meeting the Elders, and even though she was there protecting him, he couldn't shake the feeling of complete helplessness he'd had since the vampires entered that room. He knew if he ever had another encounter with *any* vampire, he would need to be much better prepared. He shuddered at the possibility. Gabrielle seemed to recognize his trepidation and gently placed her hand on his. Lucas didn't turn to her. He was afraid if he looked in her eyes, he would see something different in them. Maybe disappointment, or shame, because of the weakness he'd exhibited.

"Lucas," she said softly, which made him feel that she thought he was even more fragile than he'd imagined. "Lucas, talk to me, please."

Talk to her ... what am I supposed to say?

All Lucas could think about was how weak he was. There was absolutely nothing he could have done back at the manor to defend himself. Even if he had only one vampire to deal with, he couldn't see how he could have escaped with his life.

"Lucas." Her tone was demanding this time.

"Yes, Gabby," Lucas replied, defeated. He continued to look out the window, avoiding her eyes.

"Lucas ... will you *please* look at me?"

He heard desperation in her voice. The last thing he wanted to do was upset her more than she already was. Slowly, he turned his eyes to hers. What he saw in them was unexpected and more than he felt he deserved. Her eyes held nothing for him but compassion, more than he ever thought could be expressed in a simple look. It was breathtaking to see the love she had for him—her eyes telling him everything she hadn't spoken about her feelings. It was so powerful it was almost crushing.

For the second time today, she pulled off the road. This time it was controlled, not prompted by the terror she felt for his safety. This time, she put the car in park and turned to face him.

"What is it, Lucas? Please tell me what's on your mind." Her voice was gently insistent.

"I don't even know how to start." His voice was barely audible.

"I know what happened back there had to be pretty tough on you. I tried to warn you how profound the effect would be, to try to get you to reconsider."

"I know you did. But ... it was more than the effect they had on me. That was unnerving, to put it mildly. What I found more profound and awesome ... was *you*," he responded as he raised her hand to his lips, and, more gently than he ever had, kissed the back of it and closed his eyes.

"I didn't do anything but talk to the Elders. Well ... and keep them from sucking you dry. Which, by the way, you'll be forever indebted to me for that one."

She was trying to lift his mood, but it wasn't working.

He sighed deeply. "That's just it. Your idea of *not* doing anything is more than I could ever imagine doing as a human. Like you've already said ... I'm not your equal. I never will be."

Gabrielle's brows pulled together. She seemed to be dissecting what he was saying, trying to find the direction he was taking the conversation.

Lucas continued, his words flowing faster and his voice becoming gloomier. "Gabby, how long will it be before you get bored with me? Before you realize what I just did ... that I can offer you nothing? I'm just a human."

Gabrielle's face quickly rearranged into a combination of shock and pain. When she answered, her voice was calm but hinted at the hurt his words unintentionally caused.

"Why would you think that, Lucas?"

Lucas lowered his head.

"What am I going to do with you?" She asked as frustration seeped in. "Honestly, do you think I would even consider risking *all* I am if I wasn't completely, and totally, in love with you? You want to know just *one* thing you give me that Javan—an *angel*—was never able to in all the time we were together?"

Lucas looked back up at her, curiosity getting the better of him, as he wondered what he could possibly give her that Javan couldn't.

Gabrielle's voice and eyes became tender again.

"Lucas, in the thousands of years I was with Javan, he never brought peace to me the way you do. At first, I thought it was my imagination. But now that I've been with you, even when my lot of karma is mostly bad, somehow having you near calms my mood. Just in that one way ... *I* am in awe of *you*." A flirty, crooked smile curved her mouth. "And don't even get me started on how you make me feel when you touch me."

Lucas finally smiled and laughed lightly. "So, I make you feel pretty good, huh?"

She moved her mouth close to his. "Amazing," she whispered and gently kissed his lips. She pulled back ever so slightly and looked deeply into his eyes. He knew she meant every word that followed.

"Lucas, I don't believe I would ever be happy again without you. Don't ever think I would tire of you; it simply isn't possible." She spoke to him in such a soothing voice his concerns vanished.

My angel. He thought as he closed the short distance she'd put between them.

The remainder of their stay in London was quiet and uneventful. Gabby thought it would be best to stay in that evening, stating they'd have to get up early for their flight anyway, but he knew it was for safety.

Lucas found the sleeping arrangements to be a little more troublesome than Gabby had—she was only dealing with human desires and emotions. Her angelic conscience seemed to help keep her on the straight and narrow better than he was able to. He found himself tempted by her body snuggled up to him more than once, and they finally decided they would sleep back to back so he could do a better job of keeping his hands from wandering.

Each time sleep finally crept over Lucas, he had nightmares of fangs and red eyes coming at him from all sides—and from above. He would sit up abruptly, jolted out of his sleep, just before a set of those red eyes disappeared past his face as they moved toward the exposed skin of his neck—his eyes wide from both the horror of the image remaining in his mind and the relief of the realization it was a dream. Gabby was there every time, trying to calm his erratic, heavy breathing—concern for him clearly readable on her face.

I'm so stupid not to have listened to her. Lucas scolded himself over, and over, each time he'd woken up. He continued to scold himself until he fell back to sleep only to repeat the scenario several more times.

Now that they were back in Nashville and driving home from the airport, Lucas found he was more aware of his surroundings than he had ever been—the after effects of his newly found respect for a vampire's powers.

Gabby explained more to him about what he could do to stay safe. It all seemed pretty simple. Stay in public situations as much as possible, keep holy water handy, wear the cross she was going to give him, and his favorite, spend as much time with her as he could. The last one was something he looked forward to. Lucas watched Gabby as she drove, lost in thoughts of her own.

I wonder what she's thinking about.

He still felt the way he did after they left the Elder's house in Oxford—like he would never deserve the love Gabby so willingly gave to him. But he would have to deal with it because he wasn't going to leave her. He couldn't even bear the thought. Lucas shook his head slightly and closed his eyes, then reopened them, almost expecting to be pulled out of the dream he thought he must be immersed in. She was still there, though. Thankfully. How could he feel that way about someone he'd known for only a little over a month? He knew most people would think he was insane, but he couldn't deny his feelings for her. He knew he wanted nothing but her as soon as he looked into her green eyes that first day and was almost shocked when he was actually able to speak to her, feeling like he had a complete loss of his faculties the moment he heard her voice.

She mesmerized me from the beginning.

The first time he kissed her, what was supposed to be a quick stolen moment, turned into something he still wouldn't be able to describe even if he wanted to, which he didn't. What he and Gabby experienced together seemed somehow fated. What he felt the moment their lips touched for the first time, and every time they've kissed since, sent a feeling through him that was more pleasurable than anything he'd ever imagined. He smiled with the knowledge that, somehow, she felt the same. As he looked at her, Gabby seemed to mentally return to the car and glanced at him, released by whatever thoughts that held her captive for several miles. A simple smile curved the corners of her mouth.

"What's the dreamy look about?" she asked.

Lucas squeezed her hand and shook his head, then looked back toward the road. He was happy when she did the same, hoping she wouldn't pursue an answer to her question. He was a little embarrassed to be caught looking at her that way, imagining he must have appeared just as young as he was. She deserved so much more than a human who was just becoming a man.

I hate feeling so beneath her.

He found his thoughts wandering to Javan. How could he have ever left her? Lucas would never understand what Javan had done. Surely, he knew he would lose her forever in his act of betrayal toward God. Surely, he knew it was a direct betrayal of Gabby, as well. What would motivate him to want to lose the company of two Divine beings? One the most Divine of all.

He closed his eyes and let his head fall back slowly to meet the support of the seat's headrest, not liking the thoughts beginning to intrude. Thoughts of, one day, having absolutely no say in whether or not he and Gabby stayed together. There was a much higher power involved in the decision about their future. Someone he had no way to fight. There was also her loyalty to her angelic life—and job. Her responsibility as The Angel of Karma wasn't something she could easily walk away from.

And who am I to ask her to, anyway?

An even more troublesome question for Lucas was, would she choose to stay with him if she was given the choice? Would she regret it later if she did?

Gabby choosing him was nothing more than a dream that would disintegrate if the edges of its illusion were pulled too hard. He knew he needed to just enjoy her while he had her and face the fallout of her leaving him later—which she would.

She'd have to.

There wasn't another logical destination for the road they were on. She knew their fate as well as he did and chose to move forward as he had—like the inevitable could be changed. False hope wasn't good, but it was fantastic to be together, feeling the things they felt. But after she left, there'd never be any hope of finding the kind of passion or connection they had together.

Maybe I'll become a priest.

Lucas chuckled with the thought, and Gabrielle gave him a curious, probing look.

"What's so funny?" she asked.

"Nothing really. I was just considering what it would be like to live as a priest." He opened his eyes to look at her and gave her a playful grin and wink. "And wondering if I could abstain for my entire life."

Gabrielle snickered. "I'd give that idea some *really* deep consideration, Lucas. I'm not saying it's not a wonderful and fulfilling life, because serving Yahuwah is completely satisfying for most that choose to. But it isn't for everyone and certainly isn't easy. What made you think about that, anyway?" A slightly bewildered look changed her face, realizing he probably wasn't serious.

Lucas didn't want to share the thoughts he'd been having right before this conversation began. It was a topic he wanted to avoid discussing with her as long as he could.

"I was just thinking about how a member of the clergy would feel about all the *revelations* I've had over the past few days concerning the fairytale side of things I now know about. I was wondering how they'd handle that information, and if knowing vampires and stuff really exist, would it alter their beliefs?"

Gabrielle took time to consider his words. "You've handled the information dumped onto your lap better than most would. I'd like to think the men and women who claim to serve Yahuwah would do as well as you with the knowledge, but I wouldn't bet on it.

"So many have waned over the last century and a half, doing unspeakable things as they hide behind their status in the church, feeling immune because of the pulpit they preach from. That feeling of immunity will betray them, however. I can't stand the transgressions humans make while hiding behind the words of Yahuwah."

Gabrielle pulled into her driveway. "Be right back," she said as she got out.

Lucas looked at the area surrounding Gabby's home while he waited. Wondering what could be out there watching him, even in the daylight, that he would never know was lurking. He was glad the sun was still high in the sky, though. It made him feel safer. It wasn't really logical; he wouldn't be protected by the light like in the movies, but he allowed himself to have a little solace with the thought, anyway. He didn't think he would feel at ease between dusk and dawn ever again.

The world he had lived in his entire life and thought he understood was now unfamiliar—one he felt too weak to be in. He rested his head again and closed his eyes, but they sprung open quickly as the scene from his nightmare immediately began replaying. The red eyes descending on their target—his neck—played against his eyelids like a movie screen for his mind. Lucas let go of a sigh and began to put his fingers to his temples but stopped short. He stared at his shaking hands, cursing them for showing his fear. He didn't need them to give him away, to show Gabby how disturbed he'd been since meeting the Elders.

He concentrated on taking as many slow, deep breaths as he could before Gabby returned, clenching and unclenching his fists in an effort to make them behave. He counted only eight breaths before Gabby was sliding back into the seat beside him with her gentle smile and radiating warmth. Lucas immediately felt better when he was with her. She held her hand out—a simple, masculine silver cross with a black cord dangled from her delicate fingers. He took it from her, glad to put it around his neck.

Anything that helps.

He wasn't much for wearing jewelry, but this piece would be a constant accessory from now on.

"So crosses actually repel vampires?"

"Not exactly. But it does remind them of what they're giving up if they kill or turn a human." She gave him a weak, unconvincing smile. "And sometimes that's all it takes."

"How about holy water?"

"That will definitely get their attention … hurts like hell."

Chapter Fifty-two

Gabrielle ✝ Apologies

Gabrielle didn't know what was going on behind Lucas's eyes, and that bothered her. She didn't have a clue if he was handling what he had learned and experienced as well as he seemed to be or if he was just good at covering up what was really happening in his mind.

She sighed quietly, hoping not to alert him to her own worries.

Neither one said much until they walked into Lucas's house. Emma beamed with relief when she saw her grandson, and as she hugged her only family, she reached out to touch Gabrielle's cheek. Gabrielle smiled and touched Emma's hand in response. She could see the deep concern Emma still held, though, even with Lucas home.

"I'm so glad you're back safe!" Emma released Lucas and greeted Gabrielle with a hug of her own.

"Nonie and Nate have been wearing me out, asking where you were." Emma made her way into the kitchen and motioned for them to follow. Gabrielle could tell she was baking, and by the aroma escaping the confines of the kitchen, cinnamon was certainly involved. Emma opened the oven to check on whatever it was that smelled so good as Lucas peered over her shoulder.

"Mmm ... apple pie,'" Lucas said and turned to Gabrielle. "You're in for a treat. You'll never have better!" He gave Emma a peck on the cheek as she took the pie from the oven and placed it on the stove to cool.

Emma smiled. "You're just biased," she said, giving him a playful shove with her fingertips.

"Well, it's true. I'm biased, but my bias is firmly reinforced as soon as *anyone* puts a bite of it in their mouth." Lucas sat at the table, scooting his chair close to Gabrielle so he could lean back and place his arm around her shoulders. "So that means my opinion is based in fact. Face it, Gran, you make the best apple pie around." He winked at Emma.

Emma took the seat across from them, her worry washing away the cheerful expression brought on by their exchange. "So, want to fill me in?"

Gabrielle leaned forward and crossed her arms on the table, resting her hands on her elbows. "The Elders seemed to know nothing about an attack on Lucas and the twins. There are covens and lone Qalal in the area, of course, but no rogues they're aware of. They said they would send out some of their guard to do a little reconnaissance to see what they can find out for me, but that's the best they can do."

"Do you trust what they say?" Emma looked doubtful.

Gabrielle laughed sarcastically. "As much as you can trust Qalal. They didn't seem to be deceitful." Gabrielle sighed and placed one hand under her chin. "I'll be doing my own reconnaissance, anyway, starting tonight."

Lucas shifted uncomfortably in his chair; his expression was one of deep concern. "I thought you were going to stay with me in the evenings."

Gabrielle could see how frightened he was. Apparently, he'd been putting up a good front for her.

Emma saw it, too, and looked confused. Her eyes dropped from Lucas's face to his new necklace. The furrow between her brows deepened as she realized the reason for it.

"*Oh, Lucas!* You went in with Gabrielle to see the Elders? I thought you would stay behind at the hotel." Emma shot Gabrielle an angry look. "Why did you let him do that, Gabrielle?"

"I insisted, Gran. She told me the risk I was taking. It's not her fault. I didn't listen. You and the Daniels are all I have, and a bunch of vampires want to wipe a third of you out! I felt like I had to be there."

Emma was up now, taking her anger out on microscopic things on the counter she was attacking with her dishcloth. If she still had her former strength, the granite would have deep grooves in it already. She was mumbling to herself, but it was loud enough for them to make out what she was saying. "Of all the idiotic, immature, reckless, short-sighted things to do. *Damn it*, Lucas!"

She stopped abusing the counter and stood facing it, her arms out to each side of her supporting her upper body. Her skin was stretched so tightly against her knuckles from gripping the counter's edge that there was absolutely no blood in them. Her body began to shudder as she started to cry.

Lucas was up and standing behind her, placing his hands on her shoulders.

"Gran, I'm going to be fine. *Please,* don't cry. I'm so sorry. I should've listened to Gabby, but I refused to hear I'd be in any real danger."

Emma turned around quickly and looked up into her grandson's face, putting a hand on each cheek. She spoke in a loud whisper. "You are in grave danger, now. And I can't protect you from *this.*"

"Gabby told me what I need to do to keep safe, and she's going to stay with me as much as possible. They won't even try to do anything to me when she's around."

"But she isn't going to be around all the time. She can't protect you from this, either!" Emma shot another disapproving look in Gabrielle's direction.

"Gran, stop looking at her like it's her fault! *I'm* the one you need to be mad at."

"She knows better! She had the power to make you stay away." She slowly walked toward Gabrielle with a perplexed look on her face. "And she didn't. *Why* didn't you, Gabrielle?"

"Gran, don't take this out on her! She—"

Gabrielle interrupted his defense. "Lucas." She wasn't looking at him. She was looking at Emma. "Emma's right. I should have stopped you."

"Why didn't you?" Emma pleaded for an answer again.

Gabrielle lowered her head, ashamed for her lack of good judgment. When she spoke a few moments later, her voice was quiet and slow. "I'm sorry Emma, and I owe you the biggest apology, Lucas."

"You don't owe me, or Gran, an apology. I made the decision!"

"*Stop*—Lucas. Let me finish. This is one of the reasons I'm not supposed to become emotionally involved with a human, whether in friendship or romance. It can throw my judgment off, and my feelings for you are intense. Add to that human emotions, desires, and needs I'm still getting used to that make keeping my head 'in the game' even more of a challenge, and it's a recipe for making the wrong decisions. I let my desire to make you happy interfere with what was best for you—*regardless* of how mad it made you.

"My actions, or lack of, have put your life even more at risk. It's inexcusable." Gabrielle looked at Emma and then back at Lucas. She couldn't tell what either was thinking, but it didn't matter. She would have to work as hard as she could to make sure Lucas was safe. "I promise to do everything within my power to ensure your safety."

No one made a sound, all deep in their own thoughts about what Gabrielle had just said and all that had happened over the last several days.

Emma was the first to speak. "That's all I can ask of you now, Gabrielle. I know you'll do what you can," she said in a defeated tone, and then she addressed Lucas in a stern one. "I expect you to listen to what Gabrielle says in the future. Try not to argue with her and make her sway from what she knows is best. She's right; it's going to be more difficult for her when she is in human form. Do your best not to make it harder."

"Yes, ma'am."

"I'm not going to try and keep you from each other," Emma continued. "I can see how much there is between the two of you already. Your feelings for each other radiate off of you both, and I know it'd be useless to ask it. I also know it's the best way to keep you safe. The more the Qalal see you in Gabrielle's company, if they come around, the more they'll realize you won't be an easy target, at least. Maybe, after a long time of trying to get to you and seeing it will be more than a challenge for them, they'll give up or get bored and move on to other things."

Gabrielle saw Lucas shiver and wondered if it was the thought that Qalal would continually try to find a chance to get to him—speculating about whether or not they would ever give up. She knew they never would, though.

Never.

Chapter Fifty-three

LUCAS ✝ THE REALITY OF NIGHTMARES

Gran's hope that the vampires would get bored and give up made Lucas imagine spending his life always wondering when one would finally get him. He felt a shiver begin and tried to suppress it so Gabby wouldn't see, but he failed. He was sure she saw it, and he was sure the vampires would never get bored. Eternity allowed for a lot of time, and they would probably enjoy the challenge. They might even make some kind of vampire game out of it and have a prize for the one who eventually succeeded. They had all the time in the world.

I don't.

Lucas was still thinking about what Gabby had said about the information she'd received from the Elders. He didn't remember hearing any of it.

It must have happened when the conversation seemed so distant—when I didn't exactly have control over myself.

He felt his pulse quicken with the memory of the incident and hoped that his body wouldn't betray him further. His actions may have put him on the path to meet his maker much sooner than planned unless he was meant to do everything he had.

And this was to be the manner of my death already.

He let the thought go but knew it would be revisited again—and often. If there's a destiny for everyone, and there's a reason for everything that happens, then the events over the past week and the things that were to come had a purpose. Lucas felt the truth in his thoughts but didn't know what purpose it would serve if he, or his family, were killed by vampires.

What would that accomplish?

Lucas needed to get the subject out of his head.

"Gran, what did you tell Nonie and Nate?"

She seemed to be glad for the conversation shift. "Just that you decided to go out of town with Gabrielle to her family's resort in Florida when she heard her dad was in the hospital."

"Impressive! I had no idea you were so good at coming up with covert covers." He knew his kidding had lightened Gran's mood, at least a little, when she gave him a slight smile. "So … how 'bout some of that pie?" He looked back and forth between Emma and Gabrielle, waiting to see if there were any takers.

"Sounds good to me." Gabrielle said. "My mouth started watering as soon as I walked in the front door."

Lucas stood up and walked to the fridge. "I'll get the ice cream."

Gabrielle made her way to the cabinet. "I've got the plates and forks."

"I guess it's up to me to do the cuttin' and servin'," Emma said, "I'm all over it!"

They settled into an easier mood and tried to let their tension go. No one mentioned anything about their troubles again for quite a while even though they could see the churning of emotions and thoughts behind each other's eyes.

After finishing their pie and making small talk, Gabby took everyone's dishes to the sink and began washing as Gran excused herself to fold a load of laundry. Both seemed to be trying to act like things were moving along as they normally would have. Only things weren't normal anymore for Lucas, and his instincts were telling him that they never would be again.

It was frightening.

"Gabby, how long will you be gone tonight?"

"Not long, Lucas. Hey … try not to worry."

Lucas cringed, realizing his concern must have been evident in his tone.

"I don't see any way for them to strike this quickly, anyway," Gabby continued. "They still don't know where we are. They'll have to send out trackers and talk to their informants and allies in the Shadow World in order to find you." She finished the dishes and turned. She must not have known he had moved right behind her because she jumped a little, making them both laugh.

"Sorry, I didn't mean to startle you," he said. Lucas was glad for the laughter; it allowed him to relax his expression and tone. He put his hands on her waist and his forehead to hers.

"We have some time, Lucas," she whispered. "You can sleep easy tonight."

Gabby's words weren't making him feel better, and Lucas knew the muscles in his shoulders and neck under her hands were tight with stress. If she knew how unlikely it would be that he would sleep, she might stop trying. She *should* stop trying. Because even if vampires weren't in the room with him, threatening his life, they'd be in his nightmares—threatening his sanity.

That wasn't information he would share tonight. Lucas already felt miserable enough that he wanted his girlfriend to baby-sit and protect him from his enemy. It was embarrassing. At least she wasn't an ordinary girlfriend—and it wasn't an ordinary enemy.

"Gabby, how do you find a vampire, anyway?"

"If you're an angel, it's easy. Every living thing gives off energy, and each species has its own signature. Angels can see that energy. But there is so much of it all around that it's like white noise to us, only it's visual and not audible. It all just kind of blends together unless it's a Qalal. Because the Damned have no soul, they give a distinct, erratic signature. It disrupts the balance we're accustomed to seeing so they can't hide from us—at least not without help. It would be the equivalent of you seeing a search light a mile away in the dead of night with no other lights around for hundreds of miles. You couldn't miss it if you wanted to."

Why did she have to mention the word dead?

"When are you going to go?"

"Now. I have a lot to do and a lot of ground I want to cover tonight." She cupped his face between her hands. "The quicker I leave, the quicker I can get back to you." She smiled, and he leaned in slowly.

"Then hurry up and come back. I hate when you're not with me." He whispered to her. Her lips were only an inch away from his; her breath was sweet with apples and cinnamon.

"I can't say I like it much myself," she whispered back.

He closed the short distance between them and kissed her, tasting the sweetness of apple pie that still lingered on Gabby's lips.

Chapter Fifty-four

GABRIELLE ✟ DAMAGE CONTROL

As Gabrielle scanned Tennessee for Qalal, she found her thoughts drifting back to Lucas, wondering how she could keep him safe from the predators that would surely come for him—as well as what would happen if they achieved their goal. There were only two outcomes: death and—something far worse—becoming one of them.

Gabrielle imagined there'd be more than a few who would like to take the opportunity to not only justifiably take a human's life but the life of someone she cared about—an act of revenge against Yahuwah and her. They would know how much Lucas meant to her. Phillip smelling Lucas's scent so heavily on her body assured that, and it was something she hadn't thought of when agreeing to allow him to go with her into their haven.

The missteps she was making in her human form had already put Lucas in danger, maybe mortal danger. She knew the best thing would be to leave. She could still protect him, but she would be able to keep human emotions and desires from putting him at further risk.

She just didn't know how to do it.

Gabrielle sighed out of frustration.

I'll hurt him no matter which decision I make ... either through errors made while I'm with him, or through leaving him.

'Hey, sister.'

Gabrielle turned and smiled at Phalen as she drifted toward her in the night sky. The outline of her form was distorted by the mirror-effect illusion of the stars she used for concealment. The only reason Gabrielle could see her companion at all was because of her energy signature.

'Thanks for coming.'

'How could I say no to you? You attract adventure and trouble, and you know I'm not one to pass up on an adventure ... or trouble.'

'Let's hope there's no trouble tonight, and I am not up for an adventure.'

'Okay. What do you need?'

'First, I need to know how Grayson and Rissie are doing. Then, just an ear, really. I didn't count on all these complications when I decided to live with humans, and I need someone other than Amaziah to talk to,' Gabrielle replied.

Phalen told her their Shifter friends were healing slowly but doing a little better every day. Gabrielle still didn't feel the reassurance she was hoping for, though; she wouldn't until she saw them with her own eyes. After filling Phalen in on the last several days, the questions began to pour out of Gabrielle, almost without control.

'Am I doing the right thing? Would I have come to the same decision if I knew what the result would be? Even if it turns out that Lucas will remain unharmed and we are worrying over nothing, he would never have had the concern to begin with if he hadn't met me. What would he have wanted? Would he choose to keep things as they are, meeting and falling for me? Or go back to his life as it was before, safe from all that he now fears? Never knowing I exist?'

Gabrielle paused briefly, then proceeded to tell Phalen more of her worries.

'I can't use my ability to make him forget me because he'd still be in danger. Since that skill only works on humans, the Qalal will still remember they are free to kill him. They'll feel they are within their right to do so until word gets to them that his memory of their existence has been erased. That's time I can't risk, and they can always claim they never heard.

'If I do decide to leave him, it'll be better to do it before either of us becomes more attached. I am already so thoroughly connected to him though, I feel like we are meant to be together. Which brings up another quandary altogether. What if everything that's happened is the way it's supposed to be? What if Yahuwah intended for me to be with him for some reason that would justify putting him in mortal danger?'

She couldn't know for sure if all of this was what Yahuwah wanted and had planned, but she did feel she and Lucas were supposed to be in each other's lives regardless of how unrealistic the hope that they would remain together was. Gabrielle couldn't imagine giving up her life as an angel any more than she could imagine giving up Lucas—either sacrifice would be heart wrenching.

She left those thoughts behind as she and Phalen headed east toward the Appalachian Mountains. The further east she went, the more Qalal signatures she encountered. Phalen remained silent. They were almost to Knoxville, the sweep of Tennessee close to being over, when her thoughts diverted to another who had once been important to her—Javan.

She was still shaken from her encounter with him on Saturday night, and this was the first time she'd thought deeply about it. Javan was so different now.

Or was he?

He'd always been charismatic. Maybe he'd been delusional the entire time she'd been with him. Only she couldn't see it. By nature, angels don't doubt their brethren, so maybe she'd been fooled. But if that's the case, why did Yahuwah choose Javan for her? Why did he match her with someone who would hurt her so terribly?

Gabrielle shook her head, wanting to think about something that took her away from questioning His decisions, but the thoughts about Javan persisted. He'd said he wanted to be the most powerful being—to have all others worship him.

'You know,' Gabrielle said, breaking the silence, *'it's pretty apparent that Javan is after the Book, but how he thinks he will be able to get to Yahuwah's throne is what I can't figure out. The Fallen can't ascend back into Heaven.'*

'But,' Phalen responded, almost startling Gabrielle because she had been silent for so long, *'if that's the case, how did they do it in the battle that happened thousands of years ago? You told me that Sheridan said it reached the level of the Seraphim, and they are the closest to Yahuwah and His throne.'*

'True. I'll have to ask Amaziah when I speak to him. See what you can find out, too. Regardless, Javan seems to be well informed about the Book, more so than most angels.'

'Maybe he doesn't have all the information.' Phalen offered. *'Maybe he doesn't have things worked out as well as he thinks.'*

'I hope that's the case, and it isn't me that knows less than Javan.'

It had been far too long since Gabrielle had spoken to Amaziah. She'd been trying not to interrupt him, but too much had transpired, and she needed to catch him up. When she got back to Lucas's house, she would ascend while he slept. That way, he would feel safe and wouldn't know she was away.

One state down, eight to go.

She counted two hundred and forty-two Qalal, divided between covens in Memphis, Nashville, Chattanooga, and Knoxville, and lone Qalal scattered throughout the state.

'Two hundred and forty-two ... just in this state,' Gabrielle communicated absently.

'Did you expect so many?'

'No, but at least I have some idea, now.'

'Yeah ... that whole knowledge is power thing, huh?'

'Maybe for us, but not so much for Lucas.' Gabrielle let out the mental equivalent of a clenched-jaw scream. *'This is so frustrating! I don't know how to fix this, Phalen. I don't know how to fix it.'*

'So, don't try.'

'What do you mean?'

Phalen laughed. '*I mean it literally. Don't try. You can't really fix anything at this point. Now, unfortunately, you need to be focused on damage control. I hate to be unable to offer up a better option, but you know it's the only thing you can do.*'

Gabrielle did know, but hearing Phalen voice it helped her to let go of a little of her guilt. Not because she wasn't guilty of screwing things up pretty badly, but because it didn't help her, Lucas, or anyone else if she carried the burden around all the time.

'*I do know. Thanks for listening, Phalen. And,*' Gabrielle sighed, '*sorry for laying so much on you.*'

Phalen's laughter filled her mind again. '*No worries, sister. Even you need to have someone to talk to. All the power and abilities in the world aren't enough to overcome self-doubt and regrets. And no one angel, or person, can do this thing called living all alone. Besides, I didn't really do anything.*'

Now it was Gabrielle who laughed. '*Sure you did. You were there when I needed someone. That's not something that happens often for me.*'

'*Only because you haven't let it.*' Phalen paused. '*Gabrielle, stop making yourself stand alone all the time. I, for one, will always stand with you. Always.*'

'*Thank you, Phalen. I believe you. Now … go back to Grayson and Rissie. Give them my love, and tell them I will be visiting Corstorphine to see how they're doing for myself as soon as I can get away for a day.*'

'*I will. I can't wait to get back, actually. I like it there. Maybe more than I should.*'

And then she was gone.

Gabrielle wondered just *how* much Phalen liked it there and what—*who*—might be the cause of her affinity for the Shifter's realm. A smile spread across her face as she manifested in her human body at her home as she hoped the reason was what she imagined.

She took only enough time to shower and change clothes. After pulling a brush through her hair and putting on a little lip gloss and mascara, she was back out the door. She was anxious to see Lucas, to be near him, to feel his touch on her skin and the heat it sent through her body. It was surreal. She felt more for him than she ever felt for Javan. She would never have imagined a stronger attachment could exist, but that's what was happening.

Maybe it's intensified because of my additional human emotions and senses.

Gabrielle had been able to feel emotion and connection with Javan. But with Lucas, she could taste, smell, and physically *feel* him. Those were things she wasn't capable of without a physical body to use a nose, mouth, or skin. She loved these sensations. It made her crave him, like she could never get enough of him even if they could be together for hundreds, or thousands, of years. Gabrielle felt the weight of sorrow come over her. They wouldn't have anything close to that amount of time. The reality was that one day, even if they stayed together through his natural life, he'd die and become a spirit. Hopefully, in Heaven. But angels and human souls don't interact in Heaven, for the most part. Existence after death was different from the angels that serve Yahuwah.

There was a chance Yahuwah could make him an angel—if she asked *and* it was what Lucas wanted. But the chance wasn't great. He didn't grant Divinity casually.

She pulled onto Haber Drive a little after nine o'clock. She'd accomplished what she wanted to do quickly. As she came to a stop in front of his house, he was already coming down the steps. A huge smile told her he was doing okay. Gabrielle's heart skipped a beat; the flutters in her stomach followed. She felt a grin move across her face. She had just enough time to get out of the car and close the door before he scooped her up in a huge hug. Her feet left the ground as he spun them both in a circle, burying his face into her neck by her ear. She could hear him breathe heavy and long—breathing in her scent.

He enjoys all the sensations, too.

He placed her back on the ground, but she still felt as if she were spinning. Lucas held her face between his hands and began to kiss her softly, then his pressure and urgency increased. She matched his intensity, tracing his lips lightly with her finger as they calmed themselves.

He spoke but continued to kiss different areas of her face whenever he broke up his sentence. "I hate when you are more than a foot away from me."

Gabrielle looked at him for a long moment, enjoying having his body next to hers again. Then, she kissed him slowly and gently.

"Me, too," she whispered.

Lucas began to move her side to side as he hummed softly, beginning an easy slow-dance as cars passed on the street and the stars moved overhead. They stayed like that for what seemed like an immeasurable amount of time just smelling, tasting, touching, seeing, and listening to each other.

Just dancing.

Savoring the other as if both knew being together wouldn't—*couldn't*—last.

Chapter Fifty-Five

JAVAN ✟ PEOPLE HATERS

Javan paced in front of the massive windows of the great room in his loft—like a lion in a zoo, coveting the prey just beyond the reach of its claws and teeth. Javan knew it would be hard to get to Lucas with Gabrielle involved, but there would be an opportunity. He just had to be patient, and when it presented itself, he'd be ready.

He hadn't slept for two nights. Not since realizing he'd most likely failed to eliminate Mason Hunt's bloodline—that the baby may have somehow survived his attack. And that the baby could be Lucas.

Shadows were beginning to overtake the light of day, bringing the city into the dark fold of night. It would bring something just as dark, but entirely different, for Javan.

Cecily.

He was expecting to see her since she'd said she'd come back in three nights. In truth, he was yearning for her, hoping to enjoy another long night taking pleasure in each other after they finished their business. Mara hadn't seen the visual snitch dappling his body that remained from Cecily's last visit—fading bruises in shades of yellows and browns. Mara hadn't been trying to get him into bed, not with the mood he'd been in. He had her busy enough to keep her away for at least tonight, but his demeanor alone would have done that even if he didn't have her playing private eye.

He stopped pacing long enough to open the door to his terrace, letting in the night air that told the tale of fall with its lower humidity and chill. The breeze felt good against his face, almost calming, as it brought forth a memory in his mind. He closed his eyes and let it take him back to a time he'd spent with Gabrielle—in human form. It was very brief and only once.

He and Gabrielle had spent an entire day and most of the evening walking, running, swimming, standing at the edge of the waves to let them gently bathe their feet, and coupling until she had to ascend. It was like nothing he'd experienced before, and it was the first time he considered the possibility of him and Gabrielle doing whatever they want. It was where the seed to be free of Yahuwah had been planted.

I just don't know how to get Gabrielle to see things my way.

The breeze coming through the doorway was now moving over his skin in much the same way he remembered it coming off the ocean as they watched the sun bid farewell to another day. The air cooled just enough to make them miss the heat the sun had lent, so they used each other to warm themselves. He could feel his body reacting to the memory of the sensuality he enjoyed with Gabrielle that day, lost in every detail of the body she used. She was magnificent. He wondered how her curves would feel under his hands as they ran over the body she was using now. How warm would her skin be to his touch? How would she taste? What would her lips feel like as they moved over him? How would she feel to him as they became one?

Javan opened his eyes, discovering he was no longer alone. Cecily stood in front of him. He hadn't heard her approach. She was as enchanting as he remembered. This time, she came clothed in a fitted short black dress with heels meant to be enjoyed in more of a horizontal position than a vertical one. He didn't know what was in her eyes or in the slight smirk pulling one side of her mouth more than the other that prodded him so confidently toward her, and he didn't care. Cecily was going to be his again. With his desire already piqued by memories of Gabrielle, he took her without saying a word.

Javan and Cecily pulled themselves away from each other just as a knock came from the front door. He could sense Mara and knew she would sense him and the Qalal, as well. He contemplated not answering the door but decided she would find out about Cecily sooner or later anyway. The thought had already crossed his mind that if Cecily truly could lead him to the Book, his immediate need for Mara was going to lessen dramatically.

She'd get over it. If she didn't, he would deal with her. He didn't have the patience to play games. He had too much on his mind, far too much to accomplish, to let the little demon derail his focus.

He made himself stand, stretching his body as he did. New sore spots made themselves known, and he could see fresh bruising on his torso and arms even in the shadowed room. He gave Cecily a knowing smirk as he pulled a robe on and loosely tied it—no need to try and hide what was going on from Mara. It would be obvious.

Javan walked out of his bedroom and toward the front door as another knock sounded, this time, more aggressively. Smiling cruelly, he shook his head as if to scold himself for deriving so much pleasure from hurting Mara. But he couldn't help himself, and regardless of her being his ally, pleasure through her pain was exactly what he was about to achieve.

As soon as he opened the door, he knew he wasn't going to get the fun he was hoping for. Mara faced him with nothing but indifference held in her expression.

Ahh … come on! Where's the rage? The jealousy?

As if she read his thoughts, she cracked a detached smile.

"What?" she asked. "Are you going to let me in, or not?"

Javan opened the door further and gestured for her to enter. She walked in and looked at Cecily, smiled cordially and nodded, then looked back over her shoulder to Javan.

"Sorry for the interruption, *sweetie*, but I thought you might want to know what I've found out so far."

Javan was befuddled and more disappointed than he wanted to admit.

I thought she'd be upset, and look at her. Nothing. Absolutely nothing. And I'm getting mad at her for not getting mad at me! How absurd!

"Javan ..." Mara moved further into the main room, closer to Cecily.

It seemed to Javan that Cecily was overly curious about Mara as Mara and Cecily faced each other. He could almost see the questions forming in her mind.

Why is she so interested?

Mara smiled as she looked at Cecily. "Don't you think you should introduce us?"

Javan watched the two females check each other out. This was not the scenario he was prepared for. Cecily was more put off by Mara's presence than the other way around. Mara still seemed completely unaffected by what she had basically walked in on.

Glancing back at Javan again, Mara rolled her eyes, then refocused her attention on Cecily. "I'm Mara. Javan's other ... *friend*. I won't apologize for his lack of manners because, of course, he doesn't have any." She turned and winked at Javan.

Unbelievable!

He was stunned and surprised by Mara's nonchalant attitude. She had always seemed so weak-minded, a sycophant. He was beginning to think he had underestimated her.

Had she acted like a follower on purpose?

Mentally returning to the scene playing out in front of him, Javan became a participant in his life again instead of a momentary observer.

"Cecily stopped by with some news of her own, but we hadn't gotten around to *talking*, yet," Javan stated with definite implications. He almost wanted to sigh with the relief as his callousness returned—welcoming it like an old friend.

"Really," Mara said more as a question. "Well, I guess you'll have a lot to *chew* on with Cecily after I leave."

Javan tried not to let her detached tone and demeanor pull him back into the awkwardness only he seemed to feel. "I guess we will." Javan smiled at Cecily and tried to sound just as bored as Mara seemed to be. "What did you find that's so interesting?"

Mara turned her back to the counter and hoisted herself on it, as relaxed as you'd expect if they were actually all great friends, smiling cheerfully at them both once she was comfortably perched.

"Well, I did the research you asked me to do on Emma and Lucas, going all the way back to the day you *thought* you took care of all your little problems. Turns out … you *didn't*."

Javan felt his hands tighten into fists. This was exactly what he didn't want to hear—and exactly what he'd suspected. His voice leveled into a stern, foreboding tone as he spoke through teeth clenched from irritation with himself. "Go on."

"If you had stuck around to be positive, you would've found out the baby you killed wasn't the Watkins's son—Mason Hunt's grandson. It was the next-door neighbor's child. They were babysitting him." Mara snickered coarsely. "Apparently, Grandma Emma had Lucas at a doctor's appointment. You didn't take the time to check if it was even the right kid. All this time, he's been growing into a fine young man—*damn* good-looking one, too, I might add."

Her sarcasm was grating on Javan. He was sure she meant it to. He walked to his earlier path and began to pace again. He had been hoping he was wrong about Lucas, that he was a different family member of that *cow* he wanted revenge on. Or maybe that she was his foster parent or just a family friend who took him in because no one else wanted him. But not *this*. Not one of the only people who, according to the prophecy, would have a role in whether or not the Destroyer rose to power.

He noted Cecily was taking a deeper interest in what Mara was saying, narrowing her eyes and leaning slightly forward. They were subtle movements, but Javan caught them. Javan glanced at Mara. A smile was still teasing across her face. She wasn't finished, and Javan felt a cold knot twist in his stomach.

"*Spit it out*, Mara!" For once, his anger didn't seem to bother her.

She's enjoying this.

The evening had certainly taken a turn he hadn't anticipated.

She chuckled wryly. "Grandma, as you now know, isn't any ordinary granny. She's an angel, but not fallen. She asked permission to live as a human, and Yahuwah granted it to her. You want to know *why* she wanted to be human, Javan?"

He shot her a look full of daggers, and she seemed to decide not to push her luck any further.

"She fell in love with the boy she was ordered to protect. The one you killed twenty some-odd years later." She paused for what Javan assumed was dramatic effect. "Mason Hunt."

She waited to see if he put the pieces together, but then, like a giddy school-girl who couldn't wait to spread the latest gossip, she blurted out what he was realizing.

"*Emma* ... is Lucas's *biological* grandmother! Lucas is one-quarter angel. He has Divine blood running through his veins! He's Nephilim! Who woulda' thunk it, huh?"

She was having far too much fun with this, and it was time for her to go. Before he could say anything, she hopped off the counter, landing lightly on her feet, already in stride toward the door. With her hand raised in the air, she waved without turning around and spoke in a playful tone.

"You kids have fun! See ya later, people haters!"

Javan was seething—his pulse pumping so fast and hard he could feel the veins at his temples and neck pushing against the skin that held them in its confines.

As the door closed behind Mara, Javan was already downing his first drink.

Chapter Fifty-six

GABRIELLE ✝ A BRUISED EGO

"You know," Lucas whispered in Gabrielle's ear as they sat on his sofa. The TV was on, but neither was paying attention to anything but the warm body next to them, "I knew when you were coming tonight. I can't explain it, but I *felt* you approaching. That's why I was outside waiting on you. The closer you got, the stronger the sensation. It's happened a lot with you and sometimes with others ... like Gran and Mara. Does that make any sense to you?"

Gabrielle laughed quietly, trying not to disturb Emma as she slept in the next room. "I know what you're talking about. It's something those with Divine blood can do. We can sense when another of our kind is near, even recognize if it's someone we know. It even works with the Fallen. That's why you could sometimes sense Mara. We all have our own vibration, our own signature. Kind of like the way I described to you that the Qalal give off a distinct energy." She waited to see if he followed what she was saying. He nodded. "It doesn't surprise me that you have that ability. It's not stronger because you're mostly human. You'll possibly get better at discerning now that you're becoming aware of what you're feeling. You may even have other abilities that are hidden because they're so light in you and have never been developed."

Lucas shifted his body to face her. "Like what kind of things?"

"Well, you may have precognitive abilities or some telepathic talent. You may have already discovered you're faster, and stronger, than a human should be."

A slight smile played around the corners of his mouth.

"You may heal much quicker than normal, and you may have retained a greater capacity for compassion, love, and general kindness than most humans."

Lucas seemed to be pondering what Gabrielle told him, searching his memory for things he'd done that would corroborate what she said. If he found anything, he didn't share them with her. He kissed her hand and looked back at the TV, drifting deeper into thought. Gabrielle wondered what he was thinking about though she didn't want to pry. But after several more minutes of silence, she had to ask.

"Lucas," she put her hand lightly under his chin and guided his face to look at hers, "what's on your mind?"

Lucas smiled apprehensively and shrugged his shoulders, diverting his eyes and head away from hers. She turned him toward her again.

"Lucas, you can talk to me about *anything*. You know that, don't you?"

He rested his hand on her cheek, stroking her skin with only his thumb. He seemed to be searching her thoughts with his eyes as though he was willing them to tell him the information he was after without having to ask. After several long moments, he leaned in and kissed her forehead, speaking quietly when he pulled away.

"I know I can talk to you about anything." He sighed heavily. "I just don't know if I really want to know the answer to my question."

Gabrielle wasn't sure where this conversation was going, but she was beginning to feel like she didn't want him to ask the question any more than he wanted to let it pass his lips.

"What I want to know, I also *don't* want to know." He sighed again, then let his thoughts spill out like a freight train. "I want to know how many vampires you found tonight. How many creatures live, basically, right in my backyard that could come after me and my family? But at the same time, I don't want to know, because—well—up until four days ago, ignorance was bliss. Now I'm afraid I know too much to *ever* be blissful again. *And* now that I know what I know, I really *have* to know everything because ignorance will cost me my life. To make matters *worse*—as if *that's* possible—my girlfriend's my bodyguard." He finally paused to look deep into her eyes again, his brow furrowed from the intensity of his stress. "Do you have any idea how shitty that makes me feel? *I* should be protecting *you*."

Gabrielle was quiet after he finished, her eyes wide at his fervor. It was theatrical, and she was having a difficult time not laughing. She didn't want to make things worse for him, but regardless of how it pained her to let her amusement escape, she felt the corners of her mouth begin to curve. The more she tried to stop it, the more insistent it became. Before it escaped, she managed to get two words to sprint ahead of the laughter.

"I'm sorry ... " Then the uncontrollable laughing began.

For the first several seconds, Lucas stared at her, stunned, not understanding how she could find humor in what he'd said. He must have played over the prior spilling of his guts in his head and realized how he must have sounded because he seemed to begin to find the humor in it, as well.

When Gabrielle began to regain her composure, wiping the tears that had run down her face and catching her breath, she managed to get more words out of her mouth.

"Oh, Lucas. I'm not laughing because you're concerned, but when you have all these issues and fears about the Damned coming after you, and then you throw in your ego being bruised because I can protect you—at least to some extent—well ..."

She took a breath to make sure she could continue without letting straggling giggles creep out—waiting for their opportunity to flee her body. "In Heaven, we all protect each other. It doesn't matter who is masculine or feminine, older or younger, lower or higher rank. We take care of each other because we love each other. Try not to waste your time and energy concerning yourself over something you're fortunate to have. Let's look at the alternative. What if I were merely human with no powers or extraordinary abilities and you found yourself in the same predicament? What chance of survival would you have? Would you trade my protection to feel better?"

Lucas chuckled.

"You know—you're breathtakingly beautiful, *deliciously* sexy, fast, strong, kind, loving, *and* powerful beyond my wildest imagination. Do you have to be so damn logical, too?"

A smile moved easily across his face, and he leaned in to give her a long kiss. Gabrielle could tell it came from a sincere, grateful, overwhelmed place deep inside him, not purely passionate. Her eyes filled with tears from her own feelings of love. When he pulled away and looked into her eyes, she was sure his were shinier than usual, too.

"And," he continued, "*how* did I get so astonishingly lucky?"

Gabrielle smiled at him and whispered back, "I was just wondering the same thing about me."

They held each other for a while longer before she spoke again. "So, do you want to know or not?"

He kissed her on the top of her head. "Yeah. Go ahead. It'd probably drive me even crazier *not* to know than *to* know."

"I found two hundred and forty-two here in Tennessee, but it's the only state I covered. I'll go to the others individually, devoting a night to each of them in the coming days."

"Wow. Two hundred and forty-two, huh?" He was staring past her, letting the number sink in. "Did you expect more, or less?"

"It was more than I'd anticipated. But it doesn't really matter. You'll have to take the same precautions regardless of how many I find." She didn't want to tell him that when word got out about him being fair game, the local Qalal population would likely inflate to truly menacing numbers.

He seemed to be handling the information fairly well, at least from what he was showing outwardly. She wouldn't know for sure until she got through a few days with him.

Gabrielle looked at the clock on the mantle; it showed a quarter to eleven.

"Hey, we've had a *really* long couple of days. I think we both could use some rest, especially you."

She left out the fact that she was going to have to leave him to speak with Amaziah. He would think she was sleeping soundly next to him, and that was all he needed to know. Maybe with her here, he would be able to rest. The stress and lack of sleep showed with dark circles under his eyes, and Gabrielle didn't want him to feel even worse tomorrow.

He nodded his head in agreement and led her to his room.

Neither Gabrielle nor Lucas did more to get ready for bed than brush their teeth, take off their shoes, and fall into each other's arms on top of the covers. And both, as far as Lucas would be able to tell, fell swiftly to sleep.

Chapter Fifty-seven

JAVAN ☦ AN UNEXPECTED PARTNER

Javan and Cecily remained silent long after Mara left. Cecily seemed to understand that she shouldn't push him too hard after he learned that he failed in killing off the Watkins' bloodline. He was reeling from the information, enraged with himself for being so reckless years ago. Now he would have to eliminate Lucas just when he needed to be concentrating solely on finding the Book. It would mean precious time wasted. He'd have to go around, or through, Gabrielle to get to him—and that would be difficult. He was headed to the kitchen when Cecily spoke; her tone conveyed her boredom and agitation.

"Would you like to talk about our arrangement this evening, or would you rather I come back another time? Quite honestly, there are other things I can be doing. And they don't include watching you brood. Besides, I'm in no real hurry. It's not like I'm getting any older—well ... not in *mortal* terms, anyway. Your call."

Javan gazed at the auburn beauty sitting on his couch, one long leg crossed over the other. Her already short dress was pulled high on her thighs, exposing almost every amazing inch of her legs—legs that had been wrapped around his body just a couple of hours ago—legs he would have wrapped around him again right now if he didn't need to focus on getting the Book.

He didn't want to think about how a confrontation with Gabrielle could end, and he was glad to have a conversation for distraction. It would be difficult to kill Gabrielle, but he'd do it if he had to.

Would she struggle with the thought of killing me?

He took a sip of bourbon, sucking his lips to his teeth after he swallowed.

"Let's get down to business." He walked to Cecily and sat on the opposite end of the couch. With only a few feet between them, he found his desire prodding his mind and body again. He took a sip of his drink and placed it on the coffee table. Breaking her gaze seemed to help, so he decided to keep his eyes closed, squeezing the top of his nose between his middle finger and his thumb.

"I'll make this easy, Cecily. If you can get the Book *into* my hands, and I can keep it in my control long enough to do what I need to do, I'll honor my end of the deal and place you in the position of power you want. But that means you need to do what you can to help me maintain my possession of it. You'll need to help me do unpleasant things, and you'll need to spend a significant amount of time in my company. If you can do all of that, then I'll make you one hell of a powerful woman."

Cecily didn't respond right away, and Javan finally opened his eyes to read her expression. He saw her stunning face with a mischievous smile staring back at him. He knew she didn't really need to spend so much time with him, but he figured he may as well get any perk he could.

"I can *absolutely* get the Book into your hands, and I'm willing to do whatever I need to do to *keep* it there regardless of how unsavory you think it might be. You never know ... I might think it quite savory. And as far as spending time with you," Cecily's smile and expression became more flirtatious, "I think I can keep you from feeling like it's complete drudgery. As a matter of fact, I happen to know the loft below you is about to become available, and that would make being here when you *need* me all that much easier. At least in the daytime."

Javan felt a devilish smile take over his expression. "And how exactly do you know it's coming available?"

"Well, it seems the young man who lives there will meet someone he can't, well … *resist,* I guess you can say. This woman will be moving in with him right away. He won't want to be without her; she'll make sure of that. Then, he'll be called away to work in another country a couple of weeks later, leaving the woman to take care of his loft and affairs while he's gone. The job will be extended, repeatedly, until it becomes a permanent move." Her smile grew. "Leaving the woman free to live there as long as is needed."

"It would seem that this is something the woman has done before," Javan responded, amused again by how similar they were.

"Yes, she's accustomed to getting exactly what she wants. So far, without fail. She's resourceful."

"Sounds like it."

They looked at each other, smiling wicked smiles. Cecily was drawing closer to what she said she wanted, and Javan was getting what he needed with an unexpected and pleasurable partner. He made himself break their gaze again, not wanting to be distracted by her body just yet.

"Tell me, Cecily. How is it you came to know where the Book is?"

"It was my great, great—hundreds of years ago—great grandfather, Elijah Privett, who Ramai had commissioned, through threat of his family's death, to create a copy of the Book. He discovered that Elijah wasn't only a Seer of occurrences in time; he also had a remarkable gift to see into the mind of anyone he chose.

"Ramai used Elijah to find his memory of what the words on the pages of the Book were to make a new one. Even though Ramai promised to spare Elijah's family's life if he created the Book, Ramai killed them anyway. Elijah's sister, who was away at the time, was his only family member to survive. There was no reason Ramai killed them aside from being evil. It was purely for amusement."

Cecily paused, seeming to lose herself in thoughts. A strained expression rearranged her face for a moment. Then, she abruptly continued as if something had startled her back into reality.

"Anyway, Elijah swore revenge, but he knew it would be impossible for him to kill Ramai, so he came up with another plan. One he felt would be even better than killing him. He decided to steal the copy of the Book.

"He made some sort of pact with a demon, newly fallen, who regretted what he'd done to be cast from Heaven. Elijah convinced him that he could help him get back if the demon helped him obtain the Book of Barabbadon. The fallen angel helped him obtain the Book, and Elijah immediately hid it. He was able to tell his sister what he'd done, why he'd done it, and where it was hidden. He also told her what he'd been shown after he created the book—a prophecy about the Destroyer and the role of the Book in that prophecy. He asked her to keep it secret, to tell only those in our family she knew could be trusted. They were to pass the knowledge down through the generations but to leave the Book where he hid it until the day came when the prophecy was close to coming to pass. He was able to do all this before the demon realized Elijah wouldn't be able to help him get back to Heaven—before he was murdered." Cecily's eyes became distant. "All because he was a Seer." The same strained expression passed over her face. Only this time, it lingered longer and held sadness. Seeming to realize she was revealing more than she wanted, Cecily wiped her expression clean. "The time he spoke of is now, and it's a good thing because I'm the last of my family. And even though I'm basically immortal, we both know there are a couple of ways my existence can end."

"So, you're telling me you know where the Book is ... *right now*."

She smiled, but it grew sinister.

"That's exactly what I'm saying, Javan."

Javan's mind ran full tilt, imagining all that he was about to accomplish when the Book was his. "Well, then. Why are we still here talking? I say we get it now."

Cecily walked to the terrace and stepped outside into the cool night air. Javan followed her, feeling his mood lift at the possibility of getting his hands on what he was cast from Heaven for—*finally*.

"So," he said, speaking softly in her ear, caressing her arms, "are you ready to go?"

"I wish it were that easy, Javan."

Javan's mood began to wane again, and he turned her to face him.

"What does that mean?"

"It means it'll take a little time and planning, sweetie. But don't worry. It'll be yours."

"*Fuck*." He just wanted the damn Book in his hands. "Where is it … *exactly*?" His eyes narrowed, deepening a hard scowl.

"Where no demon would ever look—buried near one of the Gates of Hell."

Chapter Fifty-eight

GABRIELLE ✝ A PERSONAL HELL

When Gabrielle was sure Lucas had drifted into dreams, she ascended, calling to Amaziah. He was ready for her when she arrived. She was glad to see him. If she could have felt the sensation of touch in her angelic form, she would have wrapped her arms around him. Instead, the light she emanated reached for his, and the two glowed brighter as they met.

Gabrielle had an immediate sense of peace here, in her home, with her dear friend, regardless of the growing problems she faced back on Earth. But she noticed a shift in her surroundings as she felt an enormous amount of energy directed toward her. Energy from hundreds of angels all around her, passing underneath, below, and on both sides of her and Amaziah.

But why?

Just as she was about to communicate her question to Amaziah, he directed her to follow him. Gabrielle found herself missing the ability to use her lips, tongue, mouth, and air to push out what was in her mind. She wondered why. It was far easier to *think* what you wanted someone to know than go through all the motions involved with human speech. The thought of her lips reminded her of the way it felt to have Lucas kiss her, but she pushed the thought out of her mind, hoping Amaziah didn't have time to pick up on it.

Amaziah was moving her away from the main route of the angels coming and going from Heaven. There was always a constant stream of angels on their missions, but there was a lot more activity than usual. Their tasks varied: protecting humans, intervening in daily activities, escorting souls who were crossing over, teaching another angel a new position or a fledgling angel the "ropes". Normally, half the angels coming and going would be Gabrielle's own troops. She had legions assigned to her. But there was a massive amount of activity, and it made her uneasy. She suddenly felt distant from her brethren, far more than ever before.

Is it just because I've barely been back since I left?

That didn't feel like the reason. There was something else. Amaziah led her further away. Even with the numbers of angels around them lessening, she continued to feel as though they were turned toward her—*watching* her. She wondered why she'd garnered so much attention. Was it just curiosity about what her experiences have been with humans? Could it be jealousy?

Then it hit her.

This is about Lucas! Protectiveness surged through her.

She knew, at once, that's what it was. The realization made her feel like they were going to go after Lucas and maybe even her. When Amaziah finally stopped and began to speak, she could tell something was wrong. Aguish coursed through her, joining the protective response she already had. This wasn't going to be good.

'Gabrielle, I won't waste time with pleasantries. You know I love and miss you. But I'm sure the reaction to your arrival wasn't lost on you.'

Several moments of silence passed before Gabrielle received Amaziah's next thoughts.

'I was going to contact you this evening, so I was glad to hear you were coming to see me. A wealth of information has been discovered that I need to tell you. It's upsetting to us all, but it will be deeply disturbing for you.'

Gabrielle began to feel her energy quiver. She knew any of her brethren would be able to see her light pulsating right now and know something was wrong.

'Please, just continue, Amaziah.'

'We already knew Javan has dreams of grandeur—wanting to rule over everyone and everything. We felt he was delusional. But it turns out he isn't. There is a way he can achieve his goal.'

Gabrielle's energy quivered faster. She tried to calm herself. She didn't want to draw any attention to them—didn't want to increase the number of angels directing their energy at her. What Amaziah had just said was confusing, but it opened the door for her to ask a question she'd been hoping to get the answer to.

'How can he use the Book if he found it? He can't ascend back into Heaven. The guards would never allow him in. Doesn't he have to speak the words from Yahuwah's throne in order for them to be effective? How would that be possible for him to achieve?'

'He can't ascend—or enter into Heaven. But if he had an army devoted to him and declared war against Yahuwah and all His angels, Yahuwah would bring the battle and the throne to Earth. Any with Divine blood could use the Book in the same way, whether Fallen or of mixed blood. If he is able to acquire the Book, Gabrielle, all he has to have is the blood sacrifice of another fallen angel and the appropriate date to perform the ceremony. A demon, a date, and a simple ritual to summon all of Darkness to him. Once he has their attention and shows them he possesses the Book, it will be easy to persuade them to follow him. Ramai won't even try to stop him.

'Javan will be looked upon as their savior. Their deliverer. The Destroyer. Some of those in Darkness have hungered for revenge, for power to be theirs, for millenniums. But all of the Fallen have bitterness in them. They will think Javan is about to give them what they have yearned for since they fell—retribution.'

Amaziah paused as if to allow Gabrielle time to let this information take root in her mind before he continued with the next onslaught of information.

This time, it was Gabrielle who communicated first.

'What date? I haven't heard of a date associated with the prophecy.'

'You wouldn't have. It is guarded information—Ramai thought he knew all he had to know before he rebelled. He didn't. The date's necessary. Without it, it's just pages full of words.'

'So, the only way to stop Javan is to get the Book before he does?'

'There is another way. He *can* be stopped. Period.'

Gabrielle knew what he meant; Javan could be killed.

Her mind recoiled from the thought. She knew she could never be with him again; he was lost to her forever. But she also knew she'd always love him. How could she not? As much as he hurt her, *crushed* her, when he fell and left her behind, she didn't want him to *die*.

'Why wouldn't Ramai stop him?'

'He has no motivation to do so. He won't be battling Yahuwah. It's what was agreed to, to keep the fight fair. Ramai would never be a match for Yahuwah. The victor is decided by the power of the loyalty each has garnered from their followers. He needs the prophecy of the Destroyer to come to pass so that he has his champion, just as Yahuwah will have his. Because what Javan, or any other that uses the Book doesn't know, is that Yahuwah has had a secret weapon for a long, long time that will be available when the time is right … if all goes the way He hopes.'

Amaziah paused, and Gabrielle sensed more angels approaching. How could they resist the draw to her now? Her energy was frantic, and angels couldn't ignore the urge to come to the aid of another in distress. It literally hurt if another angel was upset, or in pain, in the general proximity. But she also noticed they quickly diverted away from her and Amaziah. Were they simply giving two high-ranking angels their space? Or did they know something she didn't? She couldn't be sure, and she couldn't be concerned about what they thought, or knew, right now. She gave her attention back to Amaziah.

'My dear Gabrielle, I am so sorry to be causing you distress. But you have to know everything we have found out. It affects you more than any of the rest of us.'

'Amaziah, I don't see how it affects me much more, really. I know who Javan was—still is—to me. But if he is able to achieve his goal, it will impact us all the same. We will be either enslaved or executed. Those will be our only choices. My heart cannot be broken by him anymore than it already has been. It isn't possible. He is now my adversary, whether I love him or not.'

There was a long pause while neither tried to communicate. The quiet caused even deeper anguish to rush through her than before. There was more he was going to tell her—and it was about to get worse. She wanted to flee. The instinct to be with Lucas became more prominent as the feeling of threat to him grew; it was all around her, and it was coming from her brethren. Her mind scrambled to make sense of what was going on.

'Why would they want to hurt Lucas?' She practically screamed the thought at Amaziah, who reached for her again, but she pulled her energy away.

'This is the information I most regret to give you, Gabrielle,' he said gently. 'We caught and interrogated several of Ramai's highest ranking demons. Though none gave us all the information we wanted or needed, we were able to gather enough and piece together what the prophecy foretells. We knew Lucas's grandfather was being protected by Emma and others because there was hope someone in that lineage would thwart the attempt of the Destroyer to take power. All we had to go on was that someone in Mason's bloodline would determine the outcome of whether or not a Destroyer rose to power.

'The full prophecy is more specific. It states the one who will determine whether or not the Destroyer takes power will be the only living blood relative of Mason's line, and that all others who shared his blood would be eliminated.'

Gabrielle didn't like that Lucas would be involved in this battle. But she and the rest of Yahuwah's troops could ensure his safety. So why did she feel the threat to him coming *from* them? It wasn't adding up. She could tell by Amaziah's energy beginning to show distress that her question was about to be answered.

'Gabrielle ... Lucas doesn't stand in the way of the Destroyer. The prophecy states Lucas will make the decision of whether or not he will become *the Destroyer.*'

Her energy had never been as frantic as it was at that moment.

She wanted to run to Yahuwah—yell and scream at Him as loudly as she could. Why was she being punished? What else could this be? He was omniscient—omnipotent. Why was He allowing the only two beings she'd ever loved to *both* become her enemy? At least one already had, and it looked as though she only had a fifty-fifty shot at the other. Hadn't she already suffered enough? Gabrielle wasn't sure she could handle this. What was she supposed to do with this information? How was it possible *Lucas* might be her worst enemy? How could this be happening?

'I don't understand, Amaziah. What would make Lucas want to be the Destroyer? He isn't an evil or hateful person. Quite the opposite. Because he has Divine blood, he seems to be far more compassionate than most humans.'

'I know you have a lot of questions, questions only Yahuwah can answer. But it's best if you calm down before you see Him. He knows you want answers, and He will be available to you when you are ready to ask Him. He knows you were already hurt by Javan. But you must remember, even though Yahuwah knows all that goes on in Heaven and on Earth, and most of what goes on in Hell, there are ways the Underworld veils some of what is happening and some of what they know. Gabrielle, Yahuwah didn't know what role Mason's bloodline would have. It's all determined by Lucas's decision. He doesn't know which Lucas will choose. His hope is that Lucas's choice will benefit Light—just as Ramai hopes it will benefit Darkness.

'Yahuwah knows the Destroyer is coming, and He knows the battle is coming—it's what our Lord agreed to. But He also agreed to let the Ramai have a certain amount of power in order for it to be a fair fight. Yahuwah won't force anyone to follow Him. That's part of what the Great War is all about, Gabrielle—free will and its effects. Whether good or bad. It's how the battle's victor will ultimately be decided.

'Yahuwah could manipulate Lucas into the decision He wants, but it is Lucas's decision to make. His heart aches for every one of His children, whether human or angel, who have fallen. He agreed not to sway the result of the battle with His Divine powers, but that doesn't mean Yahuwah can't try to lead someone down the path to Him.'

Gabrielle was sure where this was going, now. Lucas was to be guided to stay on the path of Light with her help along with the rest of Yahuwah's angels, which meant Ramai and his legions of demons were going to be trying to do the opposite. Obviously, if there was going to be a choice made by Lucas, there would be some victories for the side of Darkness that could make him consider becoming so malevolent.

Now, she was also sure the excessive demonic activity in the city was due to Lucas, not her. More than that, she knew for sure that her suspicion about the meaning of the crows was true.

Ramai is keeping a close eye on Lucas.

Amaziah's words echoed in her mind again. *Any with Divine blood could use the Book in the same way, whether Fallen or of mixed blood.* He was preparing her, letting her know that, even though he was only part angel, Lucas would be able to do the same. It all depended on his choice.

This was really, really bad.

Her former love believed he would be the Destroyer, and he would obviously take lives to achieve it. If Javan found out who Lucas was, he'd try to kill him. And there was a good chance Javan could end up gaining the power he needed to reach his goal. Yahuwah's angels were waiting to turn on Lucas, which she would also have to do if he didn't resist the evil coming for him. Legions of Ramai's demons would be trying everything they could to put bitterness and hatred in his heart, and then *they* would turn on Lucas if he wasn't going the direction they wanted him to. And who could forget the Damned coming after him and his family? Gabrielle had a much better idea of why the last one would probably happen. If they hurt those Lucas loved, it might push him toward Ramai's desired outcome. The vision of the attack on Lucas, Nonie, and Nate made perfect sense to her now.

'So the battle has already started. But we aren't fighting each other, yet. The battle is over Lucas's mind ... and ultimately his soul.'

She glimpsed the reason Yahuwah put her in Lucas's life, now, as well as why he decided to let her live on Earth and take on the task she had fought so long for. Gabrielle was determined not to let Darkness win. She wasn't going to let Yahuwah or Lucas down.

I love them both too much.

She filled Amaziah in on all that had happened over the last few days. He was as concerned as she was about the Qalal, especially with the bigger picture about the role Lucas would play in front of them. He assured her he would do all he could to help her keep them safe but reminded her that Ramai could operate under a veil without their awareness or detection. He stressed to her that if the Qalal she saw in her vision were working with Ramai, it would be difficult to see them coming until they were already upon them—pointing out that he could camouflage any activities he saw as a benefit to achieving his goals.

She could tell he wasn't happy about her decision to allow Lucas to see the Elders with her, but he didn't dwell on the subject. Maybe he knew she'd had enough for the day. Before she descended back to Earth, back to her body resting peacefully next to her love—potentially her future enemy—she asked him about the other angels.

'Amaziah, why is it I feel my brethren are all focused on me? Are they angry? What have I done that's causing this reaction?'

'They aren't mad at you, but they do have concerns. They know you have already lost one love, and they all know about your relationship with Lucas. They are concerned how you will handle the possibility of losing another who's dear to your heart. They don't know if you'll be able to bear it again because they don't know if they could, and they are worried about what it might cause you to do.'

'What it might cause me to do? What do they think I will—Oh. They think I might choose to stay with Lucas if he decides to choose Darkness. Wow ... they have so little faith in my love for Yahuwah. I admit, Amaziah, I won't want to leave Lucas, but if his path is one we can't travel together, I will leave him. I will do whatever I have to do to protect my home and serve my Lord. Lucas is in my heart and soul—but both belong to Yahuwah.'

Amaziah reached his energy to hers and, this time, Gabrielle reached back, welcoming his ability to soothe her a little. She heard the last words she said to Amaziah slip back into her consciousness as he murmured softly to her in Enochian. *I will leave him. I will do whatever I have to do to protect my home and serve my Lord. Lucas is in my heart and soul—but both belong to Yahuwah.*

She felt a momentary flux in her resolve as she thought of the implications of what she'd said. But it was a strong enough deviation from what she thought she would do if that circumstance presented itself that she wondered if her statement to Amaziah would turn out to be false.

Would I hesitate to stand by Yahuwah and fight for him, and my brethren, if Lucas chose Darkness?

She didn't want to admit it to herself, but that question troubled her more than anything else at that moment because she knew she couldn't honestly say she wouldn't.

How can I care for him so much that I would doubt my own loyalty to Yahuwah? What has happened to me?

She left Amaziah to return to her troubles on Earth that were now worse than before she entered her eternal home. As she did, she realized she was descending back to Earth from Heaven and entering what was becoming her personal Hell.

Chapter Fifty-nine

Javan ☩ The Kicker

"Why can't things be easy ... just once?" Javan asked without expecting an answer. There was no reason, in particular, he felt he deserved anything to be easy for him, but he could still ask the question. Cecily knew exactly where the Book was located, and he couldn't be happier about that news, but it wouldn't be easy getting it.

He was on his terrace, watching the cars on the freeway that cut the city in half. He lived on one side of that highway; Gabrielle lived on the other.

Even the city has us on different sides.

He hadn't asked why it would be difficult to get the Book. He was almost afraid to, thinking maybe they should just go and deal with whatever the issue was. Imagination could make the possibilities much worse than reality. With one exception—his first encounter with Gabrielle since he'd become one of the Fallen. That reality was far worse than his imagination ever contrived, and he was still shaken from it. She was the only thing he wanted from his former life—his former home—the only thing he longed for.

I can't take any more time thinking about something I don't have the ability to change ... yet.

"So,'" Javan began, forcing his longing for Gabrielle out of his mind, "what's so difficult about retrieving the Book? The Gates of Hell aren't exactly something I'm worried about." He hadn't turned to look at her, purposely avoiding the urge that would hit him as soon as he did.

"It's not the Gates of Hell I'm concerned about, either. For one thing, it's in a public place, and—"

"Still not concerned," he interrupted.

Cecily was now standing next to him. "Still not my concern, either. The problem is that where it's buried has gone through some changes Elijah *didn't* foresee. The spot where the Book has been concealed for all these years is close to the tomb of Marie Laveau in New Orleans."

"Is there going to come a point where you're going to just tell me why this is a dilemma? Because I'm still unsure of what's posing a problem."

"You don't have any idea who Marie Laveau is, do you, Javan?"

Javan raised his head and hands to Heaven as if asking for Divine help, which he knew better than to think he'd actually get, then let them fall to his legs with a slapping sound. "*Please.* Enlighten me."

"Marie Laveau was one of the most powerful Voodoo priestesses who ever lived. Even in death, she's still beloved and protected by those who practice Voodoo. The *protected* part is where our problem lies."

"How so?"

"Voodoo practitioners consider the location of Marie's remains a place of power. Spells are continually placed on the cemetery grounds to provide a barrier to any who are evil or intend on doing evil— powerful and efficient spells. Those who practice Voodoo are trying to keep their beliefs and practices from being turned into something Dark. The culture has suffered greatly because of how the belief and followers are portrayed by movies. They're doing what they can to ensure that image isn't inflated by certain people exploiting its power."

"That's sweet and all, but can you skip the history lesson and get to the kicker?"

"The *kicker*, Javan ... is that the Gate that's near the cemetery is simple to get to, but where the Book is located, about two hundred yards away, is off limits to those like you and me. Or to a human with ill intent. The spells confuse any who enter who are evil or want to bring about evil through their intentions. As soon as you or I walk onto those grounds, we wouldn't remember why we were there. It's subtle but intense. You can go in, but you can't get the Book. I can't, either.

"I'm Elijah's last living relative, and I can't lay my hands on it. The only person who can walk into that cemetery and keep a clear mind is someone who is pure in thought about why they are walking in to begin with. Much less why they want the Book. Now do you understand?"

Javan had intertwined his hands and placed them on the back of his neck, his arms cradling his head tightly, trying to keep from feeling as if his head was going to explode.

"Why? Why? Why? *Damn it!*"

How am I going to get someone who doesn't have ill intent to retrieve the Book? There has to be a way. I will find a way.

"No spell is going to stop me from my destiny."

He was pacing on the terrace, almost frantically, as his mind twisted through possible scenarios, trying to pinpoint a solution. He was frustrated, and adding to the frustration, images of Gabrielle and Lucas kept popping up, invading his thoughts.

He didn't mind Gabrielle, but Lucas—Lucas needed to go. And not just from his mind. He would find a way to get him when Gabrielle couldn't protect him. The fact that she cared enough to protect Lucas, an insignificant human, infuriated him further.

In that moment of fury welling up inside him, he had a moment of clarity and abruptly stopped pacing.

If Gabrielle cares that much about Lucas, if she will do everything she can to protect him, *then there is a good chance that Lucas will do anything he can to protect* her. *Especially something as simple as retrieving a book from a cemetery.*

It was worth a try. It would mean keeping Lucas alive longer than he wanted to—longer than he was comfortable with. But if it worked, it would be worth every second he let Lucas continue to draw breath into his pathetic human lungs.

Javan felt his blood pressure calm and a partial grin pushed his cheek.

This could work.

He screwed up years ago by letting the Hunt bloodline continue, but now he could use the setback to his advantage.

"Things do happen for a reason. Now I just have to figure out the logistics."

Cecily had been straddling the brick wall that acted as the terrace's railing, apparently bored. His sudden shift in demeanor and expression seemed to intrigue her, and she pushed off the wall, spanning the twelve-foot distance with little effort and landed silently in front of him.

"Do tell."

Javan looked into his cohort's eyes, allowing himself to be taken in by them again. Desire for her overtook his need for planning, prompting him to take what he wanted at that moment.

"Later."

Chapter Sixty

GABRIELLE ✟ SIMPLE PLEASURES

Gabrielle tried to rest when she got back to Lucas. But lying next to him, watching him sleep, all she could think about was the danger he was in—and what he could become. It made her stomach churn and lurch, and she spent most of the evening wondering whether or not she was going to be sick.

She needed to decide how much to tell him. He was having a difficult enough time with the threat he was already aware of—the Qalal. What would he do knowing that once Javan found out who Lucas was, he would also be on Javan's hit list—not to mention legions of demons if it looked as though Lucas would choose Light and even more Divine angels if he appeared to lean toward Darkness?

How long will it take him to realize he will be on my hit list if he chooses the path that will make him my enemy?

At about three in the morning, she couldn't take it anymore and decided to get a jumpstart on her work. She left her human body again and called to Sheridan. Ascending was more difficult this time.

Not because it was hard to do physically but because she didn't want to feel what she had earlier from her brethren again. Sheridan greeted her as she entered into Heaven, and Gabrielle could tell that she felt the same as the others, that Gabrielle might choose Lucas over Yahuwah. She tried to ignore it, but it was difficult to proceed as if there was nothing going on. She suspected her second in command would grasp anything she could use against her, so she really wasn't surprised. But she couldn't help but feel sadness creep over her, knowing so many others felt she was capable of being disloyal. For a long time, Gabrielle had thought that there was a good possibility Sheridan would try to vie for her position, but even Sheridan should know better than to think she would just abandon Yahuwah.

Work went slowly, and Gabrielle was pleased when she'd finished. Karma was balanced; her mood could go either way. But with all that was going on, and all that could happen, Gabrielle was apprehensive about getting through it without biting someone's head off. She was better when Lucas was with her, but at school, it wasn't always possible.

She returned in time to see the sun come up. Lucas was still sleeping, resting on his side with his arm draped over her, his leg entwined with hers. She wished they could stay like that forever. It was a simple thing to derive so much joy from—sleeping and waking with the one you love.

Simple and perfect.

Gabrielle lay with her eyes open, studying his face. He had masculine, intense features. Even while he slept, with no expression, he looked strong. You could tell by his dark hair and eyebrows and his sculpted face that, with the animation of a wakened state, he would be captivating. He was beautiful.

She couldn't help but reach out to touch his face, slowly tracing his high cheekbones and jaw line. She followed the bridge of his nose to his full lips, so richly colored that they looked as if they'd been soaked in red wine.

As she traced his mouth, entranced by thoughts of how much she wanted it pressed against her own, she saw his eyes begin to flutter open. She continued running her finger around his lips but looked into his eyes as he began to wake. She felt a smile stretch under her finger, and she smiled back. He caressed her face in return, and she let her eyes close so she could enjoy this simple pleasure—a moment with him she would think back on every second they'd be away from each other during the day. She felt the spinning sensation begin as it still did when they touched. She was so swept away in her feelings she almost didn't notice he'd shifted to kiss her. When his lips met hers, as she'd longed for them to, she felt the world and her worries fade away. All that mattered was that moment with his lips on hers, their bodies pressed against each other, the heat and weight of him on top of her, and their new, raw love for each other. During these few stolen moments they had alone, nothing else mattered, and Gabrielle wanted to remain swept away with him forever.

But she knew, even while lying there content in his embrace—even as an angel who was created to live forever—that forever can't exist when time is running out.

Nonie and Nate practically tackled Lucas when they saw him later that morning in the school's parking lot. They even seemed happy to see Gabrielle. She'd assumed he had gone to see them yesterday but now realized he must have stayed home, maybe wanting a break from everyone for a while.

They had a lot of questions about how Gabrielle's dad was doing. Almost too many. It felt a little too much like a probing mission. She'd almost forgotten that Emma told Nonie and Nate that she and Lucas had gone to Florida to see him in the hospital. Gabrielle told them her dad had chest pains, but the doctors determined it was stress and said he'd be fine.

Lunch brought on a flood of conversation while they lounged on the school's front lawn. It stemmed mostly from Nonie, and if anyone had been listening who didn't know better, they would have thought she hadn't seen them in weeks instead of days. Nate, on the other hand, was oddly quiet. And just as oddly, staring at Gabrielle most of the time. Gabrielle was feeling more and more like she would never gain Nate's approval to be part of Lucas's life.

The day was mild and sunny with puffy white clouds dotting the sky, like popcorn had been tossed high into the air and had become suspended—the kind of day poets write silky, flowing words about spending with the one they love or how its beauty reminds them of where their heart longed to be. The thought reminded her of a poem she'd heard once. She closed her eyes and lay down on the cool, soft grass. Wanting to remember its rhythm and words—wanting not to be, at least visually, aware of Nate's steady scrutiny.

Intent on absorbing every experience she could now that time for enjoying her human body was passing so quickly, she gave in to her senses.

She focused on the heat from the sun on her skin and how it felt hotter where she was exposed than the parts of her that were covered. She remembered, only briefly, how it felt for the sun to warm every inch of her skin as she and Javan spent the day on the beach together. It seemed as if it just happened, but it was over two hundred years ago.

The tightness that clamped her heart when she thought of Javan seemed to squeeze a little harder than usual. Gabrielle had hoped that being with Lucas and seeing what had become of Javan would cause that vice to loosen its grip on her emotions, but it didn't seem to want to entertain her hopes.

I'll never be free of him ... not really.

She let the bittersweet memory and the knowledge of her continued feelings for Javan be washed away with a cooling breeze that hinted of the change of season that was approaching. It soothed her skin that was starting to get a little too hot under the sun's assault, caressing her as it played with the fine hairs on her arms.

She smiled. Mingling with the scent of the pizza Nonie was munching on, whenever she actually stopped talking or laughing long enough to take a bite, was the earthy smell of dirt and grass, the scent of a cigarette, and her new favorite smell—Lucas. He smelled of soap, cologne, and something masculine she couldn't find the words to describe—but liked. The breeze blew against her skin again. It seemed cooler, making her shiver.

Breath warmed her ear as Lucas whispered to her. "Hey, love—you okay?"

The sound of his voice sent another chill through her for a much more enjoyable reason than the one that came a moment before. Without opening her eyes, she turned her head to briefly meet his lips.

"Right now, I'm fine," she said as she opened her eyes to look at him.

He didn't ask what she meant, but she thought he knew exactly what was behind the words she spoke, and right now … he was fine, too.

Chapter Sixty-one

LUCAS † DIDN'T HEAR MUCH

Lucas watched Gabby as she made sandwiches after school at Nonie and Nate's house. He needed to concentrate on all the schoolwork he had to make up that was spread out in front of him, but with everything that was going on, it all seemed so trivial.

What am I going to do, dazzle a vampire with my knowledge of calculus and biology?

It was easy to get distracted with Gabby near. Everything she did seemed to add to how spellbound he was. She even made the simple act of making sandwiches look alluring. He was paying attention to her for more than her obvious beauty, though.

Something is bothering her … a lot.

He'd noticed her pensiveness as soon as they started their day. All morning, she seemed to carry a sadness she tried to camouflage with her smiles. He wondered what happened since they went to sleep to cause her the unease she was trying to conceal and if she would talk to him about it when he asked her.

A flurry of activity broke out next to Gabby. As usual, Nonie and Nate were clowning around. They were wielding butter knives and had assumed fencing stances. He couldn't help but smile at his friends who were so much more than that to him. His smile was quickly erased as he thought of the danger they were in.

Because of me.

Gabby was smiling at them, too. But when she glanced at Lucas, her smile faded as she read the worry on his face. Seemingly able to understand his thoughts, she mouthed, "They'll be okay." Then she smiled and winked.

"*Touché!*" Nate called to his sister, landing a winning strike. Then he proceeded to take a victory lap around the kitchen, prompting high-fives from Lucas and Gabby in the process.

Nate's use of the word *touché* brought the memory of the conversation Lucas and Gabby had in London on the way to the hotel. He had been so sure, at the time, that he wasn't making a mistake by going to see the Elders. But that mistake had put not only him but everyone he cared about in mortal danger.

So much has changed so quickly.

"*Aww* … You totally cheated, you twit!" Nonie spouted in playful protest. "I want a rematch tomorrow. Same time, same place."

"I'm in. But you might want to prepare your ego for defeat again, sister. I am, always have been, and always will be, a better butter knivesman than you."

Nonie rolled her eyes dramatically and huffed. "Whatever. You only win when you come out of your stance. Why don't you try *staying* in it and winning tomorrow? I bet the outcome will be different. The only thing you have on your side is brute strength. I'm the one with the finesse. And by the way, brother, *knivesman* isn't even a word."

"Right, but I can't call myself a swordsman if I'm using Mom and Dad's wedding flatware as a weapon, either. So *knivesman* it is, *twit*." He shot Nonie a playful smile.

For several minutes, they all sat at the kitchen table and had casual conversation. Lucas couldn't help but notice Nate staring at Gabby.

He'd already realized earlier in the day at school that Nate's attention was almost constantly on her. Not that he blamed him. He couldn't fault any guy for having eyes for her. It was impossible not to notice how stunning she was. It would take a male without a heartbeat not to. And now that he knew there were men running around who actually *didn't* have heartbeats, he would venture to guess even they would have difficulty not being drawn to her beauty.

But there was something other than admiration in Nate's eyes. It was as if he was trying to figure something out—suspicion. What would make him feel that way was beyond Lucas. She didn't ever do anything to call attention to herself, and Nate hadn't been around her enough to see anything that revealed how different she was. Nate must have felt his friend's eyes on him because he glanced over at Lucas, then quickly looked away and took a bite of his sandwich. Everyone at the table fell quiet for several moments until Nate spoke.

"Hey, Gabrielle, Nonie and I wanted to talk to you, if you don't mi—*OUCH!*" Nate gave Nonie an irate look, and she gave him one back.

"Not now, Nate!" Nonie sort of whispered but not in the way you don't want someone to hear.

"Why not, Nee? He is our friend—*hell*—more than that. He might as well be our *brother*. I'm going to look out for him just like you or Chloe!"

"Hey ... whatever it is you want to talk to me about, I'm all ears. I don't mind." Gabrielle looked at both Nate and Nonie and waited for one of them to speak.

Nate and Nonie looked at each other for half a minute. Nonie broke the silence.

"*You* started this, brother, so don't look at me to get the conversation going now. I told you I didn't think it was something we should bring up until we find out more info. So, Mr. Jump the Gun—*enjoy.*"

Nate looked from Nonie to Gabby and then to Lucas. He sighed heavily and leaned back in his chair, crossing and resting his arms on his chest. It still took several more seconds to compose his thoughts, and then his inquisition began.

"Look, Lucas. I'm not trying to be nosy or anything, but when you were away with Gabrielle, Emma was over here quite a bit. On Monday night, she came over for dinner, and when they all thought Chloe, Nonie, and I were out of earshot, they started talking. It was kind of hard to hear, so I didn't catch everything, but I heard—" Nate squinted a little. "Were you really in London? I heard enough to know something is going on—something that has Emma concerned. And then, early this morning, she was here having coffee with my dad, and she seemed scared—*really* scared."

Lucas reached to take Gabby's hand. They didn't look at each other, though.

Nate sighed again. "So, I said I didn't hear much, but here's what I did hear. For one thing, I know you guys didn't go to Florida unless you had a stop in London to get there, which I doubt. And then this morning, I kept hearing Gabrielle's name. Something about some Elders, and that, well—that Emma was concerned for your safety. No, more than that. Your *life*."

Lucas squeezed Gabby's hand, and this time, they did look at each other, searching the other's eyes for how they were going to respond.

"Don't tell me there's nothing to this, Lucas. I've been around Emma since I was a baby, and I've never seen her like this. She's *terrified*. And I know she's not one for dramatics; she's always steady and grounded. So what's going on, and what does Gabrielle have to do with it?"

The silence seemed to stretch endlessly. Lucas understood now why Nate had been boring holes into Gabby all day, but he didn't know how to approach his questions and concerns.

Finally, Lucas spoke quietly and carefully to Gabby.

"Gabby, do you trust me?" He looked pleadingly into her eyes, begging her to let him tell them. "I really need someone to talk to about this, other than you and Gran, and I know we can trust them. They need to know for their own safety because of what you saw, because of why we went to London—*please*."

Lucas could tell by the look on Gabby's face that she wasn't sure how to proceed with this. Nonie and Nate knew just enough information to make it impossible to lie their way out of this, though.

"Here's the thing," Gabby said, "I can see you know more than we intended, but I can't just blurt out to you what's happening. Especially without Ben and Lizzie's okay. That would be wrong." She glanced at Nate who had an accusatory look in his eyes as if she was the danger herself. "I'm sorry, I can't tell you anything until I talk with them." She looked at Lucas. "And I hope you won't either. We have time to talk. Later. After their mom and dad agree."

Nonie was looking quizzically at everyone at the table, and Nate now looked more disgusted than accusatory, shaking his head.

Lucas wondered if he looked as tired as he felt. "You're right," Lucas said to Gabby and then looked at his friends. "There is something going on, and I'll tell you what I can—later."

He stood up from the table and pulled on Gabrielle's hand. They needed to get out of there. They needed to talk.

"We'll go, but I promise we'll talk soon."

He looked at his friends, who sat speechless, and turned himself and Gabby toward the door. He was almost out of the room when he turned around to speak to Nate.

"Hey man … thanks for what you said. I consider you guys to be my brother and sister, too. All of you are my family, and I don't think I've ever actually told you that before."

Nate smiled and nodded, but Nonie bolted out of her seat and into Lucas's arms.

"We love you, Lucas."

Lucas squeezed his eyes shut, trying to hold back the tears beginning to fill them, but one escaped quietly out of the corner of his eye and slipped down his cheek into Nonie's hair.

"Yeah … me, too."

Chapter Sixty-two

JAVAN ✟ EPIPHANIES

Surprisingly, Javan was able to sleep well after he and Cecily finished their discussion and she left. He'd expected his thoughts on getting Lucas away from Gabrielle to keep him awake and was caught off guard when his eyes opened and saw how brightly the sun lit his room. He'd slept though most of the day; it was well into the afternoon.

He showered immediately and dressed. There was a lot to do. He and Cecily had come up with a preliminary plan just before she left, and she was sure using Lucas would work out nicely.

Now the real fun began.

Javan enjoyed putting the wheels in motion for his games. It was more fun than the outcome because once the game was over and his goal accomplished, so was the challenge. This would be different, though. This time, he would be obtaining the one item that would make everything perfect. This time, the outcome would bring him more enjoyment than the game.

He would have to construct the plan he and Cecily devised carefully. It would be easy to fool Lucas, but not Gabrielle. Javan would have to be shiftier than ever to get this past her.

He'd already called Mara's cell and left a message that he needed to see her. He would have to involve her in his planning heavily, so it was good she didn't seem to be bothered by his relations with Cecily. It still surprised him, though, that Mara didn't seem to be affected by what she saw. She was more adaptable than he'd given her credit for and not as attached to him as he'd guessed she was.

What's she up to?

He normally wasn't so off-base about his conclusions and had been blind-sided by her reaction. His grumbling stomach interrupted his thoughts. As he made his way to the kitchen, he heard a knock at the door.

"It's open," he yelled.

He heard the door open and close and looked up to see whom he'd suspected it was.

Mara.

She looked lovely, as usual, but intoxicated by Cecily, he didn't find Mara as desirable as he once had. She still didn't seem to be phased by the prior evening's revelation.

"Hey! I thought you were leaving it locked," she chirped.

I hope she won't be this animated all day.

"Old habits," he said, then managed what he thought was a somewhat believable smile.

"Are we alone?"

"Yes."

"So … Cecily seems all right—for a Qalal, anyway." She spoke with little inflection for Javan to read. Her expression held nothing in it to help, either.

"She's proving to be helpful," he responded, matching her tone and expression.

"Is that what you call it?" she asked with the same indifference she had the night before.

"She doesn't bother you," Javan said as a statement.

"Why should she?"

"After the way you reacted to my conversation with Gabrielle last Saturday night—you know, getting all jealous and possessive—I thought you'd have a problem with Cecily, too."

"*Oh* ..." Mara smiled. "Don't you see? That's *why* I don't care about Cecily. She's no threat to me. There isn't ever going to be anyone for you other than Gabrielle. Not in *that* way. You made that obvious Saturday night. Why should I be bothered by anyone, or *anything* in Cecily's case, who will never be able to have more of you than I've already had?"

Javan was annoyed she knew how much Gabrielle still meant to him and how much he still wanted her in his life. He wasn't upset at Mara. He was mad at himself for his continuing weakness for Gabrielle and, more so, for the truth in his next thought.

I always will.

"I see," was all he said in response. It was a waste of time to argue, and now he knew Mara would see through it, anyway.

Mara took her typical position on her favorite chair, sitting sideways with one leg thrown over its arm. "Whatcha' need me for today?"

"I need you to keep tabs on Lucas and Gabrielle. *Discretely.* I want to know what their patterns are. Particularly if there's a certain time Gabrielle leaves Lucas by himself regularly. Just remember that Gabrielle will know you're around; she'll sense you."

"I can handle that. Anything else?"

"No, that's enough for you to take care of right now."

"No more digging in Emma and Lucas's past or hunting for leads on the Book?"

He could see Mara was puzzled by the shift in importance from finding the Book to keeping tabs on Lucas and Gabrielle. Javan's mouth took on one of his crooked, mischievous grins as he plopped down on the couch.

"No. No more digging into their past. I know everything I need to know about that. And ... I know where the Book is."

Mara swung herself around to face Javan so fast that he thought she was going to fall off the chair.

"WHAT? Since when?" Mara's eyes were wide with excitement.

"Since right after you left last night."

Mara threw her hands up in the air. "And you couldn't *call* me? Is that what Cecily had to tell you?"

"I didn't think about calling; there's more to it. I needed to think about some things. And yes, it's what Cecily had to tell me."

Mara settled back into the chair, scrunching her face and nose. "Yeah. I'm sure you did a lot of *thinking* after I left you and Cecily alone."

Javan laughed slightly and shook his head.

"So, what's with saying there's more to it?" Mara asked, relaxing her face.

Javan gave her the full story. Then he let Mara in on his solution, making it clear to her now why her new directive was so important.

"When are you going to try to do this?"

"I don't have a firm plan because a lot will be determined by the information I need and how fast I get it. Then I have to make sure I'm careful not to tip off Gabrielle. But if all goes well, I'll have it in my hands within the month." Javan's devilish grin spread across his face. "And Lucas's heart silenced. I'm only going to get one chance at this if I get that. If I screw it up the first time, she won't let her guard down with Lucas ever again."

"You're right about that," Mara said in a matter of fact tone. "Well, I'll get back to school. I skipped out for lunch to come here. I wasn't planning on going back to that *wretched* place, but I guess I will so I can get going on my new job. I'll call you later if I find out anything useful." Mara got up to walk toward the door.

Javan jumped in front of her—smiling a flirty, toothy smile.

"Why don't you stay a little while longer?" He asked in an alluring voice, trying to be enticing.

Mara returned a smile as if contemplating his offer but then moved past him. She looked back over her shoulder, responding to his attempt at seduction, laughing through her words. "Honestly, Javan, when did you turn into such a slut? Maybe another time." She opened the door and walked out, turning to wink at him before disappearing.

Javan stood where he'd stopped Mara, somewhat stunned and expressionless. He wasn't accustomed to being turned down.

Ever.

His crooked smile slowly returned, realizing Mara just changed things up between them.

"I'm going to enjoy this new Mara."

At least, this side of her was new to him. She might be more his equal than he'd originally thought. Her shrewdness was making an appearance, and he was looking forward to causing her to want him again—as he found himself beginning to want her more than he ever had.

"Good," he said with a smile, "another game."

After Mara had left, Javan busied himself with laying the groundwork for his scheme. He called on some old friends he'd used in trying to locate the Book to ask for their services again. Having their assistance in New Orleans before he arrived, and especially while he was there, would help things run smoother.

He hoped Mara would be able to get him the information quickly. He was so close to getting what he wanted and was already feeling more impatient. His pacing and drinking had doubled since Cecily told him that she knew where the Book was.

As Javan did what he could to get his plans going, he thought back to when he realized he was destined to become the Destroyer. The seed imbedded itself the day he and Gabrielle spent alone on the beach. But his discontent had started long before.

Javan had spent so many years having to live by Yahuwah's commands, always doing everything to help His preferred creation—humans. Javan had never understood why He loved them so much more than His angels who served so obediently. Humans tossed their faith aside in order to be able to do as they wanted all the time.

If they ever have faith at all.

Each time Javan had to help a human in some manner, his resentment grew. Everywhere he looked when he descended, Yahuwah's beloved creation would be turning their backs on Him—lying, cheating, stealing, murdering, raping, and anything else they could do against Him. And the worst of it all was that *he* had to do everything *right* or risk being cast out of Heaven. Yahuwah gave people chance after chance to be forgiven, to have the opportunity to enter into the Gates of Heaven and be in His kingdom forever.

Welcomed with open arms.

Javan never understood what made humans so special, so unique, so loved.

Angels, on the other hand, don't get a second chance. Once we're out … we're forever out. The Gates of Heaven are slammed on us for all eternity— no *redemption,* no *absolution,* no *mercy.*

To Javan, humans were utterly useless. It was one of the things that agitated him most about Gabrielle and Lucas. It would bother him to see her with anyone other than himself, but her attraction to someone he considered so worthless made it much worse. What could she possibly get out of being with him?

He should have waited until he actually found the Book before he had confronted Yahuwah, but he'd let his temper get the best of him. At least now, it seemed as though he may get his chance at vengeance, but even without the bonus of revenge, Javan would have gone after it just as vigorously. His desire for power pushed everything else out of his mind—and heart—except for one thing. Gabrielle.

Once she's released from her duty to Yahuwah, she'll see things my way. She'll be mine again.

Surely, she'd see how she'd been used and manipulated to do His bidding without any real reward for her loyalty. What did His favor really amount to, anyway? What did she gain from it?

When I take power, I'll give Gabrielle anything she desires. There will be no limit to what I'll bestow on her. How could Yahuwah's favor compare to what I will offer her?

All he wanted was for her to love him as she once had, as he knew she still did, but was unable to let herself feel out of fear.

That's all it will take for Gabrielle to be in my arms again ... freedom.

Javan smiled at his epiphany, confident that the answer was the Book and the power it would give him. He would be patient with Gabrielle until she could see that she could love him freely again—once Yahuwah and His rules were out of the way. He had to get the Book. Then he could make everything right with Gabrielle—the world would belong to them to enjoy however they wanted.

First things first. I have to get Lucas to New Orleans.

Lucas was the key to what he needed most. The best way he could see to get Lucas to help willingly was to make him believe Gabrielle's life was at stake, that the only way he could save her was if he did something for him.

It would be easy to convince Lucas he had her. The difficulty in making his plan work, as he'd already expressed to Mara and Cecily, would be getting to Lucas when Gabrielle was away from him long enough. Then he had to get Lucas to New Orleans before Gabrielle came to find him. As soon as she knew there was trouble, she'd locate Lucas eventually, no matter where he took him. The veiling abilities he'd use wouldn't be much of a match for her locating skills, especially since he didn't have the power to sustain it as long as he once could. If things played out as he hoped, it would be enough.

The Gentry might be able to help him with that, as well. He had been hearing rumors about some of the Gentry having powers they'd never possessed before—powers that could add to a demon's and could be bought for the right price.

If there is power to be had ... I will have it.

The only other thing he wanted to accomplish, once he had the Book in his possession, was to kill Lucas.

Javan poured a drink and then fell comfortably into the soft leather couch and closed his eyes. He wondered if he should be so relaxed while having so much left to do. Somehow, he felt everything would work out just as he wanted. The Book would be his. Soon.

"And with it, everything and *everyone* I want will also be mine."

He wondered how long it would take for Gabrielle to come around and see things as he did. After all, they spent so many centuries together; they had to be more alike than she knew. There had to be times she disagreed with, or doubted, Yahuwah.

At least more than she's willing to admit.

How could she not when she saw, first-hand, how much more gracious and forgiving He was to humans every time she did her job?

Javan let his mind wander into daydreams of Gabrielle, of the two of them together again like the day they stole away to the beach. Without noticing, he fell asleep. A smile was still curving the corners of his mouth. It was a smile more honest than any he'd had in over a hundred years, but he would never know that it had even been there. He would never know how much he missed the way it felt to smile the way he once was able to.

When he was still in Heaven. When he was still with Gabrielle.

Chapter Sixty-three

GABRIELLE ✝ SAFETY IN NUMBERS

"Gabby," Lucas said as he closed his front door, "they have a right to know what you saw. They're involved whether we want them to be or not. I'd want to know I was likely to be attacked if it were me. Especially by something I don't even believe exists. What do you think will happen if a bunch of vampires attack them? They'll think what's coming after them only lives in fantasies—books and movies. They'll *die*."

Lucas was right; she knew he was, but she still had to talk to Ben and Lizzie first. She wasn't positive their parents knew the full extent of what was going on or whom she truly was.

"Lucas, I agree with what you're saying. But we have to consider what they can handle. What they should know is up to their parents, not us."

She could tell her argument wasn't working as he sat at the opposite end of the couch, staring stubbornly at each other, both firmly rooted in their side of the argument. Gabrielle was relieved when she heard Emma pull into the driveway. They heard her car door close, then the sound of her shoes meeting the wood porch steps. She was opening the door and stepping into the house before Gabrielle and Lucas broke their gaze.

"Hey, you two." Emma sat her things on the dining room table and turned to face them. A smile stretched from ear to ear. It melted away as soon as she took a good look at them, grasping there was something wrong by their lack of expressions. She briskly walked over and sat across from them.

"What's wrong?" she asked, her face contorting from the fear welling up in her.

Gabrielle looked at Lucas. "Do you want to tell her or do you want me to?"

"They're my friends. I'll tell her." He turned his attention to Emma and proceeded to tell her everything so fast that Gabrielle didn't know if Emma could even understand what he was saying. When he finished, Emma's expression showed she'd understood every word.

"I'm so sorry, Lucas. We didn't … I didn't know anyone could hear us talking. I should've been more careful. I was just so worried, and I had to talk to someone. Ben and Lizzie are the only people I can safely confide in."

"Emma, how much do they know, exactly?" Gabrielle asked.

"Everything. They already know what I am—or was. They know who you are, Gabrielle, but not until a couple of days ago. I would never have told them if all this hadn't happened. After you two left Sunday night, I couldn't sleep. And after spending the day making myself crazy, they asked me over to dinner. As soon as the kids left us, it all just poured out of me. I told them everything you told me. And this morning, I needed to talk to them again. After what you told me last night, I was so frightened. I wanted to ask Ben to bring home about a hundred gallons of holy water." She laughed nervously.

"How'd they handle it, Gran? What'd they say?"

"They were silent for a little bit. I know I can trust them, but I'm not positive they've completely believed me all these years. Until two days ago, we never spoke about my origins again. They seemed really concerned, of course. I think they were a bit stunned and needed to let it all sink in. It's one thing to believe I was an angel and that Gabrielle is one, but now, they have to wrap their minds around the reality of *vampires* existing on top of everything else. Considering Ben's profession, the angel thing isn't hard for him to believe, but there isn't much that can prepare someone for the other."

"Tell me about it," Lucas said with an exasperated sigh.

Gabrielle felt awful about the situation Emma and Lucas were in. If she'd stayed away, maybe this wouldn't be happening. But if she wasn't involved, Javan could have still found out about Lucas, only she wouldn't be around to protect him. She had to believe it was better that she came into their lives, and she was sure it was what Yahuwah had intended.

"So," Gabrielle said, "now that Nonie and Nate know something is going on, the question is, how much do we tell them?"

Emma looked back and forth between Gabrielle and Lucas. "I agree with Lucas; they should know everything. If your premonition becomes reality, they'll be in mortal danger."

Lucas looked pleased and relieved.

"But," she continued, holding a finger up to Lucas, "I also agree with Gabrielle. This is a decision for Ben and Lizzie. They are their kids, Lucas. They have more right to decide than *any* of us. Including you."

Lucas sighed heavy and slow, closing his eyes as he slumped back into the couch in partial defeat. "When can we talk to them?" he asked in a flat tone.

Emma picked up her cell phone. "I'll call them right now."

It was just before five when Ben and Lizzie walked through the door, without knocking, just as Lucas had done at their house. The two families' comfort with each other was nice, and Gabrielle hoped nothing would happen to change their bond.

They told Emma when she called that they'd talked all day and wanted to know how much their kids were involved in the premonition. Gabrielle hadn't gone into too much detail with Emma before leaving for London, only telling her what she had to in order to save time.

Everyone made themselves comfortable. Or *tried* to. Gabrielle and Lucas sat at one end of the couch with Emma on the other end, and Ben and Lizzie each took one of the chairs opposite them.

Emma, Ben, and Lizzie all tried to talk at the same time, leading to uneasy laughter.

"So ... Ben, Lizzie," Gabrielle said, deciding to take control. "I'm sure there are some things you'd like to ask me. Please, don't hesitate to bring up anything. Emma assures me that you both can be trusted." She smiled, hoping to ease the tension a little.

Ben and Lizzie looked at each other. Lizzie nodded to her husband to speak for both of them. He looked at his friends, then at Gabrielle and smiled.

"Well, Gabrielle ... I'm sure you can understand that this, even considering the work I do, is a lot to comprehend. If it wasn't for our strong faith, we might think you were all crazy. If it weren't for how much we respect and trust Emma and know she's sane, it would be more difficult. We know Lucas wants to tell Nonie and Nate, and we know that they already overheard some things. I guess what we need to find out is exactly what you saw in your vision."

"It was fast, but there was an attack on Lucas by several vampires. It was during winter—heavy snow was falling. The only other thing I have to go on for a timeline is that everyone looked about the same as they do now." She paused before answering what they were really asking. "And, yes. Nonie and Nate were there during the attack."

Concern filled Ben's eyes as he went to Lizzie's side, who was trying to stifle tears. He knelt by his wife, taking the hand that wasn't covering her mouth to give her comfort.

"I didn't see Nonie and Nate being attacked. The focus of the Qalal was definitely on Lucas, but because it was just a quick snippet, I have no way of knowing everything that happened."

There was a brief silence, and then Lizzie spoke.

"Gabrielle," she began through nothing more than a desperate whisper, "what can we do?"

"There are only a few precautions that can be taken."

"Will you tell us what to do?" Ben asked with a look in his eyes that mimicked Lizzie's. "I mean, to help protect *everyone*. Not just us. We would be devastated if anything happened to Lucas or Emma."

"Considering what's going on," Lucas began, "I think everyone involved needs to know everything."

"I agree with Lucas," Gabrielle said. "I only felt we should leave the decision up to you. There is something to be said for safety in numbers, especially educated numbers. If everyone knows what to do, what to watch out for, and what *not* to do, at least no one will be caught off-guard."

"Even Chloe?" Lizzie asked.

"That's your call. But think about what it would do to her if she knew *nothing* and the attack happened in her presence. I don't think she needs to know specifics, but I believe she should be prepared to some extent. Even if she says something to someone about angels and demons, or even vampires, they'll likely chalk it up to an active imagination. You'll need to handle Chloe differently than Nonie and Nate, for obvious reasons."

Ben walked slowly and somewhat dazed to the front window and parted the blinds to look toward his home—where his children were. "Is this really happening?" he asked but didn't turn around.

"Yes," Gabrielle responded to him. "It is, Ben."

"Well, then ... I have a lot of questions, some simply out of curiosity, as you might imagine." He turned and smiled warmly at Gabrielle. "But I guess we better get the kids. Nonie and Nate, I mean. We'll decide what to tell Chloe later. Maybe you could sit with her for a little while at our house, Emma? So Lizzie, the kids, and I can hear everything, all at once. That'll keep Gabrielle from repeating herself."

"I'll send Nonie and Nate right over." Emma kissed Lizzie on her head as she walked past, pausing when she reached Ben. She placed her hand in his. "Take all the time you need. Chloe and I will be having a big time."

Chapter Sixty-four

GABRIELLE ✝ SEEING IS BELIEVING

Nonie and Nate came over right away. Gabrielle laughed to herself, thinking about the two of them wondering what was going on across the street. They had probably been driving each other crazy with questions and ideas about what all the fuss was about. Angels, demons, and vampires were not likely in the forefront of their imaginings. It wasn't amusement behind the laughter, though. It was disbelief at how things were getting so out of control.

I'm really messing things up.

She hoped they wouldn't completely flip out. It would be hard not to believe what they were about to hear, though. When your parents are as solid as theirs, and knowing Emma and Lucas weren't imbeciles, how could they not believe them? Even if they bucked it at first, they'd have to come to terms with it. Soon. There wasn't time to let doubt take over. They needed to take it seriously.

Nonie and Nate squeezed on the couch with Gabrielle and Lucas, looking at everyone with matching quizzical expressions. Nate had more reservation in his eyes, though.

"Kids," Ben started, "we understand you have some questions and concerns because of some things Nate overheard."

Both nodded.

"There are some things Gabrielle and Lucas have to tell you that Emma, your mom, and I am already aware of. I want to let you know that what you're about to hear might be more than a little unbelievable, but I *promise* both of you that it's real, and you need to listen with an open mind."

Nonie and Nate's expressions changed to concern, and both looked quickly between Lucas and Gabrielle.

"Ooh!" Nonie said, her expression perking up. "Is Gabrielle royalty? Is that why you went to London?"

Gabrielle smiled at them, shaking her head, then looked to Lucas to see if he wanted her to begin. She took his nervous gaze as her answer.

"I'll just come right out with it and spare you the long story. I'm an angel, and Emma was one, as well, until she fell in love with Lucas's grandfather and chose to live as a human." She waited for that information to sink in, studying the reaction from each of them.

Nate looked to his dad for confirmation, which he got with Ben's nod. He raised his eyebrows and looked back to Gabrielle, then Lucas, then back to Gabrielle again. Nonie just squinted at Gabrielle.

"So, what?" Nate asked. "Are you the Angel of Death or something? Cause, whatever you are has Emma pretty freaked out." He looked back at his dad. "Really?" he asked in a 'you've got to be kidding me, right?' kind of way.

Ben nodded again. "Really, Nate."

Angel of Death—The Reaper. The situation Lucas was in made her feel a little closer to the description than she ever wanted to be, making her even more annoyed at the comparison. Gabrielle glanced at Nonie and was sure she hadn't blinked.

"Angel of Death?" Nate repeated in an agitated, questioning tone.

"There's more to it than that, Nate," Lucas said, his tone defensive. "She's *not* the Angel of Death. *She's* not the enemy."

Lucas's glare and tone was more aggressive than the situation called for.

Why?

"It's okay, Lucas. This is a lot to take in."

"Then he'll *really* have a hard time with the next part," Lucas said under his breath and seemed to calm.

Nonie finally blinked and looked at Lucas, mentally rejoining the group. "You mean the rest is going to be *more* ludicrous?" she asked with raised brows.

"Yes," Lucas said. "And also completely true." He looked back at Gabrielle.

Gabrielle couldn't sit any longer as the tension in the room thickened and eyes seemed to bore into her. She stood and slowly paced as she continued.

"Again, I'm not going to waste time in trying to prep you. I don't know how I could." She stopped pacing and faced the twins. "I had a premonition that Lucas was going to be attacked by Qalal, what humans call vampires, and that's why we went away. We went to see the Qalal Elders outside of London."

"*What*? Okay, wait a minute. You had a *premonition*—a *dream*—about vampires, and you believed it?" Nate asked, clearly exasperated. He let out a hard, sarcastic huff. "I have dreams about little men and women flitting about the yard and house—some with wings—but, it doesn't mean they're *real*!" he retorted.

"Yeah. Me, too." Nonie said in passing, furrowing her brows, lost in thought again as if she was trying to piece something together.

Lucas looked at his two friends with a puzzled expression. "Me, too."

Gabrielle studied them for a few moments, her expression resembling Lucas's, though hers carried concern more heavily. "When did you start having these dreams?" She posed the question to all of them, but Lucas was the first to answer.

"I have since I can remember ... maybe three or four years old. But I had another one last night." He paused to look at the others who only nodded in agreement as if they'd been caught saying something they shouldn't and didn't want to make it worse by adding anything. Lucas looked back at Gabrielle. "Why does it matter, Gabby?"

Gabrielle started pacing again, this time a little faster. Her mind was working overtime. Why would the Gentry have any part in this? She needed to find out what they looked like so she could determine what kind they were, and then she'd be able to figure out their intent better. But she had to get the subject of vampires checked off her list before moving on to other fantastical creatures.

"We'll talk about that later. Like I said, Nate, I think the information about the existence of the Qalal is going to be more difficult for you to accept, and rightfully so. People are encouraged to believe in Yahuwah—God, as you call Him—and if you believe in Him, angels follow. With your upbringing, it's only natural to not have any real doubts about angels existing. But you were brought up to think of vampires as creatures of fantasy—not something to be truly feared. The only problem with that is that this fantasy is a reality that can kill you."

"Let's not jump the gun," Nate said. "Just because I believe in angels doesn't mean I believe *you're* an angel. Or Emma."

Gabrielle sighed. Her level of patience wasn't what it needed to be to deal with their doubts when their lives relied upon the acceptance of the information she was giving them.

She spoke in a slightly agitated tone. "I haven't done this in front of a human in hundreds of years, but we don't have the luxury of time. You both need to believe what's being said to you ... now."

She closed her eyes and pulled her shoulder blades apart, then brought her shoulders back to stand in a normal posture. As she did, a set of large white wings burst free. The air in the room whirled, making the curtains dance and everyone's hair lift as if being played with by invisible hands.

The onlookers in the room sat in shock, speechless, with the exception of Nate, who was indeed speechless but no longer sitting where he'd been. He was now perched on the top of the couch, his landing spot after he leaped out of his seat. Gabrielle had to stifle a laugh as she saw Nate's expression, not wanting to make light of things right now.

Slowly, she looked at Lucas. Wondering, as her eyes met his, what his reaction was going to be. Lucas gaped at Gabrielle, then a huge grin reshaped his stunned face. His eyes were wide with wonder. He stood and walked toward her.

"You're even more beautiful with your wings. Is it okay if I touch them?"

Gabrielle smiled and nodded.

He stepped close and put his hand out, his smile growing as he did. Just before his hand touched them, he drew back slightly, glancing at Gabrielle as he did to meet her eyes as if asking permission again. Gabrielle nodded once more for reassurance. Lucas's hand moved toward her wings and gently met them. A soft chuckle escaped him as he moved his hand over the feathers that covered them. His eyes sparkled as he spoke in whispered awe.

"They seemed to be nothing more than many layers of smoke, only thicker, but … they're so solid. I thought my hand would go right through them. They're so soft—softer than anything I've ever touched—but at the same time, I can tell that they're far stronger than they look."

Lucas became quiet again as he caressed hundreds of feathers, studying them. Gabrielle wondered if he noted all the different sizes or the colors, ranging from a silvery white at the lowest points to an almost blinding white at the top. He would surely realize that they gave off a soft, shimmering glow, but what he wouldn't know is that they would light even the darkest dark. He locked eyes with her. Gabrielle's eyes began to fill with tears. He reached for her face and drew them together to lightly kiss her lips, then moved close to her ear to whisper to her.

"What's wrong, love?"

She blinked, and a tear slipped past her lashes that he brushed away with his thumb. She lowered her head slightly as she spoke, breaking his gaze.

"I'm more than a little embarrassed by my theatrics just now. I shouldn't have done this. There are other ways of convincing a human. I guess they're all pretty theatrical, though. They kind of have to be for them to believe that the person in front of them is really an angel. Not many take us at our word unless we prove it to them in some Divine way." She sighed again, and Lucas pulled her face back up to his, seeming to disapprove of her not wanting to look at him. "And I'm afraid of what you might be thinking." She looked at Lucas. He smiled and then started to laugh.

He spoke to her in as quiet a whisper as he could. "Gabby, I can't tell you everything I'm thinking right now because, well … " he motioned with his eyes toward the others in the room, "it wouldn't be entirely appropriate. But let me assure you, it's only positive. How could it not be? You're *breathtaking*."

Gabrielle couldn't help her reaction as she threw her arms around Lucas, holding him tightly, burying her face in the curve of his neck so she could smell his wonderful scent. When she finally released him, she saw that Nate had settled back into his seat, his eyes fixed on her. The color in his face was not back to normal. He looked like he might even be a little queasy, judging by the sallow tone of his skin.

Nonie, on the other hand, appeared to have made a complete recovery. In typical Nonie fashion, she was wearing an enormous smile, busting at the seams to say something. Gabrielle glanced at Ben and was a little unprepared by what she saw.

He sat back against his chair, his legs crossed, one hand covering his mouth. He kept shifting his eyes to the floor in front of his chair, then to her face and wings, and then back to the floor. Gabrielle noticed Lizzie smiling at her. Then Lizzie gave the hand her husband still held a squeeze.

Gabrielle turned and walked to him, kneeling down and placing her hand on his shoulder when she reached him. "Ben … are you all right?" She spoke gently, hoping to soothe him. He looked at her, and after several seconds, he placed his hand on the one she'd placed on his shoulder. A sheepish smile played at the corners of his mouth.

"I'm fine, Gabrielle. So much better than fine."

She looked at him and cocked her head slightly, not understanding what he meant.

"I've spent my whole life, my career, going on nothing but faith and instincts that I was right about God. After Emma told us what she was, I believed her to a point, but I have to be honest ... not completely. I have proof that most people wish for, *beg* for. You just gave it to me. Do you know what an amazing gift it is?"

Gabrielle squeezed his shoulder and smiled, and then she stood to face Nonie and Nate again. "Nate, do you believe me now?" Nate nodded, and Gabrielle thought the color was coming back into his face a little more. "Nonie, any doubts for you?"

Nonie was still sporting an enormous smile, and she shook her head enthusiastically. "*Man*, Gabrielle. That was *amazing*!"

Gabrielle smiled fondly. She was glad to know Nonie could still talk. She wasn't accustomed to her being as quiet as she'd been. She could tell a long talk was coming as soon as Nonie was able to pin her down.

"Back to the Qalal," Gabrielle said, concealing her wings. If they had blinked at the same moment, they would've missed it. After she looked like an ordinary human again, she sat on the couch. Lucas joined her, making her give up the end seat. He immediately pulled her against him and wrapped his arms around her. She sank into him, fitting perfectly against his body—as if she belonged there, as if she was made for him. Although he would have been made for her. She'd been around just a little bit longer than Lucas.

Nate looked concerned again. "*Please*, tell me that you're not going to summon a vampire or wave some magic wand to make one appear just to prove to us they're real, too."

Gabrielle laughed. "No, Nate. I'm sorry if I freaked you out. But I really need you to believe what I'm telling you—what Lucas will be telling you. It's important ... more important than you know."

Nate nodded.

"The premonition I had, the one of the attack, the two of you were also there." She waited again, wanting to give them as much time to let her words settle as she felt they needed. "We want you to have all the information Lucas and I do so you can be as prepared as possible when, and if, my vision comes to pass."

Nonie motioned to Gabrielle that she wanted to say something. "You said *if* it comes to pass. Is there a chance it won't?"

"There is a chance. But my premonitions are rarely unavoidable. It's only happened a few times in my life." She smiled at Nonie. "And I've been around for a *long* time." She looked at Lucas, then back to Nonie and Nate. "I hope with everything in me that this one doesn't come to pass."

Or any of the other horrible things that could be in Lucas's future.

She still needed to talk to him about what she found out from Amaziah, but she hadn't had a chance to and wasn't even sure how to bring it up to him. How do you tell someone information like that?

Gabrielle answered all the questions Nate and Nonie had for her the best she could, requesting that they leave what they wanted to know about her for later when there would be time for matters of curiosity. She wanted them to concentrate on learning as much information about the Qalal as possible and how to protect themselves and each other. After answering their questions, she filled them in on the back story of the Qalal's existence, correcting their misconceptions. When they seemed satisfied and returned to questions that would satisfy their interest in her, Gabrielle cut them off.

"There are some other things I need to cover, and we've already been talking for a long time." She motioned towards the clock above the fireplace. It was just past seven, and they still weren't done. "So like I said, let's stick to what we really need to cover for the sake of your safety. I'll order pizza tomorrow, and we can sit around and talk all you want about Yahuwah and me and Heaven and Hell and whatever else you want to know." Gabrielle looked at the Daniels crew sitting around her. "Is that a deal?"

"Pizza's good," Nate said.

"Oh, Gabrielle," Ben said. "I hope you have a lot of money. You've never seen how much pizza Nate and Lucas can put down in one sitting. I'm sure Lizzie would be thrilled to have the night off from cooking, though."

Lizzie smiled and nodded. "Definitely."

"Dad's right. Deep pockets are good with these two. I'll be there just to see an angel sit in amazement of two humans eating so much. If you're as stunned as I think you're going to be when you see them devour a whole pizza each and then go back an hour later for more, maybe I won't feel so bad about the way we've gawked at you tonight," Nonie said a little sleepily.

"Good. We'll move on." Gabrielle shifted her position, sitting with her back against the couch again so she could see Lucas, too. "Now, about these *dreams*."

Chapter Sixty-Five

GABRIELLE ✝ THE GENTRY

Lucas, Nonie, and Nate looked quizzically at Gabrielle, but before she could begin her questions, Lucas stood and spoke.

"You know, Gabby, we mere mortals need food to survive. As you already pointed out, it's getting kinda late, and we still haven't eaten. How 'bout we move this into the kitchen?"

"I could use something to drink," Nate said as he stood to follow Lucas. "But I don't think I could eat much right now."

Lucas looked at his friend with surprise.

Nate raised his brow at Lucas. "Look, man ... you've had some time for all this to sink in. This is unsettling to hear, much less to believe, and I *do* believe you guys." Nate paused and looked at Nonie, then back to Lucas and Gabrielle. "I feel a little sick ... if you want to know the truth."

"Not me!" Nonie practically leapt from her seat and gave Gabrielle a huge hug. "I knew there was something different about you, but I never could have imagined anything *this* cool!"

Nonie had her typical perpetual grin as though nothing could faze her good mood. Even though Gabrielle couldn't resist the urge to return Nonie's smile, she knew there was a good possibility of things happening that would wipe Nonie's smile away.

Possibly forever.

The knowledge left her feeling as though her stomach had plummeted to the floor. Sometimes she hated knowing the things she did.

Everyone followed Lucas into the kitchen and began to raid Emma's fridge and pantry, taking out cheese and crackers, chips, fruit, some cold fried chicken, and a pitcher of sweet tea. Then, they all sat at the kitchen table. After several minutes of everyone passing around food and taking a few bites to satisfy their hunger, Gabrielle began with her questions.

"You *all* said you've had dreams about little people around outside and sometimes in your houses. Is that right?" She received nods of agreement.

Gabrielle looked at Lizzie and Ben. "Have either of you ever had any weird dreams about little people?"

Both shook their heads.

"Lucas, you said you've had these as long as you can remember?"

"Yeah."

"What usually happens in them?"

A furrow appeared between his brows as he thought. "They mostly peer through the windows at me. Sometimes, though, they're in the room."

"When they're in the room with you, what are they doing?"

"Well, usually they're only looking at me—studying me." Lucas paused, his expression turning slightly grimmer. "But other times, they form a circle around my bed, close their eyes, and chant. I don't understand what they're saying."

Gabrielle could see Lucas becoming unsettled as he shifted in his seat.

"I feel like they're doing a ritual or something." Lucas looked at Gabrielle for a moment as though searching for some kind of understanding from her about what his dreams meant, concern creating deeper lines around his eyes. "Gabby, why are you worried? They *are* just dreams … aren't they?"

Gabrielle squeezed his hand under the table.

"That's what I'm trying to determine, Lucas. But I have to find out more first. Is there anything else you can remember that stands out about them?"

"No. Not that I can think of right now, anyway."

"Okay." Gabrielle shifted in her seat to face Lucas more. "Now, this is really important, Lucas. What did they look like? Can you remember?"

"Yeah. They always freaked me out a little even if I was dreaming. There are two kinds I saw the most. But there are others I've seen only a few times. I won't be able to describe those very well."

"That's okay. Just tell me what the two main ones looked like."

"Well, they're little, but sometimes they start out, or end up, bigger. Like they can change their size. They're slim in build with narrow noses and large eyes that slant upwards slightly. In a creepy way, I would even say they're attractive. They have really skinny, pointed teeth—and their eyes … they're black. The *entire* eye. There's no white at all. They wear dark clothes—mostly things like vests and fitted pants with leather boots. And they all wear wide, silver-cuff bracelets and carry staffs.

"The other ones, they're scarier. They're shorter, but like the first ones, they seem to change sizes when they want. But even though I mostly see them small in height, they're *big* in every other way. I mean with muscles. Not big as in fat. They almost seem *dead* if that makes sense. Their faces are skeletal, but there's still flesh. They really don't have much of a nose, more of just the space where one should be. And I don't think they have what we would consider eyes. There just seems to be a faint red *glow,* like hot coals, that comes from the sockets. They wear a lot of long necklaces—all of them have pendants that are the same, but they also have others that are different. They seem to mostly wear long, tattered robes or dresses, and carry battle axes. They're definitely the creepier of the two."

Gabrielle turned her attention to Nonie and Nate. "What can you all tell me?"

Nonie was the first to answer. "Jeez ... that's so weird. Pretty much the same as Lucas. Right down to the description, but he remembers more than I do. What he described helped me to remember what I'd seen. The only difference is that I've never seen them doing any kind of ritual. They just seem to be nosing around." Nonie paused and appeared to be considering something. "You know ... I was thinking while Lucas was describing what he'd seen. I don't think I have ever had these dreams unless Lucas was staying the night with us or us with him, until a few nights ago. That's the only time I can remember dreaming about them when Lucas wasn't in the same room or house. I actually hadn't had a dream about them in years—since we were younger. Do you think that's because we haven't been staying at each other's houses over-night now that we're older? If so, why am I dreaming about them now, away from Lucas?"

Gabrielle shrugged. "I don't know. How 'bout you, Nate. Anything else you want to add?"

Nate shook his head. "No, not really. But I agree with Nonie. I don't think I've ever had the dreams unless I was with Lucas. Until a few nights ago. And like Nonie, I also hadn't dreamt about them in a really long time."

She turned back to Lucas. "And for you, these dreams have continued without a break in frequency?"

Lucas nodded.

Gabrielle picked at the food on her plate. She was sure, now, which of the Gentry were visiting. After several minutes, Lucas interrupted her thoughts.

"Gabby, are they just dreams or something else?"

Gabrielle looked at all of them sitting around Emma's kitchen table. They had the same expression on their faces—a jumble of curiosity and apprehension.

"You aren't having dreams. You're experiencing encounters with the Gentry. I don't know why, though. It helps to know what kinds are visiting you, but I'll have to do some digging to find out the reason, or reasons, they're coming around so much." She looked at Lucas. "Especially where you're concerned. This seems to be more about you than Nonie and Nate."

"The *Gentry*? I thought you were going to tell me that they were fairies or something. What are the Gentry?" Lucas almost sounded relieved.

"You would call them fairies because that's what they're commonly referred to by humans in today's world. But don't let them hear you call them that unless you want to make them mad. As a human, you don't want to make them upset with you. They can be edgy and unforgiving. It's rude, insulting, to call them fairies. They prefer the Gentry, the Old People, People of Peace, Pixies, the Seelie, the Fair Folk, and that's only some of the names."

Nate held a finger up to get her attention. Gabrielle could see from his frustrated demeanor that it wasn't going to be easy to convince him about this, either. "You said it helps to know what kinds are coming around. How many different kinds are there?"

"There are four classifications of the Gentry—hosts of the air, people of the mounds, dwellers of the waters, and those that live in the depths. But there are many types of Gentry within each of those classifications."

"What kind are we dealing with?" Nonie asked.

"Unfortunately, they're from the depths."

Gabrielle waited for the next question. It was Nonie who asked.

"Why's that bad?"

"If I had to choose, they're the ones I would want to come around the least. Even though you can't ever be sure of the intent any of the Gentry have until whatever they're doing is over, the ones from the depths are, more often than not, up to no good."

"Why's that?" Lucas asked.

"The Gentry are the offspring of fallen angels and humans. So they have powers people don't. But, because they're part human and part fallen angel, it's hard to predict where they'll fall in the spectrum between good and evil. They tend to make it easier for us to tell because they'll choose to live closer to, or further away from, Yahuwah depending on their natural dispositions."

Lucas looked at Gabrielle, confusion written deep in his expression. "Sorry, love. You've lost me."

She wasn't making this clear, but it was confusing to explain. "First of all, Lucas, this doesn't apply to you. Emma didn't fall. She chose to become human, and Yahuwah granted it to her." Gabrielle waited for Lucas to show he understood, which he did with a relieved smile and nod. "Basically, the Fallen have varying degrees of betrayal that caused them to be cast out of Heaven; some are more treacherous than others. Similarly, humans have varying levels of good or evil that lives within them. Depending on the combination of the fallen angel and the human, you can have anything from fairly *good* Gentry to evil Gentry that result from the coupling. Do you follow me so far?"

Gabrielle looked to each of them, and they all nodded. She then turned to Ben and Lizzie, who also nodded, but remained in a state of quiet attention.

"The best of the Gentry are the hosts of the air, which is why they're found closest to Heaven, then the people of the mounds, next the water dwellers, and lastly, the ones that live in the depths—the closest to Ramai and Hell. It's especially unwise to trust them. Do you see how the best of them live closer to Yahuwah, and then it goes downhill from there?"

Everyone nodded again.

"From what you described to me, Lucas, I believe the first ones are the huli jing, the second are most likely dwarves. The huli jing are definitely not to be underestimated, but dwarves are quite foreboding and dangerous. If dwarves are visiting, there's definitely a wicked intent, even if they haven't done anything physical … *yet*."

Lucas put his elbows on the table and rested his forehead in his hands. "Great … vampires *and* little people are after me."

"They aren't always little, Lucas. Your observation was correct; they can change their size anytime they choose. That's why the Gentry have been described so differently throughout the centuries. Sometimes small and other times the size of humans and every size in between. All are correct, but none are accurate a hundred percent of the time."

Nate pushed his chair back and stood to lean against the kitchen counter. "So, Gabrielle, do these *Gentry* all have supernatural powers? What can they do?"

"The powers they possess vary from classification to classification. And the different types of Gentry within each classification have different abilities. Even within those specific types, the abilities will vary to some degree with some being more powerful than another of their own species." Gabrielle knew this topic would cause them a great deal of confusion. "It would be too time consuming and way too much information to retain right now if I told you all the specifics. But because the Gentry are part angel and, therefore, have Divine blood, their abilities and powers are great. Add to that the knowledge of magic and the use of nature's Elementals that they've learned over thousands of years, and they've become a formidable order."

"What are we supposed to do, Gabrielle? How do we protect ourselves?" Nonie asked worriedly.

"As frustrating as it is for me to keep saying this, you do nothing. At least not right now. You can't do much as humans unless you have Divine protection. The Gentry won't normally attack a human unless provoked. They value their anonymity, like the Qalal. It's better for fantastical creatures to exist only in the imaginings of humans. If their reality is discovered, especially in the days we're in now, they risk substantial losses of their own kind as well as their homes. Even though they are powerful and have abilities far beyond a human's, they can be killed. They aren't *completely* immortal, but they do heal quickly. Unless you destroy them, they'll continue to regenerate. It's better if you just keep acting as you always have—like they're only a dream. Just pay more attention now. The more information you can give me about what they're doing, what they look like, and what they're saying—*if* you can understand them—will help me to get to the bottom of this."

"Gabrielle," Nate said in a slightly agitated tone, "since you're an angel, why can't you just *find out* what they are doing and what they want by twitching your nose, or snapping your finger, or whatever it is you do to find stuff out?"

"I assure you, it won't be by twitching my nose or snapping my fingers. The only thing that'll possibly hinder me in finding out what's going on is if Yahuwah doesn't want me to know or if it's Ramai's doing."

"But isn't God more powerful than Satan?" Nate pulled himself up to sit on the counter.

"Without a doubt, Nate, He is. But He has an agreement with Ramai, allowing a fair fight—so to speak."

"An agreement?" Nate's eyebrows raised, matching his rising voice. He was definitely irritated. "You mean *God*—made a deal—with the *devil*?"

"Yes, Nate. That's exactly what He did."

Nonie got up from her seat and made her way to her brother as if she intended to either support him or calm him down. Maybe both. As soon as his sister pulled herself up next to him, his demeanor relaxed.

Ben and Lizzie had adjusted their positions, leaning in closer to the table.

"Gabrielle," Nonie held her voice in a calm tone, and Gabrielle was glad she was taking the reins of the conversation away from Nate. Gabrielle didn't want this to become a heated argument because he doesn't understand all that goes on in Heaven. "What kind of deal did He make? And ... why?"

Lucas was more interested in the conversation now, too. Gabrielle realized this was information she still hadn't shared with him.

"When Ramai defied Yahuwah, one of the reasons was because he didn't understand why Yahuwah favored humans. In particular, he didn't understand why He gave them free will. Ramai was bestowed with more favor than any other angel Yahuwah created. He gave Ramai tremendous power and beauty. One of the things He charged Ramai with was taking care of Earth. Only Yahuwah himself, and Ramai, know exactly what came about to cause him to rebel, but we do know he wanted to be exalted higher than Yahuwah. Ramai argued with Him about how humans weren't worthy of His favor and forgiveness. Ramai is extremely prideful and arrogant, and that's his downfall. He felt Yahuwah favored humans more than him—he couldn't share Yahuwah's love with people, and he didn't feel they should be held in as high a regard as he was.

"While Ramai took care of his duties protecting Earth, his feelings for humans darkened as he spent more and more time among them. When he rebelled against Yahuwah, he gathered a third of His angels to attack with him. You already know Ramai and the other rebelling angels were defeated and cast from Heaven permanently. Before Yahuwah expelled them, though, Ramai asked for the ability to prove he was right and Yahuwah was wrong to hold humans in such high regard and favor. Yahuwah agreed to allow Ramai to keep his powers on Earth to try to sway humans toward the evil and sin that lives within them, while Yahuwah's angels do what we can to keep love and righteousness growing inside you. Ramai is convinced he'll win this battle because he believes humans, as a whole, will turn away from Yahuwah's love.

"Since Yahuwah is all knowing, he also agreed to let Ramai and his legions operate with a certain amount of obscurity. In this way, He is allowing for humans to truly have free will with little interference from Him. Just as Ramai is sure humans will fail—Yahuwah is sure you won't. But He won't force anyone to follow Him, and since this was the way He felt before Ramai asked for His cooperation, He agreed."

Gabrielle took in their expressions. They all looked deep in thought and tired.

"Does that make it any clearer?"

Nate shook his head. "I still don't understand why God would make a deal with an angel who betrayed Him so thoroughly."

"One of the first things that will help you to understand Yahuwah, and what He does and doesn't do, is to try not to understand at all."

"Huh?" Lucas said as he made an exasperated gesture.

Gabrielle knew it was difficult for humans to understand why Yahuwah lets what they considered bad things happen, but she was hoping Lucas would be more accepting of what she was saying, especially with what she knew about the decision he'd have to make in the future. His scowl showed the agitation that he wasn't speaking with words, but Gabrielle was able to hear it anyway.

How am I going to keep Darkness from him?

The thought was not one she could dwell on, and she didn't feel she had the mental energy even if she wanted to.

"Look. Yahuwah is all-knowing. There's no other in the universe who is. There's so much He sees that we don't, and because of that, He allows certain things to happen and disallows others. That's why *He's* God. It's not our job, whether angel or human, to understand Him. What He asks of us, what our job is, is to have faith. Faith that there are reasons why and that He always has our best interests in mind. Our *faith* in Him, and all He does, makes Him the most joyous." She paused to look at all of them again. "Is that really so much to ask of the One who created you?"

Gabrielle was weary from the discussion, and she still had a lot to take care of. She needed a break from all of the talking—the explaining. If she were honest with herself, she'd admit she wasn't only trying to convince *them* of Yahuwah's good intentions—she was beginning to question them herself. She'd never doubted Him before. She didn't know if the thoughts, the uncertainties, were a result of the information Amaziah had given her or if it was because of her human feelings and emotions interfering. Maybe it was a combination, but it was upsetting. She wanted to leave her human form and just be an angel again, at least for a little while—shed all the tethers that bound humans to their mental turmoil.

"We have enough to digest for one night," Nate said as he hopped down from the counter. "It's getting late, and I still have school stuff to do before I can go to bed—not that I'll be able to concentrate. Or even sleep."

"Yeah," Nonie agreed with her brother. "I have things to do, too."

Lucas got up from the table, and they started toward the door. Gabrielle nodded her goodbye to the Daniels family. She was spent and didn't want to move.

She heard Lucas say good night and close the door, then his footfall, much slower than his normal pace, as he made his way back to her. He was as wiped out as she was. Probably even more so. He walked up behind her and placed his hands on her shoulders, then bent down to softly kiss her neck just below her ear and whispered into it.

"I have some things to get done, too. Do you mind if I get started? Or, would you like to talk some more?"

Gabrielle did need to talk to Lucas. But she didn't even know where to begin. Things were so much worse, and far more complicated, than he knew right now. And he thought he knew everything he was facing. Her heart felt as if it was being squeezed in someone's fist. He'd already seemed so upset about Yahuwah's deal with the devil. She wasn't sure he needed to hear it right now, anyway. There didn't seem to be a need for him to know tonight.

"No. You go ahead and do what you need to, and I'll get to my work. I still have a lot I have to take care of myself. Even more now that I know about the Gentry's visits."

Gabrielle stood up and faced Lucas, wrapping her arms around his neck, then pulled back enough to look in his eyes.

"We have plenty of time for more talking."

She leaned toward him to meet his lips and closed her eyes, once again, aware that she wasn't sure how much time they really did have together. No matter how much was theirs to enjoy, the clock was counting down. She thought she could hear the seconds relentlessly ticking, getting louder as the time given for her to accomplish her goals grew shorter. She tried to block it out, but it was still there. It didn't make it go away—didn't make it less real. It was just like her love for Javan—as much as she tried to ignore it, it remained. She couldn't deny that she still loved him. And she couldn't deny that her time with Lucas, who she also loved, was slipping away. When it did, she'd lose Lucas.

Just like I lost Javan.

Chapter Sixty-Six

GABRIELLE + SOMETHING TO CONSIDER

Gabrielle left Lucas as soon as she could. She'd never felt the need for space more. Not to get away from Lucas, she just needed time to herself to clear her mind. When she escaped her human form, it was much easier for her to think clearly.

She thought back to all she'd learned over the past several days, especially the evening's conversation. It disturbed her that the Gentry were interested in Lucas, Nonie, and Nate, but knowing the decision facing Lucas, the reason for their interest would likely be traced back to Ramai—trying to find ways Lucas could be swayed toward him. Her instinct told her she was right. She needed to discover what they were trying to accomplish.

The devil is in the details.

The saying had never had more meaning to her than now. The devil seemed to be in every detail, behind the scenes of every obstacle Lucas faced. She felt a shiver trail down her spine thinking of Ramai being so interested in Lucas—so involved in his life.

There wasn't much she could do to stop him from pushing Lucas toward what he desired, though. She was a powerful angel, but Ramai was more powerful. However, she did have a much larger arsenal now. She suspected her new powers would be needed when she faced the things coming for Lucas, things lurking in Shadows that had been around him his entire life, and it was only going to get worse.

As torn as she had been about falling for Lucas, she believed that Yahuwah wanted her in his life. She couldn't have as big of an influence on him if they weren't close.

He knew we'd fall in love ... He must have wanted us to.

Anger crept in again. Having another she loved taken from her as she knew Lucas would be—as Yahuwah knew—was a crushing blow. She pushed the negative feelings down, wondering how long she'd be able to.

Not in a hurry to get to her Heavenly duties, enjoying her freedom—more mental than physical—she moved over the landscape, leaving the rolling hills of Tennessee and the flat fields of southern Georgia. There was somewhere she wanted to go, and before long, she began to see the outline of the coast.

She loved being near the ocean no matter what part of the world, but she was partial to the white sands and emerald or turquoise waters from the Florida panhandle down into the Caribbean. Something made her want to be near palm trees and the constant breeze that made them sway as if they were dancing for joy because of the beauty they lived among.

She sat at the water's edge and allowed herself to get lost in thought as she appreciated the bright moon that hung low on the horizon. Capturing its light momentarily, the waves glistened as they crested and again as they reached the shore and pushed toward the thirsty grains of sand, pulling some back into their fold with every reach.

She looked toward Heaven, searching the night sky for any of her brethren, looking past the stars themselves, trying to see her eternal home. She knew it was impossible, even for an angel, to see into Heaven from Earth, but she could see it clearly in her mind.

As she was about to call Sheridan to bring her the day's lot, she heard a familiar voice. It made her smile as soon as she heard it—Amaziah.

'Gabrielle, I couldn't help but feel you needed me. Are you okay?'

His voice soothed her worries. He made everything seem as if it was going to be all right.

Even when it wasn't.

'I'm okay. I just needed to clear my head for a while and think with the mind of an angel, instead of a human.'

She heard him chuckle.

'I understand it can be difficult. But I can't say that I have any real knowledge.'

'You haven't ever taken a human form other than recently, with me?'

'I have never had a need, or desire, to be anything other than what I am. I may never want to again after seeing how much it affects you, my dear.'

'It's not all bad, Amaziah. The physical sensations we don't get to experience as angels are interesting.'

He laughed again, 'I know you have enjoyed that part. But is it worth it, Gabrielle? Is it worth all the doubts? The temptations? It is a lot to risk, you know.'

Gabrielle was confused. 'What do you mean—risk?'

'Haven't you realized, Gabrielle? The longer you are in your human body, the more you will think and feel as a human. It's part of the reason you were limited to a six month stay on Earth.'

She had noticed it seemed harder for her to think as an angel, but she hadn't realized it would get more difficult.

'You weren't supposed to be in that form nearly as much as you have been. It was only going to be while you were in school for the day and for social activities. You spend almost every second of the day, and night, as a human.'

She hadn't considered how little time she chose to be in her true form. She hadn't planned on Lucas, wanting to spend every moment possible experiencing what she felt when she was with him . And now, even knowing how much it was affecting her, she couldn't imagine giving up time with him.

'I hadn't realized it would affect me so much. When I'm in my true form, I don't feel its effects anymore.'

'I wouldn't expect you to. Not physically. It's your mind that is of most concern to me ... and should be to you. I don't want your missteps to result in you falling.'

There was a long silence, and Gabrielle thought back to the momentary flux in faith if Lucas chose Darkness. She was thankful when Amaziah continued speaking, ending the troubling memory.

'Gabrielle, I know you don't want to, but you should try to find more time out of your human body so you are in better control of your thoughts and actions. It will help you to make the right decisions, at the right time, when you are with Lucas or your other human friends. Otherwise, you may find yourself doing things you would never consider while thinking as you are now—as an angel.'

'I will consider it.'

Gabrielle meant what she said, and she knew he was right. It had already affected her judgment. If she continued to spend as much of her time as a human as she'd grown accustomed to, it would become an even bigger problem. It was too easy to get lost in the love and contentment she felt with Lucas.

'I'm glad you knew I was thinking of you. I guess I needed to talk to you and didn't realize it. Thank you for being my friend and confidant, Amaziah.'

'You know I don't need or desire your thanks, Gabrielle. I love you. I always will. It makes me happy to be able to be the one you turn to.'

'I love you, too, Amaziah.'

Chapter Sixty-seven

GABRIELLE ✝ AN UPRISING

Gabrielle could feel her mood lift as if the veil that protected Corstorphine from the outside realm also cleansed Gabrielle of her burdens. She didn't stop to enjoy the scenery this time. She wanted to see Grayson, Rissie, and her bubble-blowing friend.

I can't believe I miss the grape bubblegum.

Gabrielle smiled, and the thought of seeing her three friends made her hasten to Mareschall Castle. She received nods with accompanying smiles and some "Good mornings" from Shifters.

I don't know if they'd be so pleasant to me if they weren't doing well.

The heavy wood doors of the castle opened before she made it to them. Gabrielle laughed as soon as her gaze settled on who opened them. With a huge smile, quickly shielded by a decent size bubble, stood Phalen. She looked well and exactly the same except for a ponytail she'd never worn her hair in before and the brown and white dappled arrow fletching splaying at an angle behind her head and shoulder—making her look like she was sporting some futuristic, feathery hairstyle. Gabrielle took a deep breath, knowing the conversation she wanted to have with her friend would need to wait.

"'Bout time ye gave the invalids a visit, sis!"

"Ye?" Gabrielle responded in amusement at Phalen's attempt at a Shifter's accent. She greeted Phalen with a hug and laughter.

"Well … you know. These Shifters have a way about them. It's rubbing off on me."

"Anything else rub off on you?" Gabrielle asked as she pointed to what was on her back.

Phalen pointed to the quiver that held about a dozen arrows.

"What … this?" She asked with a playful smile. "I'm practicing so I can *really* beat Grayson when he's better, not just barely take him. These Shifters know how to shoot!"

Gabrielle's laughter subsided as she considered the other two friends she was there to see. Her hopes lifted with Phalen's comment about beating Grayson.

He must be doing better, then.

Phalen smiled. "He is, Gabrielle … he is. Come on." Phalen turned and took Gabrielle's hand. "Come see for yourself. They're both doing fantastic."

Gabrielle let a hopeful smile slip across her lips as they walked through the wide stone halls of Mareschall. Large, colorful tapestries hung on its walls, alternated with intricate murals lovingly painted by talented artists among the Shifters. The halls, and their art and tapestries, told stories of each of the realms of Shifters—four realms, four sides of the castle, three levels on each side, each side dedicated to one realm. They walked along the hall for Corstorphine. It was, as far as Gabrielle was concerned, the most beautiful of the Shifter realms. She glanced at the scenes of people, battles, animals, landscapes, legends, and myths as they walked purposefully to Grayson's quarters.

When they reached the door to his room, Phalen gently knocked. Gabrielle heard the shuffle of soft-soled shoes on stone. As they drew closer, her stomach did a bit of a flip. She was nervous, regardless of Phalen's nonchalance.

He almost died because I asked him to be there for me.

Phalen glanced at her with a raised eyebrow, and Gabrielle met her eyes.

"Not everything is your fault, sister."

Gabrielle let out a slight humorless laugh and looked away. "Feels like it, lately."

"Sounds like we have a lot to talk about."

Nodding but not looking back at her friend, she responded. "Yeah."

The door to Grayson's room opened, casting bright light from its many windows into the hall. An older woman that Gabrielle knew as Razz stood in front of her. Razz was a nickname. No one was free from her jokes, and all loved to banter with the jovial woman. Gabrielle wasn't sure what her real name even was, and she nervously let herself wonder what it could be as she waited to see if Razz would hold a grudge against her for putting two Shifters in a situation that almost got them killed—one being the Shifter's leader.

A leader who happened to be her son.

Gabrielle studied Razz's face, looking for some sign of her thoughts. She was not only pleasant in humor but in looks. A head full of large, loose, blond curls was tied back in an intricate half braid. It would be difficult to recreate, but the Shifters seemed to have a way with things like that, and she wondered what they could do with her own. Razz was apparently the one responsible for Grayson's blue eyes, though hers were darker than his, and for his smile that made her eyes to light up just like Grayson's. It was magical when they smiled, like their eyes infected everyone with the happiness contained in their bodies at that moment.

It's a beautiful thing.

It was even more beautiful to Gabrielle when she saw that smile spread across Razz's face as she greeted Gabrielle.

"Hello, m'lady! So good to see ye!" Razz moved in to hug Gabrielle.

Gabrielle let out a quiet sigh of relief as she hugged her back tightly. Razz gave her one last tight, reassuring squeeze before she let her go.

"Hello, Razz. How are you?"

"I'm quite well, but we both know yer here to see m'son. You and I can catch up later." Razz's expression changed to playful and quizzical. "Less yer here to do 'im in this time," she said, then offered a wink.

Gabrielle chuckled lightly. "No. I think I'd like him to live a bit longer."

"Good. He hasn't given me any gran'children, yet. And I want gran'children," she said, raising her voice and turning her head toward the room behind her. "*Lots* and *lots* of gran'children. Ye hear me?"

"It may ne'er happen, mum," Grayson said loud enough to carry across his large room, "if I can't find a female who'll put up with me."

Gabrielle looked around Razz to see Grayson awake and propped in bed with several pillows. An authentic smile spread broadly across his face. Gabrielle felt a huge sense of relief move through her as she fought back tears.

'Thank you, Yahuwah.'

'I told you he was doing well, sister.'

Gabrielle sat carefully and slowly on the bed next to Grayson. His smile grew, and he laughed as he extended his hands to hers.

"I'm not that fragile, m'lady."

Gabrielle took his hands in hers, and she leaned down to rest her forehead on them. She tried but couldn't stop the tears from pooling and then slipping from her eyes. The cry was silent, though. At least until Grayson spoke.

"Aww ... ther'll be none of that. I'm fine."

Gabrielle couldn't help but hug him, and when he hugged her back, her crying was no longer silent. He held her and stroked her hair, whispering that he was okay.

But his words didn't make what had happened any better, any easier, or her any less responsible.

After Gabrielle pridelessly cried in Grayson's arms for several minutes, she was able to get hold of herself again. He told her that, in no time at all, he would be back on his feet, fighting the good fight.

She hoped he was right.

Gabrielle could tell he was in more pain than he let on, and he was certainly still weak. All she could do was wait for the healing process to finish. She wouldn't feel entirely at ease until he was fully recovered.

She checked on Rissie. Her leg had been set, the wound caused by the break stitched up. Gabrielle found her on the back lawn of the castle grounds being lifted by two muscular, rather attractive, young men. Rissie joked as she was carried into the Mareschall that being injured had its benefits, motioning to her transportation. She assured Gabrielle during their long talk that she was also doing just fine.

Gabrielle and Phalen walked around Corstorphine. Silently. Neither one seemed to want to interrupt the other's enjoyment of the scenery. The sun's descent was almost complete, and the stars above them were beginning to make themselves known. The moon, always much larger and brighter in Corstorphine, was full and starting to peek over the horizon into the Shifter's realm to begin its vigil for the night.

A cool breeze carried the scent of dinner preparations and of wood burning in fireplaces from the village across the rolling hills. When they topped one of those hills, Gabrielle stopped and sat on the ground facing the village and the setting sun behind it. Light from candles and lanterns spilled onto the streets from the windows of homes and businesses, softly illuminating cobblestones, grass, and dirt. Mareschall was within view, perched on ground far higher than the rest of the village. There was also light coming from many of its rooms. Gabrielle could see Grayson's from where they were sitting. It had far more windows than any other room of Mareschall except for the ones that mirrored his, each sitting on the corners of the castle. They were the largest of the private quarters and were kept for the leaders of the Shifter realms. Grayson had told her that their visits were far less frequent over the past couple of decades. Phalen made it obvious that she heard her thoughts.

"Why aren't the leaders from the other realms visiting, anymore?"

Gabrielle laid flat on the ground and studied the heavens as she answered.

"Apparently," she began, "Grayson thinks there's an uprising brewing."

"Uprising? Why?"

"He thinks it has something to do with his family being in power for so long. There aren't really rules about it, and they aren't officially royalty; it's just how it's always been. There are other clans who feel they should have a shot for a while."

"Hmmm …" Phalen responded . "What does Grayson think of it?"

"That he doesn't want anyone who thinks they *deserve* power to have much of it, and being looked upon as royalty could embolden them to a level of tyranny. He says that he's considering calling for a vote to put an official title on someone as king. That way, there isn't any question. But he wants *all* Shifters to have a say in it, not just the current leaders. It will be the first Shifter election in history. That way it will set up who *is* royalty, and from that point on, it will be law and can't be changed. Unless by war."

"Ugh … no more war."

"My thoughts exactly."

They listened to the crickets begin their nightly chorus, spending several minutes in silence. An owl hooting in the distance and laughter from the village broke that silence between them.

"I hope it doesn't come to that, sister."

"Me, too."

"Let's change the subject," Phalen said as she popped a piece of gum in her mouth and lay down next to Gabrielle. "What's been going on back in the human world?"

This subject wouldn't prove to be any lighter, but Gabrielle did want to share what she knew with Phalen. It would help, she hoped, to discuss it with someone other than just Amaziah.

"More deep stuff, I'm afraid," Gabrielle said through a heavy breath. She turned her head toward Phalen and found she was already looking back at her.

"What is it?" Phalen asked.

"It turns out that not only will Lucas play a part in whether or not the Destroyer comes into power ..." Gabrielle paused, not for dramatic effect but because a large lump had formed in her throat, stalling her words—like it thought that if she didn't speak them out loud it wouldn't all be real. She swallowed hard.

"He will choose whether or not *he* will become the Destroyer."

Phalen just eyed her for several moments, mouth agape, eyes wide, and apparently having as much difficulty in understanding as Gabrielle did when Amaziah spoke the same words to her.

"*No ...*" Phalen finally responded.

"Yes."

Phalen quickly sat up and turned toward Gabrielle, her legs crossed like a pretzel.

"Gabrielle ... I am *so* sorry."

"I am, too."

"What does he think about all of this?"

"He doesn't know."

"You haven't told him?" Phalen asked with surprise.

Gabrielle shook her head, pursing her lips.

"You *have* to tell him, Gabrielle."

A sigh was her first response. "I know. I will ... eventually."

Phalen studied her, silence lingering longer than before. Her friend lay back down next to her, but this time, she took Gabrielle's hand in hers, giving it a long, firm squeeze. They stayed there, looking at the stars for a long time, watching as they became brighter and more numerous while the world around them darkened. They thought their private thoughts and listened as the Shifters began their night filled with friends and family, food and drink, laughter and music. All while Gabrielle wondered if their world, the human one, and her own would survive the Great War.

And Lucas's decision.

Chapter Sixty-eight

Gabrielle ✟ Unseen Dangers

For many weeks after Gabrielle's big reveal to the Daniels family, everything seemed to be business as usual for Lucas, Nonie, and Nate. Gabrielle thought it was too normal. Fall had firmly claimed its time; it was the end of October, and the seconds were ticking off louder in her head every day.

She watched Lucas and her friends looking through racks of Halloween costumes, kidding with each other about the four of them going to the school's annual costume party as Lucy, Ricky, Fred, and Ethel from *I Love Lucy*. Gabrielle was amazed how they acted as if they'd never learned of her being an angel or of any of the other fantastical creatures they found out were more than imagined.

Nonie and Nate did have plenty of questions when they all got together for pizza the night after they found out. As expected, they wanted to learn more about Yahuwah, angels, and fantastical beings. But they seemed most fascinated by Gabrielle's powers and abilities and wanted to know what Heaven was like.

Nothing strange or dangerous had happened since she and Lucas returned from their trip to see the Elders—not even a mosquito bite. It bothered Gabrielle, but Lucas seemed to be at ease, which was both good and bad. Good because he was able to relax and return, as much as he could, to being a regular seventeen-year-old. Bad because Gabrielle didn't want him to let his guard down—big problems still loomed.

Gabrielle hadn't been able to bring herself to tell him about the decision he faced, and she felt she was betraying Lucas with every second that passed. She wasn't sure if it was better if he knew or if he remained oblivious until the decision had to be made.

There was no way for her to tell if knowing would have a positive or negative impact on him. He could use the information to make decisions that would keep him on the path of Light, or that same information could lead him to become angry and bitter, which could cause him to make decisions that would turn him toward Darkness.

Gabrielle let her thoughts divert to Nonie and Nate, still kidding around with the costumes. When an employee brought more options to consider, Lucas turned his attention to Gabrielle. His face shifted from ease to concern when he saw how far off she was in thought.

"Love, what's on your mind?"

Gabrielle tried to lighten her expression as Nonie and Nate cast their attention toward her and Lucas, walking over to where they were.

"I was just thinking how this is the first Halloween I'll be spending as a human. It's all sort of silly, the way you all celebrate it."

"What do you mean?" Lucas asked as the twins reached them.

"Halloween is the most dangerous time of the year for a human."

"How is it dangerous? I mean, other than razors in candy and pedophiles, what's so risky?"

"It's when the veil between this world, the Shadow World, and the Underworld is thinnest. Those who live in either of the other realms have far more power that night than at any other time of the year." Gabrielle looked at the three staring at her with matching puzzlement.

"Just because you don't see the danger, doesn't mean it isn't there."

"What is the Shadow World and Underworld? What's the difference, and what lives in them?" Nate asked in a tone dipped in exasperation.

"The spirits of those who can't, or won't, move on to the next stop of their journey—meaning Heaven or Hell—exist in the Shadow World. Their unrest can make them malevolent and troublesome. The Gentry, some of the darker elemental spirits, and other fantastical beings also live in what we call the Shadow World. But there are far too many to go into—definitely more than you'll want to know about. The only residents of the Underworld are the Fallen, though any who live in Shadows can cross to that realm if they desire.

"One of the bigger dangers of Halloween is that it's easiest to see the Gentry in their true form then. It's common for humans to be taken back to their world if they see one, and the Gentry know it."

"Why's it bad to be taken back to their world?" Nonie asked.

"The only way you'll ever make it back is if they decide to bring you back. That's a fifty-fifty chance. Even if you are returned, time in their world moves differently than your own, just as time in Heaven moves at a different pace. You could come back decades later, maybe longer. You wouldn't have aged as though that time had passed, but everyone you knew might either be much older or dead.

"On top of that, if you did come back and anyone you knew was still alive, you may find they never even knew you were gone because they'd seen you the entire time. At least, who they thought was you."

Nate shifted his weight. He still seemed uncomfortable with anything that had to do with angels, demons, or fantastical beings. She realized that just because the three of them acted as though they'd put what they'd learned out of their mind, they were really just covering for the worries they had.

"How could they still see someone if they weren't there?" Nate asked.

"The Gentry are talented at becoming a doppelganger, or they can produce a changeling. They can recreate any appearance they want including animals."

"So why don't we know about all of this?" Nonie asked as she sat next to Gabrielle.

"It isn't something that's kept from you. The information is there, but most of modern society doesn't believe in the fantastical world. They believe what science says is real; the rest are myths or fairytales. Humanity's lack of belief in that world, of Heaven and Hell, Yahuwah and Ramai, have left all of you vulnerable—easy targets. That's part of the reason I'm here … to figure out how to make you all believe once more."

"Well, you have three believers here," Nate said as he shifted his weight again and dropped his eyes.

"That may be true, Nate, but that's only because you've been made privy to information most humans never are. If you didn't know me, would you have been convinced so easily?"

Nate shook his head. "No offense, Gabrielle," he said without looking up, "but you kinda know how to take the fun out of things sometimes."

Gabrielle chuckled humorlessly. "I'm just telling you the facts. You can carry on with your normal Halloween festivities. It's not likely you would ever have any encounters."

"Then, why tell us at all?" Nonie asked.

"Because Lucas asked, and you walked up when I was talking to him," Gabrielle snapped back. Three sets of eyes widened in surprise at her tone. The effects of her lot from the night before were showing up, filtering into her tone and patience. It hadn't been a good night for the side of Light. She was particularly irritable today and having a difficult time masking it. "It wasn't my intent to spoil anything for any of you, Nonie. I'm sorry I messed up your holiday." Gabrielle turned to Lucas. "I think I better go. Why don't you catch a ride home with them? I'll see you later tonight."

Nonie put her hand on Gabrielle's shoulder. "Hey, Gabrielle … I didn't mean to upset you. I'm sorry."

"Yeah," Nate chimed in, "me either. Don't leave. It's just a lot to hear."

Gabrielle tried smiling to put them at ease, but she knew it wasn't convincing. She looked back at Lucas who had taken her hand in his.

"I wish you'd stay." He asked with his eyes as much as his words.

"I need to go. The more I think about it, the less I want to participate. Maybe it'd be best if you go as The Three Musketeers or Three Blind Mice … or something."

"Why? It will be fun."

"I don't feel comfortable celebrating a holiday steeped in Dark undertones."

Under different circumstances, she might have attended, but she didn't want to prove Nate right about spoiling their fun by being too informative or concerned about the evening's dangers. She didn't want to tell them that because of all the spiritual and fantastical attention surrounding them, Lucas in particular, there would be considerable curiosity. And that the added curiosity would, most likely, bring a lot more Shadow World and Underworld activity to the area.

"Really, Lucas, I don't mind just doing some work and keeping an eye on things. I think it's best. That way, you all will know I'm watching without any distractions, and you'll be safer because of it."

Lucas waited for several moments before he responded, and Gabrielle could see him considering every angle of what she'd just said.

"If that's what you really want to do, and if you think it's the best thing. I won't lie, Gabby, I want you with me, but I'm not going to guilt you into something you don't feel comfortable taking part in." He smiled a little crooked smile at her and then added, "Don't hold it against me if I try to change your mind, though."

Gabrielle smiled back and put her arms around him for a long embrace, then kissed him. She said bye to Nonie and Nate as she made her way to the front of the store.

As she passed people looking at costumes, makeup, and masks of all kinds, she was too caught up in her own thoughts and too in tune with her human senses to notice two things she normally would have never missed: the black-haired, yellow-eyed beauty she knew as Mara, acting like she was looking at a wall of masks, and the now completely black eyes of the employee who'd been helping them with their costume selection intently watching her as she walked out the front door.

Chapter Sixty-nine

JAVAN ✛ AN OPPORTUNITY

Several weeks earlier Javan had woken up just as he had when he fell asleep—thinking about Gabrielle. He was confident that day that Gabrielle would return to him once she had freedom from Yahuwah. He was also confident his plans to get the Book would work. He allowed himself to let his guard down—to rest. But by the time he'd opened his eyes from that nap, his certainty about both outcomes had waned—considerably.

He hadn't rested since.

Now, as Javan continued to busy himself laying the groundwork for his plans, he tried to remember what it was he'd dreamt about that day that so radically altered his outlook. He was unable to bring the reason back from the sleeping world and was still unable to revive the memory now. Whatever was in his dreams that day caused him to immediately doubt his intended outcome.

In the days since, agitation and a sense of urgency replaced any light mood his nap began with, relentlessly becoming a part of his demeanor. Whatever he couldn't bring forth in his mind was still spurring him on subconsciously, making sure he was doing everything he could to ensure success.

At one time, when he was still in Yahuwah's fold, he had the same Knowings all angels possessed. Since falling, the Knowings disappeared, semi-prophetic dreams taking their place. But they were rarely lucid or easy to recall, always just out of memory's reach. He could barely remember even the smallest detail.

Quite a bit of time had passed since he had begun putting his plans in place to get Lucas to New Orleans, more than he'd realized. He was so busy setting everything up and trying to guarantee no holes were left that he hadn't realized it was the end of October—three days before Halloween.

Mara and Cecily had been in and out of his loft for weeks, sometimes at the same time, but there never seemed to be any tension between them. It still bothered Javan but not enough to be distracted. He wouldn't let his ego get in the way of his purpose.

All the effort he and others had been putting into finding an opportunity to get Lucas away from Gabrielle had been for nothing, and it was beginning to infuriate him. He might need to take the risk of creating a reason that would make Gabrielle leave Lucas alone. Putting something like that in place was risky, though. She wasn't stupid, and it wouldn't take much to tip her off. If that happened, he'd lose his chance.

Javan considered using a different person to retrieve the Book, and though he could force someone to do it, he wouldn't get the same satisfaction. He wasn't ready to give up on having Lucas carry out his plan.

As he looked out the window of his great room onto another morning, he felt the chilly northern wind push through the open door to his balcony. It pulled at branches, attempting to pluck more leaves off limbs that had succumbed to autumn's possession. Javan imagined that the wind wanted to bring the leaves to their end, hurrying up the process of being returned to the earth through their decay. He couldn't help but feel as if the same wind was pulling at him, encouraging him to accompany it on its plunge deeper south, toward what he wanted most—toward bringing his search for the Book and Lucas's life to an end.

It was too soon, though. Javan closed the door, ending the goading wind's intrusion on his day. As he turned toward his room and the awaiting hot shower, he was interrupted by a knock at the door.

He opened it, expecting either Mara or Cecily, but saw no one. He stepped into the hallway and looked, listening to try and catch even the most subtle sound, but there was nothing to hear. He wondered if he'd imagined it as he turned to re-enter his loft. Instead of an open doorway, he ran into a dwarf.

"Damn it, Som! What the hell are you doing here?" Javan peered to one end of the hallway, then the other. Satisfied no one had seen him, he closed the door.

Som looked amused—as much as a mature, large dwarf was capable of looking.

Javan had called on Som to help him with his endeavors since before he'd fallen, and he was who had first confirmed the existence of the Book.

He always wore the same clothes: a long, faded black robe tattered and torn from many years of use loosely tied with a thick, brown, frayed rope, and well-worn black leather boots intended for battle. Javan was surprised he had missed the presence of his musky smell that now wafted around him.

The battles of his long life were declared by scars on his face, neck, hands, and arms. Dwarves were notorious fighters and looked for any opportunity to wield their axes and daggers.

Necklaces of heavy chains or leather cording hung from his muscular neck, each adorned with at least one pendent. Some were announcements of heritage or tribe; others were trophies from battles won; the rest were a mystery to Javan. As he looked into the unsettling red glow of Som's eyes, Som spoke. Javan was struck, as usual, by his deep, gruff voice. On its own, it would make a human shudder with fear.

"Stop wasting time seeing if I was noticed. If I hadn't used a

Glamour, how could I have gotten past you at your own front door? I know what I'm doing, *demon*. Why don't you concern yourself with something that needs it, like how things are going in New Orleans?"

Javan smirked. Som certainly didn't make up for his appearance with a pleasant personality.

"Tell me," Javan said as he walked past him toward the kitchen. Som would want the strongest drink he could pour, so he opened a bottle of whiskey. "How are things going in New Orleans? On schedule, I suspect."

Som looked around at the seating options as he always did. He would complain, sometimes verbally and sometimes, like now, with his expression and body language that said everything Javan had to sit on was too soft.

'Made for humans and their frailty,' he would say in a caustic tone.

It's something a dwarf never wanted to be anything like—a human. Som preferred a hard rock or trunk of a fallen tree to sit on, if he even acted as if he was in need of rest at all since dwarves also never wanted anyone to think they were tired.

As was also customary for Som when he visited, he chose to stand.

Javan gave Som his drink. He downed it in one large swallow and indicated he wanted another. As Javan started to pour, Som answered his question.

"Would you have asked me to help you if you thought I wouldn't have everything ready? All we need is for you to tell us you're on your way."

Som always answered a question with one of his own first. A way to make you stroke his ego. Then, he would give a direct answer to what you'd asked.

"You're right. I wouldn't have if I didn't have faith in your ability to get the job done," Javan answered, playing along. "I'm glad to hear something's going according to plan."

"What do you mean?" Som asked and tossed back his second drink. He made himself at home and poured himself another shot.

"Putting my plan into action isn't happening as quickly as I'd hoped."

Som looked at Javan with squinted eyes, the red glow seeming even more targeted, and then he huffed disapprovingly.

"Why don't you just make things happen then? If I had your abilities, I wouldn't wait. I'd move things along on my schedule."

"I don't think you understand my situation. If you think my powers are something to be appreciated, then you would be quite impressed with Gabrielle. She can put a stop to everything I'm trying to accomplish, and I'm too close to screw it up by being impatient."

"Gabrielle ... as in *your* Gabrielle? Isn't she all cozy and comfy up there?" Som gestured to Heaven with a dismissive wave.

"Yes, my Gabrielle. And no, Gabrielle isn't up there. She's down here. And she's involved—*closely*—with the human I have to get to New Orleans."

Som scrutinized Javan as if trying to look deep inside him to gain more information that he knew Javan wouldn't divulge.

"I see," Som responded, discontinuing his attempt to gain more insight.

He walked over to where Javan stood—bottle in hand. After pouring Javan another drink, he added more to his own.

A dwarf's thirst for alcohol was as unquenchable as their thirst for battle.

It wasn't so much the sudden realization of dwarf tendencies that captured Javan's attention, but his desire not to have Gabrielle, or at least Gabrielle being close to Lucas, in his mind. He let his thoughts drift further into the ways of dwarves as he walked over to the terrace windows and peered out into the bright, chilly morning.

He wasn't sure how long he'd been standing there, entranced by his mind's wanderings. When he finally snapped out of it, he realized Som had left. The only evidence that showed Som hadn't been something of Javan's imaginings was a now empty bottle of whiskey and glass on the kitchen counter.

The day drug on after Som left. It was proving difficult, as was common now, for Javan to keep Gabrielle off his mind. Maybe it was because he hadn't allowed himself the physical distraction Cecily or Mara could offer. He'd been telling himself that he wanted to stay focused on his planning, and he didn't want problems between the two females to interfere. The truth was that it was almost impossible to know Gabrielle was so near and not miss her more than normal. He longed to be with her again. To talk and laugh together. He'd been able to push those feelings away since falling, but that was when she was far away in a place he was forbidden to enter ever again. It was easier then. Now, she wasn't just on Earth, she was within a few miles every day. The desire to be with her pulled him like the waters of the ocean by the moon.

It's just as inescapable. She's *just as inescapable … she has to feel it, too.*

Staring blankly at the brick wall of his great room, he hadn't noticed it steadily darkening from dusk settling. He also didn't notice another with Divine blood nearing until he heard the knock at his door. He was abruptly aware he'd been deeply lost in his thoughts again.

Cursing himself for wasting the afternoon dwelling on something he had no control over, he opened the door to find Mara smiling broadly back at him. She walked past him without saying a word and pulled herself up on the kitchen counter, swinging her dangling legs.

Javan pulled himself up next to her, trying to seem himself. He didn't want her to realize something was off about him. When he looked at Mara again, she was still smiling at him, but now her smile appeared even larger, and there was an expectant look in her eyes. She seemed to become giddier by the second

"Spit it out, Mara. You're wasting my time."

As if she was simply waiting for Javan to do his usual barking of a command, and now had the all clear, she spilled the information almost quicker than Javan could keep up.

"I know when Gabrielle is going to be away from Lucas—at least kinda!"

Javan felt his eyes widen and a smile form. But then his brain caught up with the speed of her words, and his expression rearranged back into a scowl. "What do you mean by kinda?"

She gracefully jumped down from the counter and sat on the arm of the chair to face him.

"I followed the three stooges and Gabrielle to a costume store and heard Gabrielle say she had no intention of participating with them in their Halloween escapades. So she'll be away from him."

Elation filled Javan. This was what he'd been waiting weeks to hear, but he still needed to hear the catch. "Fantastic. But what's the *kinda* about, Mara?" He felt himself return to normal—the way he was when his love for Gabrielle wasn't trying to take over. Mara seemed to sense a shift, too. With a much less playful demeanor, she began to fill him in.

"She told Lucas she wouldn't be participating, but she'd still be near him so he shouldn't worry about his safety."

Javan didn't think she'd been tipped off to his plans, so why was she or Lucas concerned about his safety? Javan was frustrated. He still couldn't figure out how to distract Gabrielle long enough to get Lucas to New Orleans. If she was that concerned about his safety, she'd be watching him even if she wasn't physically next to him.

"Have you heard them talk about any specific concerns?" Javan asked.

"They talk some about the Qalal and the Gentry."

"The Qalal and the Gentry. Why would she be so concerned about them? Why would his safety be at risk?"

"I think I can answer that."

Javan and Mara looked toward the voice coming from the terrace. Cecily sauntered toward them—her eyes fixed on Javan. She looked stunning as usual, wearing all black, and her long auburn hair bounced past her shoulders as she moved.

"Cecily." Javan said, jumping off the counter and greeting her with a kiss on the cheek. He knew he was being friendlier than normal, but Cecily was hard to resist. "Where've you been? I haven't seen you in a week."

Cecily gave Mara a look of satisfaction as he stepped back from her, but when he looked at Mara, she didn't seem to be bothered.

"Hi, Cecily," Mara almost cooed her greeting as if she actually liked her. But Javan knew, even if Mara was unaffected by sharing him with Cecily, she wouldn't like her, simply because she was Qalal. Regardless of what side they seemed to be on, Mara didn't trust them.

Cecily nodded toward Mara and smiled. It was more an obligatory expression than one of sincerity. "Mara, you look well," Cecily said coolly.

She turned her attention back to Javan as she sat on the couch. Javan and Mara had to position themselves to see her. He was realizing Cecily had to feel she was in as much control of a situation as possible. He'd let her have it for a moment. When she'd settled herself comfortably and felt she had the others complete attention, she spoke.

"Like I said, I believe I can shed some light on Gabrielle's concern for Lucas's safety."

Cecily paused and seemed to be wanting to be asked for her knowledge. Biting his tongue—to keep from biting her head off—so he could satisfy Cecily's need for importance to be confirmed by others was going to prove to be a challenge.

"Yes, Cecily. What is it you can tell me?"

"While traveling, recruiting I guess you could say, I heard it was open season on a human who voluntarily made his knowledge of the Qalal known in Europe."

"What does that have to do with Lucas?"

Cecily laughed snidely and cast her eyes to the ceiling. "Javan—*Lucas* is the human."

Javan's eyes widened again, realizing Gabrielle must have taken him.

Why would she do that?

Was she closer to Lucas than he thought? He felt a slow, quiet growl begin to rumble deep inside of him, but another thought stopped it, and he felt the curve of a smile begin. It spread across his face as he began to laugh as one does when satisfied at another's expense. Lucas was, in fact, in a ton of trouble and danger. When he stopped, he asked for more information.

Cecily told them of Lucas and Gabrielle's trip to see the Elders because of a vision Gabrielle had of an attack. When she finished the story, Javan felt much better about everything. He now knew when Gabrielle would be away from Lucas, and he knew how to make that distance, and time, grow.

"Cecily," he said as he sat next to her on the couch, still smiling broadly, "I have a job for you and your minions if you think they'll help."

Cecily smiled back. "I have quite the little coven started, Javan. They'll do what I ask. They know I'm going to be powerful, soon, and they want to be on my good side."

"Great. Tell them you're going to need them on Halloween."

Chapter Seventy

GABRIELLE AND LUCAS ✟ DOUBTS

Gabrielle watched Lucas from her car as he made his way down the steps of his front porch, hitting only two of them. He jogged toward her with his hands pushed deep in his jean pockets, attempting to shield his ears from the brisk wind greeting him by lowering his head and raising his shoulders.

She took a deep breath as he let himself in. She was going to do her best not to ruin the day with feelings of dread. She'd keep him safe, so there was no need for him to worry more. Still, she struggled with wondering if he would've been better off never meeting her, remaining as he was on the first day of school when they met—just a typical teenager with typical teenager concerns.

He's had a choice to face since birth that guaranteed he'd never be typical.

Lucas leaned over and put his hand on her cheek. It was cold even though it had been in his pocket. Gabrielle placed her hand over his to warm it.

"Hi, love," he said as he moved closer. Their lips touched gently.

Gabrielle felt the warmth of his kiss travel through her body. It was a sensation she longed for, and now that it was sweeping through her, she closed her eyes, settled into the feeling, and lingered there. When she opened them, Lucas was staring back at her with a crooked smile that parted his lips slightly.

"Sorry," she said as she sat back in her seat and put the car in drive. "I got caught up. I'm glad to have you near me again."

Lucas put his hand in hers as she turned the car around. "Don't ever apologize for that, Gabby. I'm glad you're not bored with me."

Gabrielle looked at him with an amused expression. "Why on Earth would I be bored with you?"

"Let's not forget, you're a powerful angel. I'm just a normal human."

Gabrielle glanced sideways as she turned off his road, smiling at him as he caught her eye.

"Lucas, you're right. I am an angel, and you are human. But I believe we established weeks ago you aren't quite *normal*." She gave his hand a squeeze and snickered playfully. She tried to figure out how to tell him how much he meant to her without sounding too sappy but gave up. If she sounded sappy, that was just the way it would be.

"Hey," she said and waited for him to look at her. When he did, she was concerned by how sad he seemed to be. "You mean more to me than I can put into words, Lucas. I don't think you understand how much I love you."

He smiled and let his eyes drop from hers.

She tugged his hand to get him to look back at her again. "I mean it."

His smiled remained, but she could tell he was still unsure. Would he ever believe her? She knew from their conversation right after meeting the Elders that Lucas felt he didn't deserve, or have anything to offer, her.

It was frustrating.

They loved each other. That was all she needed. Not some knight in shining armor who could come to her rescue. But feeling capable of the act was important to Lucas. She wondered how she could make him feel like her equal so he'd be as content as she was.

She drove several blocks before she spoke again.

"So, what do you still need to pick up?"

Lucas, along with Nonie and Nate, had decided to go as two vampires and their victim. It was a bad joke. Nonie and Nate were the vampires; Lucas was the victim. Of course, no one but them and Gabrielle would understand the meaning behind it, but the three of them thought it fitting. Gabrielle kept her opinion to herself.

"I still need to get the waxy stuff to put on my neck to make puncture marks, makeup to make it look like skin, and fake blood." He spoke without looking at her, gazing out the window instead. The leaves being stripped from trees were no match for the strong autumn wind. Gabrielle knew he wasn't as entranced with the foliage as he acted. He was avoiding her eyes, knowing she didn't like the costumes even though she hadn't said anything.

She tried not to sound displeased. "So, where do you want to go to pick those up?"

"Back to the costume shop we were at a couple of days ago. I need to pick up black capes for Nonie and Nate while we're there also."

Gabrielle couldn't help but laugh at how far into the Hollywood version of vampire attire and appearance the teens were going. Lucas looked at her with a puzzled expression.

"It's nothing—" she searched her thoughts for a different subject. "Where all are you guys going tonight?"

They'd already told her, but she couldn't think of anything else to say. He would feel belittled if she told him how silly they were being about their costumes.

Lucas responded in a careful tone. "Just to the Halloween party at the school, then to Nonie and Nate's afterward to watch some horror flicks. Are you at least going to come by for that?"

Lucas didn't like that Gabrielle wasn't planning on spending any time with him. He didn't understand that she needed to be watching for trouble, and the best way for her to do that was in her angelic form. Spending more time as an angel than a human, as Amaziah had urged her to do, was proving to be difficult, and it was affecting her senses while in human form more and more.

"I don't think I will, Lucas." She could see her answer wasn't what he wanted to hear. "Horror movies just aren't my thing, you know?"

Lucas looked back out the window. "I guess, but I was hoping you'd come so we could be together for a while."

"I'll think about it. Okay? Regardless, I'll see you when you're back home."

Lucas gave her a slight nod and smile, but his disappointment wasn't concealed.

Normally, the quiet moments between Lucas and Gabby didn't concern him, but she seemed to be keeping something from him, and the silence between them seemed to grow with every turn of the car's tires. He could feel the tension pushing on him, believing it would shove him out the door and onto the ground as soon as he tried to exit the car. When it didn't happen— when he was able to stand and walk without picking pieces of pavement out of his skin—it almost surprised him.

Gabrielle made her way to his side faster than he thought she could have walked, and he wondered if she'd somehow manifested next to him. There was still a lot about her he hadn't figured out, and she didn't seem to want to show him all she could do. He'd asked her to once, but she said it wasn't important, and she didn't want to make a spectacle of herself—especially to him. He wondered, though, if it wasn't more about not wanting him to feel even more inferior to her than he already did.

Lucas laughed to himself and shook his head. He wasn't finding actual humor in his thoughts. He was questioning, once again, what he could ever offer her. He wished he knew how she felt about Javan, if what she said she felt about the two of them even began to compare to what she had with the fallen angel, and, more importantly, if those feelings still existed. He thought back to how she'd said he made her feel things Javan never had been able to.

Wouldn't it also be true that Javan made her feel things I'll never be able to, as well?

Gabrielle moved past him toward the restroom. He watched her, feeling the distance expanding between them. It wasn't the physical distance he was aware of, however. There was something going on between them he couldn't explain. He wasn't even sure who was the cause, him or her. Maybe it was simply what was to be expected. They really had no business being together. How would it ever work between them? Short term wasn't the problem; long term realities were the issue.

He didn't know when it was all going to end, but it would. It was the only logical outcome for an angel and a human being in love unless the angel chose to give up their life to be a human, like his grandmother had done for his grandfather. He would never let Gabrielle do that for him. He'd feel guilty the rest of his life. The more he thought about how he felt they were growing apart, the more he was sure the reason was because he wasn't good enough, or *right*, for her.

As the shop's employee returned to the register with what he needed, Lucas could see Gabrielle approaching in the periphery of his vision. He didn't turn to look at her as he would normally have done, afraid of what she'd see in his eyes—believing his concerns and insecurities would be known to her right away. Even though he felt like parting ways was inevitable, he wasn't going to encourage the conversation. He wanted to be with her as long as he could, and the things on his mind would surely bring about their separation sooner if they were made known to her.

Gabrielle waited for him. After he'd paid, he turned toward the door, away from Gabrielle, and started to walk, wishing he could leave his thoughts behind as he moved closer to the exit. He felt her hand reach for his, then she laced their fingers. As soon as his eyes met hers, he felt the warmth of his love for her begin to push away the negative thoughts. He leaned down to kiss her, and when she raised her head so her lips could meet his, the desire consuming his mind and body chased away any lingering doubts—at least for now.

Chapter Seventy-one

JAVAN ✝ ROMEO

Javan was pacing his usual path in front of the windows of his great room as he waited. He didn't know how long he'd been moving from one end of the room to the other until he looked at his watch and was frustrated to see not nearly enough time had passed. All his plans were put in place, and there was little he could do but wait. He had a hard time not wishing time to hurry so that he, Mara, and Shea could leave.

Shea was his newest pawn, and right now, the most important.

She was Gentry, a huli jing, and Mara had recruited her only yesterday. He hoped she was as skilled with changing her appearance as she claimed. Shea said it would be risky for her to change and then turn around and do it again the next day, explaining how it took a lot of energy. She didn't want to risk being able to transform herself convincingly twenty-four hours later.

Javan veered off his pacing course to pour himself a drink. Just as he was about to tip the bottle and fill his glass, he stopped.

"Fuck it."

Javan put the bottle to his lips and began to drink, righting it when he heard a knock. He abandoned his beverage and jogged to the door, reminding himself to calm down as he reached for the knob and opened the door.

Through a breathy whisper, he said her name. "*Gabrielle.*"

He had to remind himself to breathe, stunned by her beauty. Her hair hung in loose waves far past her shoulders. Her eyes seemed to capture all available light, giving them a sparkling effect. A fitted red sweater and jeans embellished her curves. He didn't know what to say. Why was she there? Javan felt his hopes rise. A smile spread wide across his face. Was she coming back to him? A smile parted the lips he longed to press against his. As he was about to do what he'd wanted since he'd first seen her in this body weeks earlier, she spoke.

"You're pleased by the likeness?"

She waited for him to respond. He couldn't.

The smile that had spread across his face slowly reversed, along with the hope that sprung with it. He was as disheartened as he was amazed. Shea had convinced even him.

He studied her more carefully. From what he remembered of Gabrielle's appearance in her human form, Shea was a dead ringer. Even her voice sounded similar. She'd be in his embrace then if she hadn't said something that made him realize whom she was.

Javan didn't notice that her own smile had vanished into a scowl. She crossed her arms and threw her hip out one way, pointing the opposite side's foot and knee the other direction.

It was the universal stance of an annoyed woman.

"Hello?" Shea voiced her agitation.

Javan looked back to what he thought were Gabrielle's piercing green eyes and was once again torn by what he'd hoped for only moments before.

But she isn't Gabrielle.

And there was still work to do before he could make her see things his way so she would return to his arms. He nodded his head to Shea and moved aside so she could enter.

"Are you happy with what I've done or not?" she asked curtly as she entered, turning in time to see him checking out her backside.

Javan's gaze traveled up her body to her eyes—eyes he could get lost in if he allowed himself to believe it really was Gabrielle for just a little while. He moved close to Shea. So close she arched her body. He took one of the dark waves of hair and wrapped it loosely around his finger, trailing its length. His hand remained where the lock ended, and he didn't resist the desire to caress the area it rested upon. Shea closed her eyes, and Javan saw a smile part her lips. As he put his other hand on her face, she pushed into it.

As he was about to press his lips to hers—to Gabrielle's—he prompted her with a breathy whisper. "Open your eyes."

When she did, he knew she was going to allow him to do what he wanted while looking into them—believe it really was Gabrielle in his arms.

Javan relaxed a little after being with Shea, just enough to be somewhat patient while he waited for Mara. He didn't have to wait long. He heard her knock on the door, and Mara let herself in. He was glad she arrived later than Shea.

He looked at Shea and smiled. He knew she wasn't Gabrielle, but it was nice to think of her being there, anyway. It would be satisfying when she sat in his loft as casual and content as Shea was at that moment.

Mara's eyes fixed on Shea. "Holy shit! If I didn't know what we were about to do, I would've sworn you really were Gabrielle."

Mara sat in her usual chair, in her usual manner. Only this time, she was turned the other way so she could continue to analyze Shea's transformation. She spoke to Javan without turning around at all.

"Are you happy, Javan?"

He didn't get a chance to answer. Shea beat him to it.

"I think it's safe to say he's more than happy. You were right,

Mara. He seized the moment."

The two of them laughed.

Javan didn't really mind that the two had expected this of him, but it did bother him how Mara seemed to have figured him out. He wanted to stay more of a mystery to her, knowing that the less she knew or expected would give him an advantage. As it now stood, it seemed that advantage was gone, and Mara was several steps ahead of him. That shift in power might prove to be a problem. He would have to correct his mistake some other time. He looked at his watch. They needed to leave. The minutes that had seemed to be dragging now moved at a normal pace.

"Ladies," Javan said and took another drink straight from the bottle. "I'm glad to have amused you, but we need to get ready for tonight. Let's wrap up comparing notes and move on to what we need to focus on." Javan spoke in a tone that made it clear not to test him.

Shea was quick to take the cue from Mara as she swung her body around and stood. Shea followed her into the kitchen area. Mara was apparently ready to make him feel like he was back in control. Now that he sensed the shift with Mara, he wouldn't let her gain any more footing. He would keep a closer eye on her from now on, which meant finding a way to spend more time together. It was something he wouldn't have looked forward to three months ago, but now that he knew he'd underestimated her, he was far more intrigued. She was becoming desirable, instead of a convenience.

As she looked at him, he could see confidence in her he'd never noticed before. She gave him a subtle, crooked smile that seemed to be both flirty and knowing. He found himself smiling back, enticed by the demon he didn't know, but thought he'd figured out many years ago.

"Okay," he said to break himself away from unproductive thoughts. "I don't think we need to go over the plan again, but if there's anything either of you have a question about, now's the time to ask. Don't piss me off later because you hesitate. This has to be perfect and quick." When he felt they had plenty of time to say something, he continued.

"Cecily is already in place to start her diversion, but Gabrielle won't be thrown off of her game for long. As soon as Gabrielle leaves Cecily, Cecily and the others are going straight to New Orleans to wait for us. I'm counting on Gabrielle being overly cautious tonight because of Halloween."

"You really think she'll be taking extra precautions?" Shea asked.

"Based on what Mara has heard, yes. But even if she goes overboard in trying to protect Lucas's mortality, she isn't stupid. Far from it. She has extremely sharp instincts. I don't think she'll be diverted for long. That's why I am stressing there's absolutely zero time for mistakes, or wavering, on your part."

Javan studied Mara and Shea, wanting to make sure he had their attention so he could drive the next point as hard as possible.

"I know both of you have been told how powerful Gabrielle is, but I've seen her in action. From what I've been hearing, Yahuwah has granted her even more powers than she had when I was with her. She isn't someone you want to make an enemy, so do yourselves a favor and make sure you don't screw up. If you do and she catches us, I'll be the least of your worries." Javan looked at Mara directly. "You think I'm a dick when I get upset—Gabrielle makes me look like a newborn kitten when she loses her temper."

Mara nodded in understanding, and when he looked at Shea, she did the same.

"Let's go, then. We still have time, but I'd rather get there early."

Javan picked up his keys and grabbed a duffle bag he'd already prepared. Before he opened the door, he turned to Mara and Shea.

"One last thing. If things do go bad tonight, it's every man for himself. Don't expect me to turn hero." Neither responded. "Got it?"

Mara was the only one to say anything. "Loud and clear—*Romeo*."

Javan smiled at her and turned to leave his loft, not knowing what the evening would hold for him or if he would be alive to return.

If he did, he hoped to be carrying the Book of Barabbadon.

Chapter Seventy-two

Gabrielle ☩ Dark Vision

Gabrielle dropped Lucas off at his home after they left the costume shop. She could tell he was a little off with his affection and hoped it was only because he was disappointed she wasn't going to join their festivities—aware that she was ignoring the nagging impression that there was more to it. She sighed and tried to push the thoughts out of her mind the way she pushed air out of her body.

It didn't work.

She couldn't help but think about what was happening to Lucas—to them. Even now, when out of the restraints of her human form, the thoughts were still there. She'd hoped at least one benefit of being away from Lucas, and in her Divine form, was that her thoughts would be less focused on their problems. But in the early stages of tonight's watch, she was finding absolutely no reprieve from the panic she was beginning to feel about their relationship.

She still hadn't told Lucas about the decision he'd have to make and wondered if that's part of why she felt distance growing. She figured that was part of it but certainly not the entire reason. The most troublesome thing to her about not telling him was not understanding what her motivation was for keeping the truth to herself. In the beginning, she didn't know how to tell him. But since weeks had passed, she wondered if her fear of losing him was more involved. If that was the real reason, it'd be the first time she had acted so selfishly. She felt the truth in that, and shame followed on the realization's heels. She decided she would tell Lucas as soon as she was alone with him again—whether or not the time was right.

There will never be a right time.

The simple act of making the decision brought relief she'd not expected. She realized what a burden the secret had been.

I should have told him right away.

For now, though, she had to get him through the night safely so she'd have the opportunity to tell him. In order to do that, she was going to have to concentrate on what was going on in their surroundings and stop obsessing on their relationship.

Gabrielle spent the next part of the evening scanning Shadow World and Underworld energies flitting about in the night. Nothing in particular caught her attention. The Gentry's activity was more than normal, but that was expected. She'd also not been surprised by the number of spirits moving in and out of the human realm or that the activity seemed to be so prominent in the Nashville area.

The only thing she kept focusing on was a group of Qalal just over the border in Kentucky. She wasn't too concerned about them. They seemed to be moving slowly north. But with the danger Lucas was in from their kind, she would keep a close eye on any in, or near, the city. The number of Qalal she'd originally tallied in Tennessee and its bordering states had stayed roughly the same, and she was glad for that.

Lucas, Nonie, and Nate had been at the school Halloween party for a little less than an hour, and she knew they were planning on staying until about ten before they made their way back to the Daniels' home. She was amazed by how realistic Nonie had made the bite marks and blood on Lucas's neck appear, and her reaction had convinced her that she did the right thing by staying to herself.

Having to look at Lucas all night with realistic signs of a Qalal attack would've made her more edgy.

Lately, she found herself feeling increasingly angry at the three of them, especially Lucas. They seemed to be aloof about the dangers they knew existed for them. It was as if they thought making light of the situation would make it go away when, in fact, all it would do is make them more vulnerable. She definitely thought Lucas was slipping into denial, and there was a possibility that his denial was one of the reasons for the coolness she felt from him. If he was pushing away the reality of Shadow World and Underworld beings, it would also mean denying angels.

At least for a few hours, she felt the three were safe enough for her to do her job without watching them constantly. It lessened her concern with them around so many other people. No Shadow Worlder would dare do anything when Lucas was around so many humans, and that meant Nonie and Nate would be safe, too. Those who lived outside of human's perceived reality would know they would be hunted down and killed for something as brazen as attacking a human with scores of witnesses. They would be an immediate target of those with Divine blood and any who feel the need to live only in people's imaginings.

Gabrielle relaxed for a minute and took in the night.

It was a chilly evening. The moon was taking its time rising, still hugging the horizon that partially framed a cloudless sky. Sporadic outbursts of laughter were carried up to her by the light breeze that accompanied the evening. They were mostly the contagious giggles of children, but occasionally, she'd pick out deeper adult tones. She'd heard someone say earlier that they wished it felt more like spring than autumn, like the last few Halloween's had.

She would love to know what spring felt like, imagining how the new blooms would smell and how welcome the scent would be the first time the grass was cut. The warm temperatures and breeze that brought the spring scents would feel more like summer than a mild day after the cold winter months as everyone pulled out shorts and tank-tops and made their way to the nearest park.

It probably feels like their skin has just been released from some kind of cloth prison.

It was only a dream. She wouldn't be on Earth in the spring. She wouldn't get to experience that transition, know those smells, or have those sensations in a human body. She would have enjoyed the experience though, and she let out a frustrated sigh.

Two more months.

Thoughts of how much she might enjoy spring were abruptly replaced with darker ones, with her … *without* Lucas. As the vision in her mind appeared, sadness pushed through every part of her mind and body, heart and soul. She couldn't tell if it was because he wasn't in her life or something worse …

Is he dead?

Gabrielle felt her energy shudder as the vision continued.

Now the image was just … *dark*. But she knew she was in that darkness somewhere. A shadow would have been no easier for her to make out wherever she was than a human trying to pick out their idea of a ghost in a thick fog. She was alone—alone and scared. And more than a little angry. She felt something she never had, and it sent terror screaming through her body and mind.

I'm powerless! How could that be? What could render me powerless? Why did I feel so utterly alone?

The vision didn't bode well for her or any of her brethren or allies, either.

Or Lucas.

She hoped it wasn't a premonition at all. Just her imagination getting the better of her.

As she was trying to clear her dark thoughts, a bright flicker of energy in the north caught her attention. The energy was Qalal. As she watched for a few more moments, her mind began to race with the realization that it was the group she'd dismissed earlier. They were no longer moving slowly north; they were moving south—with a quickness. Toward Nashville.

Toward Lucas.

Chapter Seventy-three

Javan ✝ The Human

Javan made his move as soon as Cecily called. He was situated close enough to Lucas to get to him quickly, but far enough away that Gabrielle wouldn't be alerted to their proximity.

The anticipation that had been steadily increasing in him all day was absent now. He was so focused on his goal that he felt nothing but his limbs moving, his mind methodically working through every step of his plan. All he had to do was convince Lucas that Gabrielle's life was in his hands and that all Lucas would have to do to save her was obtain a simple little book. After that, he would let Gabrielle go.

He smiled wickedly at the next part—Lucas experiencing more than one type of pain before his death.

After arriving at the school, he let Mara take the driver's seat so she and Shea could get in position while he lured Lucas outside. Before he made his way into the gym, Javan took a look around to make sure Gabrielle was out of the area. Once he was satisfied, he swiftly covered the remaining twenty yards to the doors. He would have enjoyed the attention from the teenage girls as he passed, but he had no time tonight to delight in young human flesh.

Once inside, Javan scanned the large rectangular room for his target. All the teens behind makeup and masks might have been a hindrance if Mara hadn't known what Lucas and his friends were dressing up as. Javan had found quite a bit of humor in their selection.

Javan spotted Lucas within seconds. Even if he hadn't known what to look for, Lucas's regular clothes, with only puncture wounds and blood for makeup, made him easy to spot. Javan made his way through the clusters of high school cliques. Even in costume, you could tell who hung out together, all dressed in their group's chosen theme.

How pathetic.

They were so ready to follow anyone who showed an ounce of leadership. Those leaders would be just as worthless but have overblown egos and an ability to delude a more simple-minded group of people that they were worthy of being followed. He loathed them, and the thought inflated his desire to acquire the Book of Barabbadon.

Lucas was turned toward Nonie and Nate, so he didn't see Javan approaching. But Nate spotted him, and he must have seen something about Javan that made it known his demeanor and appearance weren't part of any costume. Nonie noticed her brother stiffen, and her head snapped in the direction of Nate's gaze.

I could have fun with her.

Lucas was quick to notice his two friends' abrupt change and followed their eyes. When his met Javan's, he looked like a deer transfixed by a spotlight in the deep black of night.

Javan didn't slow and came upon Lucas so fast that Lucas stumbled. Javan stood, staring into Lucas's blue eyes with his own black ones. Lucas's brows pulled together, but he seemed too stunned to speak.

Javan studied his face as a sneer pulled at the corner of his mouth.

"I'm going to have a hard time refraining from putting my hand through your chest and ripping your heart out, *human*, just so I can feel life leave you with its last beat." He had to fight that urge, especially when he saw the look of terror grow in Lucas's eyes. But he knew he'd have even more fun with Lucas later. He moved closer and whispered. "If you want to save Gabrielle, I suggest you come with me—*now*." Javan waited for his response, but Nate spoke.

"I don't think so, man. He's not going anywhere with you."

Javan turned his hostility toward Nate, growling. It was a long and grumbling warning. He contorted his face as he'd done with the policeman weeks before but didn't unleash the full force of it. Javan didn't need an audience, only for Nate and Nonie to fear for their own lives enough to give him time to get Lucas away. Nate stumbled back until he hit the wall. Nonie went to his side. He was dazed, but Javan knew he would snap out of it soon enough.

Javan looked back to Lucas who was about to say something. He let out another low growl in warning and put his hand firmly around Lucas's arm. Lucas winced from the pressure as Javan turned him toward the side door a dozen feet away.

He led Lucas to the exit as swiftly as he could without anyone noticing. Luckily, the music was loud and had changed to something that was apparently popular just as he had reached the threesome . Most everyone was dancing or bobbing their heads as they watched the mob of high schoolers thrash about on the dance floor. As he pushed through the side door into the night air, turning to shut it again, he felt something stop it from closing.

The now angry, red-faced blond stepped into the night, letting the door close behind her. She spread her feet apart as if she was bracing for an attack, her hands pulled into fists next to her hips.

Javan smirked, amused by the girl's bold show of guardian instinct, but he didn't have time to test how far she'd go. She opened her mouth and took half a step toward Javan; he sent her against the brick wall. Nonie hit her head so hard that Javan and Lucas heard the thud. She fell in a heap, moving only slightly after she landed.

Lucas gasped, but Javan squeezed his arm harder, making sure pain ripped through Lucas's thoughts so he could think of nothing but feeling like his bone was about to break.

Javan hissed a warning in Lucas's ear. "Your little friend is fine, just taking a nap. I think you need to be more concerned about your precious *Gabby*. If you don't concentrate on her, I can assure you that she won't live to see the rise of tomorrow's sun."

Javan spun him toward the black car idling before them. Lucas watched the rear window drop slowly to reveal something that he was sure the human would have never thought he'd see.

Chapter Seventy-four

LUCAS ✣ WIN-WIN

Lucas's heart sank when he saw Gabby, making him forget the pain he felt from the vice grip on his arm. She was held by someone who stayed partially out of view. Shadows cast into the car, making the golden glow of something wrapped several times around Gabby's chest create an eerie effect. He wasn't sure what it was, but Gabby had told him the only things that could harm an angel were Divine weapons. She seemed only somewhat aware, drifting in and out of consciousness. Lucas made a move to reach her, and pain tore through his arm again. His knees buckled.

"What the hell!" Lucas screamed in protest.

"Shut up," Javan said through clenched teeth as he pulled Lucas back to his feet toward the other side of the car where the door seemed to open for him by some invisible hand. He threw Lucas into the backseat on the other side of the person, or *thing*, holding Gabby.

He felt something wrapping around his chest, and then he was being pushed back in the seat. He looked down to see he'd also been bound, ensnaring his arms tightly to his sides. The movement was swift. Lucas barely had time to take in a full breath and exhale before his entrapment was complete. He knew before he looked next to him there was no way they could be human. But he didn't expect to see who was there when he gathered the courage to glance. Mara was smiling at him innocently.

"Hey, *lover*," she said, then leaned in as if she was going to kiss him.

"Mara! Enough!" his captor commanded her from the driver's seat. "We don't have time for your games."

"Who are you?" Lucas asked who he assumed was a demon that had drug him out of the building, away from his friends—away from safety. It was the first real sentence he was able to form in his mind and get his mouth to cooperate in articulating. He'd felt almost mute since he'd turned to see whomever this was descending on him in the gym.

"I'm sure you've heard of me. Gabrielle most likely would have told you my name already."

"Javan." Lucas had suspected when he saw Mara. Gabby had told him she was palling around with him. Now he was sure her ex was in the driver's seat, and he was in that seat in more ways than the literal one since Javan had him and Gabby under his control.

"I'd ask what Gabrielle has told you about me, but I'm sure I'd rather not know. Besides, she doesn't have time to spare for our small talk."

"What do you mean?" Lucas tried to see her better, but Mara wouldn't let him get a good look. "Gabby! Gabby, can you hear me?"

"Lucas?"

Gabby's voice was barely a whisper. Whatever they'd done to her, she didn't seem to be doing well.

Lucas felt the car gun forward as Javan sped through the school's parking lot toward who knows where. As the school slipped away behind him, any hope of human intervention slipped away with it. He was on his own to deal with two demons and no telling what else.

He couldn't see the speedometer, but Lucas thought they were going fast—so fast he felt there was no way the natural world could create that speed.

He wondered how many miles of his former reality they'd already left in their wake.

"What the hell did you do to her?"

"Easy. She'll be just fine as long as you do *exactly* what I ask of you tonight."

Lucas looked back at Gabrielle. He thought he saw her trying to open her eyes. Fear gripped his insides even more. He had to do anything he could to save her. He steeled himself, not wanting to let her down.

"What do you want me to do?"

Javan snickered caustically. "That was easy. You must really think you love her. More than that, you must *really think* she loves you." He snickered again, this time heartier.

"What would you know about love, Javan? You gave her up. For what? Selfish desires? Yeah … I love her. And I would never willingly give her up like you."

"Stupid human. You have no idea about anything you *think* you know." Javan paused. "But you didn't say you *know* she loves you, too. So maybe you're not so stupid after all. Tell me, are you starting to feel as inferior and unequal to her as you are? I bet you're feeling her slip away from you."

Silence filled the car—an uncomfortable, telling silence. Lucas was sure Javan knew he'd struck a nerve, and he would apply as much pressure to it as he could.

"Lucas, let me help you out here before you get in any deeper. You have no way of being what she needs for any real length of time. You see that, don't you? You're just a *human*. You're mortal. She's not only an angel, she's one of the *most* powerful angels Yahuwah has ever created. Do you have *any* idea what that means?" Javan let loose a disgusted laugh. "Why am I asking? Of course you don't. Like I said, you're just a lowly human. It wasn't that long ago your kind believed the Earth was flat—idiots. You don't have the capacity in your tiny minds to understand beyond the thoughts Yahuwah allows you to have—which isn't much."

"That's all true, Javan. But He apparently didn't think much of you, did He? I think you just hate humans because you're jealous," Lucas ended in a matter-of-fact tone.

"Jealous? Of what? What do *humans* have I'd be jealous of, Lucas? What do you have that I don't?"

The superiority that Javan felt was apparent in his tone. It seemed to drip from his mouth as he spoke. Lucas's pulse rose from his anger even more than from his fear.

"That's easy—we have God's forgiveness. Since you can never get back into Heaven again, my guess is forgiveness isn't something He'll offer to you. Am I right?"

It was Javan's turn to sit in silence. Lucas wondered if he was doing so not only out of frustration, but also out of the need to calm himself so he didn't throw Lucas out of the car to his death.

When Javan did speak, Lucas could tell by his tone that he was stifling his anger. Lucas felt a sense of victory in knowing that he'd gotten to the demon, but he knew that feeling was also probably going to be short-lived.

"Let's get down to business, Lucas. Here's what you'll do if you want to keep Gabrielle alive. It's simple. Get a book for me and place it safely into my hands."

Lucas considered what was being asked of him. It sounded simple. Lucas wondered what kind of book was so important to him. A feeling of dread passed through him as he considered the possibilities.

"Why don't you get it yourself? Why do you need me?"

"Your only concern should be Gabrielle's safety. Do you not care what happens to her?"

"Of course I care. I just don't understand why you have to use me to get a book if it's as simple as you say."

"Again, it's really not your concern. I will tell you, though, that what's easy for you isn't as easy for me or any of my kind. So, you see,

I do need you. And I had to make sure you needed something from me, too. Gabrielle. It's a win-win, Lucas."

Lucas tried to look out the window of the car, but the tint was so black that he couldn't make anything out. He glanced back over to Gabby. He was getting more concerned. She hadn't made any movement for a while, and the only sound she made was an occasional low moan.

Mara looked at him, and the sight of her eyes glowing that creepy shade of chartreuse made him shiver. Was the girl he'd originally met still anywhere in there?

"Don't worry, lover. She's still breathing—for now." Mara smiled an innocent smile as if this was a sick double-date. As if he and Gabby weren't living what may well be their last night.

"What do you say, Lucas? Are you going to be the *champion* for your angel in distress? Or are you going to let her die?"

"I'll do what you want," Lucas answered. He had no way to save Gabby and *not* do what Javan wanted. Javan knew what the answer would be before he asked.

"No hesitation—valiant. I'm sure Gabrielle would be touched by your bravery, but only for a little while. She'd continue to grow tired of you."

It sucked that Javan was probably right. It didn't matter, though. Not while she needed him. Right now, all that mattered was making her safe, again.

"Even if I knew she was going to grow tired of me, Javan … I love her. I'll do anything I can not to let her down."

Lucas couldn't see Javan's face but was sure he'd see a triumphant, smug smile if he could. He hated being so weak, and he seemed to be increasingly surrounded by others with epic strength and abilities—making that weakness even more apparent.

Javan was right; he was just a lowly human. Now that he knew it, he wished it could be changed. But he couldn't see how he would ever be anything more than a simple mortal or how Gabrielle could ever continue to want him.

"Where are you taking me?" Lucas asked in a defeated tone.

"New Orleans."

Lucas tried to make himself more comfortable, but it wasn't working. It was no surprise that bondage wasn't conducive to relaxation. He sighed heavily and closed his eyes anyway. Sleep wasn't something he thought he'd actually achieve, but he didn't want to see the inky view outside the car's windows or the creepy glow of Mara's eyes every time he tried to look at Gabby.

As soon as his eyes closed, though, he felt the car slowing—and he was sure they were descending.

"We're already there? How? New Orleans is at least a seven hour drive." He opened his eyes and tried to see out the window he was resting his head against, but all he saw was the same ebony expanse of nothingness.

He heard Javan snicker again as the car settled. "Like I said, you have a tiny mind, Lucas."

Javan got out of the car and closed the door. By the time he opened Lucas's, Mara had freed him from his bindings, and Javan had a vice grip on his arm again. When he emerged into the night, he had to shield his eyes until they adjusted; even though the moon was temporarily behind a low cloud, the light was still brighter than what he'd grown accustomed to during the car ride.

Once he was able to open his eyes and focus on the surroundings, there was no mistaking New Orleans. Javan had parked right beside one of the city's famous above-ground cemeteries.

Chapter Seventy-Five

GABRIELLE ✟ THE COVEN

Gabrielle didn't know what the Qalal might be up to or if they were after Lucas, but she wasn't going to wait to see if they made it all the way to where he was. Maybe she was wrong. Maybe they were brazen enough to attack. Or maybe they were positioning themselves to strike when there were less witnesses.

Gabrielle had already moved to intercept them as she went through the different possibilities, and it wasn't until she was closing in on their location that she stopped and realized she'd left Lucas unprotected—unprotected when he thought she was watching over him. She weighed the danger and decided again he was probably safe with so many others around even if she wasn't right outside. She started toward the Qalal, once more.

Lucas is safe, but someone else might not be.

He wasn't the only human she was supposed to protect, and the Qalal were acting too erratic to do nothing.

Drawing closer to them, she noticed a glow of yellow and orange leap from the ground ahead of her. The Qalal had stopped as suddenly as they'd begun to move and did so just outside the glow.

The yellow and orange light was from a bonfire, and six Qalal now surrounded it. They remained unmoving in the cloak of blackness, undisturbed by the light cast from the billowing flames. Within the circle of light was a group of teenagers.

They were in mortal danger. They were far enough away from any other human eyes that an attack on them wouldn't be seen. The closest house was at least two miles away, too far for their cries for help to be heard.

Her thoughts went back to Lucas again, but right now, he wasn't the one in danger. The ten unknowing teens, laughing and drinking beer, oblivious to the advance of the silent predators around them, were. The Qalal were so close that the teens nearest to the edges of light would have been able to feel their breath if the Damned actually had need of pushing air in and out of their mouths—mouths that were used for something more lethal.

Gabrielle sensed something moving up behind her—quickly. She swung around in time to recognize the erratic energy of another of the Damned. She raised her hand, about to attack, when it halted about twenty yards away. It proceeded to circle her slowly—like a wildcat waiting for its chance to pounce.

"You know, *angel*, you have no right to strike. We haven't done anything to warrant your attack," the Qalal said. "You should remember the *rules* your Lord binds you to follow when dealing with us."

"I forget nothing, Qalal. I need no reminder from you. But one move from your friends, and I will be happy to hold up the end of the bargain Yahuwah made with your kind—with a swiftness." Gabrielle took in the appearance of the female who circled her.

She was quite beautiful. Her hair was as long as Gabrielle's, but unlike her almost black shade that blended into the night sky, the Qalal's had a red hue that glowed like an ember in the moonlight. Her skin was pale against the night's shadow, and her deep red eyes filled with contempt as she looked at Gabrielle as if she was this Qalal's enemy even before this encounter.

"Do you really think you can take on so many Qalal at once?"

Gabrielle almost laughed. "Without a doubt."

The ground beneath the Qalal's feet trembled, causing her to spring back. She looked down, then back at Gabrielle. The Qalal showed a glint of white teeth between lips parted by a smile.

"You're no *ordinary* angel—are you?"

"There are none of Divine blood you should ever think of as ordinary. Do so at your own peril. It makes no difference to me what befalls a rogue Qalal or any of her coven."

"Ooh … harsh." The Qalal was beginning to circle again. "What makes you think it's *my* coven?"

"You approached me for confrontation. Only the highest member of a coven would have the feeling of power that would cause them to be comfortable with an angel fixated on them. You think you can take me." Gabrielle smirked. "I know I can take you. Your followers are too smart, or you're too foolish. Both are probably true. So many times, the smart ones stay in the shadows of those who want to shine the brightest." Gabrielle paused and closed the distance between her and the female Qalal by half. "Did you know a star shines brightest right before it dies?" She waited for a response that didn't come. "You haven't been a Qalal for long, have you? Little more than a few hundred years would be my guess."

"How can you tell?"

"Your kind are slow to learn."

Gabrielle could tell she struck a nerve. The woman's smile turned into a sneer accompanied by a guttural growl. Gabrielle was amused to have rattled the young Qalal so easily. It only showed her youth and inexperience.

"Do you have a name, or would you like me to call you Damned?"

"Cecily."

Cecily glared at Gabrielle as the two waited for the other to make a move. Gabrielle didn't care for most Qalal, especially those obviously not interested in regaining their soul. Cecily definitely seemed to be the kind she liked least, and there was something about the look in her eyes that told Gabrielle that something was particularly off about her.

Cecily cocked her head slightly, allowing the light from the moon to catch a pendant that hung from the choker around her neck. Gabrielle tried to see it better, thinking it looked like the one that Ka'awa and the demons at Yosemite wore. Cecily shifted, blocking the light again before she could be sure.

"You know my name … are you going to tell me yours?"

"Gabrielle."

Cecily laughed loudly enough that the teenagers quieted. After several moments, they resumed their partying.

"*The* Gabrielle?"

"I suppose so."

Cecily stopped circling "I've heard a lot about you. From one of your kind, actually."

"Really? And who would that be?"

"Just a mutual—*friend*."

"I don't believe any of my kind who would speak to you about me would be classified as my friend, Cecily."

"Well—maybe he's more like an *ex*-friend. If you have to be so technical about it."

Gabrielle was growing tired of the chitchat. "Since I really don't care much about who you're friends with who I was once friends with, how about we move on to what you and your coven are intending to do here tonight?"

Cecily bent over in laughter. When she returned upright, Gabrielle caught something else in her eyes that hinted to her that she wasn't going to like where the conversation was heading.

"Oh, no. On the contrary, I think you would be interested in this particular old friend who is now a *very* good friend of mine."

Gabrielle sighed. She wished she wasn't bound to guidelines concerning Cecily's kind.

"Enlighten me."

"This *particular* friend was once much more than your friend. Much, much more."

Gabrielle felt the crush in her heart again. She didn't have to hear his name. There could only be one she could be speaking of.

Now, it was her turn to be rattled.

Gabrielle didn't say anything for a moment. Cecily seemed to be more than happy to let the information, and its meaning, seep in without interruption.

Javan had certainly made the rounds, and as much as she didn't want it to, it hurt her deeply. It didn't seem to bother him at all to be with *anyone* that crossed his path, making her feel she never really mattered to him at all.

Why does he seem to want me back so badly? Am I just a challenge? A trophy?

After several long moments of her thoughts twisting with the hurt she felt trying to surface, Gabrielle was finally able to regain her composure and break the silence.

"Tell Javan hello. But back to the matter at hand. What's your intention with these humans?"

Gabrielle was hoping for the worst so she could do whatever she wanted with Cecily. The other six Qalal held steady in their positions, not making any move toward the fire or the humans huddled close to it. If they did, she'd have to take care of them before she could turn her wrath on Cecily. The lives of the teens were more important than her personal vengeance.

Gabrielle was suddenly struck by the track her thoughts had taken. Why did she care whether Cecily had been with Javan? She certainly wasn't the first female he'd had trysts with, and she was now sure there were many, many more.

Obviously, he has no desire to spare my feelings in any way.

She tried to shake off her desire for revenge, not wanting her decisions to get muddied with emotions.

"We just wanted to join their little party."

"That wouldn't be advisable. I don't think you would do well resisting your urges."

"Maybe not. Or maybe we're trying to change our ways. You know, regain our mortal souls and such. Regardless, you can't stop us from being around humans, Gabrielle. Even you can only interfere if we're going to kill one." Cecily looked toward the bonfire. "Or ten."

Gabrielle hated that Cecily was right, and her hue began to take on a hint of red.

"So, Gabrielle, are you going to baby-sit us all night? Or are you going to just trust we aren't going to have a midnight snack?"

Staying all night to watch the coven wasn't an option. She looked at the position of the moon, now well above the horizon, and could tell immediately she'd been gone longer than she'd intended. She'd have to call in some of her troops to oversee the Damned so she could get back to Lucas and still ensure the safety of the teenagers at the bonfire.

Just as she was about to call to them, Cecily spoke again. "How about I make the decision easier for you?"

"And how are you going to do that?"

This time when Cecily spoke, it wasn't quiet, and it wasn't to Gabrielle.

"NOW!"

Gabrielle threw up her hand to pause human time and keep the Qalal from attacking. The effect didn't work. They were still moving toward the now frozen teens. Gabrielle immediately released her hold on time so that the humans could react and descended upon the first Qalal before he even broke the shadow's edge that mingled the darkness of Halloween night and the glow of flames. She was sure he didn't even know his head had been torn off. She tossed it the length of a football field and threw his body just as far in the opposite direction, putting as much distance between the two until she could dispose of him permanently. Even as quick as she was moving, she noticed a black stone pendant reflecting the flames as it fell to the ground.

She produced a disruption in the air just inside the circle of the fire's light and thrust it outward with more force than a bomb's repercussion, sending the others in the coven flying far enough that she'd have time to deal with them all one by one.

The teens' attention was complete. They huddled together as close to the fire as they could get. They had no idea what was going on in the inky blackness around them, but they were smart enough to be scared.

As she made her way to the next Qalal, a female, Gabrielle scanned the area for Cecily. She saw her faint energy vibrating in the distance, moving swiftly to the east.

I'll catch up with you later, Cecily.

Gabrielle ripped the head of the female off next, discarding it in the same way as the first. The next one came to her as if he was going to fight. He had no chance, but she wasn't about to stop to let him in on that information and made quick work of his disposal as well.

By this time, two of the remaining three had regrouped and were fleeing north. Gabrielle put her hands before her, clapping them solidly together. The two Qalal stopped as the ground beneath their feet began to tremble, then roll violently. Before they could try to move away from the lurching earth, Gabrielle opened her hands again, ripping the ground apart angrily. When she saw them fall toward the bowels of Hell, she slapped her hands together again. The earth closed its mouth, plumes of dirt and rock erupting from the rejoining. The sound it made, like the loudest clap of thunder, echoed for several moments.

She turned to see where the final Qalal had fled. To her surprise, he hadn't fled at all. He was just below where she hovered—on his knees. He was bent over, hands palms down on the ground in a show of surrender. Gabrielle descended, slowly.

"*Please*, angel. This wasn't what she said would happen. We weren't going to actually hurt anyone. She said we were supposed to scare them. She said it was what you wanted us to do because they were in some kind of wannabe vampire coven. She said you wanted us to scare them so they would realize what they wanted to get involved in."

Gabrielle was stunned. *Why would Cecily do something like this?*

"How do I know you're telling me the truth?"

"She said you were Gabrielle, The Angel of Karma, and if we helped you, you would help us get our souls back—so we would have another chance for salvation."

He looked up at her, his red eyes pleading with her as much as a soulless creature's could. Another pendant with a black stone at its center swung from the chain dangling around his neck.

Gabrielle realized the look she'd seen in Cecily's eyes hadn't been imagined. The female Qalal had known exactly whom she was all along and exactly what Gabrielle was capable of doing to her coven.

"She sent them into a slaughter under the guise of redemption," Gabrielle said in a whisper.

Cecily knew who she was. She knew Javan. What would be the motivation be to lure Gabrielle out to the middle of nowhere for a fake attack on a group of teenagers?

All at once, Gabrielle knew why.

"Lucas!"

Chapter Seventy-Six

LUCAS ✝ THE BOOK OF BARABBADON

Javan walked to the rear of his car, and like the door that seemed to open by itself back at the gym, the trunk opened for him before he put a hand on it. It was as if an invisible chauffeur was always several steps ahead of him.

Lucas didn't know what Javan was getting, and he didn't care. He took the opportunity to look back in the car at Gabby, who still seemed to be out of it. He sighed and started to turn back around. He hoped Javan would let her go after he got the book, but he wasn't sure if either of them would make it out of this.

Just as he was about to fully face the direction he'd originally turned from, something landed hard against his chest, knocking him into the car. What had felt like a railroad tie when it hit him was now in his arms, and was just a simple long-handled shovel. He looked up at Javan. The smug smile plastering his face was exactly what Lucas had imagined during their conversation in the car.

"I have to dig up the book you want?"

"That's right." The voice didn't come from Javan or either of the occupants in the car. It came from his left, and it belonged to a female.

Because of the shadow she was walking through, all he could see of the woman was her black knee-high boots. As she moved closer, the light rose up her body until he could see her face. He knew from the red eyes that she was a vampire.

An exceptionally beautiful vampire.

Like with the Elders, once he looked at her eyes, he was unable to look away. He hated this feeling. And tonight he didn't need to feel any weaker or more useless than he already did. Once again, he was caught in the midst of yet another being who was more powerful than he was in every way.

She stopped in front of him. She was so close he could smell her—rosemary and lemon. His two favorite scents. Lucas felt the desire to move closer to her so he could enjoy the scent more.

She leaned in, inhaling deeply near his neck, then moved back enough to meet his gaze. "Mmm ... yummy." She licked her lips slowly.

He was suddenly aware he couldn't, or didn't want to, move. His heart pounded harder in his chest than he thought possible. She was surely able to see the rhythm of the blood thrust through the veins traveling up his neck that she was staring at intently.

"Cecily," Javan said from behind her.

Cecily looked away briefly. It was long enough to release Lucas from the hold she had on him. His hand flew to his chest, and he sharply sucked in air. He hadn't realized he'd failed to take a breath since she first looked at him. It was the same experience he had the last time he was face to face with a vampire, only this time, Gabrielle wasn't capable of saving him.

"Cecily, I know you'd like to have fun with Lucas," Javan said as he made his way to her, "but we need him alive. And we don't have time for games—even though I'd love to play a few of my own." Javan glared at Lucas, then smiled and kissed Cecily from behind on her neck. Cecily didn't hide her enjoyment. She closed her eyes and placed her hand behind Javan's head, pressing him harder into her.

When he was finished, Javan moved away from Cecily, positioning himself between her and Lucas. "Here's what you need to do. Take these directions into the cemetery, and when you get to the point where it's buried, dig. When you find it, bring it back to me, and I'll release Gabrielle. Do you think you can handle that, *human*?" Javan continued to glare; his black eyes seemed to be rummaging through Lucas's mind. Lucas wondered if he'd always been like this.

How could Gabby love someone so malicious?

"Yeah," Lucas answered dryly. "I can handle it."

Lucas studied the small piece of paper in his hand. A rough map of the cemetery and its tombs were drawn on it. There were simple instructions written below the map. Lucas glanced at Javan, avoiding Cecily's gaze. He didn't want to be spellbound again.

"Are you going with me?"

Javan grinned. It wasn't meant to be friendly. "You're on your own. We'll be waiting here—with Gabrielle." Javan's smile turned back into a sneer. "Make sure you move quickly and quietly. I've taken steps to ensure a certain amount of time for you to be alone in there, but I won't be able to keep people away long. Especially tonight."

Javan stood and stared; the expression on his face showed his growing annoyance. "GO!"

The sound of his voice was less than human. Lucas jumped, his heart lurching for several beats, remedying the feeling of being unable to move. Lucas's feet seemed to be moving without his prompting, likely his mind trying to force his body to flee to safety. He knew that wasn't possible, so he forced his mind to slow down.

He stopped at the opening of the cemetery and looked at the unadorned white pillars flanking the passage between the walls that ran the entire border of the cemetery grounds. Spanning across the top between the pillars was an iron cross that any who entered would have to pass under. Lucas recognized where he was. As he read the simple plaque on the side of the entry, the words confirmed it.

"Saint Louis Cemetery Number One." Lucas spoke the words aloud and stepped into one of New Orleans's cities of the dead.

The caw of a crow came from above. Hair stood on the back of his neck and down his arms. He didn't bother to look up. He knew by now what he'd see. The crow cawed again as if to protest not gaining his attention. Lucas kept his eyes down, focusing on the piece of paper in his hand. He read the directions and went to his left as it indicated, then proceeded to the next to last walkway on the right.

As he walked, Lucas tried to calm his mind and nerves. He recalled the trip he took two years earlier with his grandmother to try to stop focusing on Javan, Cecily, Mara, and Gabby's condition—to distract himself from thinking of crows.

They'd come here on a cemetery tour during a long weekend getaway because it was supposed to be one of the most haunted places in the world. Lucas found the idea silly at the time, and he caught himself laughing humorlessly at his ignorance. Now, he knew spirits and far worse existed.

He came to the next step in the directions and made the right, then the next to last right. The cemetery was spookier now than the first time he'd been there. He was here at night then, too, but this time, he was aware there were things lurking in shadows.

"Now I believe in monsters and fairytales," he said under his breath.

The map showed he needed to follow the path he was on to its end. It wasn't far, according to the drawing, and made an L shape. He was supposed to dig where the path ended, so he followed it until it did. Except for a narrow space between the tombs to his left that led to another path, he was completely shielded from view.

Lucas stuffed the piece of paper into his front pocket and slammed the spade into the earth. Maybe it was soft ground or anger trying to escape his body. Maybe it was the book, under who knew how many layers of soil, helping in some way because it wanted to be free, but for whatever reason, Lucas was able to remove the dirt with little effort.

He felt eyes on him, watching what he was doing. He didn't want to see whatever the eyes belonged to, so he never took his attention off the ground he was butchering. Every time he stabbed it, he wished it was Javan, or a vampire, that he was ripping apart instead of a bunch of dirt. Through the anger and terror, he had a profound need to hold Gabby safely in his arms.

She's all that matters right now.

He didn't know if he'd survive the night, but he would do anything he could to save her.

As he raised the shovel again and thrust it into the ground, it hit something hard. The force caused his hand to slip down the wood handle, shoving a splinter that felt like a chopstick into his palm.

Lucas dropped the shovel and grasped his hand, bending over in pain as he tried to stifle a cry. The last thing he needed was to give Javan another reason to get rid of him. He could stay quiet if it kept the situation he was in more stable.

As he stared at his palm, a stream of blood dripped from his hand onto the dirt he'd ripped from its home. He looked at the fresh earth he had exposed—smelling its scent, realizing the pain it would have been in from his abuse if it were capable of feeling. With all that he had learned existed in the world, what he thought were impossible things, that lived and breathed—could *feel*—the idea that dirt could feel pain from the beating he inflicted upon it became less unrealistic.

"I guess you got me back," he said to the dirt.

Lucas turned his attention to his palm and picked as much of the splinter out of his hand as he could. It came out mostly in one big, painful piece, but little ones were still embedded in his skin. Something he'd have to take care of later.

"If I have a later," he mumbled, not wanting to speak the words too loudly. He hoped he and Gabby would make it through all of this somehow.

He directed his attention back to the hole, more specifically to whatever it was he'd hit. Alternating between his hands and the shovel, he finally was able to bring up a box. He studied it for a few seconds, wiping dirt from it as he did. The box was made out of wood. It didn't look like much. He wondered how old it was and why the book in it was so important. More importantly, he wondered why it needed to be buried in order to keep it out of someone's, or something's, possession?

Lucas placed the box on the ground. He raised the spade, bringing it down just above the lock. It didn't break. He was surprised by its resolve, considering the decaying timber it was attached to. He raised the shovel again, and with this attempt, he dredged up as much strength, anger, and frustration as he could and struck it again. It surrendered, along with most of the front panel. A gust of cold wind pushed around him. Lucas crouched down and tried to look into what remained of the book's coffin. He could see a deep red cloth but nothing else. He reached into the box, moving the remaining pieces of wood that continued to keep it in its confines.

When he pulled it out, he was amazed at how heavy it was. He'd thought the weight was the result of the box, but it was the book. It didn't appear to be big, maybe the size of a small paperback. And even though it must have been in the ground for a long time, it looked as if it had just been placed inside. The fabric was unfaded, clean, and completely dry. As he unwrapped the book, it seemed to get heavier and bigger. By the time it was entirely lit by moonlight, it was the size of a coffee table book and at least four inches thick. The cover was made from leather, embossed with a symbol of a sword with a snake coiling up its blade. Raised lettering made out of some kind of metal was attached. Lucas ran his fingers over the cover.

A foggy image of a man dressed in clothes from long ago, sobbing over a body, flashed in his mind—the faint scream of a woman and children crying for their father accompanied the vision. Lucas shook his head, trying to clear his mind. The image and sounds disappeared.

What was that?

Lucas didn't have time to dwell on it. He angled the book to catch more of the light, wanting to read the title.

"The Book of Barabbadon."

Lucas felt another movement in the air, this time from directly above him. It pushed down around his body. He froze, not sure of what to do. He closed his eyes and said a quick prayer and began to wrap the Book back in the cloth. He felt its size and weight change. This time, in reverse, larger and heavier to lighter and smaller. He would've studied it more carefully out of sheer curiosity if it weren't for feeling he was being scrutinized by a growing number of eyes. He really didn't want to stay around and find out what had just disturbed the air above him, either.

Once he had it wrapped and secured again, he turned and started back, all the while feeling eyes boring into him.

At one point, he was sure he heard his name called from above, but there was no chance he was going to look up and chitchat with something flying silently over him. He almost did, thinking it might be an angel who would help him, but he decided his luck hadn't been the best lately and continued to make his way back to Gabby. As soon as he turned the corner to where he'd left her, his heart skipped a beat. Gabby stood between Mara and Javan but was still in need of support. Javan had his arm around her back and waist. Her head rested on his shoulder, and her eyes were still closed.

But she was alive.

Lucas didn't know how much longer she could have those bindings around her before it was too late, and he wondered how long it would be before she would be strong enough for the two of them to get back home.

If that moment ever came.

As he approached, Javan's stony face split into a true smile of self-gratification. He'd gotten what he wanted. Lucas stopped about fifteen feet from where the three stood. Someone was missing.

Cecily was nowhere to be seen.

Then, she dropped out of the sky beside Javan and gracefully landed next to him, leaning to whisper something to him.

Javan's smile broadened. "You have the Book." Javan put his hand out to Lucas.

"I have it. But I want you to send Gabby over to me without the bindings."

Lucas tried his best to look stern while he struggled to keep from losing the contents of his stomach. The corners of Javan's mouth dropped; his eyes seemed to grow an even murkier shade of black.

He raised Gabby's head and whispered something in her ear, then unbound her—letting the bindings drop to the ground. They immediately lost their glow and looked like a length of ordinary thick rope you'd get from any hardware store.

Gabrielle opened her eyes briefly and looked at Lucas. "Lucas."

She barely got his name out. She was weak.

"I'm right here, Gabby. It's almost over."

Lucas didn't know *how* over it was about to be, whether this nightmare was about to be over or if their lives would be. He didn't want to alarm her, though. For once, he actually did feel as if he might be able to save her—something he never thought he'd be able to experience.

"I'm going to walk a few steps with her until she steadies herself enough to come the rest of the way to you." Javan said.

Lucas nodded and watched as Gabby stumbled slightly with her first step, then seemed to get a little more sure-footed as she took a few more toward him.

Javan let go of her and stepped back again; his smug smile returned.

Gabby made it almost all the way to him, then Lucas closed the gap between them as she began to stumble. He caught her with his free arm and pulled her tightly to his chest. He took a deep breath, feeling it was the first one to enter his lungs since he'd seen her in the backseat of Javan's car. He bent his head to hers and whispered to her without taking his eyes off Javan, Mara, and Cecily.

"I've got you, love."

He could feel how cold she was even through their clothes and wondered how much longer she would've been able to withstand whatever those bindings were doing to her.

"The Book, Lucas," Javan prompted as he held out his hand again.

"I'll bring it to you," Gabby said.

Lucas stiffened. It couldn't have been her.

As he was about to look down at his angel, he felt her rise strong and steady. He looked at her, stunned, and she smiled at him.

Gabby backed away from him and took the Book out of his hand. He didn't try to stop her. He wasn't sure he had the strength in him at that moment to even move his mouth. He felt as if the life had just been sucked out of him.

Gabby turned and walked back to Javan.

"Gabby?" Lucas was amazed that he was actually able to make his mouth and throat cooperate enough to say her name, but he couldn't seem to make any other words come out. There was so much he wanted to say—so many questions he needed to ask.

She turned and smiled but never stopped walking. When she reached Javan, she handed him the Book. Javan looked at her and smiled, then snatched her to him, kissing her almost ravenously. What was worse, Gabby put her hands into his hair and forced his lips harder into hers, kissing him back just as greedily.

Watching her in Javan's embrace, Lucas had too many thoughts and feelings to know what to do with. Anger, jealousy, sadness, betrayal, disbelief—all tried to claim the forefront in his mind. None of them could withstand the swirl of commotion in his head, though. Lucas felt his world begin to spin, and he could no longer keep the bile in his stomach from surfacing. He bent over, retching for what seemed to be forever. With every purge, he heard them laughing at him and heard more laughter coming from others he guessed were the ones he felt had been watching him. With every lurch of his stomach, anger became increasingly rooted in his emotion. Finally, he had something to focus on, and he began to regain control of not only his body but his thoughts.

When he stood back up, he couldn't bring himself to look at Gabby, focusing on Javan instead. Now that he had Gabby happily draped on one side of his body, he wore the look of superiority even more than before.

"I tried to tell you, Lucas. You could never have held her interest or retained her love. She's loved me for *thousands* of years. Did you really think a couple of months would have even a minuscule chance of comparing to what we've had together?"

Lucas felt the words cut through him, and he finally looked at Gabby, hoping to see some sign in her eyes that told him to just play along—that *somehow*, this was part of her plan. But the look he wanted to see wasn't there. He only saw the eyes of the angel he loved coldly looking back at him. He saw no feeling for him in them at all, not even remorse for what she'd done—was doing—to him.

He'd only been a pawn to her. She had never been in danger. He looked down at the ground by her feet where the once glowing rope still rested. That's all they were—plain ropes. Nothing damaging to an angel at all. They probably wouldn't even give her skin a rope burn.

He couldn't find the words to answer Javan. What was he supposed to say, anyway? He just wished they'd leave. Javan had what he wanted, and apparently, so did Gabby. All he wanted was to be away from the eyes on him. The ones across from him and the ones he knew were waiting in the shadows.

A strong wind came from above again. Javan looked up and didn't seem to like what he saw. He looked back to Lucas, then to his left to address Cecily.

"We have to be going, so if there is anything left that you want to do here, I suggest you get on with it. Otherwise, I'll take care of him."

Lucas saw her smile, showing the sharp white teeth he'd seen in his nightmares; then she slammed into his body. He felt himself lift high off the ground as her teeth plunged into his neck.

His eyes were wide with fear and pain. He couldn't seem to focus on anything until he was finally able to see the ground ahead and below him where he saw Mara getting into Javan's car. He shifted his eyes to find Gabby and found her being led to the car by Javan.

"Gabby," Lucas whispered, unable to say her name any louder as Cecily drank heartily.

Gabby seemed to hear him, though, and looked up to where Cecily had him suspended a dozen feet off the ground. The last thing he remembered seeing was her smirk at him as she disappeared into the car—then he closed his eyes.

He wanted death to come.

He didn't know how he could live anyway.

Cecily removed her mouth from his neck abruptly; then he heard her hiss before feeling her release her grip. His body met the ground again.

Hard.

He heard Javan's voice and maybe Gabby's, but all the while, he continued to hear Cecily hiss, and now he thought she might be growling, too. She sounded like she was in pain, but he wasn't sure.

He didn't care.

He let himself drift away into the quiet and darkness that was consuming him. Hoping it would take him to a place where he would no longer have to feel his heart that felt as if it had just been crushed in his mortal chest. As his life faded away, so did the voices—so did the pain in his body. But what he was most happy to feel leaving him, what death was sparing him from feeling any longer, was the pain in his mind and heart.

Wherever this darkness was taking him, he hoped he would never have to feel anything again.

Chapter Seventy-seven

GABRIELLE ✝ INTO THE UNDERWORLD

Gabrielle hoped she was overreacting, and that since she'd been expecting the worst, her imagination was getting the best of her. But if she was, why did she feel like time was running out to save Lucas?

She moved from one location to another faster than she ever had, but even with speed, she knew she wasn't going to get to him fast enough. Thoughts of what could have happened while she'd left Lucas alone screamed through her mind. She manifested behind the gym, and as she turned the corner to make her way to the front, her stomach dropped.

Ahead of her, next to the side door of the building, was an ambulance. A body was being tended to by paramedics. As she made her way to the scene, tears began to blur her vision. She tried to blink them away, swallowing hard as she did. She couldn't let human emotions take control right now, no matter who was on the ground. She closed her eyes and said a prayer before she opened them and looked down. She wasn't expecting who she saw—Nonie was lying unconscious where she was sure she'd see Lucas.

"Gabrielle!"

She saw Nate stand up from beside Nonie and make his way to her.

"Nate, what happened?"

He took her by the arm and moved away from the crowd around his sister. When he seemed satisfied no one would be able to hear him, he turned to face her.

Gabrielle looked at the concern in his eyes and asked again. "What happened? Where's Lucas?"

Nate just stared at her and shook his head.

"NATE!" Gabrielle put her hands on his shoulders and shook him a little harder than she meant to, but it seemed to do the trick.

"I don't know where Lucas is. What happened to you? Are you okay?"

"What. Happened. Nate?"

"The last thing I remember was some guy looking at me and feeling like he was dissecting my mind. Then, I was drenched with water and had half the student body standing over me." Nate paused, ran his hand half way through his hair, and stopped as he looked up into the night sky. "I came to look for Lucas and Nonie when they weren't anywhere in the gym. I found Nonie unconscious against the building. She still hasn't woken up." He looked back at Gabrielle. "I haven't been able to find Lucas."

Gabrielle felt her pulse ratchet up its pace as her mind began to spin. "Nate, what did this guy look like?"

Nate started to pace a short path in front of Gabrielle, one hand on his hip and the other still on top of his head as if it would help him remember something. "Umm, I don't know … black hair, black eyes, model looks—even with the scar. Evil as hell, from what I could tell. He scared the shit out of me."

It had to be Javan. "What did he say?"

"The only thing I heard was to Lucas. He said, 'If you want to save Gabrielle, I suggest you come with me now'. That was it, nothing else … at least not while I was lucid." He paused and squinted at Gabrielle. "Where were you? I thought you were going to be close in case something happened."

"I was distracted, apparently on purpose. I don't have time to explain. How long do you think it's been since the guy confronted Lucas?"

Nate kept squinting at Gabrielle as he answered her. "Thirty minutes, hour—maybe. It's hard to say—I was out of it for a while."

"I have to go." Gabrielle looked back to Nonie, then back at Nate. "She's going to be fine, Nate."

Gabrielle ran as fast as she could with people around until she got to the rear of the building again, then ascended. She didn't know what Javan was up to or why it would involve Lucas. But she knew she was going to need help finding them.

'Amaziah. Sheridan. I need your help. Now.'

It was only a moment before they were both with her, and it took only seconds for them to understand what was happening and what Gabrielle needed. They sent the call out to any angels who could be spared to find Lucas and Javan; then they went to search themselves.

It wasn't going to be easy; Javan would be using his ability to camouflage himself and Lucas. While all of her comrades looked for them above ground, she was going to go below, hoping to see him from there or somehow get one of the Fallen to tell her where Javan was.

It would be dangerous for any angel and was particularly so for her even with her exceptional abilities, especially since some who lived in the Shadow World and Underworld could now be somewhat immune to them. She suspected the pendants she'd been seeing some wear were the reason. She didn't know how many had them—how many could get closer to killing her than any ever had because of them. The thought didn't make her feel better about what she was about to do, but it didn't matter. Lucas's life was at stake, and she believed it was the quickest way to find them. She didn't think Javan would consider shielding his and Lucas's energy from below, so below was where she was going.

Into the Underworld.

Time didn't allow for her to be choosy about where to enter Ramai's domain, and she wasn't going to look for an entrance—she would make her own. Descending to the landscape below, she opened the earth and was enveloped by the bleakness that was the Underworld.

When she stopped to get her bearings, she couldn't help but notice the eyes that turned on her to see who had invaded their domain. Shiny, solid black eyes that glinted in the sparse moonlight filtering in from the rift she had created.

Chapter Seventy-eight

Gabrielle ✛ The Battle Begins

A dozen Underworlders approached Gabrielle, and none looked like they were welcoming her to the neighborhood. From the looks of them, they had been below for a long time. Their skin was so pale it almost glowed, and their eyes were larger than they should be.

One seemed to be leading the others as they approached. As he neared, she thought she recognized him. He passed out of the shadows into the moonlight shining into the deep cavern Gabrielle had just created.

"Mylek?" she said, surprised she recognized him.

Mylek was once a commander in her own troop who decided he wanted to have some of the things humans enjoyed on Earth. When he was refused by Yahuwah, he rebelled and was cast from Heaven. It had been close to a thousand years since she'd seen him, and the only reason she recognized him was from his energy. Even now, it was strong.

He continued his approach but waved the other demons off. As he drew closer to her, he moved more slowly, cocking his head as if trying to remember who she was.

"Mylek, it's Gabrielle. I mean no harm to you or any Underworlder tonight."

Mylek paused, and after several moments, she saw a strange smile cross his face—strange because it must have been some time since his face pulled the muscles of his mouth in the directions it was now attempting. Though it seemed genuine, it also appeared strained. He straightened, leaving the stance of a predator and adopting a friendlier one.

It was something Gabrielle hadn't expected.

"Gabrielle. You may not believe it, but I'm glad to see you. It's been so long since I've seen any of my former brethren. I didn't think I ever would again." Mylek clasped his hands in front of him and let them rest against his body. It was a gesture she knew well, any angel would. "If you aren't here to hunt any of—*us*," he said, and Gabrielle noticed he almost choked on the last word, "then why are you here? You have to admit, your approach was confrontational."

"It's not my intent, but I have limited time, and this was the best way."

"Maybe I can …" Mylek paused, "help."

"I'm looking for Javan and a human. Javan is camouflaging, and I have to find them—*now.*"

Mylek scowled, and Gabrielle could see him clench and unclench his fists.

"Javan, huh? He's caused me a bit of trouble since he's fallen. Arrogant ass." Mylek started walking toward her again. He stopped in front of her and looked her hard in the eyes.

"I think I know where they are. Word down here is he's going to obtain the Book of Barabbadon. Tonight. He's recruited an impressive amount of Shadow Worlders and Underworlders, and some are helping him now."

Why would he need Lucas to get the Book?

"Where are they, Mylek?"

"New Orleans, near one of the Gates of Hell."

"I know where that is. I have to go." Gabrielle began to ascend, and as she did, she called back to Mylek.

"Thank you ... old friend."

"Maybe I'll be a *new* friend," he said before she completely ascended.

Gabrielle arrived near the Gate in New Orleans and began to search. She had a good chance of finding them now that she knew where to look. She flew in a circular pattern about a half a mile wide using the Gate as a central point, causing a substantial disturbance in the air as she flew as close to the ground as she could without being seen. She was about to abandon the area and look further out when she noticed several different energy signatures.

She'd seen those energies together before ... in her vision. She recognized three of the four moving swiftly north. She turned her attention to the energy fading on the ground.

Lucas.

His energy was faint. She made her way to him, terrified of what she'd find. Her heart plummeted. He was lying on his side, motionless. His heart was beating slowly, and it was steadily growing weaker.

Gabrielle descended and scooped Lucas up, not caring if there were human eyes to see the expanse of wings or the glow of energy. All she wanted was to hold Lucas and try to save him.

'Amaziah! I have Lucas. He's dying, Amaziah! Please, help me!'

He was with her immediately along with several others.

'Amaziah, please help him. Is there anything we can do?'

He reached out for her to hand him over, but even as she did, she could tell his body hung too lifeless.

She'd failed him.

Gabrielle grew angry as her arms emptied Lucas into Amaziah's outstretched ones, hearing the last beats of his heart as she did. Gabrielle remained motionless. She was stunned to a point that she felt nothing but numbness that seemed to filter slowly into her entire being.

Amaziah held Lucas for a long time without saying anything. She managed to choke out a question even though she felt no life left in her to do it.

'What is it? Why are you looking at him as if you've never seen a dead body?'

'Have you not noticed, Gabrielle? His soul hasn't left him. He's not dead.'

'That's not possible. I heard his heart take its last beats as I placed him in your arms.'

As she said the words, she heard Lucas's heart beat again, but there was something different about it. She waited, and it beat again.

'He's still alive! Help him!'

Gabrielle moved closer to Amaziah, but he moved back as she did.

'I want to hold him. Why are you keeping him from me?'

He hesitated before he answered, and she noticed the others had backed away from them.

'You're right, Gabrielle. He is still alive. But not like he was before.'

'What do you mean, not like before? He's either alive or not alive. There is no in between.'

'What happened to him?'

'I don't know. I found him on the ground and came straight for help. No one else was around, at least not by the time I reached him. What are you getting at?'

'As you can hear, his heart is strong, and he breathes.'

'Yes. Which means he's alive.'

'What else have you noticed?'

Gabrielle studied Lucas for several moments.

'Nothing, Amaziah. I don't want cryptic enlightenment, either. Please, just tell me what you think is going on!'

'Lucas breathes and his heart beats, but there's an abnormal amount of time between either breath or heartbeat.'

Gabrielle hadn't thought too much about it, happy to believe he might survive, but more than a minute passed before she heard his heart pump again or his lungs moving air.

'He's been bleeding from his neck. It's stopped now, but it's fresh.'

She was almost amused by his observation. 'No, it's part of his costume. It's fake blood.'

'Gabrielle, I know the difference between fake and life-giving blood. So do you. Accept what has happened. This blood is real.'

Gabrielle moved Lucas's head so she could see his neck. She stared at the puncture wounds next to the ones Nonie had created. The other set was definitely the real thing.

'He's Qalal. But why does his heart beat at all? Qalal don't breathe.'

'I know. I've never known of a human being bitten and not turning or dying. Take him home. He'll be better off with you and Emma looking after him. I'll post some of your comrades around the home for protection so you can tend to him without worrying about another attack.'

He placed Lucas back in her arms, and she looked at his face. She wondered what was happening to him now and what was going to happen to him later.

'Go now, Gabrielle. I'll be back to you soon, I promise. This won't take long.'

Amaziah and the others were gone before she could reply, although really, there was nothing to say. She made her way back to Emma's home, looking at Lucas's face the entire time. He hadn't moved at all in her arms, except for an occasional rise and fall of his chest, too far apart to be humanly possible.

She couldn't believe how rapidly everything went wrong. She was almost to Emma's when he tried to say something. It was barely a whisper, but she thought he said her name and then the word why. A few moments later, she heard him say, "How could you, Gabby"? It didn't make sense to her.

Maybe he was wondering how she could have stopped watching

for trouble, why she let him be taken, why she wasn't there to protect him. She didn't know, but she was happier than she could have ever imagined being just because he said those few words. If there were words, there was a Lucas, and no matter what happened to him or what he became, she loved him.

When she entered the living room, she found not only Emma but the entire Daniels family, minus Chloe. Gabrielle scanned the room and realized she would be rather awe inspiring to everyone except for Emma, so she manifested her human form.

"Emma, get me a glass of water and some warm clothes for Lucas. I want every human in this house to make sure they have a cross in their hand or around their neck at all times."

She looked at Ben, Lizzie, Nonie, and Nate, who all shared stunned expressions with a look in her eyes and scowl that said *now*, and everyone went out the door except Lizzie. Gabrielle stared at her to see why she wasn't listening.

Lizzie must have understood. She reached her hand under the neck of the sweater and pulled out a cross that hung on a short chain.

"Never take it off."

Gabrielle moved through the house toward Lucas's room, laid him on the bed, then grabbed an afghan and covered him. Lizzie entered the room right behind her. Gabrielle heard Emma come in and place the items she'd requested on the nightstand.

"Gabrielle, what's wrong with Lucas?" Emma asked.

"I'm not sure," Gabrielle responded as she was getting Lucas situated. "When I found him, he was alone on the ground." She turned to face Emma, placed her hands on her arms, and moved to sit on the end of the bed. "There's a problem, but we don't know what to make of it yet. So please, try to stay calm. Amaziah has sought council. Until we know, we have to take precautions."

"Precautions?" Emma looked at Gabrielle and then to Lizzie, who was rubbing the cross between her fingers. She looked back at Gabrielle and then back at the cross.

Lizzie stopped playing with the pendant. Both women understood at the same time. Lizzie let out her breath hard and put her hand to her mouth as she stared at Lucas.

Emma sat on the edge of the bed. Tears began to spill from her eyes as Gabrielle held her. They stayed like that until they heard footsteps near the room.

Ben, Nate, and Nonie entered, took one look at the scene in front of them, and immediately thought the worst—that Lucas was dead. They didn't know that death wasn't necessarily the worst thing that could have happened to him. Lizzie shook her head and hushed them with her finger before they had a chance to say anything. Everyone looked at her, waiting for an explanation. She motioned for Lizzie to take her place next to Emma and stood to face them while she explained what she knew.

"I don't know everything that happened tonight. But at some point," she said, speaking through a knot that had been in her chest since she realized that she was purposely distracted by Cecily, "Lucas was attacked by a Qalal." The room was silent. She knew she couldn't offer them much more, but she continued talking for lack of knowing what else to do. "There's something wrong, though."

Nate spat out a sarcastic snicker. "Like there isn't something already *very* wrong about this?"

"Nate Daniels!" That was all Lizzie had to say.

"Of course, Nate, that's wrong enough. But the real questions are: Why is his heart still beating? And why is he still breathing?"

Nonie stepped forward and walked over to Lucas. She stared at him for a moment before she spoke. "What *normally* happens?"

"Normally, if the person isn't killed, their heart would completely stop beating from the infection, their breath would cease, and they would become a Qalal. That's it. No other variation has ever happened."

"So what?" Nate asked as he joined his sister. "Lucas is going to live through a vampire attack?" Nate smiled and looked at Gabrielle. "That's good, right?"

Gabrielle raised her brow and shook her head. "We just don't know. But with his heart and breath being so slow, it isn't a good sign he's going to come out of this unscathed." Gabrielle was about to say more, but she sensed Amaziah manifesting in the next room. "Amaziah's here. Maybe now we'll have an answer," she said as she looked toward the door.

Amaziah came into the room and walked over to Emma. She stood quickly, throwing her arms around him. "Amaziah. Please help him."

He moved her back from him slightly and smiled.

"This is something no angel can fix, Emma … I'm sorry."

Emma sat back on the bed again, and a fresh stream of tears ran quietly down her cheeks.

"What did you find out?" Gabrielle asked.

He nodded to the Daniels family, then turned his attention back to Gabrielle.

"It's a mystery. Yahuwah knows why he wasn't killed and why he's not a Qalal, but not what he will become. That remains to be seen."

"What do you mean? How can He not know?" Gabrielle sat next to Lucas. She looked at his face. He seemed so peaceful. She couldn't imagine anything bad was going on beneath his skin—behind his eyes.

"His blood isn't completely human. It's part Divine. That's why he wasn't killed and why his transformation to a Qalal appears to be only partial."

"Of course." Gabrielle stood and walked to the window, raising the blinds. "A Qalal can't kill an angel or turn them. I hadn't thought about that."

Emma spoke, and Gabrielle could hear the hope in her voice when she did. "Then he'll be okay?"

"Emma," Amaziah began, "he's still mostly human. Just *how* human he remains—we can't calculate. Yahuwah did not create whatever it is that Lucas will become … which is why even He isn't sure what Lucas is now. As hard as it's going to be, we have to wait and see."

"How long?" The desperation was heavy in Emma's voice.

Gabrielle closed her eyes to fight back her own tears. She'd messed things up so badly. She should never have chosen to live among humans. This was all her fault, and she couldn't change any of it.

"We don't know that either. His body will change, but because of the circumstances, the changes will be very different and may take longer than what's normal in these cases. Or it may be more brief in its duration. Patience—"

"Amaziah, if you say patience is a virtue, I'll do anything I can to make you regret it." Gabrielle didn't turn to look at her friend, but she felt bad as soon as the words escaped her lips. He was so good to her, and all he was trying to do was comfort everyone the best he could.

She felt his energy draw closer to her until she knew he was right behind her.

"I'm sorry, Amaziah. I didn't mean to—"

"I know, Gabrielle." She felt his hands on her shoulders, and she couldn't hold her tears back anymore.

She turned and buried her face in his shoulder, crying harder than she ever had before. The tears weren't only for Lucas or their love being in peril but also for her shame. She'd fallen so far. Not like Javan. Not like the thousands of others cast from Heaven, but she'd fallen in her own way. She was so far from what she'd intended that she wasn't sure where she was going anymore or if Heaven would lend a hand to help her redeem this mammoth mess she created.

She just wanted to cry. To not be strong for herself or anyone else. To feel all her pain, all her shame, all her fears—feel it, and somehow come out the other side with the answers to the problems she faced.

So that's what she did. She cried into the shoulder of the angel who'd been there through it all and still held his arms out to her. She wasn't sure how long she wept, but when she let go of Amaziah, the only person left in the room other than Lucas, who still lay just as he did when she put him in bed, was Emma. She had pulled a chair from the front room and was sitting in it, staring at Lucas.

Gabrielle looked into the face that was her friend's. He smiled warmly at her, and she hugged him tightly. "What would I do without you?"

She felt him chuckle quietly.

"Let's not find out." He held her a little longer, and then he made her look at him. "You're being too hard on yourself, Gabrielle. This isn't your fault."

"But it is. If I'd stayed and kept watch over him like I was supposed to, this wouldn't have happened."

"But it would."

Gabrielle looked at him quizzically. "What do you mean?"

"Your vision. The attack on Lucas was going to happen. There were things done by Lucas or the twins, maybe even you, that changed the *how* of it, but the result was the same."

"So no matter what I would have done, Lucas was going to be attacked." Gabrielle paused for a moment to let that fact sink in. "Then what was the point of Yahuwah putting me in his life to protect him?"

"Lucas's real need for protection and guidance is just beginning."

"The choice he has to make," she murmured. The battle for Lucas's soul, for the existence of every living thing, had begun tonight. And it was her job to help him make the right decision. Maybe, she was the only one who could.

As she watched his resting body, struck by how frail and precious human life truly was, she prayed his love for her, their love for each other, would be enough. If it wasn't, hope for every living thing was lost.

Chapter Seventy-nine

GABRIELLE ✝ AWAKENINGS

Two days passed before Lucas began to move, and even then, he didn't wake.

Gabrielle stayed with him continually, pausing time when she needed to work. No one could predict how Lucas was going to act when he woke, and she didn't want to take the chance of someone getting hurt.

While she watched him, he still seemed like her Lucas. His face and body appeared the same. His infrequent breathing and heartbeat had remained unchanged. So far, the only difference she noted was that his skin seemed smoother. She thought it was her imagination, but his lips appeared more red, too.

Emma had held it together after her initial meltdown. Since then, she'd devoted herself to tending to Lucas and Gabrielle. The two of them spent many hours talking, sometimes even laughing, because of something Emma told Gabrielle about Lucas as a child. If she felt animosity toward Gabrielle for what had happened to Lucas, she was doing a good job of hiding it. It might have something to do with the long conversation Emma had with Amaziah after he comforted Gabrielle two nights earlier. She never asked Emma what they'd talked about, but when she returned from the conversation, she seemed to be more focused and smiled at her as if she understood something.

Gabrielle walked to the window. Outside the light was growing dim as the sun relinquished its hold on the day, turning control over to the moon and shadows. It had been a sunny day, and now the stars were beginning to speckle the cloudless sky. She'd been standing there for some time when she suddenly felt an energy right behind her. She spun quickly and found herself staring into Lucas's eyes.

Only they were different.

They were still blue, but more brilliant, and had taken on violet strands that constantly mingled with the blue. They were mesmerizing.

She wanted to throw her arms around him, but she felt the need to be cautious. His expression and body language were unreadable, and more than his eyes were different; he'd been able to move out of the bed and across the room without a sound. Even a full Qalal couldn't move quietly enough for Gabrielle not to hear them coming. His stealth unnerved her.

"Lucas … how are you feeling?" Gabrielle didn't move, but she readied herself in case she had to switch forms. Lucas looked at her with the same lack of expression. After several moments, Gabrielle reached out to touch his face.

He stopped her hand with a movement that was so fast she barely saw it. She continued to look in his eyes. Something was clearly wrong, and it wasn't just that he was something that had never existed. It was in his eyes, something she felt was directed at her. After a few more seconds, Lucas let go of her hand, turned around, and began to make his way down the hall.

"Leave, Gabrielle." It was his voice but silkier, deeper, like he'd grown from a teenager into a man in the two days that had passed.

"Why? Lucas, wait!" Gabrielle manifested in front of him. They were in the hall that led to the rest of the house, facing each other. Lucas didn't stop moving. When he reached her, he just moved her to the side without making eye contact.

Why is he treating me this way?

She expected he might be different, but she got better treatment from Qalal she'd never met, much less one that was still part human or at least part angel—someone she loved and she thought loved her, too.

Lucas stopped at the kitchen sink and bent over to drink straight from the tap like it was a water fountain. Gabrielle waited for him to finish, knowing water wouldn't quench his thirst. When he did, he fluidly moved the three steps to the refrigerator and opened it, taking out a can of soda. He popped the tab and tilted his head back to drink, then tossed the empty can into the sink.

"I told you to leave," he said, bitterness spiking his tone.

"I asked you why." Gabrielle wasn't going to just leave even if that really was what he wanted. There was too much he needed to know and too much she still didn't know about him and his condition. He was going to have to deal with her whether he liked it or not.

"After what you did, I don't think I owe you an explanation. What happened? Did Javan let you down again?" Lucas shut the door to the fridge and turned his exquisite, pooling eyes on her. "Did you decide you still wanted to *play* with the human?"

"Lucas, I don't know what you're talking about. Javan won't ever have the opportunity to let me down again. I told you I could never be with him again after his betrayal. Why are we discussing him, anyway?"

Lucas smirked, then let out a sarcastic laugh that sent a chill through Gabrielle. There was definitely a more malicious side to Lucas, now.

"Were you the one who had the life sucked out of you, Gabrielle? You're not *really* going to act like you didn't betray *me* with Javan the other night, are you? Are you going to deny you pretended to be on the brink of death, helping Javan sucker me into getting him that book by saying it was the only way he would release you?"

"The Book of Barabbadon?"

"Yes. The fucking Book of Barabbadon."

Lucas started toward Gabrielle aggressively. She transformed before he reached her, stopping him temporarily, but then he closed the rest of the distance in two more quick steps.

He didn't touch her. Just glared.

"What was worse," he continued, "you stood and watched as that *bitch* made a snack out of me." Lucas narrowed his eyes. "You *smiled*. Are you going to try and deny that, too? Or were you hoping, since she didn't kill me, I would somehow forget?"

Gabrielle felt like she was going to break into pieces. She manifested her human form again.

"I deny all of that, Lucas."

He sneered and turned. She turned him back, and he shoved her hand off his arm.

"Lucas, what you *think* you saw wasn't real. It wasn't *me*."

"What? Are you going to tell me he had you under a spell or something?"

"It *wasn't* me!"

How was she going to convince Lucas it wasn't her he saw? She frantically searched her mind to try and figure out a way to make him believe her. Whatever happened to him, whatever he thought he saw *her* doing, was embedded in his mind. And she didn't know what to do about it.

She couldn't imagine what he must have gone through—thinking she was doing those things to him or that she stood by and watched him being killed with a smile on her face. How was she ever going to get him to see the truth when he saw it with his own eyes? Gabrielle didn't think she was going to be able to get through to him, but she had to try to help him work through what had happened.

"Do you remember the attack?"

"It's a little hard to forget something like that." Lucas's tone seemed to have softened but only a little. He turned to face her, then took a seat at the table. Gabrielle sat across from him. He didn't look at her as he continued. "Even if I didn't remember, I heard enough about what happened from you, Amaziah, and Gran to put it together."

"I didn't realize you could hear us. I'm sorry. If I'd known, I would've made everyone talk about it somewhere else."

"It's not a problem. Besides, I think you would've had to go a couple of blocks away—*at least*. My improved hearing is annoying, but I'm starting to figure out how to tune in to only what I want to hear. At least, I think I am."

Gabrielle raised a brow and wondered what other abilities he now had. *'Lucas, can you hear me?'*

She waited several seconds and tried again.

'Lucas, can you hear me?'

Lucas turned his head toward her slowly. She heard his voice, but not with her ears.

'Are you kidding me? Am I hearing your thoughts?'

Gabrielle smiled. Whatever he held locked away in his angelic DNA had apparently been awakened.

'Not my thoughts, exactly. Just the communication I want you to hear. It's selective, for not only what I want to be transmitted to someone else, but also who I want to hear that information.'

'Wow—can I do the same thing?'

'You already are. You just have to learn how to perfect it.'

"Cool," Lucas said aloud and smiled. Gabrielle smiled at his reaction. But she couldn't help noticing how white his teeth were. There was definitely some Qalal in him.

"How do you feel, Lucas?"

Gabrielle was surprised by how quickly he seemed to calm down after being in almost a rage a few minutes ago.

"I feel kinda great, actually. I thought I'd feel all empty and emotionless. You know—*dead*. Instead, all my emotions seem to be enhanced. Like with you I feel angrier than I ever have in my life. So much so, I can feel it twisting inside me. Like it's got a life of its own. I'm having a really hard time not physically throwing you out right now, to be honest. The only reason I haven't is *because* I've heard you all talking over the last couple of days." Lucas studied her for a moment. "Maybe there's some truth to what you're claiming. I have to find out what really happened. If it wasn't you, then you aren't the one I need to go after—Javan is … and whoever impersonated you. And Mara …" he said, then seemed to go somewhere deep within his thoughts.

While he was far away in his mind, she thought she saw black playing around the edges of his eyes. A grave tone accompanied his next words.

"I'll go after them … *all* of them. I'll make them pay."

Chapter Eighty

GABRIELLE ✢ BITTERSWEET

Gabrielle watched Lucas from her solitude high above him. It hadn't been easy between them over the last couple of weeks. Lucas still didn't know what to believe about Halloween night. His only contact with anyone since then had been with Gabrielle, Emma, and Amaziah. But now that she felt he was safe for Nonie and Nate to be around, she'd agreed to let them see Lucas. She left after the initial reunion, and the long hugs had ended without Lucas gnawing on his best friends' necks. She still wasn't comfortable not being close by, though, so she thought she'd stay and keep an eye on things without him knowing she was around.

The way Lucas had dealt with the changes in his body, in his life, had been amazing, to say the least. What was more remarkable were the changes themselves. He was stronger and faster than any Qalal she'd ever seen. He'd even almost beaten her in an all-out sprint. *Almost*. His vision and hearing were far beyond human capability and even pushed very close to the abilities of an angel.

He'd also gotten quite good at telepathy, purposely making idle conversation with Gabrielle when he knew she was working, even communicating with Amaziah about his new body and abilities. She'd wondered if he'd tried to communicate with Javan, but it wasn't likely he'd be able to. Javan's ability to use telepathy would've been weakened, maybe eliminated, after he'd fallen.

Gabrielle was still disturbed, and sometimes unnerved, by some of Lucas's actions and demeanor. He was more imposing than she would have ever thought he could be, and he seemed to enjoy using his new-found ability to persuade others. She caught him trying to use it on Emma one day, but as soon as he realized Gabrielle was in the room, he stopped. She never said anything, hoping he was just trying to fine-tune a new gift, not meaning any harm.

The gift of Persuasion was very rare. One that even Gabrielle didn't have. It worried her, and she hoped he would never do anything negative with the ability. Now that he was probably more Qalal than anything, he was going to be far more prone to Darkness and its ways. The only thing that could help keep it at bay was his Divine side that had awakened within him. But they didn't have any idea how strong that side was.

Emma seemed to be adjusting to her grandson's change. Lucas still wasn't showing a strong urge for blood. The steaks and burgers he ate, cooked rare, seemed to be enough to stave off any intense desires. Emma even joked that Lucas was going to have to get a job to help her rising grocery bill. It was good to see everyone becoming so light-hearted in a way, but it was also troubling. As much as Gabrielle wanted to think this transformation was going to be easier than anyone hoped for, she still believed it was far from complete. She sensed a struggle within Lucas, something she wasn't sure he was aware of.

At times, she could see it in his eyes when the blue and violet swirling would briefly change into a violet and black duet. Gabrielle wondered if the sporadic color shift ever pushed out the blue altogether, if the Lucas she loved would be pushed out, too. She noticed the change most when she and Lucas talked about the night he was attacked or about Javan. She knew his hatred for her former Reyah was deep, and she felt if those negative feelings increased, he would slip further toward Darkness.

Even with some of the more disturbing new traits, though, he still seemed to be very *Lucas* to her most of the time. At least for now. She did wonder if his battling sides would keep shifting at all times, causing him to be in a constant state of instability. And if he would have days he didn't seem to be at all the Lucas she'd fallen in love with. The most disturbing thing was not knowing if those bad days came, would they increase to the point that his more menacing side would be the only one she could find anymore.

That was what Ramai hoped for so Lucas could try to bring about the end of Light's rule over Darkness. She'd do everything in her power to make sure that didn't happen. The first step was to get him to trust her again. To trust the love she had for him, and she hoped he still had for her. They hadn't touched in more than a friendly gesture since he'd changed. Not because she didn't want to. It was everything she could do to not fling her arms around him, show him how much she loved and missed him. Her heart became an ever-tightening knot in her chest when she allowed herself to think about it—like it was at that moment.

She closed her eyes, trying to block the thought. She wasn't keen on letting her mind dwell in that gloom, preferring to just keep trying to help Lucas adjust in hopes he would be the one to pull her into his arms. Then, she would know he still loved her.

Then ... maybe I could breathe again.

Gabrielle shifted her thoughts to the Book of Barabbadon. Javan had it. But Amaziah assured her they had time to get it back. Even knowing the date, knowing exactly how much time they had to try to get the Book back, she still had moments when she felt defeated.

When she opened her eyes, her focus targeted a familiar energy in the distance. Her anger surged.

Javan.

She hadn't seen him since Halloween night, and now that he was close, she wouldn't lose the opportunity to confront him. She made her way toward him, but he swiftly shifted direction away from her. She should have known he'd see her coming, but he wouldn't be able to outrun her. She'd been faster than him even when he still held Yahuwah's favor, so he had no chance now.

She closed the distance so quickly he must have pulled up on his attempt to flee, stopping completely. Gabrielle changed into her human form as she reached the ground in front of him, facing the fallen angel who was once her Reyah.

"Hello, dear," Javan said, smiling innocently. "How have you been?"

Gabrielle calmed herself. She couldn't strike out at any living thing without direct orders or just cause. Javan knew the rules, too. He wouldn't be concerned right now as long as he gave her no reason to fear for her safety.

Her desire for revenge warred against her restraint, ebbing and flowing through her, testing for a weak spot in her resolve—trying to break free. Though it didn't manifest physically, it latched onto her words, lacing her tone with venom.

"I've been better than you might expect."

"Really? I thought you might be in mourning."

"Why's that, Javan?"

"I heard your little boy toy's ability to breathe had ceased." Javan's smile turned sinister.

He doesn't know Lucas survived.

She weighed whether or not it would be better for Javan to know the truth at this point. He was going to find out soon, though, and Gabrielle wanted to see the look on his face when he learned the truth.

She smiled back at Javan. "I think you've been misinformed—*dear*. Lucas didn't die. All you did was make him stronger."

Javan's upper lip pulled into a sneer. Knowing he'd failed to kill Lucas would be a terrible blow to his ego. Gabrielle seized the moment to dig into the open wound a little deeper.

"You failed, Javan. You did not kill Lucas."

"You're lying! A human can't survive the bite of a Qalal unless they're turned themselves." Javan's smile returned again. "So. He's one of the Damned, then." He laughed, the sound vicious in its intent.

"No ... no." Gabrielle shook her head slowly, and Javan's smile slipped away. "You're right about one thing, though. A human can't survive a Qalal attack *without* being turned. But there's one tiny, tiny but *crucial*, fact that you didn't take into consideration."

"What's that?" Javan asked, his words sounding more like a growl.

"Lucas was not completely human. Apparently, Nephilim *can* live through a Qalal attack."

Javan's face flushed with anger, and Gabrielle realized she was enjoying this far more than she should.

"It also turns out a Nephilim who's bitten doesn't turn all bloodsucker, either. As a matter of fact, what it *did* do to Lucas was give him all the really cool stuff. You know ... like immortality. By the way, thanks for that one. I wasn't sure how we would ever get past him being mortal. We don't have to worry about that anymore, thanks to you. He has incredible strength, vision, speed, hearing, and even *more* incredible good looks—like he needed *that*.

"His angelic DNA seems to have been enhanced. So now, he can do things you can't do anymore. Telepathy ... he's really great at that. And we're sure there's going to be more. He's a phenomenon, you know. The first of his kind. There's no telling what he'll be able to do once everything he's capable of is known."

Gabrielle let Javan simmer, and when he was about to open his mouth to say something, she used her power to Hush him. He stood there, shocked. The expression on his face was born from what she was sure was anger at her gall in silencing him.

"There's just one more thing I forgot to tell you, and I wanted to let you know before I forget. I always found Lucas incredibly desirable, but now—*whoo*! He really is amazing. I guess I should thank you for that, too. But even before all that, when he was mostly human, he made me feel things you never did."

Gabrielle released the Hush and waited for his response. He stood, motionless, except for the heaving of his chest that spoke of how furious he was. She couldn't help but smile. She'd gotten to him in a way no one had ever been able to. And what was more delicious, he had created the ammunition. When he finally spoke, few words passed his lips. It was very unlike Javan, but his bitter, dark demeanor was not lost.

"This isn't over, Gabrielle." He was back to growling more than speaking.

"You're quite right, Javan. It isn't. There is a lot to be settled and time needed for *karma* to take its course." Gabrielle lost her smile. "I promise you … it *will* take its course."

Javan turned to leave.

"Javan."

He turned, the ferocity of his anger burning in his glare.

"You don't know why you can't use the Book … do you?"

He clenched his hands into tight fists by his side, the only answer he gave. It was enough to know the truth of her words, though.

Gabrielle smiled. "I do."

Javan's scowl deepened, and then he was gone.

He may have the Book, but at least she knew he didn't know why he couldn't use it. He had at least two obstacles in his way—Lucas, and not knowing about the date—and that would buy Gabrielle more time. Until that date came, she would do everything she could to get the Book back in safe hands.

And away from anyone who would use it … especially Javan and Lucas.

She was going to be busy in the coming months.

'*Gabrielle.*'

The voice in her mind was now familiar. Lucas was calling to her.

She made her way to him, seeing Nonie and Nate climbing the steps of their home as she neared. Lucas was alone. She manifested across the room from him. Since he had changed, she learned that he didn't appreciate being startled. He was still hyper-defensive and wasn't used to his enhanced reflexes or the instincts that drove them. It was best if she stayed far enough away that he wouldn't fling her across the room if she surprised him. He didn't do it intentionally, and he didn't hurt her. She tried to reassure him she was okay the couple of times it happened, but he fell all over himself apologizing anyway. But now that she knew he was so jumpy, she chose to keep the incidents from repeating.

"Hi."

He had her in his arms so quickly, his lips parting her own, that he knocked the breath out of her. Or maybe it was the rush of emotions she felt after the long absence of his affection.

She didn't care.

All she cared about was the way he was kissing her, the way it made her feel as the heat from each other's bodies reacted the moment they touched, sending a fire through her she'd never felt before.

She couldn't believe how strong he was as he picked her up as if she weighed no more than a baby and carried her back to his room—making her feel she was his for the taking. She had no desire to resist him.

He placed her purposefully on the bed. He was no longer acting like an unsure teenager. He was confident, intent about every place he touched her with his hands and lips. His hands made her skin tingle, and even when they left one area of her body and traveled to the next spot, that sensation lingered for several moments before lifting away from her.

The feeling of their bodies as they moved together, when he pressed his rhythmically against hers, was sensational. She'd didn't know anything between a man and woman could feel so sensual. A raw hunger awakened within her. She wanted him—wanted to make him physically hers—and at that moment, it was all she could think about. Maybe it was only because she wasn't worried about hurting him by accident with her own strength, or maybe it was knowing he wasn't quite as innocent—as human—as he was prior to him changing, but she didn't want him to stop. Her body warmed, making her think she was going to throw everything away just so she could feel him in the most complete way possible. He was making her body feel so wanting that it would be hard for her to resist him if he moved things in the direction she wanted. She would have let things go further, much further, but he reduced the intensity of his kisses, changing them to gentle wisps across her neck and face, then stopped all together to look in her eyes.

"I love you, Gabby."

She smiled at once. He called her Gabby. He hadn't since he'd awoken, and it was a word of endearment that she missed every time he spoke her full name.

He looked at her longer, and she didn't say a thing. She just let the words linger in the air between them, losing herself in the slow swirl of blue and violet in his eyes.

"I know, now, what you told me was true. Nate told me about you coming to find me at the gym, not long after Javan tricked me into going with him. And I already asked Amaziah about some things he knew that happened that evening. He told me you were trying everything you could to figure out where Javan had taken me. It fits with what Nate said—I'm sorry, love." He looked at her, then kissed her lips gently, stopping again to whisper in her ear. "Will you please forgive me?"

She put her hands on his face and moved him to look in her eyes again. She answered with a long kiss of her own before answering with words.

"I love you, too, Lucas. Never doubt that again."

They lay there for a long time, mostly with their eyes closed, holding each other like they never had before—like it was the last time they ever would again. When Gabrielle finally broke their embrace to stand, she turned to see a slightly puzzled look on Lucas's face.

"What is it, Gabby?" he asked.

She didn't want to tell Lucas she'd just seen Javan, but she was already keeping so much information from Lucas.

"I just spoke with Javan."

Lucas remained seated for a moment, expressionless, but his eyes became a darker shade than Gabrielle had seen. It unnerved her. Lucas walked to the window of his room, looking out into the day that was slipping into night as he spoke.

"What happened?"

"Just a conversation. I can't do anything to him unless he attacks me or someone else in my presence." Gabrielle moved behind Lucas and wrapped her arms around him. "He didn't know you survived. He does now."

Lucas was quiet, but Gabrielle could feel the negative energy coming off him. She hugged him tighter, wishing it would make his anger stop surging. Lucas seemed to sense that she was trying to calm him, and he pulled her around to face him.

"I'm okay, love."

His words weren't convincing, not when she saw Darkness was still in his eyes. Lucas smiled, an attempt at further reassurance.

"I can't say that things will be so easy for Javan when I finally have him in front of me since I'm not bound by your rules, but I *am* okay."

He leaned in to kiss her, pulling back slightly after he did to look in her eyes. Gabrielle was pleased to see the shade of his eyes returning to what was their new normal. She kissed him again, then let him just hold her, feeling his energy lighten as anger slipped further away.

Gabrielle allowed a happier mood to settle on her in spite of not knowing what the future held for Lucas, for her, or for any who made Heaven or Earth their home. He pulled her closer, kissing her head, and she let herself melt into him.

This wouldn't be such a bad way to be together as long as I can keep him from Darkness.

"Is there anything else you need to tell me, love? I've felt like there has been since before Halloween."

She flinched inside. There was a lot she still needed to tell him, things that could steal him from her and make him her mortal enemy. She held him tighter, not wanting to look him in the eye.

"No. There's nothing I need to tell you."

She had to lie. Though the bite would be felt deeply once it was discovered. She was torn between two worlds, now. Her divine one that she had been fighting for over thousands of years, and this new one that belonged to her and Lucas that she would also fight for—caught between a mortal and immortal world. It seemed she was being pushed toward a decision, betraying one if she protected the other.

She had to do her best to protect them both for as long as she could.

While Gabrielle and Lucas lost themselves in their thoughts, in their love, there was movement outside.

In the shadows of dusk, a flock of crows descended and quietly perched on the low branches of the tree by Lucas's window. They all turned toward the soft glow of light spilling from Lucas's room onto the darkening lawn. The only thing they seemed interested in was the silhouette of a young man and woman in an embrace.

There were nine total, but just as the sun's last rays disappeared below the horizon, snuffing the light and sending the day into murky night, another crow joined the voyeuristic flock.

Bringing their numbers to ten.

Acknowledgements

So much time and effort goes into writing a book, and without the love, support, and help from the following people, it would not have been such a fulfilling and wonderful experience. I truly appreciate each and every one of you. You are my heroes.

My deepest thanks go to my mom, Dixie Schoolman, for always believing in me even when I didn't believe in myself. You have been there though it all and loved and supported me no matter what. You are my rock as well as my guiding light. Thank you to my daughter, Piper Haviland, for making me want to follow my own dreams so you could learn through my example to follow your own. To Frank Haviland for doing everything you could to support me through this process, I appreciate it … all of it. And to all my family and friends who have supported my little adventure … you all rock. Oodles of thanks to you.

To my first readers who had to schlep through a very rough first draft, to my latter beta readers who still suffered through my unedited manuscript, thank you, thank you, thank you. The feedback you *all* offered was so incredibly helpful. I would especially like to thank Mekisha Elias, Wendy Felber, Karen Hollis, Beth Lelman, and Bethany Cotton for their early insight and suggestions, and for making me believe that The Reaping Chronicles was worthy of completing.

To two my two priceless editors, Crystal Bryant and Wendy Felber, you ladies exceeded my expectations and have helped tame the beast that was the unedited version of Inception. I couldn't have done this without you, and I have enormous gratitude for all you have done for me.

To KP Simmon of InkSlinger PR, I am so very pleased to have you on my side. Thank you for believing in my book and taking on this author who is a nobody.

My amazing cover designer, Damon of Damonza.com, and my formatter/interior designer, Benjamin of Damonza's Awesome Book Layout, thank you for making my vision for my cover and interior become a reality. You both rocked it! And, of course, without the contributions of photographer Cathleen Tarawhiti, model Emerald Reid, and artist Dana Mubarak M, I would not have the original image that captured the feel of The Reaping Chronicles ~ Inception so well. Thank you, ladies!

A special thanks to all of my friends who are writers, bloggers, the Nashville Writer's Meetup Group, and for the admins for book promotion pages on that big ol' social networking site, thank you so, so much for all you have done to cheer me on and for the guidance I have received from many. In particular, I would like to thank Brittany Carrigan, Paul Brown, M.R. Polish, Jamie Anderson, Janet Wallace, Willow Cross, Carol Kohnert Kunz, Alan Lewis, Amy Sun, Erin Fitzpatrick, Bella Belikov Colella, Jessie Peacock, KB Miller, Madison Daniel, and my-oh-my so many others that this list could go on for a very long time. Please know if I didn't include your name here, it is no reflection on my gratitude.

And, last but not least, to the One who gave me my desire and talent to write and fills my imagination with stories, I am forever grateful and humbled for all you have done, and will continue to do, for me. I hope what I do with your gift makes you smile.

Author Note

I did not create the counting rhyme about crows. As of the publication date of this book, I have still been unable to find out who the original author is. It appears to be a very old nursery rhyme by an unknown author and there are various versions to be found. This one is the version I felt fit the purpose of my book best.

About The Author

Teal Haviland lives in Tennessee with her daughter and her four-legged friends. She enjoys photography, travel, reading, music, cooking, daydreaming, writing (of course), and above all spending time with her family and friends.

Teal grew up with a love for anything fantastical or outrageous. After years of dreaming of worlds where fairies, angels, demons, and shape shifters (to name a few) exist, she finally decided to begin writing her stories down. Inception, book one in her series The Reaping Chronicles, is her first published novel.

Visit and talk to Teal online at: www.tealhaviland.com, or find her on Facebook www.facebook.com/thereapingchronicles
www.facebook.com/authortealhaviland and
Twitter www.twitter.com/tealhaviland

For further information about any of the wonderful people who helped in putting together The Reaping Chronicles ~ Inception, please use the following links:

~ For Cathleen Tarawhiti:
   http://cathleentarawhiti.deviantart.com/
~ For Dana Mubarak M:
   http://pure-poison89.deviantart.com/
~ For Damon and Benjamin Carrancho:
   http://damonza.com/

"Books you might enjoy
from authors I happen to adore."

Ageless Sea
by M.R. Polish

In Book One of The Ageless Series, M.R. Polish tapestries into a world where myths are real. Deception lurks in the shadows, and destiny brings two lost souls together to fight as one.

Silent Orchids
by Morgan Wylie

The Orchids have been silenced... but for how long?